PENGUIN BOOKS

The Affair

Hilary Boyd was a nurse, marriage counsellor and ran a small cancer charity before becoming an author. She has written eight books, including *Thursdays in the Park*, her debut novel which sold over half a million copies and was an international bestseller.

The Affair

HILARY BOYD

PENGUIN BOOKS

PENGUIN BOOKS

UK | USA | Canada | Ireland | Australia
India | New Zealand | South Africa

20 Vauxhall Bridge Road
London SW1V 2SA

Penguin Books is part of the Penguin Random House group of companies
whose addresses can be found at global.penguinrandomhouse.com.

First published 2021
005

Set in 12.5/14.75 pt Garamond MT Std
Typeset by Jouve (UK), Milton Keynes
Printed and bound in Great Britain by Clays Ltd, Elcograf S.p.A.

The authorized representative in the EEA is Penguin Random House Ireland,
Morrison Chambers, 32 Nassau Street, Dublin D02 YH68

A CIP catalogue record for this book is available from the British Library

ISBN: 978–1–405–94390–1

www.greenpenguin.co.uk

To my dear friend Suzie, with love

A happy marriage is the union of two good forgivers

Robert Quillen

I

Connie McCabe was an honest woman. At least, she'd always considered herself as such. It wasn't something she prided herself on: it was just her default position, as another person's might be to slide away from the truth when it didn't suit them. But she was never brutal – if asked her opinion of a friend's new dress, she wouldn't say, 'That yellow makes you look as if your liver's packed up,' when the friend was stuck in the outfit for the foreseeable. So the events of that summer shocked Connie to the core and made her question everything she thought she knew about herself.

On the 2 p.m. xxx, Connie texted her husband, Devan. They lived in a large village – almost a small town, or 'tillage', as the locals referred to it – south of the Mendips, on the Somerset Levels, and her train journey, starting from Paddington, would take close to three hours.

See you at the station x, Devan replied.

She sat back in the crowded carriage, the heating turned up way too high for the mild April day, and closed her eyes, letting out a luxurious sigh of relief. For the past ten days she'd been on call, responsible for thirty-nine people's welfare – one passenger had cried off sick at the last minute – on a rail journey through the tulip fields of Holland. According to company guidelines, it was frowned upon to read or listen to anything – heaven forbid snooze – while accompanying her passengers across Europe. She should stay alert, poised to deal with any concerns her flock might have. So, despite loving every minute of her job as a tour manager, just sitting here, alone, with no responsibility to anyone but herself, was bliss.

Connie felt herself begin to unwind as the train travelled west, past Reading and Swindon, the countryside awash with bright blossoms and deliciously pale spring green. It had been a good tour. Only one really irritating couple who'd picked holes in everything, from the pillows to the narrow steam-train seats and rain on the day they'd toured Amsterdam. She'd been waiting for them to kick off about the colours of the spectacular tulip displays. There was always one.

Now would be the time, she thought sadly, *when I'd ring Mum and fill her in about my trip.* Her mother, Sheila, had died in January, in her sleep, at eighty-six, after barely a day's illness in her life. She'd been quietly independent to the last, living alone in her small South London flat with no fuss, miles from both of her daughters. But Connie would ring most days and they would chat away. Sheila was wise, someone who really listened. But she also loved a good rant, a good gossip, a good laugh. *I miss you so much, Mum*, Connie whispered silently, her eyes filling with tears, which she quickly blinked away in the crowded carriage. *And I really need your advice. I'm worried. I don't know what to do about Devan.*

Her train arrived fifteen minutes late. But there was no sign of her husband or the red Honda in the semi-circle of cars waiting on the station forecourt. She got out her mobile.

'Hi,' her husband said, sounding disoriented. 'Where are you?'

'At the station.' She tried to keep the irritation out of her voice, but she was dying to get home and take off her 'cruise wear', as she called the outfits deemed suitable for her job, and have a long, hot soak in her own bath. She knew Devan had probably fallen asleep in front of some rugby match or other. It was all he seemed to do, these days, since his retirement last summer as the village GP – a post he'd held for the past thirty years.

There was a moment's silence and she heard scuffling in the background. 'God! Sorry – didn't realize the time. On my way,' Devan said, and clicked off.

'Good trip?' her husband asked, smiling briefly at her as she climbed into the car, but not removing his hand from the gear stick or leaning over to kiss her. His handsome face looked crumpled, his grey jumper had a large stain just below the crew neck and his chin sported a day's growth, the stubble sprouting silvery, although it was only the very edges of his dark hair that showed signs of grey. But Connie wasn't in the mood to comment or criticize.

'Yes, great. Weather was a bit rubbish the day we were in Amsterdam, but otherwise it went pretty smoothly, apart from the usual PPs.' Which stood for Perfect

3

Passengers and was their ironic acronym for any awkward customers on her tours. 'The wife kicked off because there wasn't a "pillow menu" at any of the hotels.'

Devan glanced at her, his thoughtful blue eyes, deep set beneath heavy brows – people likened him to the footballer George Best in his prime – coming suddenly to life. He had such a charming smile, which she'd instantly fallen in love with, that long-ago night in the festival medical tent. 'Is that even a thing?'

Connie nodded. 'These days, if you're in four- or five-star luxury, yes.'

He gave a disbelieving snort. 'Does it include starters and a main?'

'Well, I've seen buckwheat pillows listed – filled with buckwheat hulls, apparently – and one with herbs and essential oils. So you're not far off the mark.'

'Preposterous.' Devan chuckled.

They drove in silence for a while. 'How have you been?' Connie asked.

'Oh, you know . . .' Devan's words were lost in the roar and rattle of a passing tractor.

'Your back? Are the exercises helping at all?'

Her husband's mouth clamped in a thin line of warning. He'd been plagued, on and off, by a degenerating disc in his lower back for the past couple of years, for which he'd been given a slew of exercises by the physio. But he never did them, as far as Connie could tell. 'God, Connie, don't start.'

His words were spoken softly, but she was taken aback by the veiled antagonism. She sympathized with someone in constant pain, obviously, but it was frustrating, watching him do nothing to alleviate the problem – Devan, a doctor who'd endlessly ranted about patients not being prepared to help themselves.

It was on the tip of her tongue to retort, but she took a deep breath instead. 'Hope it stays fine for the Hutchisons tomorrow,' she said, changing the subject as the atmosphere in the car grew thick with the unsaid. 'I got Carole a kitsch pair of clogs in Amsterdam and they painted her name on the side.' Tim and Carole Hutchison owned an impressive Victorian villa at the top of the village, with spectacular views over the Somerset Levels. They always threw a spring party for Carole's birthday, and although Connie wouldn't call them close friends – in fact she thought Tim, a retired fund-manager, pompous in the extreme – an invitation to the yearly bash was much coveted and a matter of pride in the village.

Devan didn't reply at once. 'I suppose we have to go,' he said eventually, as they pulled onto the paved parking space at the side of their house and he turned off the engine. They sat in silence for a moment, a weak evening sun breaking through the clouds and bathing their still faces in light pouring through the windscreen.

Connie frowned as she turned to him. 'You love their parties. You always say it's the best champagne in the county.'

He gave a weary nod. 'Yeah, well . . .'

Connie was about to remonstrate, but she heard Riley, their beloved Welsh terrier, barking excitedly, and jumped out of the car. Biting her lip with disappointment at her husband, she pushed open the front door, bending to enjoy his enthusiastic welcome, to bury her fingers in his soft black and caramel fur and watch the perfect arc of his tail wagging furiously at seeing her.

Every time she went away these days – even if only for a week – she hoped, in her absence, things might shift for Devan. Hoped he might begin to shake off the pall of lethargy that broke her heart. Hoped to see the light in his eyes again. Her trips were like a bubble. She would escape into another world, swept up in round-the-clock responsibility for the tour and its passengers, the extra-ordinary scenery, the diverse smells, the delicious local food – even the sun's rays seeming to fall differently abroad. Her problems with Devan faded into the background for those few short days. But coming home, however much she looked forward to it, forced her to face up to reality again.

The house was as messy as Connie had anticipated – sofa cushions squashed to Devan's shape, newspapers strewn, a dirty wine glass on the coffee table, some dried-up olive stones in a ramekin. She took a deep breath as she entered the cosy farmhouse kitchen at the back of the house, where they'd spent a lot of family time when Caitlin – named after one of Devan's Irish grandmothers – was growing up. It wasn't bad, she conceded, casting an eye over the worktops and range, the oak refectory table. But Devan had never got to grips with surface wiping: the cooker was spattered from the endless fry-ups in which he'd no doubt been indulging, the worktop strewn with toast crumbs and greasy smears, tea and coffee stains ringing the area around the kettle, a pile of used teabags mouldering on a saucer.

She stopped herself seizing a cloth and getting down to it immediately, knowing she was more pernickety than some and not wanting to wade in the second she was through the door in such an obviously censorious fashion. She would unpack first, have the bath she'd been longing for. She didn't want to pick a fight on her first night back.

'Think I'll go up. Been a long day,' Connie said later, pulling herself off the sofa and yawning as she reached for her reading glasses on the side table. They'd spent the evening with a bowl of ready-meal shepherd's pie, frozen peas and ketchup in front of the next episode of a Belgian-police box set. Devan had held it over while she was away, although now she couldn't remember a single thing about who'd been bumped off or why – and was too tired to concentrate anyway.

Devan glanced up from his phone – which, these days, seemed to have become a physical extension of his hand. 'I'm sure it has,' he said absentmindedly, but made no move to join her. 'I might stay up for a bit.'

Connie felt a pang of disappointment. She just wanted to connect with him again, to be close. They had barely spoken all evening, except to catch up with trivial domestic news – such as the flush button coming loose in the downstairs loo and Rees, the gormless plumber's apprentice, coming to fix it. If she went to bed now, she would be dead to the world by the time he crept in beside her. Then in the morning, he would still be asleep when she got up.

'Please . . . come with me,' she said quietly, and saw his face go still for a moment. Then he sighed and nodded.

'Sure, OK,' he said. But his reluctance was evident, and she was upset.

Does he worry I'm after sex or something? she wondered wryly, as she climbed the stairs to their bedroom, placing her glass of water and specs on the bedside table. But she'd stopped having expectations in that arena after a number of humiliatingly unsuccessful seductions on her part during the previous two years.

The last, months ago now, had been the worst – and such a sorry cliché. She had put on a slinky silk camisole in delicate lilac and matching knickers – saved at the back of her drawer from years ago and barely worn – then waited for him to finish in the bathroom, heart knocking as she sat on the bed, hair fluffed and loose. When Devan had seen her, he'd stopped short and stared, eyes wide, as if a woolly mammoth had landed on the duvet. From his twitchy, but resigned expression, he might have been anticipating an unwelcome appointment with the dentist.

He'd recovered sufficiently to force a smile and come over to sit beside her on the bed, picking up her hand and kissing it. But she'd seen the effort it took and she'd snatched it away, leaping up from the bed and shutting herself in the bathroom. She'd felt so utterly mortified – so unsexy, unattractive – that even the thought of it now made her cringe.

Although there had been many wonderful times in the past when they'd made love in this very bed, over the thirty-three years of their marriage. They'd always been good together, their attitude to sex one of relaxed mutual pleasure. No bells and whistles or swinging from the chandelier, neither of them trying to prove anything. Just a light-hearted lust for each other – which she sorely missed.

She realized with a jolt that it was over two years since they'd properly made love – if you didn't count that night last summer when Neil, Connie's best friend, and his husband, Brooks, had asked them over, inventing this lethal cocktail of something green and sweet and fizzy, then burned the chicken pie in the Aga. The only thing they'd eaten all evening was a handful of crisps and a piece of toast. Neither she nor Devan had known which way was up and they'd fallen into bed, heads spinning, and fumbled around in some half-hearted rendition of sex. Because although her husband had only just retired, things had been difficult between them for much longer than that: the strain Devan had been under at the surgery had taken a heavy toll.

He lay beside her now, his book – the usual weighty siege-and-massacre tome – propped on his chest. Connie tried to read, but the sentences swam before her eyes and she knew she was wasting her time. She put down the reader and her glasses and switched off the light, turning on her pillow to face her husband. Despite implying earlier that he wasn't tired, his book was swaying back and forth in his hands, his eyelids fluttering. A small fly was spinning in the beam of the desk lamp he read by, and she watched it for a while, then gently removed his book from his hands, turning down the page corner and closing it.

Devan jerked. 'Hey, I was reading.'

'You were almost asleep.'

He sighed and didn't object, removing his second pillow and slinging it to the floor, then turning off his own light. Their bedroom faced the main street of the village, and a car passed, headlights raking the ceiling in the semi-darkness. Connie placed her palm on his chest and stroked his warm skin. She just wanted some sign of affection, but he made no move to offer any. All he did was clamp her hand to his chest to still her stroking. She could feel the tension flowing off him, like steam from a kettle.

'A cuddle would be nice,' she said.

After a moment's hesitation, Devan lifted his arm so she could lie against him, her head on his shoulder. She felt his hand pull her in, bringing her closer, and she wanted to cry.

'Love you,' she said softly.

'Love you too, Con,' he replied automatically.

She sensed his heart wasn't fully behind his words. Despite that, Connie luxuriated in his embrace. He smelt musty, but she didn't mind. His body was so comforting, so familiar, even in the state he was in, that she didn't want to let him go. When she woke around three in the morning to pee, she remembered that she'd gone to sleep in his arms, something she hadn't done for a very long time.

2

'Oh, come on, Devan.' Tim Hutchison snorted his loud, confident laugh, his jowls wobbling above his pink Ralph Lauren polo shirt, champagne flute waving in Devan's face. 'Admit it! You're a true-blue Conservative at heart. All this whiny-liberal bollocks is just a throwback from your student days.'

Connie watched her husband's mouth twitch. The discussion about immigration, despite Tim's joshing, had been bordering on rancorous, like most current debate in the country. But the difference today was that Devan had got stuck in. As the village doctor, he'd made it his business to stay neutral – except in private – when it came to politics. 'I don't need to know what my patients think about the world,' he always told Connie. 'If I did, I might not want to treat them.' But today he'd been truculent, almost aggressive, when Tim blamed the current crisis in the NHS – which Devan believed in passionately and knew was wobbling for a whole variety of reasons – on migrants.

Connie nudged him surreptitiously, but all she got in return was a glare. She knew he'd had a lot to drink, the delicious champagne flowing from a seemingly bottomless well. But she didn't want him falling out with Tim, who nonetheless possessed the precision of a brain surgeon in his ability to stick the needle in where it would have the most effect.

'Well, if you're a good example of conservatism, I'll take whiny liberal any day of the week,' Devan said.

It was spoken in the same jokey tone, but Tim's eyebrows rose just a fraction and he turned away.

'That was rude,' Connie hissed. 'He's our host.' They were standing by the French windows, from which there was usually a spectacular view across the Somerset Levels, but this afternoon she could barely see past the end of the garden because of low cloud, brought on by a sudden spring squall raging outside.

Devan just shrugged. 'He's an arse, is what he is,' he said. 'We shouldn't even be here.' He bent awkwardly to set his empty glass down against the wall on the strip of parquet floor not hidden by the vintage Turkish rug – where, no doubt, it would be knocked over and broken. She immediately picked it up, then felt his hand in the small of her back, beginning to guide her away.

The large sitting room was full, people standing around in groups and pairs, the hot air reverberating with laughter and chatter, heavy male voices and lighter female ones vying for dominance. A couple of girls from the village were weaving in and out, refilling the glasses and offering trays of unidentifiable one-bite canapés, while Carole bustled and twittered nervously around her guests.

'We can't go yet,' Connie said, resisting the pressure on her back. 'They haven't cut the cake.'

Devan let out a pained sigh. 'Honestly, Connie, I

can't deal with this right now. I feel as if I'm going to explode.'

She looked up into his face. He was blinking rapidly, his mouth twisting, his fists now thrust deep into his trouser pockets. She was hesitating, not knowing what to do, when a man approached them, holding out his hand to Devan, a big grin on his face. He was in his mid-thirties, she thought, blond and broad and blandly tidy in beige chinos. She heard Devan groan quietly.

'All I need,' he muttered.

'The legendary Dr Mac!' the man said, pumping Devan's hand up and down. 'Such a pleasure to see you again.'

Connie had no idea who he was.

'Will Beauregard,' he said, turning to her with his hand held out and the same cheerful grin, as he waited for Devan to respond.

Devan, Connie could see, was settling his features in a gargantuan effort to be nice. 'William,' he said, producing from the depths of his soul his very best smile – the one that had stunned people into submission so often in the past but now looked frayed at the edges. 'A pleasure indeed.'

So this is one of the new GPs, she thought. The two doctors had taken over the practice since Devan's retirement. His back problem had been cited as the reason for him going, but really it was because he couldn't cope any more with the pressure of a single-GP practice in this day and age. He'd had two permanent locums who worked part-time alongside him and a loyal support team, but it was still too much. For years Connie had witnessed the strain he'd been under – her husband put his work before anything else. She'd thought at the time that he'd welcome being free of such a massive responsibility when he was still young enough, at sixty-one, to do all the things he'd never had time for. But so far it hadn't worked out that way.

After a few short weeks, when he was on a 'school's-out' high, Devan had begun to sink. As the days went by he did less and less, his initial enthusiasm for retirement turning into a listless rant about petty stuff: someone stopping across their parking space for ten minutes, the noise of a hedge trimmer, the next-door neighbour's climber invading the trellis on their side of the wall. This wasn't the Devan Connie knew. These petty fixations were ageing him. The vital, charming doctor had turned into an old man overnight. He'd always been so enthusiastic, so full of energy, it never entered her head that he wouldn't embrace retirement with the same verve – maybe, after a break, take on some consultancies or volunteer, write articles and contribute to journals and websites, as many of his colleagues did when they left the health service. Devan had mentioned these options over the years, although never in direct relation to himself.

'How's it going? You know you can always be in touch if you or Rob need help with anything. It can be a little overwhelming at first,' he was saying to Will, assuming the tone of elder statesman.

Will smiled his thanks. 'Our only problem is the

patients all want to be seen by the brilliant Dr Mac. We both feel like the poor relations at the moment.'

Devan gave a self-deprecating laugh, although Connie noted the gratified flush on his cheeks. 'They complained enough when they had me,' he joked.

Ting, ting, ting . . . The spoon tapping insistently against Tim's glass interrupted further conversation and Connie turned to see that the cake had been brought through and placed on a round, polished walnut table in the centre of the room. It was a towering three-tier confection of chocolate icing, raspberries and white chocolate flakes, two sparkler candles in the numbers six and four adorning the top tier.

Tim, his arm round the shoulders of his timid wife – seeming, to Connie, as if he were crushing the very life out of her – began to expound on her virtues, as he did every year, and Connie switched off. She laughed when everyone else did, but surreptitiously she was eyeing the new doctor standing at her side. It was strange, after thirty years, to imagine someone else in the role that Devan had inhabited so authoritatively for so long. He was, as Beauregard suggested, a legend in the area, his diagnostic nous, dedication and impeccable bedside manner vastly appreciated by the sick and dying. *Where has that man gone?* she wondered sadly.

Connie and Devan walked the mile home across the field and down the steep lane to their house in silence. It was chilly and grey. Although the squall had passed, the wind was still strong across the Levels.

'William bloody Beauregard,' Devan muttered sourly, as they tramped on. 'Sounds like something out of the American Civil War. Wasn't there a General Beauregard who got killed for doing something brave and foolish?'

Connie laughed. 'He seems OK. The solid, cheerful sort.'

'He won't be cheerful for long,' Devan harrumphed.

She grabbed his arm, gave him a squeeze. 'Stop it, will you? You've had a really good career out of that surgery.' Her husband was silent. 'And there'll be two of them,' she added.

Still no response. Then Devan said, 'I think he's a bit of a smug twat, if I'm honest.'

Connie snatched away her hand. She was worn out from trying to sympathize with him. 'Fine,' she said. 'Be a miserable old bastard. Will was only being friendly. You could tell he really respected you and your reputation.'

Later that night she lay in bed alone. She'd had a long talk with her daughter as soon as Devan declared he was going to the pub after supper. The Skittle House – 'Skittles' to the locals – was on the corner of the main street, the publican a Yorkshireman called Stacy, friend to them both.

'Are you worried?' Caitlin had asked, after Connie had filled her in about her father's mood. 'He sounded very grumpy when I called him last week. Said he was really missing you.'

Connie sighed. 'So he keeps telling me. But when

I'm here, he does nothing but avoid me. All he seems to want to do is stare at his phone, watch sport and drink too much. He's at the pub right now, despite boozing all day at the Hutchisons'.'

'And he won't consider antidepressants?'

'Well, no . . . because he's not depressed, is he? According to his own expert medical opinion, your dad's merely "adjusting" to a big life change.'

'Well, I suppose he might have a point. It's not even a year since he stopped working.'

Connie had sighed, aware that Devan's distress dated much further back than that. 'I know, but . . .'

'Poor Mum. Must be hell, having him so grouchy all the time.' Caitlin paused. 'I hope he's not being mean to you.'

'God, no. Your dad would never be mean,' Connie said firmly, anxious to dispel her daughter's concern. Although she'd almost rather he *was* mean – that he'd say something she could really get her teeth into and they could have a good old-fashioned row. They'd always been good at rowing, and even better at making up. Instead, the constant drip, drip of dyspeptic sniping and lack of motivation dragged her down so much that she was beginning to dread being in his company for any length of time.

Mother and daughter had talked on for a while, mainly about Bash, Connie's three-year-old grandson – who'd apparently sprayed the sitting room with quantities of suntan lotion while his mum was making his tea, leaving pockets of gunk in the loop pile of the

17

sisal carpet, which Caitlin was finding impossible to get out.

Connie read after the call, finally drifting off around eleven. Devan was still not home, but Stacy sometimes had a lock-in for his mates on a Sunday night. She wasn't worried.

The sound of her mobile woke her from a very deep sleep. Devan's number came up on the screen, but it wasn't her husband who spoke. 'Connie, it's Stacy here. Slight problem. 'Fraid your old man's kaylied, can't seem to stand up on his own. Thought I'd bring him home, but he doesn't have his keys on him . . . I worried you wouldn't hear the bell.'

Connie sat up. 'God, Stacy, I'm so sorry. I'll come and get him.'

'It's no bother. If you'd just open the door.'

She thanked him and tumbled out of bed, pulling her dressing gown over her pyjamas as she hurried downstairs. She saw her husband's keys immediately, sitting on the ledge by the front door.

The following morning Devan staggered down to the kitchen around ten o'clock. Connie and Stacy had tried to give him water, then coffee, the night before, but their attempts had just met with flailing arms and angry grunts. So they'd dragged him upstairs and dropped his dead weight onto the spare bed – in what used to be Caitlin's room. Connie, mortified at her husband's behaviour, had thanked the publican profusely, then ripped off Devan's trainers and wrapped him in the section of duvet not already squashed under his prone, fully clothed body. She'd spent a sleepless night worrying that he might vomit, choke and die. But she was too angry to sleep in the same room as his chain-saw snoring and make sure he didn't. By morning she was not in the greatest of moods.

'Hi.' Devan slumped into a kitchen chair and eyed her cautiously as she began to unload the dishwasher on the far side of the room. When she saw him sitting there, so pathetic, so wasted, she began to slam the plates and cups onto the shelves, hurl the cutlery into the drawer, clank the pans and bang the cupboard doors shut. The cacophony made her ears sing, but she didn't care.

Her husband didn't flinch, however, and when she eventually shut the last cupboard door and leaned on the other side of the kitchen table, slightly out of breath and glaring at him, he gave her a sad smile.

'Made your point.' He straightened up, still in his clothes from the day before. 'Listen, I'm really sorry about last night. I don't know what got into me. I think it was seeing that shiny new doctor, bursting with vim and vigour. It just reminded me of myself, all those years ago . . .'

Connie gazed at him. 'Retirement doesn't have to be grim, you know,' she said gently. Despite her irritation, she did feel sorry for him. She understood how hard it could be for anyone, going full tilt for so many years, then having nothing to get out of bed for. But that was months ago now and, if anything, he seemed even more unhappy. The problem was, he'd never made an actual plan about what he would do when he stopped working. Suggestions had been bandied about, but neither of them had given it proper, serious thought. He'd been too stressed at the time, and since then, apparently too low.

He stared at her for a second, a calculating edge appearing in those deep blue eyes. 'Really? Maybe you should try it sometime,' he said, raising his eyebrows in question, the faint smile that accompanied it barely reaching his eyes.

Connie shook her head. This subject had been slowly building a head of steam over the past year. Now hardly a week passed when Devan didn't try his luck. 'I've told you a million times . . .' she sat down so she could meet his eye '. . . *I'm not ready*. It's different for you. You got to the stage where you hated your work. I still love mine.'

Devan's expression hardened as she watched him rasp his fingers roughly across the day-old stubble on his chin. 'I *didn't* hate my work,' he said dully. 'I always hoped I'd keep going till I was at least seventy. It just became impossible . . . too many patients, not enough time or money.' He gave a dispirited sigh. 'I keep thinking I've made a terrible mistake, giving it all up. But then I remember the reality.'

She'd heard the same thing so often she felt she was running out of ways to respond helpfully. He was, she was certain, using her retirement as a peg upon which to pin his unhappiness. 'But there are loads of things you could do now,' she said encouragingly. 'You were going to ring Lillian, weren't you, find out about that medical website she works for? Or you could talk to your mates at the Royal College of GPs – they're bound to have some ideas. With your expertise . . .'

Devan gave a dismissive shrug. 'There was one thing that cheered me up, Connie, when things were getting on top of me at the surgery and I knew I'd have to quit,' he said, completely ignoring her suggestions. 'It was the thought you and I would finally have time, after all these manic years of work, to do stuff together – hang out with the family, go places, see things, meet people.' He levelled his gaze at her, clearly on a mission to make her understand. 'We've always wanted to do South America, the Great Wall . . . You haven't even been to Australia yet. And little Bash, you hardly see him because you're always away. He won't be young for ever, you know.'

Connie frowned, her face set. She also looked forward to doing some of the travelling Devan was suggesting. But her summer tours didn't preclude that. She was only away – sporadically – from April to October, which left five months free. What upset her now was the below-the-belt accusation about their grandson. She was the first to admit she didn't see enough of him when she was working, but she tried really hard to make up for it during the rest of the year.

'You're not being fair, Devan. I never said I'd retire when you did.' Stupidly, she'd come to realize, she hadn't considered it might be a problem. When Devan didn't immediately agree with her, she went on more gently, 'Did I?'

He gave her a sulky look. 'Maybe not as such. But I assumed, once I did, that you would too.'

'We never talked about it, though, did we?' Connie kept her tone reasonable, but his voice rose.

'So? You're going to keep on doing this silly job for the next ten years, just to spite me?'

'"Silly"?' She was hurt. He sounded like Lynne, her elder sister. Lynne was the one who'd been to college, eventually becoming head of admissions at Aberystwyth University, unlike Connie, who'd dropped out of school at seventeen. She always seemed to put patronizing quote marks round the word 'job', when talking about Connie's trips.

Not that Connie needed validation for what she did. It was her dream job, always had been. She'd previously worked – not as happily – for a self-styled lifestyle guru with an emporium in Bridgwater. Fiona Raven was a chef, designer and broadcaster, who wrote cookery and party books, and produced her own range of gourmet foods, such as jars of cooking sauces, fruit compôtes and nut butters. Connie was her Girl – then Woman – Friday, a difficult job she knew she did well, but for which she got scant credit from Fiona. So as soon as Caitlin had left home – twelve years ago now – Connie had applied for a manager's job with a railway-tours company and never looked back. Having found, so much later in life, the job she loved, she had no desire to give it all up just yet.

Now Devan reached out for her across the table. 'I didn't mean silly, you know I didn't. I'm sorry.' He looked so weary, suddenly, that she thought he might fall asleep where he sat. 'I think your job is great, and I know you love it. But what about us, Connie? I'm sure it hasn't escaped your notice that we're not getting any younger.'

'Oh, please.' She pulled her hand from his and stood up. *How did the conversation twist away from yesterday's horrendous binge, so that now it appears to be all my fault?*

Shaking her head in frustration, she moved round the table, wrapped her arms around her husband's shoulders, kissed his bent head and tried another tack. 'I'm worried about you, Devan,' she said softly. 'This drinking thing, it isn't you.'

For a moment he let her comfort him. But then he nudged her arms off and straightened, heaving himself to his feet. He looked wrecked, his tone bleak. 'I've said I'm sorry.'

Connie took in a big breath to give it a final go. 'You don't think you should at least talk to one of the new doctors?'

The stare he gave her was withering. 'About what?'

She didn't dare mention depression again, as she had so many times. But this time she didn't need to.

'I'm sick to death of you and Caty implying I'm depressed,' he said wearily. 'Depression is an illness, Connie, like lung cancer or diabetes. Its symptoms are well categorized.' He raised his hand and began ticking off on his fingers. 'I don't feel hopeless about the future. I'm not tearful. I'm not anxious. I still take real pleasure in lots of things – like a good glass of wine or a rugby match.' He gave her a tight smile. 'I'm not depressed.'

She didn't speak, noting there was no mention of herself in his current list of pleasures.

'Maybe I'm not on top form at the moment,' he went on, 'but that's mostly to do with my bloody back. And if you seriously think I'm going to share my innermost thoughts with either of those smug twelve-year-olds, then you've got another think coming.'

His look challenged her to disagree. But she still said nothing. What was the point?

'I'm going to take a shower,' he said, turning away.

Connie heard him slowly climb the stairs, then a minute later the sound of the shower pump from the bathroom. She sat down again, exhausted. She had no idea how best to help him. He'd always been wilful – it was what had made him a good doctor. He would fight to the bitter end to secure the care he thought a patient needed. But when it came to himself, he was blind as to how his actions were affecting himself and all those around him.

Tears pricked behind her eyes as she thought back to his repeated pleas that she should retire, or scale back her tours. She didn't feel her age in the same way Devan clearly did. Her shoulder-length auburn hair had help from Janine at the village hairdresser, these days, and her grey eyes required drops because they were dry. She needed reading glasses, but she'd recently ordered varifocal contact lenses, *Which I must pick up before I go away again*, she reminded herself. But she was still slim – despite the irritating pad of post-menopausal stomach fat that seemed resistant to all her efforts – and her fair, freckle-prone skin still smooth because it never went in the sun without Factor 50 and a hat. But it wasn't really about looks. Connie didn't feel like a woman in her sixties on any level. She was fit and energetic still, and she knew she was good at her job. Her tours provided so much pleasure: to give them up now might crush her.

If Devan keeps going on at me like this, she thought, *it's not going to end well*. She didn't examine what she meant by this, not then, but she felt her stubbornness limbering up, like a substitute on the touchline waiting to run onto the pitch. Throughout her childhood, as her mother had often reminded her, Connie's stubborn nature had been a thorn in her side.

3

The family were coming for Easter. Connie had been so looking forward to it – they rarely had time to make the trek to Somerset. Ash's punishing schedule as a television producer and the demands of his extensive family in Manchester usually resulted in Caitlin coming with just Bashir. But she had been worried about how Devan would cope with having a small child in the house for two days, even though he adored his grandson.

She remembered the day they'd met Bash for the first time. It was the morning after the birth, the hospital room boiling hot, Caitlin flushed and puffy, dazed as she carefully handed Devan the baby. Connie would never forget the absolute absorption on her husband's face, the intense love in his eyes as he tenderly cradled his grandson for the first time, the little bundle so small and frail in his man-sized arms. She had been overwhelmed, realizing that the huge love she felt for Devan, and he for her, had now spawned two further generations of love. Thinking of that moment now, she told herself nothing had really changed. But the unquestioned closeness, the feeling of being part of a loving team, no longer seemed so evident.

The days since the drunken binge had been quiet at home. Connie had not thought at the time that he'd heard what she said, but he did seem to be making more effort, pointedly doing things about the house – like sanding the scarred kitchen table, a job he'd been talking about for months. He couldn't keep it up for long, though, and she would come home from shopping or coffee with a friend to find him slumped in front of some match or other, one hand clutching his phone, the other cradling a glass of red wine – often fast asleep. He was utterly resistant to going out, even for a walk, and sent Connie on her own to supper with friends. 'Tell them it's my back,' he'd say. And when she'd raise her eyebrows at him, he merely snapped, 'It's true.'

But the prospect of seeing his daughter and grandson seemed to spark him up, and Saturday morning saw a version of the old Devan, spruced up and standing straight, even coming with her to the supermarket and offering to make his famous sausage pasta for supper. Connie held her breath, hoping this resurgence would last at least till Sunday night.

As Devan fussed over which brand of penne was best, she leaned on the trolley in the supermarket aisle and remembered with a pang the first time he'd cooked her sausage pasta, about twenty years ago now. She had always been the family cook, but that January weekend she'd slipped on black ice on the pavement outside the house when she'd taken their previous dog, a rescue greyhound called Corky, for a walk just before it got dark.

Devan had examined the painful area, gently

manipulating her foot, then held a packet of frozen peas to her ankle and rubbed in pain-relief gel. He'd settled her on the sofa, her foot elevated on a cushion, then handed her a cup of tea. Caitlin, about twelve at the time, was having a sleepover with a friend, so they had the house to themselves. Devan could not have been more solicitous.

He'd stroked her head as she lay there. 'I'm doing supper. Going to surprise you.'

She'd laughed, looking sceptical. 'Beans on toast?'

He'd tapped his nose with his finger. 'Trust me, I'm a doctor.'

Over the next hour or so, Connie had been aware of waves of intense and focused industry emanating from the kitchen. Occasionally, as she dozed or read her book, Devan would pop his head round the sitting-room door, cheeks flushed with his exertions. 'Where's the sieve?' or 'Have you seen that small knife with the black handle?'

Eventually he summoned her to the table, almost carrying her into the kitchen, where candles lined the centre of the carefully laid table. The smell was mouth-watering. She noticed her *River Café* cookbook open on the side – which she'd read, but never cooked from, the ingredients mostly high-end Italian and not available locally. *He never does things by halves*, she'd thought, amused at the rooky cook's ambition.

Devan had uncorked a bottle of wine, and her tummy rumbled in anticipation at the dish of steaming penne and bowl of tossed green salad he set before her.

'Hope it's OK,' he said anxiously, as she prepared to take the first bite. 'I couldn't get proper Italian spicy sausages, so these are just normal ones and I added more chilli.' He watched her closely, seeming to hold his breath as she lifted her fork to her mouth.

The pasta was gorgeous, rich and robust but . . . She gasped. Her mouth was suddenly on fire, her eyes spouting water, her head feeling as if it were about to explode. She spluttered and grabbed for her glass, gulping the wine as if it were water. But it did no good, only made her choke.

She could see Devan's stare – clearly offended – through the blur of her tears.

'Hot . . . hot . . .' She tried to speak, fanning her open mouth. And as she saw him lifting his own fork to his lips, she held out her hand. 'Don't.'

But Devan kept going, thrusting in a huge mouthful of pasta, his scornful expression implying she was being pathetic. She watched as he chewed for a moment. Then his face, too, contorted and he dropped his fork with a clatter. She could almost see steam coming out of his ears.

A second later they were laughing – huge gasps of mirth that had them clutching their napkins to their burning mouths, tears of laughter and pain running down their bright red, sweating faces.

'Didn't you check it?' she managed to ask, when she could finally get her breath.

Devan wiped his eyes, his face crumpling with laughter again. 'I thought it tasted a bit insipid, so I threw in three of those dried chillies from that old plastic bag in the herb drawer.'

'Oh, my God, you're kidding! Those are the ones I got from that roadside stall in Turkey last year, remember? They're absolutely lethal.'

Once they'd calmed down and their mouths were smarting but no longer on fire, Devan suggested, 'Beans on toast?' which set them off again.

Despite the chilli assault and her sore ankle, they'd ended up making love that night. She remembered it because, without their daughter in the next room, she had relaxed and allowed herself to cry out, uninhibited, as he eventually, after a delicious hour or so, brought her to orgasm. He was a good lover. *Was.*

She felt a tingling wave of longing pass through her body now, at the memory. But Devan was asking her something about bay leaves and she forced herself back to the present.

Bash was a beautiful child, and not just because his doting grandmother said so. Ash, his Indian father, had given him huge dark eyes, luscious lashes straight as a die, and a head of shiny dark hair. His mother had given him her wide, full mouth and cheeky grin, his grandfather the dimple in his chin. He was sturdy and even-tempered, liking to potter around getting on with things on his own. But if you turned your back, his telescopic arms would grab anything you assumed was out of reach, and it would be gone, hoarded in some secret place, perhaps never to see the light of day again.

This had been the fate of Caitlin's passport on a recent trip to France, resulting in a tedious and very expensive visit to the British Embassy, and Ash's mobile, lost for two days inside a Playmobile recycling truck they'd given Bash for his second birthday.

They had just finished a roast chicken lunch – with Connie's famously crunchy roast potatoes – on Easter Sunday and were lounging around the sitting room. Bash was playing with a pile of ivory mahjong tiles from Connie's parents' time in Singapore after the war, as the adults discussed the timing of Caitlin and Ash's journey back to Shoreditch.

'I'll give him supper and get him into his jammies before we go,' Caitlin said, 'so we can just transfer him when we get home.' She gave a wry laugh. 'It sometimes works.' She was sitting next to her father, and now she nudged him in the ribs. 'Stroll before we go, Dad?'

Connie saw Devan hesitate. He'd looked tired today and a bit twitchy, she thought, at being dragged from his solitary routines by the unaccustomed activity in the house. But the weekend had been a success. She was pleased that he'd made an effort for them all.

'You go,' he said to Caitlin. 'My back . . .'

'Poor Dad.' She stroked his arm. 'What are you doing about that?'

'Oh, you know, stretches and stuff . . . I've got a sheet of exercises as long as your arm from the physio.'

Caitlin cast Connie a glance, with a questioning arched eyebrow. 'And are you doing them?'

Devan gave a short laugh. 'Don't you start. Your mother's on at me day and night.' His tone was unfairly resentful, Connie thought, given she hadn't mentioned the exercises in weeks.

'Well, it's important, Dad.'

He nodded. 'Yeah, yeah, I do know.' He got to his feet, perhaps to prove that he could, without too much trouble. 'You lot had better get off for that walk, if you're going.'

For a moment he stood there, looking lost. Then he frowned. 'By the way, has anyone seen my pen?' He was talking about his Mont Blanc biro, sleek and black, which Connie had given him for his sixtieth as a designated crossword pen. 'It's always on the table, there.' He pointed to the one at the end of the sofa where he usually sat.

Everyone looked around vaguely, and shook their heads.

'It probably rolled off,' Ash said, obligingly kneeling down and laying his head on the wood floor to peer under the sofa, pulling out a square of yellow Lego and – embarrassingly – an old crisp, plus a used tissue from the dusty space. But no pen.

Connie considered Ash Mistry the perfect son-in-law. Her daughter, who was a script editor, had met him at a BBC script conference. Ash, despite his high-octane job, was the calm one of the two, the most practical, Caitlin more volatile and given to bouts of anxiety that meant she spent too much time catastrophizing – mostly about ill health and accidents

33

happening to those she loved. Ash grounded her, and Connie loved him for it.

'Maybe you took it upstairs,' she suggested to her husband.

But Devan was eyeing Bash, who looked up from his mahjong tiles, obviously sensing the atmosphere. 'Bash, sweetheart, did you see Grandpa's pen?' Devan went over to the little boy and sat on the nearest armchair, leaning forward to bring his face close to his grandson's. 'Did you move my black pen somewhere?'

Bash shook his head solemnly.

'I won't be cross if you did,' Devan went on, although he already sounded stern to Connie. When his grandson didn't respond, just stared, wide-eyed, he added, 'Maybe you were drawing with it.'

'I wasn't,' Bash said, blinking his long lashes anxiously and glancing at his mother.

'Did you hide it in one of your trucks then . . . just for fun? *Did you?*'

His tone was sharp now and Bash's chin began to wobble, his eyes filling with tears as he backed away from his grandfather.

'Stop it, Dad,' Caitlin butted in. 'You're upsetting him. He doesn't know where your pen is.'

Devan frowned at his daughter. 'I was just asking. He's got form, Caitlin. Remember the passport?'

'I know, and I'll check around. But don't badger him.'

There was an uncomfortable tension as Caitlin swiftly bent to pick up her son and carry him out of the room. Ash hurried after them with an apologetic grin.

'I wasn't badgering him,' Devan said grumpily. 'Was I?' He looked at Connie, suddenly bewildered.

'A bit. You could see he was getting upset.'

He sighed. 'I didn't mean to.'

Connie went over and put her arms round him. For a moment they embraced in silence. She felt his body almost limp against hers, as if the life had gone out of him. Pulling back, she looked into his face and saw tears in his eyes.

'I don't know . . . I just can't seem to get anything right these days.'

She wanted to say that was ridiculous, but it wasn't. She wanted to reiterate that he should get help, but she knew it would be pointless. She had a strong urge to shake him and make him wake up to what was going on, but she knew that was cruel and would be completely unhelpful. So she just hugged him again, until she heard her daughter talking to Ash in the hall.

Connie pushed Bash in the buggy as they made their way down the high street in the direction of the sub-post office and the Wells road, where they would turn right and come back into the village on a loop. It was a cool, breezy day, the spring sun briefly warm on their faces as it emerged from behind the scudding clouds. Ash strolled ahead, hands in his jacket pockets, seemingly deep in thought.

'Dad's in a right old state,' Caitlin said.

'Oh . . . I thought he'd been OK over the weekend.'

'Really, Mum?' Caitlin glanced at her, eyes wide.

'Well, yes. Until the pen incident . . . and he didn't mean to get at Bash.'

'Mum! He looks dreadful,' her daughter said, clearly shocked at Connie's blindness. 'Sort of defeated, don't you think? And unnecessarily snippy all the time.'

She sighed. 'Maybe I'm just used to it.'

'Can't you talk to that new doctor Dad was carping on about?'

Connie snorted. 'And get us both killed?'

They turned the corner, Ash now a long way ahead.

'So what *are* you going to do?'

She shrugged, mildly irritated that her daughter thought she could wave a magic wand and make Devan happy again. 'I've suggested a million things he might enjoy. Things that keep him in the medical loop, where he can use his substantial know-how. All of which he's aware of himself, of course. But I irritate him enough as it is, just by asking him, for instance, to take Riley for a walk or have the occasional shower.'

They walked on in silence. Connie greeted someone she knew, who was raking old leaves from the flower-bed near his fence as they passed. Riley barked at their snuffling old pug, which gave a half-hearted woof in response.

'He'll be OK, once he's adjusted,' Connie said finally.

'And his back?'

'I'm pretty sure that's not as bad as he makes out. He's using it as an excuse not to do anything at the moment. But, of course, the less he does, the worse it'll get.'

Caitlin put her arm round Connie's shoulders as they walked. She was taller than her mother, with shiny dark auburn – almost plum – hair and her father's deep-set blue eyes in an intelligent, open face. 'Very tough on you, all this,' she said, giving her a squeeze.

'We'll get through it,' Connie replied. 'We always do.'

But she realized, despite her confident words, that there hadn't been anything very significant to 'get through' till now. Their marriage simply hadn't been tested. *We've been lucky*, she thought, looking back on decades during which they had shared their life on a mostly even keel. She felt a pang of self-pity. She spent so much time trying to work around Devan's moods, these days, but it was wearing her down. And she didn't even have her mum to confide in any more.

Connie thought back wistfully to the night they had met. She had been just twenty-four and had gone to Glastonbury with her American friend, Gaby. It was the first time the festival had been called 'Glastonbury' and the first year of the new Pyramid stage, which looked huge and impressive but was actually shed-work standard: metal sheeting and telegraph poles. Gaby was a dedicated Hawkwind fan and although Connie was a bit vague about space rock – her preference being Motown – she went along because she loved music, loved dancing, loved meeting new people.

But Gaby had surreptitiously taken one of the many unidentified substances circulating in the summer darkness and had suddenly begun to sweat and puke, becoming quickly disoriented. Connie, realizing that something was very wrong, managed to stagger for what seemed like miles through the swaying, intoxicated crowds, the cold, churned-up mud squelching between her toes, clutching her limp friend against her shoulder, until she reached the medical tent on the outer edges of the field, where she almost threw Gaby into the volunteer doctor's arms.

Devan and the nurse – who seemed to be the one in charge and way more experienced than the trainee doctor – took over, while Connie stared anxiously on, although Gaby was already coming round by the time they reached the tent.

To tell the truth, Connie was quickly distracted from her friend's drama as she basked in the beam of Devan McCabe's extraordinary, reassuring smile. It was as if she herself had been drugged, aware that she couldn't help gazing back into those blue eyes. He'd looked so funny, so conservative and self-conscious in his tidy jeans and blue shirt, compared to the drunken, barefoot, T-shirt-and-shorts mob outside the tent. She wanted to hug him.

This is only a passing phase, she told herself now. But she was conscious of a new wariness when she was around her husband, these days. He was pushing her away and she was worried about losing the strength – and inclination – to push back.

Another tour beckoned in a week, which Connie decided would do her the world of good. She couldn't keep worrying about what Devan was up to while she was gone. She had to focus on her job, enjoy her time away. Maybe by looking after herself, she'd feel stronger and better able to sympathize with Devan when she was at home.

After the family had gone back to London, she became busy checking all the travel details and touching base with the thirty-two travellers, introducing herself and enquiring about any special requirements they might have. The new data protection laws prevented her knowing their ages or addresses in advance, so during those calls she had to find out as much as she could with some subtle, well-placed questioning. The more she knew, the more she could help them enjoy the perfect holiday.

They seemed a chatty, easy-going lot this time – she didn't detect any obvious troublemakers. Not at first. A night in Strasbourg, the Bernina Express across the Alps and a luxurious week beside Lake Como was one of her favourite tours and she was ashamed to say that she was almost holding her breath until she could leave.

4

As Connie re-entered the grand foyer of the lakeside hotel on day three, she heard her name called. A couple of her charges were hurrying anxiously towards her across the expanse of mosaic marble, which gleamed in the light of the sun pouring through the open doors to the street.

'I've been calling you, Sandra,' Connie said, as they reached her. 'The minibus has just left for the ferry. They couldn't wait any longer.'

Sandra, a plump woman in her late sixties with aubergine candy-floss hair in a halo round her powdery face and a determined, wilful air, was wheezy with indignation. 'You said we were leaving at nine thirty and we're barely ten minutes late.' She frowned at Connie, clearly convinced it was her fault.

Connie glanced at the ornate gold clock above the reception desk. It said nine fifty-five. 'I did try to reach you.'

Sandra's husband, Terry – thin and mild-mannered by contrast and never allowed to say much – nodded. 'We –' He was silenced by a glare from his wife.

'So would you like me to order you a taxi?' Connie asked quickly, to stem the flow of Sandra's annoyance. 'The ferry doesn't go till ten past so you should just make it if you leave now.' She paused. 'And if you don't, there's another in an hour.'

'Will the taxi be free?' Sandra demanded. 'We've already paid for the minibus.'

'I'm afraid not. But it's not far – it won't be more than ten euros.'

'Hmm.' Sandra snorted angrily. 'This really isn't good enough. We were only in the dining room and you knew we were booked on the ferry.'

Connie gave Sandra her best smile. She had checked the dining room when they didn't turn up and rung Sandra's mobile twice. 'Let's get the taxi organized.'

After she'd seen the still-grumbling Sandra and her long-suffering husband off to the ferry, she stood for a moment beneath the arches of the hotel frontage, looking out across the lake. It was a gorgeous spring day, the sunlight catching the small ruffles on the water in hundreds of glinting flashes that hurt her eyes, the hills on the far side a soft grey-green, contrasting with the pink and cream walls and terracotta roofs of numerous lakeside villas. She watched a white ferry gliding past with an Italian flag flapping at the stern, bright orange lifebelts decorating the bow, and smiled to herself, taking in slow lungfuls of the clean, invigorating air. She loved the Italian lakes.

Half of the group had been taken into Como itself – an hour's drive from the hotel – the other half to Bellagio. Neither would be back for lunch, so she had the day to herself. Sometimes she would go with them on the day trips – there was so much to see – but she'd visited Bellagio many times over her twelve years as a tour manager. Today she felt like having a bit of time for herself. She might risk a swim in the hotel pool, then indulge in a light lunch on the terrace overlooking the lake. It was frowned upon to swim with the tour guests, so Connie had to slip in her swims while her flock was off sightseeing or after they'd gone in to shower and change for dinner.

The pool was set in the mature gardens behind the hotel, currently alive with the purple and pink blooms of banks of azaleas. It was unheated and would be freezing at this time of year, the outside temperature a moderate sixteen degrees today. But Connie and her friend Neil had begun wild swimming the previous year and regularly took off for a morning in one of the nearby rivers. The shivering anticipation, the adrenalin punch of the cold water, the stinging, reddened skin, the exhilaration afterwards – they both found it addictive. So she was looking forward to a dip in the chilly pool.

Connie brought her book with her to lunch, but she didn't read it. The view from the cool first-floor terrace was compelling as she ate her tricolore salad – the drizzled olive oil bright green, the tomatoes softly ripe, the buffalo mozzarella piquant and creamy – and sipped a small glass of chilled Chardonnay, gazing across the water towards the distant hills.

She was thinking of Devan. She knew she should message him – as she did every day, religiously, while she was away – but he hadn't responded to her last two

43

and she was reluctant to send another. When she'd first started touring, she'd sent emails – there was no Whats-App in those days – crammed with photographs of lakes, mountains and ferries, churches, monuments and tulips. Her family had seen it all. So now she just sent short anecdotes: an amusing incident on the train or a thumbnail sketch of a colourful passenger. She wasn't sure Devan even read them any more, not in his current state, but she persevered nonetheless, not wanting the weeks to go by with them both revolving in a totally separate universe.

In the days before she left this time, her husband had seemed to shut down, maintaining an almost impenetrable silence, greeting her attempts at conversation with an indifferent 'Mmm,' or a vague nod, as if she'd interrupted him in the middle of something important. She had tried not to be hurt by it, but in the end had given up and retreated into her own wounded silence.

'Hope it goes well,' Devan had said, as they drew up at the station for her to take the train to London, then the tube to St Pancras. He sounded sheepish suddenly, as if he might be ashamed of himself and his behaviour. So Connie had reached over and kissed his cheek. He'd smiled briefly, and she'd seen a flash of sadness in his eyes.

'Love you,' she said. He had merely nodded.

Tears sprang to her eyes now, and she was grateful for the sunglasses she wore against the glare off the lake. *Does he still love me?* It was something she had never, until this moment, questioned. But now it occurred to her – shockingly – that his low mood, the way he was distancing himself from her, might not just be a retirement issue. It might be related to *her*, to *them*. *Is it me who's the problem? Is he unhappy because of our marriage?* It was a very painful thought.

She shook herself, then turned to catch the waiter's attention and ordered a double espresso. The swim had been gorgeous, the pool empty except for one ageing American lady in a white swimming hat and goggles, doing steady breaststroke lengths despite the water being numbingly cold. Connie hadn't lingered afterwards on a poolside lounger, the early May sun not warm enough for that. She'd just wrapped herself in the ample white towelling robe provided in her room and hurried upstairs for a divine shower.

The sheet of hot water pouring down her naked body from the overhead fitting – which she estimated was an impressive ten inches across – made her wish Devan were there to enjoy it too. They used to shower together sometimes, in the past, soaping each other and themselves, chatting and laughing about nothing in particular in the steamy warmth of the capacious shower Devan had insisted on installing when they'd first bought the house. It wasn't a sexual thing – although occasionally it led to that – just a cosy ritual they both enjoyed.

As she sat at her table, stirring a small brown-sugar cube into her coffee, a voice behind her dragged her back to the present.

'Is it too breezy out here?' The carefully modulated vowels were instantly recognizable. Dinah Worthington, in her early eighties, was on the tour with her godson. She was like a duchess, Connie thought – although she'd never met a real one – with her gracious but slightly condescending politeness and the obvious expectation that doors would be opened, chairs pulled out and an arm always at the ready for her to lean on. All of which her godson, Jared, patiently and apparently willingly supplied.

Connie turned. 'How was Como?'

Dinah started. 'Gosh, Connie, I didn't see you there.' She pulled her floppy straw hat from her white curls and sat down with a grateful sigh at the vacant table next to Connie's. The terrace was nearly empty now. It was gone three and the restaurant in a lull between lunch and dinner.

Jared hovered for a moment, looking around as if he were checking there wasn't somewhere better, then sat down opposite Dinah. With his grey polo shirt, sunglasses hooked on the top button, rust-red trousers and deck shoes with no socks, he would have passed unnoticed in a crowd of British holidaymakers, except for his eye-catching Bradley Cooper hair – thick, shiny brown with golden natural highlights and falling, one length, to the collar of his shirt. It would flop, at regular intervals, across his face, and he would sweep it back over his head, like a film star.

In the few exchanges she'd had with him so far – mostly pertaining to his godmother, such as managing the air-conditioning controls in her room or whether Connie thought Dinah would cope with the steep Varenna streets – she'd found him reserved, bordering on standoffish. Not unpleasant, it was just as if he wasn't quite comfortable being on the tour. Which maybe had something to do with his age – early fifties, Connie reckoned. Almost twenty years younger than the majority of the group.

She watched as the waiter poured mineral water into their glasses, Dinah taking a long draught, then sighing gratefully. 'We did the stunning cathedral, then the Garibaldi place, which was a trifle dull, I thought. The others were off up to Brunate in the funicular, but I simply can't do heights any more. So Jared, bless him, organized a cab.' She gave her godson an apologetic smile, patting his hand across the table. 'I feel bad, depriving you of all those marvellous views, darling.'

Jared shook his head. 'I've seen them before, Dinah. Much nicer to sit here with you, having a nice cool drink, than be stuffed into a lurching tin box, forced to listen to oohing and aahing in six different languages.'

Connie gave a dutiful laugh, but eyed him, thinking he was being unnecessarily derogatory about his fellow tourists.

'It is maddening being old,' Dinah said wistfully. 'I used to love funiculars, ski lifts, views from the tops of mountains.'

Jared's voice was suddenly full of kindness. 'There's lots of other things to enjoy. We've got the Villa Cipressi gardens tomorrow. You'll love them. Maybe the wisteria will still be out.' He turned to Connie with a charming smile. 'Are you coming with us?'

Feeling bad for her hasty initial assessment, she nodded. 'So you've been here before?'

'Absolutely,' Jared replied airily. 'Travelling is my thing.'

She realized he was unusually tanned for an Englishman in early May and wondered where else he had been.

At dinner that night she sat with Ruth and Ginty, friends from college, now in their late sixties, who met up every year for a holiday without their husbands. Connie always ate with her flock, but moved around to sit at different tables, so that by the end of a tour she had engaged with everyone at least once. The group tended to form their own allegiances, making friends and pairing up as the week went on. Sometimes she was eating with five or six, sometimes only two. A solitary traveller could pose a problem – she had to make sure he or she was accommodated and never left to eat alone.

Connie occasionally found supper conversation heavy going, but mostly her fellow diners were buzzing with what they'd seen that day and eager to chat about what was coming up tomorrow. Tonight would be easy: Ruth and Ginty were lively, mischievous and loved nothing better than a good gossip.

'So, the godson.' Ginty lowered her voice and widened her blue eyes dramatically at Connie. Jared and Dinah were tucked against the wall on the far side of the large dining room, whose windows looked out onto what was now a breathtaking indigo and gold sunset. 'I'm thinking he might be gay. But Ruth insists otherwise.'

They both waited expectantly for Connie to reply.

'You know I can't comment,' she said, with an amused smile.

'No, no, of course not.' A fair-skinned blonde with a rounded figure she liked to show off, with clinging fabrics and low necklines, Ruth chuckled. 'Ginty's reasons for thinking he's gay are totally spurious. She says no straight man would be so kind and good-tempered with his godmother – who's obviously a bit of a handful, however gracious she pretends to be.'

'Unless, of course, she was about to leave him her fortune . . . I hadn't thought of that,' Ginty mused, as she shot a sneaky glance across the room towards the pair in question, who were deep in conversation.

'Stop staring! He'll think you fancy him,' Ruth hissed, playfully cuffing her friend's arm and causing them both to break into schoolgirl giggles – fuelled, no doubt, by the copious quantities of Soave they'd consumed.

Connie had not, so far, considered Jared's sexuality. He was certainly not a flirt – at least, not with her. Her overriding impression was of well-mannered reserve. She agreed with Ruth, though, that kindness certainly wasn't exclusive to gay men, remembering Devan's numerous acts of kindness over the years. Such as the hours he had taken patiently explaining – over and over again until he must have been nearly mad with irritation – the various tests and their significance to her frightened sister, when she was diagnosed with breast cancer, years ago now.

She tried not to stare at Jared, although he and his godmother were in her direct line of sight whenever she looked up from her plate of delicious grilled sea bass and courgette fries. *A dark horse*, she decided, as the women chattered on.

The following day, Luca Pozzi, their guide, leaned against the stone wall near the jetty where the ferry docked, close to the tiny harbour in Varenna. He had a cigarette cupped furtively in his palm and tucked behind his right thigh, from which he took swift, shifty drags.

'They know you're smoking, Luca,' Connie teased, checking the straggle of tourists taking final photos of each other against the backdrop of the lake as they emerged from the narrow streets after an afternoon in the pretty lakeside town. 'The clue's in those fumes pouring from your mouth.'

Smoking was supposedly forbidden for employees of the tour company, but Luca, who looked like the clichéd ageing Lothario with his tan and improbably gleaming white teeth, his turquoise open-necked shirt and dyed black hair, gave her a wide grin.

'*Che importa?*' He shrugged, then patted his chest proudly. '*Tutti mi amano.*'

And it was true: they all did love Luca. His English

was impeccable, although still lyrically Italian, and he was so knowledgeable, so charming – he had a degree in Italian history, he was always keen to point out – that he had the whole group eating out of his hand.

As she waited for them all to gather before boarding the ferry, Connie checked her phone again. There was still nothing from Devan in response to her message nearly two days ago now. She felt a small spike of worry, suddenly visualizing all the things that might have happened to him. Maybe his back had seized up and he couldn't reach the phone. Or he'd fallen in the shower. She dismissed the doomy scenarios. *I'll call as soon as we get back to the hotel.*

Looking up from her screen, she saw Terry, Sandra's husband, approaching at a run, his face a picture of concern.

'It's Walter, Connie. He's come over faint and says he can't walk.' Terry spoke breathlessly, his normally solemn face suddenly animated. 'Sandra's with him. And Jared. But we don't know what to do.'

Connie and Luca hurried after Terry to the café-bar, a short way up one of the town's narrow streets. Walter – a tall American from Ohio in his seventies, who seemed to wear exclusively beige, even to his cotton flat cap – was sitting at an outside table. Sandra was beside him, self-consciously holding his hand, Jared and Dinah hovering nearby. His face was pale, with a sheen of sweat, his breathing shallow.

Connie bent down, a gentle arm around his shoulders. 'Walter?' She knew, from their pre-trip phone call, that he had a heart condition. But he had assured her it was under control with a battery of daily drugs. 'Do you have any chest pain?'

'No, no.' He glanced up at the sound of her voice and seemed suddenly to become aware of the ring of concerned faces looking down at him. 'Just give me a second, I'll be fine. This happens sometimes . . .'

'Do you have your medication with you?'

He stared at her blankly for a second, then nodded slowly, indicating his canvas man-bag, lying at his feet. Luca lifted it and handed it to Connie.

'May I look?' she asked Walter.

He nodded again and she began to rummage, quickly finding a white plastic bottle of pills, which she handed to him.

'I ought to take them three times a day,' he said, with an apologetic smile, 'but sometimes I forget, you know.'

'Shouldn't he go to hospital?' Jared asked, his phone poised in his hand. 'I can call an ambulance.'

Connie hesitated. Getting an ambulance down the narrow Varenna streets would be a nightmare and take for ever. 'Hold off for a moment, Jared. Let's see if he's all right when the pills have had a chance to kick in.'

She could tell from his face that Jared wasn't convinced. 'There must be a doctor somewhere here. I could ask at the bar,' he said, glancing around, as if he thought help might spring out from one of the low bushes bordering the café garden.

'That's very kind,' Connie said, noticing for the first

time his unusual eyes, almost turquoise as they caught the light from the sun reflecting off the lake.

'No doctor,' Walter said agitatedly. 'I don't need a doctor. Just give me a minute.' He clutched Connie's hand.

'We can get someone to check you out at the hotel,' she told Walter, then turned to Luca. 'You'll be OK with the others?' She knew the last ferry didn't go for a couple of hours, but she didn't want the whole group hanging around until Walter had recovered sufficiently to be able to walk to the boat.

Luca nodded his agreement. They were a good team. She knew he was completely reliable and would shepherd the passengers onto the ferry, then the minibuses at Menaggio.

'I can stay and help you with Walter,' Terry said quietly. 'You might need two.'

Connie was grateful, but she saw the frown on Sandra's face. She obviously didn't approve of her husband's uncharacteristic bid for freedom.

'Thanks, Terry. But I think I can manage,' she said, although Walter was tall and heavily built. If he was still wobbly . . .

'I'll do it. You take Sandra and Dinah back,' Jared told Terry, his voice firm, as if he were taking charge.

Dinah nodded her approval. 'Yes. Jared can help you, Connie.'

Connie saw Terry's fleeting look of disappointment and smiled at him. She would rather have waited with Terry than Jared – with whom she felt slightly awkward.

But the decision had been made and she was not going to argue, with Walter still pale and silent beside her.

Connie watched the retreating figures of the group as they hurried back down the cobbled street and turned the corner towards the waiting ferry. Walter still appeared a bit vacant, clearly bemused by what had happened. But the colour was returning slowly to his cheeks, helped, presumably, by the pill he'd swallowed and the cup of tea – a pallid Lipton's teabag, of course – that Jared had acquired from the concerned waiter behind the bar.

'So what's the company protocol in a situation like this?' Jared sipped the double espresso he'd ordered for himself. Connie had asked for a latte.

She eyed him, trying to gauge if there was any criticism behind his words. But she couldn't detect an edge to his question. 'Well ... company rules state that I should stay with the group *at all times*,' she replied, with a smile. 'I'm not even allowed to pick up a passenger who's fallen or put a plaster on a cut. Dear old Elf and Safety. But, finally, I'm supposed to use my common sense.'

Jared laughed. 'A commodity in short supply, these days.'

As he laughed, his face lit up and he looked properly at ease for the first time since Connie had met him. It was as if he'd stepped out of the stiff, slightly diffident costume he'd been wearing for the tour. *Is he cowed by his indomitable godmother?*

'It's a bit like being a parent,' she said. Which was true. You had to keep a constant eye open, be aware on a visceral level of the integrity of the group at every minute of the day. When she'd first started, she'd been so terrified she would lose the tickets, their luggage, even one of the passengers, or miss the trains, that she'd hardly slept, arriving home after a week abroad a nervous wreck. But very soon she had realized she was capable of sorting out most situations thrown at her with comparative ease.

'Hear that, Walter?' Jared nudged the American. 'Connie's your new mum.'

Walter smiled weakly. 'Fine by me.'

There was silence for a moment between the three of them. It was getting chilly: the evening sky had clouded over and a breeze was filtering up from the lake.

Then Jared said, 'Well, I think you're brilliant.'

His words were delivered so simply, but with such feeling, that Connie was taken aback and felt an instant blush rise to her cheeks. She gave an embarrassed laugh, quickly looking back to the American.

'How's it going, Walter?' she asked. 'Do you think you're OK to start walking down to the harbour? You can lean on me. We'll go really slowly.' She knew her tone was slightly forced, but she was confused by Jared and needed to shift the focus. He'd said nothing much, certainly nothing contentious. But it was the way he'd said it – and being in the beam of his strange eyes – that unnerved her.

Connie was glad when Walter nodded. 'Let's give it a go.'

*

Later that evening, Walter in bed and given the all-clear by the brusque Italian doctor the hotel had summoned, Connie closed the door of her bedroom with relief. Although she was pretty sure that Walter had never been in mortal danger, there was always the chance that he might have become really ill and needed hospital treatment – with all the attendant worries that would have entailed.

She undressed and washed, taking a few minutes to open the French windows and step out onto the balcony in her bare feet. Her room faced the gardens at the back of the hotel – no lake view for the tour manager – but the air felt cool and soothing on her face, the stars an extraordinary display in the clear spring night.

It was gone eleven, but only ten o'clock in England, so she got into bed and reached for her phone. 'Did I wake you?' she asked, because Devan sounded groggy.

'No, no. Just watching some dross on the television.'

'How are you? You didn't answer my messages.'

She heard him shifting about, a low grunt.

'Are you OK?' she asked, when he didn't reply.

'Yeah . . .'

'You don't sound it, Devan.'

There was an irritable harrumph. 'Sorry about that.'

Connie winced at his sarcastic tone. She knew he must have been drinking and regretted calling. 'OK, well, I'll leave you to it, then,' she said curtly, and was about to hang up when she heard his voice.

'Connie, wait. Sorry, sorry . . . I've just had a bad day with my back and I'm feeling a bit low . . . missing you.'

Now she felt terrible. 'Poor you,' she said, more gently, searching around for something she could tell him that might cheer him up, and finding nothing. Recounting what a beautiful day it had been here would hardly cut it. This was new, the lack of spontaneity in their exchanges – they'd never been short of something to say to each other.

'How's it going with you?' she heard Devan ask, obviously making an effort now. 'Any PPs so far?'

She pulled herself together and adopted her brightest tone. 'Ha! Well, I think that title goes to Sandra, who's seriously Hyacinth Bucket and makes me nervous, because she always seems to be brewing a kick-off. But, to be fair, she hasn't been too bad, and the rest seem reassuringly normal.' As she said it, though, her thoughts returned to Jared Temple and his grand godmother. 'Well, perhaps not entirely normal . . .'

She heard him chuckle and it lifted her heart. 'I miss you too, you know,' she said sincerely. Because in that moment she would have liked nothing better than to be sitting curled up on the sofa between Devan and Riley, pulling apart the TV drama they'd just watched, a glass of wine in her hand, the dog's head warming her bare toes. 'You'd like Varenna, where we were today. You come in on the ferry and there are these ranks of cute houses – terracotta and ochre, cream and red – nestling on the hillside around this gorgeous harbour. It takes your breath away.'

She heard him sigh. 'Maybe you can show me one day.'

Connie loved the idea, but wondered if she ever would. Devan generally preferred to take his holidays in the Highlands, the Lake District or Northumberland, with the accompanying horizontal rain and peat bogs. And, although he seemed obsessed with them travelling the world, she wasn't sure either of them was in the mood, at the moment, to take any trip together.

They talked on for a while, an easy, companionable conversation at this distance, during which Connie was able to daydream that Devan was back to normal and that things would always be good like this between them.

But when she said goodbye and lay down beneath the soft hotel duvet, she felt the sadness return. *Can we only communicate properly these days when we're nine hundred miles apart?* she wondered, as she drifted off to sleep.

Dinah waved her over. 'Our turn,' she said, smiling, as Connie sat down at their table for dinner on the last day. They were not eating in the hotel that night, but at a restaurant just along the lake.

It had been hot for two days now, in the mid-twenties, but the evenings were still cool in May and Connie had assumed they would eat inside. But while most of the group chose to, Dinah and Jared had brought their jackets – Dinah also wore a beautiful cashmere wrap, in delicate blues and greens – and were determined to brave the potential chill and eat al fresco on the restaurant's terrace. The space, jutting out over the water, was covered with a wicker canopy and dotted with terracotta pots planted with lemon trees, their star-shaped white blossoms glowing in candlelight from the tables.

'Isn't it romantic?' Dinah gave a long sigh as she gazed towards the coral sky and the setting sun throwing gold splinters across the lake. 'I wish I were twenty again.' Then she laughed. 'Although, come to think of it, I was on the verge of marrying the ghastly Ambrose then. Such a brute. So maybe not.'

'How could you tell, at twenty?' Jared commented.

'Exactly,' Dinah agreed, then turned to Connie and

laid a hand confidentially on her sleeve. 'Do you have a family? You know all about us and we know absolutely nothing about you.'

Connie grinned. 'I prefer to keep it that way.'

She saw Jared smiling too, but Dinah was not giving up. 'A husband? Children?'

'I have one daughter and a husband, Devan. He's a doctor, a GP.'

'Devon with an *o*, like the county?' Dinah queried.

'No, an *a*. He's Irish, from Dublin originally, although he was brought up mainly in Scotland. His father worked as a golf professional in the Borders.'

'Golf . . . Oh dear.' Dinah's face fell. 'My second was a fanatical golfer. He practically lived at the club. When he wasn't playing, he was drinking himself to death with his cronies in the clubhouse. Ghastly game. Poor you.'

Connie wondered how many husbands she'd had. She caught Jared's eye and saw an amused smile playing around his mouth as if he knew exactly what she was thinking. 'The golfer was Connie's father-in-law, Dinah. Her husband is a doctor,' he said.

For a moment Dinah seemed confused. But she quickly recovered. 'I'm not dotty,' she said reprovingly, and turned to Connie. 'So, tell me about Devan.'

'Well, he's recently retired –'

Dinah interrupted with a wave of her hand. 'I really do *not* approve of retirement. It's a lot of nonsense, putting a perfectly capable person out to grass just because he's not in his first flush. My third husband retired – foolishly, I did warn him – and died within the month.'

Jared began to laugh, his turquoise eyes lit by the candle in the middle of the table. 'He was ninety-two . . .'

Dinah shot her godson a sharp look, then her face broke into a tender smile. 'Gordon was such a dear, wasn't he? The best of a very bad lot.' She laid a hand on Jared's arm. 'I wish you'd settle down, darling. You're always rushing off hither and yon. Never in one place long enough . . . I do worry.'

Connie thought Jared looked distinctly uncomfortable. He took a hasty sip of wine, his mouth twitching in a half-smile. 'You know me, Dinah.'

His godmother gave him a considering look, one eyebrow slightly raised, implying she was not sure she did. Then she said, 'I suppose after that dreadful business with Charlotte –'

'Please,' Jared interrupted, frowning beseechingly at Dinah. 'Connie doesn't want to know about that.'

Dinah turned, as if surprised to see Connie still sitting there. But with a lifetime of honed social skills, she segued seamlessly into an amusing anecdote about a visit to Monte Carlo with the dastardly Ambrose for her twenty-first birthday.

Connie's meal was delicious: pumpkin and pecorino ravioli, lake fish *fritto misto*, a green salad with a dressing to die for. Dinah entertained them with hilarious and frequently naughty tales of her four husbands: it turned out Gordon was not the last – a misguided interlude with one charming but profligate Thurston being her final hurrah. Connie was so entertained, she almost forgot she was on tour and working.

Dinah was nothing like her mother, but they were of the same generation, and her vocabulary, her attitudes, her independent mind reminded Connie of Sheila. Throughout the meal, it felt as if she and Jared were strangely allied, laughing as much with Dinah as at her foibles. He obviously loved his godmother very much but saw her clearly for what she was.

It was such a beautiful night, the air crisp and fresh, the lights along the lake piercing the darkness like clusters of winking fireflies, the sky a sea of stars. They opted to walk back to the hotel. Even Dinah, leaning heavily on Jared's arm, insisted a taxi would be an insult on a night like this. Connie agreed. She was feeling lightheaded and even light-hearted this evening. A combination of more wine than she usually allowed herself and the lively company had relaxed her. She wanted to enjoy these moments before the long slog home and what awaited her there.

Some of the group were already back at the hotel, gathered in the bar adjoining the foyer. As Dinah said her goodnights, Jared still supporting her towards the lifts, she made a small *moue* of regret at what she was missing.

'There was a time I'd have closed the bar in the early hours,' she said to Connie, standing straighter for a moment, head swept back, allowing her a small glimpse of what must have been the striking, magnificent woman of her youth.

'Join us, Connie?' She heard Ginty's drunken tones

and turned to see her and Ruth beckoning her from where they sat with the others, around two tables pushed together. *It's the last night at the lake*, she thought. Tomorrow they would take the train to Paris, spend a night there, then onwards to London. So maybe she could stay for a quick one. She had no desire to go to bed right now.

Almost before she had sat down, Ruth plonked a glass containing amber liquid and crushed ice in front of her.

'We're on to the Amaretto,' she said.

Connie thanked her and took a sip, the sweet bitter-almond taste rolling smoothly over her tongue. She and Devan weren't big spirits drinkers, their preferred poison a good red wine. But this was hitting the spot for her tonight and she smiled, raising her glass to the group, all clearly in a celebratory mood.

'We've had the best time.' Ruth beamed at her, clinking her glass. 'You've made it perfect for us.'

'She really is the best,' a voice from behind her agreed.

Turning, Connie saw Jared. As before, when he had remarked so emphatically that she was 'brilliant', she felt embarrassed by his praise. It didn't sound quite the same as Ruth's or Ginty's. It had a note of something else that unsettled her – although not in an altogether unpleasant way.

He pulled up a chair next to her, peering into her glass. 'What's that you've got?'

She told him and he pulled a face. When he came

back from the bar with a tumbler of whisky and chinking ice, he turned to her. 'Listen, I'm so sorry you had to endure all Dinah's stories tonight. Neither of us got a word in edgewise. But that's how it always is with her.'

'Goodness, don't apologize,' Connie said. 'I loved it. She's a force of nature, your godmother.'

Jared chuckled. 'She's wicked about her poor husbands. I only met two of them, but they were nothing like as bad as she makes out. Just outmanoeuvred and outclassed, poor sods. They didn't stand a chance.'

For a while the conversation became general. Favourite moments of the tour were mooted and challenged. But all the while Connie was conscious of Jared by her side, contributing little, but quietly attentive to what she was saying. She found she was enjoying it.

By the time she got up to her room she was pleasantly drunk. She twirled in front of the mirror and smiled a goofy grin to herself, smoothing her hands down her hips, the jersey of her blue and white paisley dress warm beneath her fingers. Then she sighed and sat down on the bed. She would be home in a couple of days and she returned to the question that had been flitting uneasily around her brain during the tour. *If I retire, will it change things for Devan?* Or did his discontent go much deeper? It was pointless for her to throw in the towel – this, for example, had been such a fun trip – if the real problem was not her work at all but something else that was wrong.

A knock at the door interrupted her thoughts.

Opening it, she found Jared, barefoot, his linen shirt pulled out of his trousers, looking apologetic.

'Sorry to disturb you so late, Connie.' He glanced up and down the corridor. 'I wondered if I could have a quick word.'

Connie hesitated. He was looking as if he didn't want to be overheard, so she opened the door more fully, leaning against the edge to prevent the spring lock banging it shut again. Jared took a step forward, stopping respectfully on the threshold, although Connie found herself instinctively crossing her arms at the sudden intimacy she sensed between them.

'Dinah asked me to give you this.' He pulled from his pocket a cream envelope – one of the hotel's, with the pale, cursive script of the establishment's name in the top left-hand corner – and held it out to her.

It was normal for passengers on tours to tip the tour manager at the end. Given a comments sheet on the last train home – to rate the tour itself and her performance – they were encouraged to include a tip for Connie when they handed back the forms. But this envelope was bulging.

'Oh.' Connie took it and they stood there in silence. 'Wow, thank you.' She gave Jared a self-conscious grin. 'That's very kind of Dinah.'

He shrugged. 'I keep telling you, you've been marvellous.'

There it was again, the tone that kept making her cheeks hot.

'I'm just doing my job, Jared.'

His gaze seemed serious, as if he were giving great weight to her reply. She felt his presence strongly, the warm smell of him, his face lit only by the bedside lamp from inside the room and the glow through the open French windows from the security lights in the garden. As the silence lengthened, the atmosphere thickened between them. Connie didn't want to examine why, to name the feeling that was making her breath stutter in her throat. *He should go*, she thought. But it was as if someone had stopped the clock.

Jared said nothing. She didn't like to dismiss him, not when he had just pressed what looked like a substantial tip into her hand – even if it hadn't come specifically from him. But she wished he would leave.

'I should let you get to bed,' Jared said, finally releasing the deadlock. He began backing into the corridor with a final lingering glance.

Connie took a deep breath. 'Yes, long day tomorrow,' she said, her voice faint. She waved the envelope. 'Thank you so much for this.'

She breathed a sigh of relief as she let the door go. But Jared had stopped and was holding it back with the flat of his hand. As if in slow motion – a second seeming to stretch into eternity – he stepped forward and dropped a very gentle, very composed kiss on her mouth. A strand of his hair brushed her cheek. She had time to be shocked, time to clock the faint tang of mint on his breath and also to feel a sharp tingle at the touch of his lips against her own. On some unacknowledged level she had known what he was going to do, but she'd done nothing to stop it.

'Goodnight,' he said, sweeping his hair back, no trace of awkwardness in his eyes. He reached out, his fingers briefly pressing the bare skin above her elbow, then slowly walked off down the corridor.

Her door slammed shut. Connie was stunned. She walked unsteadily over to the window, fanning herself with the envelope still clutched in her hand and taking big gulps of cool night air. She could feel a warm vibration washing through her body and swallowed, trying to compose herself. *What just happened?* she asked herself, leaning her hot cheek against the smooth cold of the glass door. She knew she should feel guilt, knew full well she could have avoided the kiss. But right now all she felt was a breathless arousal.

6

Connie was up before dawn with a muzzy head and scratchy eyes. She'd barely slept, and began packing without her usual care. Normally she loved the process of filling a case with the utmost precision until it was a work of art with its neatly arranged layers, no space unemployed. But today she was hardly aware as she folded and piled and squashed her clothes any old how into the small wheelie.

It was going to be a long day, herding her passengers, plus luggage, tickets and passports – which someone always managed to mislay – onto the bus, then the train to Paris, across the city in another bus, then settling them into the hotel, before getting them back on the Eurostar in the morning. But she could cope with that. What she was really dreading was seeing Jared.

In the long dark hours of the night, Connie had attempted to analyse the kiss. Over the years, there had been the occasional passenger who'd tried it on with her. Just a mild flirtation – unsuccessful in every case – and harmless, occasioning the odd raised eyebrow from an irritated wife. On an Edinburgh tour to see the Tattoo, a burly Mancunian called Roy – who'd been putting it away, but was not so drunk he didn't know what he was doing – had come up behind her, pinned her to the hotel bar and attempted to kiss her. Connie, horrified, had used the wooden bar as leverage and shoved him violently off, sending the man flying into a table and landing in an ignominious heap on the patterned carpet. His wife long since in bed, another man in the group had helped him to his feet and carried him off upstairs.

Roy had made a complaint about Connie, saying she was lazy and unhelpful. But Connie had got in first, immediately reporting the incident to her boss at the company, who knew beyond question that the adjectives 'lazy' and 'unhelpful' could never in a million years be applied to Connie McCabe. Roy was put on the banned list thereafter.

It was different with Jared. It had never even crossed her mind that he found her attractive. *Why on earth would he?* Connie had been told she looked good for her age, but there it was, her age. She was probably ten years older than he. As she thought back over their interactions during the week, though, she did accept that, after the first awkwardness, she'd begun to enjoy his company and find him amusing . . . sympathetic to chat to. They had bonded over Dinah, mostly. But also everything Italian and travel in general. It was good to talk to someone who shared her passion – Devan saw Italy as a rival, not a conversation.

But a kiss? And not just a random kiss: one that had set her body buzzing. She had been entirely faithful for the thirty-three years of their marriage, had never even been close to kissing another man, *not once*. Which was no hardship, just an unconscious faith in the love she bore for Devan. Sometimes, inevitably, she met men she found attractive, but she and Devan would joke about it, just as they did about women who caught his eye. She would not be joking about Jared.

After she'd finished packing, she sat down on the bed in a daze. *It was a stupid moment*, she told herself. *I'll never have to see him again after tomorrow.* The thought was a relief, but the memory of his mouth against hers would not go away. A wave of panic swept through her. Would Devan detect something in her eyes? *It was just a kiss*, she tried to console herself. But she couldn't escape the fact that she had enjoyed it . . . She had enjoyed another man's kiss.

In her confusion, she realized she hadn't opened the envelope, which was currently lying on the bedside table. She reached for it now and lifted the flap, withdrawing the wad of English notes. Counting, she saw Dinah had given her two hundred pounds. A fortune! The average tip from a couple might be between twenty and forty pounds, occasionally a bit more from warm-hearted Americans. But two hundred? She wondered if Jared had put her up to it.

Entering the breakfast room, she spotted Jared and his godmother at the hot-food section of the buffet, Dinah looking suspiciously under one of the domed stainless-steel covers. Taking a deep breath, Connie put her key on her table and went – head down to avoid Jared's eye – to fetch some grapefruit juice and a bowl of fresh fruit salad. She wasn't hungry, her stomach was in knots, but she knew she should eat something.

The young Polish waitress who had been serving them all week accosted her as she filled her bowl. 'I bring you coffee?' She grinned. 'Black, hot milk on the side.'

Connie found a smile from somewhere and nodded, thanking her.

'Morning, Connie.' She turned to find Dinah at her side, holding in front of her a plate of scrambled eggs and a sad-looking grilled tomato as if it were contaminated. 'I shan't be sorry to leave these miserable offerings behind,' she said, in a voice that must have carried clear across to Bellagio. 'They cook it at five in the morning then leave it to wither till nine.'

Connie gave an embarrassed laugh. 'I'm sticking to fruit.'

Dinah leaned closer, her voice lowered to conspiratorial level. 'I love fruit, but it plays havoc with my innards. I simply can't risk it when we're stuck with rackety train loos all day.'

Connie sensed, rather than saw, Jared approaching. 'Listen, Dinah,' she said, quickly, 'thank you so much for the incredibly generous tip. But it's way too much.'

Dinah waved her free hand imperiously. 'Nonsense, Connie. Not another word. You're worth twice that.'

Before she had time to object further, Jared was beside them.

'Hi,' he said, his turquoise eyes gazing steadily at her as Dinah made her way slowly towards their table. He didn't immediately follow. 'I couldn't sleep,' he added. 'I . . .' He stopped, gave her a warm, brief smile that might have carried an apology, Connie wasn't sure, before turning away without another word.

She stood stock still. Her breath was shallow in her chest. She saw out of the corner of her eye the waitress setting her coffee on the white cloth. Luckily there were tables between hers and Dinah's and she chose a seat with her back to them. The fruit salad was too cold, the chunks of unripe melon so big they almost choked her. The coffee was perfect, though, hot and strong, made from her favourite arabica beans. It would probably cause her to shake even more than she already was. But she badly needed a hit to get through the day.

The journey home passed in an anxious daze for Connie. The long hours to Paris, with all her passengers safely stowed, gave her too much time for reflection – especially as she wasn't occupied with a book or music.

At St Pancras the following day, she found she couldn't wait to be shot of them all. She often felt weary as she waved her passengers goodbye and shed the responsibilities of the week, but this time it was more a need to be free from the temptation of Jared's gaze. They had barely talked since leaving the lake. Dinah had old friends in Paris, so she and Jared had been whisked away for dinner the previous night. And Connie's seat had been in a separate carriage on both trains.

Now Dinah was approaching, enveloping her in a

warm hug. She smelt the reassuring fragrance of Chanel, felt the softness of the powdered skin. 'Connie, my dear. How sad. It's been such a pleasure meeting you.'

'You, too, Dinah. I'll miss you both.' Which was true, although not quite in the context implied.

Jared held out his arms. 'The wonderful Connie,' he said, and wrapped her close against him, lowering his head to drop an unseen kiss to the side of her mouth. She stiffened in his embrace, terrified that Dinah would think them too intimate, and he let her go.

'Come on.' He gave his godmother a friendly grin. 'Let's get you home.'

Connie breathed a deep sigh of relief as she watched the pair make their way slowly across the busy station concourse in the direction of the taxi rank. *I will forget it ever happened*, she told herself firmly.

7

'Sandwich at the pub?' Connie suggested brightly, two mornings after her return.

Devan glanced up from his phone. Every time she met his eyes, now, she was sure he would see a change in her. But his gaze was dull. 'Umm, could do.'

Connie sighed. 'Bit more enthusiasm would be nice.'

Her husband's brow creased. 'Just because you suggested it, Con, doesn't make it a good plan.' He accompanied his words with a sham smile, behind which she could sense the stubbornness not to be seduced, to maintain his huffy position of a child abandoned by his mother.

Since she'd got back, she'd really tried. Guilt was partially driving her, it was true – and maybe he could sense that, without knowing why. But her efforts to be loving and sympathetic were not a pretence: she did, of course, love Devan. But she'd been shocked at how easy it was to slip into attraction to someone else. Treacherous attraction that still tormented her, the facile notion that she could forget what had been, after all, merely a fleeting aberration not proving so easy.

It was as if she were existing in a different zone, where the echo of arousal engendered by Jared's kiss swirled constantly around her, like a miasma. She wanted release, wanted Devan to snatch her up in his arms and make wild, possessive love to her, let the kiss be deleted from her body's memory bank. But she also felt like a traitor in wanting his hands caressing her as a substitute for what she would never have.

'OK,' she said now. 'Forget it, then.'

Clutching his phone in front of him, as if it were a shield against her hostile invasion of his space, Devan sighed. 'No . . . no, the pub would be good.'

Connie didn't argue. She took the scraps he offered. 'I'm having a coffee with Neil in a minute. Meet you there at twelve thirty?'

'Sure. Say hi to Neil.'

She thought he looked relieved that she was going out.

Neil and Connie had been friends almost as long as she had been with Devan. He was a successful food stylist, whom she'd met while she was working for Fiona Raven. He'd created all the illustrations for Fiona's glossy cookery books and they'd bonded early on over the chef's diva ways – although Neil was initially flavour of the month to the predatory Fiona.

It would be 'Neil, my darling boy' and 'Neil, sweetie' and 'Come here, gorgeous one,' all accompanied by intimate strokes and arms pressed round his shoulders, private whispers in his ear. Neil – who was still 'gorgeous' with his blue-eyed, blond-haired charm, even in his mid-fifties – suffered her attentions stoically at first, but rolled his eyes and pulled faces at Connie whenever the chance arose. Things changed, however, when Neil asked his boyfriend of the moment to meet him at the Bridgwater emporium.

'She must have known I'm gay,' he'd complained to Connie at the time, when Fiona's *froideur* became glacial.

Neil, though, was too good a stylist to be dispensed with. Gradually he and Fiona had settled into a new working relationship, of sorts. But he, too, became the victim of what Connie and the others suffered daily: her bitchy putdowns and imperious demands.

It was eight years since he and his husband, Brooks, had bought a house in the next village to Connie's – much to her delight. She and Neil would often meet for coffee in the rickety wooden barn-conversion that passed as a mini arts centre in the corner of the recreation ground near his house. The cakes were to be avoided – flapjacks and millionaire's shortbread, oversweet and bordering on stale – but the coffee was delicious.

Angela, who owned and ran the place in a cheerfully haphazard way, was a middle-aged, purple-haired Londoner, her wrists bandaged with multicoloured woven bracelets, sleeveless vests showing off the daisy chains tattooed on the inside of her ropy upper arms. She took her coffee seriously and was always demanding Connie and Neil try out her latest blend – Yemen Mocha with Sumatra Mandheling, dark roast Colombian with light roast Colombian – which she brewed in small cafetières and served with frothed milk in a tin jug. It was way more expensive than any other cup of coffee in the county, but they liked Angela, preferred the offbeat ambience to the chintzy local tea rooms designed for Cheddar Gorge tourists – and loved the coffee.

'I'm exhausted,' Neil announced dramatically, flopping onto a chair and leaning on the folding metal garden table, which wobbled alarmingly and threatened to deposit the potted lavender and sugar bowl on the barn floor. 'I've been working my tushi off on this job for weeks now. I'm still there at ten o'clock at night . . . "Just one more tiny thing, Neil, if you wouldn't mind."' He mimicked a fussy, high-pitched voice, then laughed. 'He doesn't sound even remotely like that, but you get the gist.'

Connie smiled as she listened to him talk. But her concentration was elsewhere, her thoughts in disarray. On one hand, she wanted desperately to splurge her secret to her friend, to get Neil to make sense of it and reassure her that she wasn't mad or even particularly bad to have received, and found tempting, an unsolicited kiss from a virtual stranger. But she hesitated. 'A shared secret is not a secret,' her wise mother frequently warned her. And although she trusted Neil with her life, she didn't want to give such a fleeting moment any currency. Didn't want it to become a thing between her and Neil. Didn't want, in fact, to make it more real than it deserved.

'Enough about me,' Neil was saying. 'Tell me about your latest trip.' His brow furrowed. 'Como, wasn't it?'

Connie couldn't meet his eye. She fussed with the cafetière, pouring coffee into Neil's cup, then her own.

'Yeah . . . It was fine.' When she did look up, Neil was eyeing her.

'Something up, Con?'

'No. Well . . .'

'Devan?'

She nodded quickly – easier by far to talk about her husband than the recent trip to Lake Como. 'He's still on about me retiring.'

'Well, I suppose it's not unreasonable –'

'Neil! Whose side are you on?'

He laughed. 'OK. It's just you did say a while back that you wanted to travel.'

'I *am* travelling. It's what I do for a living, in case you hadn't noticed.'

'Yeah, but you said you and Devan wanted to go places together.'

Connie sighed. 'I know I did.' But the conversations Neil was referring to had been merely idle speculation, about trips she might like to take with Devan some-time in the future, Neil and Brooks being keen travellers. The trips, in her mind, were *as well as*, not instead of, her tour job. Now she looked at her friend entreatingly. 'You think I should?'

Neil held up his hands. 'I don't think anything, Con. Just reminding you of what you said.'

They sat in silence.

'It's not just that. He's not being very nice. He spends every minute of every day on his wretched phone. Even when he's watching a match, he's still got the bloody thing in his hand. I can't have a proper conversation with him any more.' She sipped her coffee. 'I mean, what's he doing on it?'

Neil was frowning. 'Have you asked him?'

'Of course I have. He says things like "Just the usual", whatever that means.'

'Hmm . . . You don't think . . .' He stared at her.

'What?' She spoke sharply, not herself this morning.

'Well, porn springs to mind. Or gambling.' He looked at her quizzically. 'Or maybe he's hooked up with someone.'

Connie practically choked on her coffee. 'You think Devan's having –'

Neil shrugged. 'Maybe.'

Connie thought about it. 'He wouldn't do that,' she said flatly, aware, uncomfortably, of the hypocrisy of her reaction.

Her friend grinned. 'You look like you swallowed a spider.'

She didn't reply as she trawled back through her husband's behaviour over recent months. *Could that be why he's so distant with me?* But it didn't feel right.

'I really don't think it's that,' she said, after another silence. 'He'd be more furtive . . . and, I dare say, a lot happier.' She gave a sad laugh. 'I just wonder if he still loves me, Neil,' she said.

He snorted. 'Oh, come on, Connie. That's ridiculous. He adores you. You know he does. I didn't mean to wind you up.'

'You aren't,' she said, but felt tears behind her eyes. 'Would I even know, if he was having a thing with someone else, when we communicate so little these days?' she asked.

'Of course you would.' Neil was firm. 'He'd be weird and secretive, giving you far-fetched excuses for where he's going, then coming back late, smelling of someone else's soap. Devan never goes anywhere, you say.'

But what Connie was really asking was whether Devan would know that *she* had been – however fleetingly, however unintentionally – tempted by someone else.

She waited a quarter of an hour before seeing her husband's head appear round the pub door, then braced herself.

'Sorry,' Devan said, not explaining why he was late. He sat down, laying his phone carefully on the table between them. Connie had bought two glasses of red wine. It was a Monday and the place empty so early, except for Dix – the resident drunk – perched on his habitual stool at the far end of the bar.

'How's Neil?' Devan asked eventually, as if he were madly searching for a topic of conversation with his own wife.

'Fine. Sends his love.' Connie did not elaborate. She was on a mission and not going to be diverted, given the suspicions Neil had planted in her mind. 'Devan, can we talk about something? Your phone, what exactly are you doing on it all day?'

He looked surprised, then frowned. 'Why? Does it bother you?' His tone was not quite rude, more nonchalant as he reached for his glass and took a large gulp.

She was pretty sure she couldn't detect any shiftiness in his expression.

She ploughed on regardless, accompanying her words with a poor attempt at a laugh. 'I feel like Princess Diana, these days. There are three of us in this marriage.'

Devan was silent. Then he said quietly, 'Or one.'

Confused and taken aback, she just stared at him.

The glance he shot her implied she was being disingenuous.

'I need to spell it out?' He took another gulp of wine. 'You spend virtually seven months of the year on your trips. Then you come home and all you do is monitor me, criticize me.' He let out a pained sigh. 'As soon as you step through the door, I feel judged. The house isn't tidy enough, the surfaces not wiped enough. I haven't been *doing* stuff. Plus, I'm not chipper, I drink too much and don't give you enough sex. And now my phone's an issue?' He raised his eyebrows in apparent exasperation.

Connie squirmed. There was some truth in what he'd said – although he chose to exaggerate, as always, the time she spent away. But it was his tone that dismayed her. It was so totally devoid of tenderness. 'Don't you wonder why I behave like that?'

He gave a careless shrug. 'Because you're feeling guilty? You know I hate you going away, so when you're home you pile in and try to polish me up . . . so you won't have to worry about me when you leave the next time.'

Again, his assessment was not far off the mark. She did worry about him and would rather not have to. 'I only feel guilty because you make me,' she said quietly. She hadn't tasted her wine. The quantities of strong coffee she'd recently consumed had turned to acid in her stomach.

He stared stonily ahead, as if she hadn't spoken.

'Are you saying you're fine as you are, if only I would stop nagging you?'

'No. I'm not saying that. I'm not fine. I'm bloody lonely when you're away. That's why I'm on my phone all day. With my back playing up, it's my only companion.' At another time, his blatant self-pity would have made Connie laugh. 'And I can't properly settle to anything because then you come home and interrupt, expect me to be on tap again.'

'Settle to what?' She knew she sounded dismissive, but he, a grown man, was being so childish, so unfair, she could barely control her irritation.

Devan drew himself up, crossing his arms. 'OK, I'll tell you. I want to do a history degree with the Open University. I want to learn to sail. I want to walk the Pennine Way . . . like you always said we would.'

Connie was silenced. Yes, they'd often discussed that walk over the years. But the history degree and the sailing were entirely new. He'd never suggested he might be interested in doing either. Was this real, or was he just making something up to throw her? She barely knew him enough, these days, to answer her own question.

Deciding to call his bluff, she said, 'Well, that's great. Why didn't you tell me? I thought you'd do something medically related, but sailing sounds fantastic.' He didn't respond, maintaining his aggrieved expression, so she went on, 'Tell me more, Devan.' He let out another long sigh, his face softening. But he still didn't speak, just bowed his head and began picking at his thumbnail. 'I'm not stopping you doing any of those things, you know.'

Silence fell.

She remembered the days when her husband had been up at six thirty every morning, off to work with a spring in his step, totally involved with his surgery, his patients, the team with whom he worked. He'd arrive home exhausted, full of the dramas of a long day . . . although still interested in whatever Connie had been up to, how school had gone for Caitlin. *I never complained*, she thought, *about his long hours, his dedication to work. I never suggested he give it up for me, even when Caitlin was small and I was virtually a single mum.* It was just a given that she would keep the home fires burning. But he was not now returning the favour.

'When did we lose touch?' she asked eventually, pressing his hands as they lay clasped in his lap. He shrugged as she squeezed them. 'Devan?'

His fists just sat there beneath hers, unresponsive, as if he couldn't feel her touch – or couldn't bear it – and she pulled away. After what seemed like an eternity to Connie, he raised his head, his blue eyes dark with reproach. 'I don't know where we're going, you and me.'

She felt a powerful judder shoot through her body, as if she'd walked into a lamp post. 'What do you mean?'

'Surely you can see.' He gazed forlornly at her. 'This

is supposed to be *our* time, Con. We've worked all our lives. Now, we've got, what, twenty years left? And that's if we're lucky. Probably even fewer *fit* years when we can do stuff. But you intend to be gone for at least half of that.' He sighed theatrically. 'It tells me something. You'd prefer to be off with a bunch of strangers than here with me.' He stopped but he hadn't finished. 'It's making me think . . .'

Ignoring the exaggeration of her time away, Connie was surprised at how steady her voice sounded as she asked, 'Think what, Devan?' She knew in her heart of hearts that he was being unfair. But she also felt conflicted. Even Neil seemed to think her husband had a point.

This whole issue with retirement reminds me, she thought, *of how Devan never breathed a word about me smoking when we first met.* If, back then, he'd tried to make her quit, she would probably have taken years to do so. But he'd never mentioned it, despite apparently being disgusted by every puff, and she gave up soon after. If he'd taken the same approach as he did then, kept his thoughts to himself and let her retire in her own time – given her something to come home to, indeed – she would probably have set a date in the near future. But the more he backed her into a corner, the more she wanted to work till she dropped.

'About us,' Devan said. 'About what our marriage means to you.'

Connie sat up straight. She still hadn't touched her wine, although Devan had drained his. 'And what did you conclude?' she asked coolly, sick of the whole thing and furious about all the pointless effort she'd put in to help him over the hump of retirement, the worry she'd invested in his health – mental and physical – the numerous times she'd reached out to him and been rebuffed. None of the support she'd offered had been, as he suggested, a selfish act on her part, but because she loved him and hated seeing him so diminished. In return he was bullying her until she did what he wanted, bundling her into a retirement for which she wasn't yet ready.

When he didn't reply, she said, 'OK. So, hypothetically, what would happen if I did decide to retire at the end of the season?'

'What would happen?' He seemed puzzled by the question.

'You finally get me where you want me, Devan. What next?' She glared at him. 'Seeing as you don't even seem to like me any more.'

Now it was his turn to appear confused. 'Of course I like you, Connie,' he said, blinking nervously. 'We'd . . . we'd start again, wouldn't we? Recalibrate our lives.'

I don't want to recalibrate my life, she muttered silently. But aloud she said, 'And do what? You keep banging on about travelling, but we can't afford to, not all the time. Would you do this history degree you're talking about? Or take off sailing? Both things you could do right now, of course, if you were serious.'

His expression hardened. 'No need to be spiteful.'

Neither spoke, both trapped in their own affront.

Connie was the first to back down. 'Devan, please,' she begged. 'What are we doing? This is stupid.' She shuffled her chair closer and put her arm across his shoulders, which made him look around self-consciously at the other drinkers who'd been accumulating in the low-ceilinged snug during the course of their row.

Shrugging her off, he picked up his glass. 'I need another drink.'

He could have drunk hers, but he obviously wanted a break from the conversation. She watched him as he leaned on the bar, chatting amiably with Stacy as if nothing were awry, then had a smiling exchange with one of their neighbours. *Charming to everyone in the world but me*, she thought sadly. She got up. There was no point sitting here torturing each other. She didn't tell him she was going, didn't say goodbye. She'd never walked out on him in public like this before – never needed to.

Connie realized, as she covered the short distance to the house, that something very serious had just happened between her and Devan. She was pretty certain there was no cooing female voice online, consoling her husband in his outrage at her intransigence and neglect. This was worse, in a way. A significant breach had opened up in their relationship today. As if a door, long fastened and secure, were being slowly forced ajar. Devan, she saw, was using the threat to their relationship as blackmail. Forcing her to quit the tours. But she knew that if she gave in now, she would resent him for the rest of her life.

8

As Connie sat on the Eurostar, staring out of the window at the flat grey-green stretches of Normandy flashing past, she realized that each tour seemed to mark out a further decline in her relationship with Devan.

The tulip tour had seen the connection between them stuttering, as if they were coming in and out of signal, her husband's increasing lack of motivation and attention to his personal care – including drinking too much – becoming more apparent. Lake Como had witnessed a ratcheting up of his sniping about her retirement, his ongoing avoidance of any physical contact and his obsessive withdrawal behind his phone screen. And now Lake Garda seemed to have identified a new low, where the very bedrock of their marriage was being questioned.

Since the conversation in the pub, Connie felt they had been shocked into a temporary moratorium on any further discussions about their relationship. They'd tiptoed around each other in the days before she left, as if each were an invalid who couldn't cope with stress. She didn't dare explore what Devan had meant. He clearly didn't dare either. And, as had become the norm these days, Connie had not taken a proper breath until she was on the train to London and away from her husband's discontented presence. She wondered gloomily how bad it would have become by the time she was on her way to Poland next month.

'Ah, Connie! *Bentornata, cara.*' Bianca Conti, diminutive but fizzing with energy – although she was well into her seventies – kissed her warmly on both cheeks. *'Avanti! Ciao, ciao, benvenuti a tutti.'* She opened her arms to the group in the foyer with a charming smile.

Connie had been bringing tours to this family-run hotel in Desenzano for a decade now. It was Venetian in style, faded terracotta with narrow arched windows and lacy balconies overlooking the peaceful harbour for small boats on the shores of Lake Garda. Bianca ran the hotel with her two sons, Federico and Sandro, but was unquestionably in control.

As soon as the hurdle of check-in was cleared, Connie found her room and threw herself onto her bed with a sigh of relief. The journey had been unusually trying. One of her passengers, Martin, sixty-seven, from Cheltenham, had not been able to lift his case because of his bad back – although it was a company rule, made very clear at booking, that everyone was responsible for their own luggage. So Connie had had to lug his heavy suitcase on and off the trains, along with her own. Then the hotel next to where they overnighted in Turin was hosting a wedding, the shrieks and thumping music going on into the early hours. And, to cap it all, the train on to Lake Garda had been cancelled, and Cheltenham Martin had been pickpocketed as they hung about at Turin station, his wallet stolen out of his back pocket. Luckily it had only contained his bus pass, some loyalty cards and his RAC membership: his bank card had been in his shirt pocket at the time. But he was upset, and it had taken Connie a while to calm him down.

None of that matters now, she thought, as she lay on her back, looking up at the light from the water outside reflected on the cream ceiling in glinting ripples. She'd got her passengers here, safe and sound, the sun was shining, and Bianca, as always, would give them a wonderful time.

The weather had been perfect so far – sunny and hot, but with a pleasant breeze – the tourists gradually coalescing into their groups and obviously enjoying themselves, with the lake excursions, pretty squares to explore, and the pavement cafés in which to sit with a cool drink or *gelato*.

Now it was day five: Venice, Connie's all-time favourite.

They took an early train to the city, then a couple of private water taxis along the Giudecca canal to Piazza San Marco. The first sight of the city – although Connie had seen it more times than she could count – always took her breath away. It sat shimmering in the soft morning light above the water of the lagoon, its elegant skyline of domes and campaniles like a chimera: if she closed her eyes, she thought, it might vanish as if it had never been.

As the group stood on the square, phones held in

front of their faces almost before they'd even taken in the extraordinary thirteenth-century Byzantine façade of the basilica, she spotted Gianni, the guide who would lead the walking tour through the city.

'*Adesso* . . . You come with us, *bellissima*?' he asked flirtatiously, when they'd greeted each other. He was young and handsome, sunglasses perched on his dark hair, the muscles of his tanned arms stretching the short sleeves of his white polo shirt. He was relatively new to guiding, and a touch cocky, Connie thought. He seemed to think his job was almost beneath him.

'Not today,' she said. She had absorbed much of the art and culture on previous trips, but in her current mood she craved indulgence, nothing she had to concentrate on too hard. Maybe she would drink a dramatically expensive hot chocolate on the piazza to the music of the small café orchestra, then wander the shady, picturesque streets, stroke some of the soft leather handbags she couldn't afford. 'Don't drown them,' she said.

Gianni batted his eyelids in mock seduction. 'For you, signora, I do anything you ask.'

She waited till the crocodile had disappeared down one of the narrow alleyways to the south of the piazza, then went and found a table in the sunshine and ordered her hot chocolate. It came with about three inches of whipped cream sprinkled with chocolate flakes in a glass with a metal handle and she just stared at it, appreciating its beauty, before plunging in her teaspoon and dragging up some hot, creamy deliciousness, shutting her eyes to savour the sweetness rolling over her tongue.

As she sat there, she found herself thinking disloyally of Jared – Italy evoked him. And without the constraint of being with Devan, she made no attempt to quell her musings. She wondered if he'd ever thought of her since that night on Lake Como. She laughed to herself. *A fleeting kiss, yet it sets my ageing heart aflutter*, she thought wryly.

'Connie?'

She jumped as a hand dropped lightly onto her shoulder. She spun around, expecting to see one of her group, left behind already by Gianni's imperious march through the crowded back streets.

'*Jared . . .*' Her breath caught in her throat. It shocked her to see him there – almost as if she'd magicked him up with her thoughts. For a moment she thought she must be mistaken – the morning sun was so bright behind his head that it left his face in shadow.

He was entirely composed, however, as he smiled and pulled out a chair. 'May I?'

She managed a nod, her heart flapping uncomfortably beneath her ribs. 'What on earth are you doing here?'

'Just staying with friends for a few days. They own one of those damp, crumbling palazzos on the canal. Just can't resist Venice in the spring.' He nodded towards her drink. 'I see you're getting stuck into the local delights.'

'What an incredible coincidence, bumping into each

other,' Connie said, still stunned that Jared was actually there, sitting calmly at her table.

He gave her a knowing smile and tapped the side of his nose. 'Ah, well, not entirely coincidence. I over-heard a woman in the queue for the Doge's Palace chatting to her friend. "We have to be back to meet Connie by twelve," she said. And I just knew it must be you . . . so I've been wandering around looking for you ever since.'

He was wearing sunglasses and she couldn't read his eyes, but he was giving her a self-congratulatory grin. And, unlike her, seemed perfectly at ease as he ordered his coffee.

'Still strange,' she said, trying to calm herself. 'Us being here in Venice at the exact same time.'

Jared smiled. 'True. But I'm a firm believer in synergy.'

When his coffee arrived, he stirred the chocolate carefully into the foam. 'It's good to see you, Connie.'

There was an obvious reply, but Connie couldn't say it. *Is it good to see Jared?* On one level, yes. She found, against her will, that the frisson his presence engen-dered was agreeable. But on another level, no. She didn't want him here, didn't want to be reminded of that kiss.

'When you've finished your chocolate, there's some-thing I'd love to show you,' Jared was saying.

Her peaceful drink had been ruined by his presence. Now she finished it almost unconsciously, desperate for something to do, something that would distract her from his charming smile. 'I'm working, Jared. I can't just swan off.'

Ignoring her reproving tone, he replied, with a sly grin, 'You don't have to meet them till twelve, according to your client in the queue.'

She glanced at her watch. 'Twelve, yes. We've got tickets for the basilica this afternoon.'

He raised his sunglasses and she was treated to those extraordinary eyes again. 'This won't take long. Half an hour, tops.' He stood and held out his hand to her. 'Please . . . it's special.'

She did not take his proffered hand as she reluctantly got to her feet. 'OK. But I have to be back in good time.'

She followed Jared as he wove in and out of the crowded piazza then chose the same street on the south side down which Gianni had earlier led her tour. They wiggled through the maze of alleys, crossed over one canal, then another, to an unassuming white-stone Renaissance building right up against the waterside, not heralded by any billboards or crowds.

Jared pushed open the heavy wooden door. Inside was a small chapel, only dimly lit. It took Connie's eyes a moment to adjust to the dark. But what she saw took her breath away. Around the room, above head height, was an array of vividly painted panels.

'Vittore Carpaccio,' Jared whispered, although the place was empty, apart from the shadowy figure who had sold them tickets. But the atmosphere was almost reverent. 'Look, St George and the dragon . . .'

Connie was no art expert, although she had seen a lot in her time, but she immediately appreciated the vibrant charm and humour, the drama and detail of the paintings: St George's story on the left-hand wall, St Jerome's on the right.

'Don't you love the horrible dragon?' Jared said. And as they moved round, 'Look at the terrified monks fleeing from St Jerome's lion.' And then further round, 'Isn't the little dog with St Augustine cute?'

'They're fantastic,' she said, almost forgetting that her guide was Jared Temple, and that she was supposed to be working, as she studied the beautifully executed narratives. When they finally emerged into the blinding sunshine, she felt dazed.

Jared was eyeing her. 'Worth it?'

She grinned. 'Oh, my goodness, Jared. So worth it.'

He beamed. 'I knew you'd like them.' He took her arm companionably and this time she didn't resist as they walked back the way they'd come and crossed the bridge in the direction of St Mark's Square.

'Art like that is life-enhancing,' he added quietly.

When they reached the piazza, Connie immediately saw couples from her group, looking about, probably wondering where she was, and realized it was nearly twelve. They'd been much longer in the Scuola di San Giorgio than she'd intended.

'I've got to go,' she said, glancing up at Jared. 'They're waiting.' He nodded. 'Thank you for showing me the paintings. They were really wonderful,' she said.

'I've loved every minute,' he replied.

She thought, when he didn't immediately move off, that he might dare to kiss her again and became slightly flustered. But he made no attempt to do so, and absurdly she realized she was disappointed. The memory of his lips on hers that night at Lake Como came back to her again and she caught her breath.

'Bye,' she said, turning quickly away and hurrying over to her charges, hoping they hadn't seen her and Jared together. She didn't want them reporting her for dereliction of duty.

The rest of the afternoon passed in a blur of organization. Connie had to corral the group at the end of the day and pack them onto the train back to Desenzano. Not easy when everyone had dispersed into the crowds after the basilica tour. They only just made the train, one couple sauntering onto the churning water taxi, calmly licking ice creams as if they had all the time in the world.

It was not until she shut the door of her room that night, and could finally dispense with the company lanyard round her neck, take off her shoes and wipe away her make-up that she could properly think about Jared.

So strange, she mused, *him turning up like that*. Although these things did happen, she knew that. It was, as people were always pointing out, a small world. And, after the initial surprise, she had enjoyed seeing him. The Carpaccios were gorgeous and he was so knowledgeable, so interesting about the *scuola* and its history – she had been quite carried away in his company.

About Jared himself, Connie wasn't sure what to think. *Was he flirting with me?* she asked herself, as she climbed into bed. Or was he just being friendly and charming? Since she would never see him again, it didn't matter either way: the tour managers, on pain of death, were required to delete passengers' contact details when they returned from a tour, so she didn't even have his phone number . . . not that she would have used it, if she had. But, still, there was this tingling in her belly when she thought about him. And it wouldn't go away.

Verona was only a twenty-minute journey from Desenzano, and the tour set off early on the last day. It had been cloudy when Connie had woken, rain forecast on her weather app at 33 per cent during the afternoon. It would be a shame, she thought, after the brilliant weather they'd had, not to be able to take full advantage of the beautiful city.

She decided to join Serena – the Verona tour guide – on the walking tour today. She felt she hadn't been present enough or paying proper attention to her flock, her mood initially too distracted by the problems at home, then by Jared's sudden appearance two days ago. Though what she would really have liked to do today was wander round the super-chic boutiques hidden in Verona's side-streets, where she could find things that would never make the crowded Via Mazzini and its designer stores.

But she would do Juliet's balcony – always a bit of a disappointment – and the first-century Roman arena instead. She would listen to the glamorous Serena – an actress by night – making jokes about Romeo, and watch tears fill her brown eyes as she told dramatic tales of Christians waiting in the dank, gloomy tunnels before walking into the sunlit arena to be slaughtered. She would bond with the group. Do her job.

It did rain. Not hard, but drizzly and chilly enough to dampen the group's enthusiasm for standing outside for long periods in their summer clothes. Serena, chic in a short cream trench coat, matching cloche hat over her shiny hair, soldiered on, but everyone – Connie included – was pleased when the traditional *osteria* and a comforting bowl of dark, rich Amarone risotto hove into sight.

She had found herself glancing around as they stood in the echoing Roman amphitheatre, checking the tiers of stone seats raking sharply to the sky and the wide arena, as if she were expecting – ridiculously – to see Jared emerge from one of the tunnels. She was mortified by her imaginings, but couldn't help feeling his presence, couldn't help remembering with pleasure the morning they had spent together in Venice.

Connie angled the magnifying mirror in the bathroom to put on her make-up, preparatory to the last dinner of the tour. As she gazed at her reflection, foundation stick in hand, she saw the anxiety etched in her eyes, and sensed the reluctance she always felt as home and Devan loomed. She'd only messaged him a few times over the past eight days. He had replied to each with a row of three kisses – the equivalent of a cop-out on WhatsApp. She had almost rung him one night as she lay in bed trying to sleep. But she didn't want to start a conversation on the phone when he'd probably been drinking. It might only escalate the current tension between them. She knew, however, that once home, they would need a proper discussion.

Dinner was fun, the long table that Bianca had constructed in the small hotel dining room becoming more and more raucous in the face of the delicious home-cooked food – platters of local salami and *frico friabile* (crispy-fried Montasio cheese); tortellini with a shallot, scallop, basil and white wine sauce; panna cotta wobbling delicately in a sea of raspberry coulis – and quantities of local wine. Connie, as she always did on the last night, drank more than she should. But no one else was in a state to notice or care. She even made friends with Martin from Cheltenham, who had come out of his shell over the week and become quite talkative, even if his conversation about local Gloucester politics was not entirely riveting.

'Be glad to get shot of us, will you, Connie?' he said, as the party wound down, people beginning to make their way up to their beds, some still lingering in the lobby, reluctant for it all to end. 'Must be like herding cats, your job.'

'It has its moments,' she said, laughing. 'Although cats don't have wallets to steal.'

Martin grinned. 'Could have been worse, I suppose. My daughter says I'm so scatty I need a leading rein to stop me wandering off.'

'I've never lost a passenger in all the twelve years I've

been touring,' Connie told him. 'And I don't plan to start now.' She put her finger to her cheek in mock contemplation. 'A leading rein? Hmm, not such a bad idea . . .'

They were both laughing as they said goodnight. She waved to the others waiting by the lift, but she wasn't tired.

Sandro, Bianca's younger son, stood behind the desk, punching away on his computer, a frown of concentration on his face. He was in his fifties and broad, well-fed, genial. She supposed he had a pleasant existence with his lovely mum, beautiful hometown and job for life.

'It was a wonderful dinner, Sandro,' she said, leaning on the counter. 'Thank you, we've all had such a great time, as usual.'

He grinned. '*Prego!* You know how Mamma loves you, Connie.'

She yawned, peered through the open hotel doors. 'I think I'll pop out for a bit of fresh air. It seems to have stopped raining at last.' She unfolded the caramel pashmina she'd brought downstairs and pulled it round her shoulders. 'See you later.'

The night was beautiful, the hot summer dustiness cleansed by the recent rain. Connie breathed deeply as she crossed the road and walked past the line of café tables, still occupied with a few chatting diners. Ranks of small blue and white boats bobbed silently on the water, people strolling the cobbled promenade beside the lake. She knew the main squares would be heaving with the young at this time of night – she could hear the beat of disco music in the distance.

She leaned against the cold iron railing and looked out onto the lake. Lights lacing the peninsula of Sirmione twinkled to the east, dominated by the illuminated elegance of the Rocca Scaligera, the expanse of dark water stretching away from it like the ocean.

Turning to walk back the way she'd come, tiredness sweeping over her, she heard the ping of a text on her work phone. Hoping it wasn't something serious, she opened the screen.

I'm outside the hotel, if you fancy a nightcap? Jared x

She read the message and heard herself give a small gasp. For a moment she just stared at the words, glowing bright in the darkness. *He's here?* She felt panicky.

Worrying that he might go into the hotel and ask for her, Connie hurried the two minutes around the corner. She saw him before he saw her. He was waiting quietly, hands in his jeans' pockets, staring out over the water, the street lamp under which he was standing lighting up the blond streaks in his hair.

Reaching him, Connie said, 'What are you doing here?' She was angry. 'You can't keep turning up like this, Jared. It's really weird.'

Jared turned at the sound of her voice, but he didn't seem offended by her words. 'Hey, Connie. Sorry . . . You said you were staying here and I thought a glass of something might be fun. It's such a beautiful night.' He was smiling, and her heart seized in her chest.

She frowned. 'Did I say I was staying here?'

'Yeah, don't you remember? You told me all about Bianca and her sons.' When she didn't speak, unable to remember telling him, but knowing she must have done, he went on: 'I was on my way to Milan for a meeting and had some spare time. I realized I've never seen Desenzano.' He lifted his arms outwards, palms up. 'So I thought, What the heck?'

Connie was calming down. 'It's just a bit unsettling, you popping up out of the blue like this, twice in one week.'

Jared looked abashed. 'I can see that. I'm sorry. I don't want to freak you out.'

They stood in silence. Connie's tiredness had vanished in the adrenalin hit of seeing Jared. Her heartbeat was hurtling round her chest, like a runaway train.

'Now I have, though,' he went on, unable to keep the amusement out of his eyes, 'will you at least let me buy you a drink?' He indicated a vacant table by the water.

Connie hesitated. She was flattered by his attention, she couldn't deny it. But she was also wary of it. *There's no harm in one drink*, she told herself, unable to stem the pounding in her chest. 'Not an Amaretto,' she said. 'I'm not really sure I like that stuff.'

Jared disappeared into the restaurant that owned the waterside tables, leaving her sitting nervously on a cushioned aluminium chair, which wobbled on the old stone of the harbour. She noticed the chill and drew her pashmina closer around her.

The waiter set two small balloons of brandy and two tumblers of water on the table. Jared raised his glass, smiling at her as he waited for her to do the same. She touched her glass to his.

Jared said, 'To Italy. The country we both love.'

Connie smiled and nodded her agreement.

They sat in silence. Connie knew it should feel awkward, being there, late at night, in that magical setting with a virtual stranger. But Jared obviously didn't feel the need to make conversation. And his ease made her relax too. She took a sip of brandy and felt the pleasant burn as it hit the back of her throat. It made her cough, though, and her eyes water.

Jared raised his eyebrows.

She laughed. 'Not used to it.'

'This is my favourite thing,' he said. 'Sitting outside on a beautiful evening, in my favourite country, with a wonderful woman.' He accompanied his words with a slow smile that made her heart beat even faster.

But Connie was taken aback. If he had used a word such as 'gorgeous' or 'beautiful' to describe her, it would have sounded flirtatious. But 'wonderful' – spoken so sincerely – implied a whole different level of admiration.

'You barely know me, Jared.'

He looked surprised. 'Don't you have people like that in your life? The instant you meet them you feel a powerful connection?'

Connie thought of Devan, thought of Neil. 'I suppose, yes.'

'Well . . .'

Those eyes again. He was gazing at her, his expression solemn and considering. She felt a tremor pass through her body as she gazed back, as if a touchpaper had been lit. Her breath was faint, like a whispering breeze . . . that kiss. And suddenly all she wanted him to do was kiss her again.

She turned from him, looked out towards the dark lake, wanting to hide the heat bathing her cheeks. When she glanced back, he was laughing. Connie laughed, too, and somehow the tension dissolved.

Still trying to control her pounding heart, she said, with as much firmness as she could muster, 'Go away, Jared. *Please*, just go away.' Although even she could hear the quiver in her voice.

'Charming,' he said good-naturedly, tipping the last drops of brandy into his mouth and standing up.

For a moment she thought he was taking her at her word and leaving. But no. He came round to her chair and held out his hand, as he had two days ago in the piazza. But this time, hardly thinking about what she was doing, she took it.

They didn't speak, she didn't question where they were going, but before she knew it his arm was around her waist and he was turning her away from the harbour and the lights into a smaller, darker street, narrow, lined with shops – closed and shuttered and silent at this time of night. She knew she was trembling. She knew what he was going to do.

They'd walked only a short distance before he pulled her into a little recess between two buildings – not an alleyway, just a niche, really. Then his mouth was on hers, hot, breathless, insistent, as if he had waited a lifetime for that moment.

She had no idea how long they kissed. She was

gathered up in his desire, her body matching his, ready to fly into a million pieces as she felt his hand between her legs, his fingers pressing up inside her. She had no consciousness of her surroundings, no shame as she gave herself up to his urgent touch. Small, rapid gasps, then the world paused for a second, before release overtook her in a delicious surge. She moaned softly, heard Jared chuckle. Opening her eyes, she saw him smiling down at her. But she couldn't speak as she leaned against him, suddenly exhausted.

'What on earth are we *doing?*' she whispered, drawing back from his embrace, biting her swollen lips as she attempted to adjust her crumpled dress. She was suddenly acutely aware that they were in a public place, pressed up against a cold wall, making out like teenagers in a bus shelter. But the realization could not erase the intense pleasure of Jared's touch.

His hand pressed into her back as they stepped onto the deserted street. But the spell was broken. Connie pulled away in panic as she glanced at her watch. 'Shit!' She thought of Sandro at the desk. *Will he be worried, wondering where I am?* 'I've got to go back.' The cold hard fact of what she'd just done made her almost desperate to get away from Jared.

They hurried the five minutes to the hotel in silence, Jared making no attempt to touch her. When they reached the door, it was locked, but a small polished-brass bell push was labelled 'Night Bell'. Connie had never noticed it before. She looked up at Jared as she pressed it, in trepidation of who might come.

'Go,' she whispered. 'Please.' *They mustn't see him with me.* Bianca knew all about Devan and her family, always asked to see the latest photo of little Bash.

'OK . . . but will you –'

'No.' She pushed her palm flat to his chest, not wanting to hear what he was asking of her, just desperate for him to leave. 'This was so wrong. I'm sorry, I –'

But he laid his finger gently to her lips. After a moment's hesitation, he was gone, striding purposefully along the quay. She watched him until he was round the bend of the harbour road and safely out of sight.

No one was answering the bell. Anxiously, she pressed it again, smoothing her tousled hair and tucking it behind her ears, running a finger beneath her eyes to catch any errant mascara, applying lip-balm to her stinging lips. She knew she must look like somebody who'd been doing exactly what she and Jared had just done. *What if nobody comes?*

After what seemed like an eternity, she heard shuffling behind the wooden door and a gruff voice – not one she immediately recognized in her distraught state – calling, *'Chi è?'*

'It's Connie. I'm a guest.'

She tried to remember the words in Italian as the voice repeated more loudly, *'Chi è là?'*

'Io resto qui,' she said, as loudly as she dared, 'in the hotel.'

There was the sound of a key grating in the lock, then bolts being drawn, deafening in the still night. She cringed, wondering if any of her group with the lake view were awake and listening. Then the door swung open and an older man, whom Connie recognized as Franco, the hotel's handyman, was peering out at her, dressed in an old sweater and loose trousers, slippers on his feet. He'd clearly been asleep.

'Franco, it's me. *Mi dispiace tanto . . .*'

He stood aside to let her in, grumbling under his breath as he did so. But Connie didn't care. She was safe. With a mumbled '*Grazie . . . grazie mille*,' she raced up the stairs two at a time, fumbling with the key card until the green light flashed and she almost fell into her room.

Once inside she leaned against the door. The bedroom looked so normal, so exactly how she'd left it before her life had been turned upside down tonight. She began to cry. They weren't tears of sadness, or even guilt. Connie was crying because the turmoil she was experiencing was so bewildering, so all-consuming, the exhaustion so great, that sobs simply burst from her throat, propelled by the maelstrom inside.

She didn't know what to think about first: Jared, Devan, her behaviour . . . *Sex against a wall in a back alley? Me, Connie McCabe?* It was unthinkable. And she was, indeed, too tired to think. A frantic day lay ahead, including hours on trains with too much silence in which to contemplate what she'd done. When she closed her eyes at last, laying her cheek gratefully against the cool cotton of the hotel pillow, she was aware of nothing else until her phone alarm's painfully insistent buzzing.

9

Connie opened her eyes to find herself in her own bed again. She looked around, expecting to see her husband, but Devan was not there, the sheets and pillow on his side untouched. She tried to clear her head. Then she remembered.

Devan's greeting to her the previous day when he had picked her up from the station had been muted, scarcely even friendly. And she was barely through the front door when he announced he was off to the pub.

'It's Dix's birthday,' he'd said. 'Come if you like.'

Connie had no desire to sit and watch Dix fall off his stool yet again, even if it was his birthday and he had an excuse for once, so she declined.

'By the way,' Devan said, in parting, 'I've moved into the spare room. I'm sleeping really badly at the moment and I don't want to disturb you. You'll be exhausted after your trip.'

Connie had stared at his retreating back. Was this his form of punishment for her intransigence? Was his sympathy for her tiredness just veiled sarcasm? She wasn't sure: he had spoken from the hall – perhaps deliberately – as he was opening the front door, so she couldn't see his face.

In a sense it was a relief. On two counts. The tension

at bedtime in the past months had been huge – pretty much since the incident with the lilac negligee – Devan always avoiding coming up at the same time as she, then smartly turning his back. She felt like a pariah in her own bed.

And then there was Jared. On that front she deserved more punishment than her husband moving into the spare room. In the rush and busyness of the previous two days – overnighting in Turin and so on – there'd been no time to think. She'd slept on the first train. Against the rules, but no one seemed to notice or care. Then her seat had been beside Cheltenham Martin, as a single traveller, on the day-long leg to Paris and the Eurostar to London. He'd talked non-stop until somewhere south of Paris, Connie having to crane her neck awkwardly sideways as he told her about his plumbing: by some system incomprehensible to her, he'd proudly linked the renewables in his house to the fossil fuels via a clever new widget. Her head bobbed up and down, like that of a nodding dog in the back window of a seventies car, as she dropped in the occasional 'Wow, fascinating,' her mind fighting to find space to process what had happened with Jared.

When she'd woken to her alarm in the lakeside hotel the morning after, she felt as if the late-night interlude had been a dream. It still did not seem possible – although she was painfully aware of the after-effects of Jared's touch: her lips were rough and sore, and she still tingled when she remembered what he had done.

But any hope that her behaviour was a fantasy, or her

late – and dishevelled – return to the hotel might escape censure, was instantly dispelled by Bianca's level gaze as Connie checked out the group. *Franco must have said something*, she thought miserably. Bianca looked disappointed, although there was doubt in her kind eyes. Her goodbye hug was tempered, her usually effusive warmth missing, which broke Connie's heart. She couldn't meet the handyman's eye as he loaded the coach with the piles of wheelie-cases.

Now, as she lay on her back in bed, blinking in the early-morning light, she was bemused at the extraordinary licence she'd allowed an almost perfect stranger. Someone with whom she'd exchanged only brief conversation and had absolutely no future.

'It's just sex,' she remembered a cheating work associate insisting. 'I don't love her.' As if that made it perfectly fine. But now she thought she could appreciate the distinction. What had happened between her and Jared was just a one-off crazy thing and seemed to have nothing whatever to do with Devan. She felt almost detached from her behaviour, now she was home. It was as if that night by the lake was completely separate, contained in an illicit bubble, a million miles away from her marriage, her home, her friends.

She would be away again in two weeks. Auschwitz was part of the Polish tour, which she'd never done before and was quite nervous about. It would be a far cry from the lazy Italian sunshine, the decadent hot chocolate, the humorous Carpaccios ... and, thankfully, Jared. The intensity of that night would eventually fade from her memory, she was certain. She would never forget, but she would put it firmly behind her and swallow her guilt. What she needed to do now was concentrate on mending her marriage.

The door creaked open and Riley's face appeared. He trotted over to the bed and nuzzled her face. He always seemed to know when she woke, even though she hadn't made a sound.

'OK, OK,' she said, delving into his warm coat and massaging his neck with her fingers. 'I know what *you* want.'

She got out of bed and pulled on jeans and a T-shirt. It was a beautiful morning for a walk, and she felt glad to be back in the temperate English climate. She knew Devan would sleep late, and she was happy for that. Facing him would be a challenge this morning.

'Hey.' Devan emerged from the spare bedroom as Connie was taking the washing basket piled with her tour clothes down to the kitchen.

'Good night?'

He stretched, yawned. 'Great, yeah. You should have come. Everyone asked after you.'

The smile he gave her as he brushed her arm on the way to the bathroom was more giving than yesterday's and she smiled back, encouraged, keen to coax him out of his recent truculence, bombard him with sweetness and love. 'Shall I make coffee?'

When they were seated with it at the kitchen table, she asked, 'So, who was there last night?' The garden doors were open, a warm breeze wafting the scent of lilac from the bush by the wall.

'Just the usual suspects. Gloria popped in. I haven't seen her in ages. She's been on a cruise around the Galápagos with her daughter.' He took a sip of his drink. 'They snorkelled and hiked . . . The wildlife is incredible, apparently – giant tortoises, turtles, sealions and iguanas, tons of birds. She says it's stunning.' He sighed heavily. 'I would really love to go one day.'

Despite her determination to make an effort, Connie felt a spurt of irritation at his martyred sigh. But she smiled brightly. 'Well,' she said, 'we should plan a trip.' The expression on his face implied the wind had been taken out of his sails. 'Why not?' she added.

Devan shrugged. 'You're working most of the year.'

'No. As I keep repeating, there are five months when we can go wherever we want.'

Her husband seemed almost disappointed at the unexpected reduction in his firepower. 'It'll cost, I imagine,' he said. 'Gloria's not short of a bob or two.'

'You could investigate.'

He stared at her, maybe wondering if she was serious. 'OK.'

Connie felt the skirmish was over but was also aware that one cruise was not going to change the world. She genuinely wanted to hug her husband, to love away his detachment. But she could still feel, reprehensibly, the imprint of Jared's mouth on hers and she knew it would be wrong just now: it would be fraudulent.

There was a knock on the front door.

'Postman?' Devan said, getting up.

Connie heard him chatting, then laughing, thanking whoever was at the door.

'It's for you,' he said, dropping a heavy package onto the table and sliding it across to her. She picked it up, puzzled. She hadn't ordered anything. 'I'm meeting Bill later,' he added. 'He wants to look at a car and I said I'd go with him.'

Bill Kitson was married to Jill, a good friend of Connie's in the village. He was obsessed with classic cars, frequently buying wrecks, which he then lovingly restored. Jill's only objection was that he kept them all. There was now a barn on the edge of the village that had upwards of ten: MGs, Sunbeam Alpines, Morris Minors.

'Count me out for supper.' Devan grabbed his phone from the table and turned away. 'We're going over Oxford way, probably won't be back till late.'

Connie sat on at the table after Devan had disappeared upstairs to get dressed. She was worried about her husband's sudden desire to be out socializing all day, after so many months slumped comatose on the sofa. *Is it just a desire to avoid me?* But she was pleased he seemed more motivated. She stared unseeingly at the package on the table in front of her, her fingers smoothing the cardboard exterior. Then she automatically began to pull at the tab that would release the contents.

Inside was a glossy hardcover, full of illustrations: Carpaccio. She gave a small gasp. There was only one person in the world this could be from. *How did he get my address?* She felt her heart pounding.

But she was quickly reminded that she and Devan were in the phone book. She thought back to all those questions of Dinah's, that night by the lake. She didn't remember specifically mentioning the name of the village they lived in, but she knew she had talked about Somerset and the Levels. It would be a matter of minutes to trace her online, knowing her husband was a doctor.

With shaking hands, Connie examined the paperwork tucked inside the cover of the book. There was no message, no indication of where it came from, only a gift invoice from a French forwarding company called DFB – Connie was familiar with forwarders: Fiona had regularly used them for shipping her products abroad.

The book was beautiful. As she leafed through the pages, she found herself smiling at the reproductions of the panels in the Scuola di San Giorgio, lost for a moment in the artist's mastery . . . and remembering the smell of the darkened chapel, Jared close at her side. But although she felt flattered he'd been thinking of her to the extent of sending the book, marking the time they'd spent together in Venice, his attention made her instantly nervous.

'What is it?' Devan, dressed and ready to go, was standing in the doorway, jangling the car keys.

Connie jumped. 'Oh, I'd forgotten I ordered a book on Carpaccio when I was away. We saw these wonderful panels of his in one of the little churches in Venice.'

Devan seemed uninterested. 'Never heard of him.'

She didn't reply, unable to trust herself to say any more. She hoped she wasn't blushing, although her heart was beating like a bass drum as she rose, folding the cardboard from the package and squeezing it into the bulging recycling bag hanging from the kitchen-door handle. 'I thought I might ring Jill, see what she's up to, if you two are off for the day,' she said.

'You're back!' Jill shrieked, when Connie called. 'Yes, yes, *please* come over. Save me from all the grisly chores I've been avoiding.' Jill, a petite sparky brunette a few years older than Connie, had taught history at Bristol University. Since her retirement, she'd been researching a novel – a murder mystery set in France, during the great freeze of 1709.

'You know they used ice skates instead of gondolas to get around Venice in the freeze?' Jill said, when Connie had filled her in about her trip. They were taking the dogs up to the top of the village and into the woods – a walk they frequently enjoyed together. Jill's Scottie was old and not as fit as Riley, but she panted bravely in his wake as he chased elusive scents and stuck his nose down rabbit holes. 'Even the lagoon iced over.' She frowned. 'Imagine . . . it must have been hell. People burned their furniture – if they were lucky enough to have any, of course – to keep from freezing to death.'

'Horrible.' Connie shivered at the mere thought. She hated being cold. 'How are you getting on with the book?'

Jill laughed. 'Can't really call it a book yet. I'll prob-ably be researching for the rest of my life because I'm terrified of actually writing the damn thing.'

They walked in silence for a while, Connie finally beginning to calm down from the shock of the morning delivery. The Carpaccio, however well meant, felt like an invasion into her real life. Jared had been thoughtful enough not to leave any sign on the documents that it was from him – in case Devan had opened it, she supposed. But it implied a connection with her that was way too intimate. And pricked the bubble in which Connie had carefully placed him.

As they stopped at the top of the rise, looking out across to the Mendips, Connie realized Jill was eyeing her with a frown. 'Is everything all right, Connie? You seem preoccupied.'

Connie shook herself. 'Do I? Sorry. It's always tricky, settling back after a trip.' Although in the past, before things had gone so wrong with Devan, she had always loved coming home.

Jill didn't reply at once. Then she said quietly, 'I gather things aren't so good between you two at the moment.'

Connie raised an eyebrow. 'Has Devan said something?'

'Not to me. But he admitted to Bill he's struggling with retirement, and finds it tough you're still working. Said it was driving a wedge between you.'

She was stung, hearing Devan's neat, one-sided assessment on her friend's lips. Especially as Bill was acknowledged by all as a blatant, unrepentant gossip. It wasn't malicious, he just couldn't help himself. And if he'd told his wife, that was probably just the tip of the iceberg. The whole village would know by now that she and Devan were having problems and that Connie was the cause. She could just hear the twittering: *That dear Dr Mac, such a lovely man and a wonderful doctor. And her away all year. It's not right.*

'You don't have to tell me,' Jill said.

They walked down the hill in silence. The late-morning sun was hot and Connie wished she'd brought a hat. But she'd been in such a tizz about the delivery before she left home.

Jill said, 'Seems he really misses you when you're away.'

Words fizzed and boiled in Connie's mouth. She stopped so she could face her friend and swallowed hard. Her words, when they finally emerged, were pinched, as if she were squashing them in her fist. But she didn't want to rant to Jill, who would tell Bill, who would tell the whole county. 'Devan was so over-stretched before he retired that we never had the chance to put together a plan for what came next,' she said carefully. 'I think we both made the assumption he wouldn't have any trouble finding new things to do . . . and that hasn't happened. Not yet, anyway.'

Jill rubbed her arm sympathetically, clearly concerned.

'I hate him going around telling everyone I'm a rub-bish wife.'

'It's not like that. Bill said he was just a bit low, that's all.'

'Which he is. And has been, even long before he retired.' She paused, not wanting to seem too defensive.

'But I'm glad he's got Bill to talk to. He won't talk to me.'

'I think Bill sympathizes because he panics if I'm away for even a night . . . even bloody breakfast!'

When Connie couldn't bring herself to respond, hearing only the censure – intended or not – in her friend's remark, Jill spoke again. 'You two have such a great marriage, Connie.' She laughed. 'Remember that time we went to the Western Isles? The ceilidh? Devan claimed he could do the proper Scottish thing, hopping about and pointing his toes and waving his arms in the air.' Connie smiled. She did remember. 'Then he dragged you onto the dance floor and somehow, together, you managed to make it really work – although you didn't have a clue what you were doing, you said – and the pub went wild, clapping and cheering your efforts.'

'I didn't,' Connie said, 'but I've always loved to dance. God, that night was fun.' She heard the wistful note in her voice and Jill must have too.

'You're so good together, Connie.' She gave her an encouraging smile. 'I'm sure you'll sort it out.'

When they arrived at Jill's rambling thatched cottage, Connie excused herself, refusing her friend's offer of tea and one of her famous madeleines. She couldn't face any more discussion about her marriage. Not least because, although Jill had not said as much, she could tell her sympathy – Bill's too – was tipping in Devan's favour. After all, Jill was retired and clearly loving it. She probably couldn't see the problem. *Jill, Bill, even Neil . . . they're sort of implying I'm on the wrong foot about my job*, she thought, after she'd said goodbye to Jill. Not for the first time, she wondered if they were right.

Her phone rang as she was walking home. Her sister, Lynne. The very last person she wanted to speak to right now.

'Connie, it's me, Lynne,' she said, never having grasped that her name came up on Connie's screen. 'I'll be there about four, if that's OK?'

Connie gulped. She'd entirely forgotten that Lynne was staying the night, en route from Aberystwyth to give a lecture at Southampton University. 'Great,' she replied, with a forced enthusiasm she hoped her sister wouldn't detect. 'See you later.'

She was glad Devan would be late: he and Lynne had never got on. Lynne had called Devan 'Dr God' in the early days. She thought him too handsome, too pleased with himself. But she'd been dismissing Connie's choices since they were both small.

This could not be put down exclusively to sibling rivalry, Connie had always felt, because Lynne was the clever, successful daughter, approved of by both their parents, but particularly by her solemn, hardworking father – a civil servant in the Department for Education. Connie, by contrast, had been the troublemaker, the one who'd caused her father to clutch his brow in despair for her lack of focus on school-work and general dislike of authority and rules. She'd been much closer to her mum, who didn't care so much about such things.

Devan had tried, in the early days, to get on with Lynne. But when he saw his efforts were futile, he'd stepped back. 'She always makes me feel as if I've done something wrong. As if I'm not good enough,' he would complain.

'Join the club,' Connie had responded.

But she'd found as she got older that her position towards her sister had softened – especially now both parents were dead. She loved Lynne, and if they kept their exposure to each other sporadic, they got along fine. Tonight, she would keep things simple: open a nice bottle of red wine, cook a tomato and pepper spaghetti – Lynne didn't eat meat – and get lots of chocolate in. She'd be gone after breakfast.

'God, am I ever glad to be here,' Lynne said, plonking her overnight bag on the kitchen tiles and letting out a long sigh. 'Bloody roadworks on the four seven nine, then an accident just before the bridge. It's taken me almost five hours!' She was taller than Connie and neurotically thin, her dyed dark-blonde hair cut to her shoulders with a fringe that was too short and neat, giving her face a severe look. They were nothing like each other. Lynne was the spit of their father while Connie, with her auburn hair and fair skin, resembled absolutely no one in her family.

'Where's Devan?' Lynne asked, accepting the glass of wine Connie pressed on her.

'With a friend. They're checking out a car.'

'And getting up to no good, I expect.' She winked at Connie.

Connie wasn't sure what that was supposed to mean

so she smiled and turned back to skinning the red peppers she'd just scorched under the grill. 'How's Roddy?'

Lynne wriggled on her kitchen chair, adjusting her gold disc pendant on its fine chain and settling the collar of her cream blouse. 'Happy as a sandboy. Our life is now regulated to the nth degree.'

Connie frowned.

Her sister's voice had dropped to a dull monotone. 'We shop in the same supermarket on the same day at the same time. We park in the same spot and buy the same food, which we eat in the same rotation each week. We go to the pub on Friday nights for two hours, then get fish and chips on the way home. Roddy has his rugby on Saturday, then there's church on Sunday, we change the sheets on Monday . . . We do everything together.' She stopped, giving a light shrug.

Connie winced. Not just at the horrendous-sounding schedule of her sister's life, but at the weariness in Lynne's voice. Rhodri had been a bull of a man in his youth, a talented tight-head for his local rugby team, a loud, laughing, good-natured person. He still was, to a degree. But his body had gone to seed: he was now seriously overweight and idle since retiring from BT. 'You're OK with that?'

Her sister didn't reply, her face very still. 'It is what it is,' she said quietly. 'I'd love to get away once in a while. But Roddy doesn't like the heat, hates being squeezed into plane seats – which I can understand at his size – so we never go anywhere.' She shot Connie a half-smile. 'Not like you, gadding about all over Europe.'

Connie wasn't sure 'gadding' quite described her job, but she let it go. 'Can't you go with a friend?'

Lynne gave a sad laugh. 'I couldn't leave Roddy.'

They're living Devan's dream, she thought, with a wry smile. Her sister appeared to be pandering to Roddy's whim just to keep the peace. *Or is it because that's what Lynne wants to do and is blaming it on him?*

'What would happen if you did?' Connie slid the charred chopped peppers into the saucepan with the sautéed onions and garlic, the tinned tomatoes, then lit the hob, poking a bay leaf beneath the surface and grinding in some black pepper. She would add fresh basil at the last minute.

Her sister looked as if she were confused by the question. 'Well . . .' she took a sip of wine '. . . it's not worth the hassle, to be honest. He'd fret and I'd have to cook all the food before I went and freeze it . . . I'd worry about him. Even me being away tonight was winding him up.'

Connie was shocked. She laid the wooden spoon on the chopping board and turned to her. 'That sounds dreadful, Lynne.'

'Does it?'

Connie thought she detected tears in her sister's blue eyes. Knowing Lynne would hate it if she went over and put an arm around her, she just said, 'Don't give up. You're too young for that. Find a friend who wants to travel and plan a trip. I'll help you.'

Lynne glanced at her, her expression unreadable, but said nothing.

'You might be surprised by how well Roddy copes.'

Connie dragged out the pasta pot from the bottom of the pan drawer and put it under the tap. Lynne had been so independent, so highly thought of in her professional life – it staggered her that she should be reduced to this.

'I've got the vegetable garden,' she heard her sister say, almost defensively. 'That takes up a lot of my time. And I'm learning the ukulele – there's a man in the village who gives classes. I'm pretty crap, but it's fun.'

Connie smiled encouragingly and refilled her sister's glass. She was just opening the fridge to get out the lettuce when the front door banged and Devan appeared. It was clear to Connie that he'd been drinking from his loose expression and the way in which he leaned to starboard, resting his head against the jamb.

Lynne jumped. 'Hi, Devan.'

'Lynne . . . didn't know you were going to be here.'

'I did tell you,' Connie objected, but remembered she, too, had forgotten her sister's visit. 'I thought you'd be late.'

Devan shrugged off his jacket and slung it onto a chair, immediately going to the cupboard and bringing out a wine glass. 'Bill wasn't interested in the car.'

'Have you eaten?'

'No, I'm starving. We stopped off at a pub on the way back, but all I had was a packet of pork scratchings.'

'Nice healthy snack,' Lynne commented drily. She couldn't help herself when it came to Devan.

Ignoring her, he sat down heavily at the head of the table and filled his glass. The atmosphere had changed.

Devan said barely a word over supper, just shovelled spaghetti into his mouth and drank large quantities of Chianti. Connie felt constrained by his brooding presence. Lynne was also wary, her remarks brittle and loaded as Devan's drunkenness became more acute. Conversation stuttered and finally died out altogether as Connie emptied a carton of fresh pineapple chunks into a bowl and put it, with a slab of local Cheddar, on the table.

'So,' Devan looked over at Lynne, 'I suppose Connie's been filling you in . . . about her lover.'

Her sister looked puzzled.

Connie's heart jolted. She tried to breathe, daring her cheeks to colour on pain of death, wanting immediately to refute the allegation. No words would come. Devan was staring at her now.

'No? Go on, then. Tell your sister all about it.' His tone was almost menacing, although his words were slurred.

What does he know? Her thoughts were spinning frantically about her brain. *The book.* Had he realized it wasn't she who'd ordered it?

Devan shifted his chair, banging the table leg as he moved his foot, which made the wine in the glasses splash, the cutlery judder. 'For Christ's sake, Connie . . .' That was all he said as he closed his eyes and leaned back in his chair.

Connie looked at Lynne. Her sister's eyes widened in question.

'What are you trying to say?' Connie asked her husband, her chest constricted.

His arms crossed defiantly across his chest, Devan viewed her through half-open lids. 'Italy. You're in love with Italy. You come home all starry-eyed and distracted . . . like you've been with your lover.'

Connie got up quickly. The threatened flush was on the march, she could feel it. 'You're drunk,' she said curtly, beginning vigorously to scrub out the pasta pan and turning the tap on full as if the noise might hide her shame.

She heard Lynne say brightly, 'How lovely for her. I'd take Italy for a lover tomorrow if I had the chance – Roddy or no Roddy.'

Either her words had stunned Devan into silence, or he'd passed out – Connie didn't want to turn around and confirm which – but she silently blessed her sister.

Her husband hadn't finished, though. 'Seriously, Lynne. Explain what you would do, if you were me? Should I just sit here like the pathetic cuckold I am and wait for this love affair to run its course?' He gave a sardonic laugh. 'Or find my own diversion, perhaps.'

As Connie listened to the exchange behind her, she knew Devan wasn't – couldn't be – talking about Jared. But he seemed to be right there, in the Somerset kitchen, and she couldn't prevent the spike of desire that washed over her at the memory of the cool bricks through her cotton dress, the warmth of Jared's fingers on her bare thigh. She felt the supper she'd just eaten churning dangerously in her rigid belly as she upended the pan on the draining-board and turned to face them.

'If I were you, Devan,' Lynne was replying coolly, 'I'd sod off to bed before I said something even more stupid. And when I woke up tomorrow, I'd wonder why my devoted wife might want to take a lover.'

Connie felt tears filling her eyes at her sister's spirited defence. She blinked them quickly away as Devan got to his feet.

'Lucky you're not me, then,' he growled, swaying on his feet. Then he lurched towards the door and was gone.

The kitchen was silent, both women listening to his progress upstairs and the slam of the bathroom door.

'Sorry,' Connie said.

Her sister waved her hand, dismissing the apology. But she was eyeing Connie steadily. After another silence, she said, 'A bit too close to the bone?'

Connie let out a breath she seemed to have been holding all her life and sagged into a chair, covering her face with her hands. *A secret is not a secret if you tell someone* . . . Her mother's words rang in her ears. But she couldn't lie to Lynne. Although they weren't close, her sister had always been able to intuit when Connie wasn't telling the truth – and always called her on it.

'Someone on one of the tours. He kissed me. Then he turned up by accident in the next place, and we kissed again.' She spoke as nonchalantly as she could. But Lynne wasn't fooled.

'Christ, Connie. That's awful.'

Connie knew what she'd done was awful, but Jared didn't seem to fit into real life. He was there, then he wasn't. The badness was a step removed from tangible guilt. Part of her almost expected her sister to sympathize, after witnessing Devan's drunken, aggressive behaviour. 'I know,' she said. 'It won't happen again. I won't see him again, *ever*.' She wouldn't, she was certain of that.

Lynne was still frowning. 'What possessed you?'

Connie couldn't answer. She didn't know. But 'possessed' she had been. 'Devan doesn't know, obviously.'

'Really? I'd never have guessed.' Lynne grinned mischievously: the first proper smile Connie had seen from her sister all evening.

Connie smiled back. 'Thanks for rescuing me,' she said, and this time Lynne gave herself up to Connie's grateful hug.

'She's so uptight, your sister.'

Lynne had left early, refusing breakfast, just filling her Thermos-mug with hot black coffee for the journey to Southampton. Connie was sad to see her go. There had been a bond between them this time that had not been apparent in a while. She'd sat with a cup of coffee in the morning sunshine after waving Lynne off, but found she was nagged by tormenting thoughts of Jared in the wake of her confession to her sister. She needed action and quickly drained her cup. Opening the creaking door of the potting shed, breathing in the warm, dusty, earth smell she loved, she'd pulled on her gardening gloves and grabbed her secateurs.

It was nearly eleven when Devan wandered out onto the terrace, clutching a mug of tea, hair dishevelled, still in his pyjama bottoms and a tatty grey T-shirt. He'd clearly just climbed out of bed.

'Because she noticed you were legless?' Connie didn't turn, just kept snipping at the bamboo stalks that had made a run for it from the clump at the bottom of the garden, popping up in the back of the rose bed.

'I wasn't "legless". If I had a bit too much it was because Lynne was there, disapproving of me every time I breathed.'

Connie straightened up, bamboo fronds clutched in one hand, brushing her hair out of her eyes with the back of her gardening glove. It was hot and she was sweating from her exertions. She hadn't slept well and felt nervy and out of control, worried that somehow things had escalated with Jared at the arrival of the book . . . and her sister knowing.

Although, she kept telling herself, Jared belonged to Italy, and she wasn't due for another Italian tour this year. He was hardly going to pitch up in Warsaw. *It was just a mad moment.* Connie knew she should feel relieved by this certainty, but somehow she did not. 'Let's not argue, Devan,' she said quietly.

Her husband was staring off down the garden. When his gaze returned to her, she saw a softening in his face that matched her own. He gave her a tired smile. 'Sorry about last night,' he said.

Later that morning, Connie and Devan drove over to Wells to potter round the outdoor market. The stalls were set up in the square outside the Bishop's Palace, with all manner of goods, from cheese and home-made pies to silver bracelets and wooden ducks. Connie felt awkward with her husband. It seemed such a long time since they had done that sort of thing together, and she wanted it to be fun, for them to find some common ground again. He hadn't seemed particularly enthusiastic when she'd suggested a day out so she felt the pressure was on her to make it work.

'Lunch?' she asked brightly, when they'd exhausted

the stalls, buying local goat's cheese, some spicy sausages and a cotton sweater with a train on it for Bash. 'I
need a sit-down.'

Devan grinned and nodded. 'The Close?' It was
their favourite restaurant, although they hadn't been
there for over a year now.

When they arrived the place was empty, a sticker
on the streaked plate glass of the window saying it had
closed down sometime in April.

'No!' Connie felt unreasonably disappointed. They
stood staring through at the interior, remembering the
many lovely meals they had enjoyed there. It had been
a romantic spot for them in the past, one they'd chosen
for birthdays and anniversaries, the food not fancy,
mostly steaks and grilled fish, but beautifully cooked.
In her overwrought state it felt like a portent.

'We could get a hog-roast bun from that stall and sit
on a bench?' Devan suggested half-heartedly. 'Or find
a pub . . .'

But the joy seemed to have left them. They were two
people going through the motions, when really they
would have liked just to go home and get on with things
separately, reduce the need to avoid topics of conversation that were contentious – Italy, tours, travel of any
sort, retirement, her sister, Bill, alcohol consumption.
The list was getting ever longer.

'Maybe get a bun, then,' Connie agreed, and they
trailed wearily back to the market. She had wanted to
sit opposite Devan in a quiet place, with a good meal
and a glass of wine, so she could talk things through

with him. But as she walked along the crowded streets, she realized nothing would be solved between them until either she agreed to retire or Devan found something to do that he enjoyed and stopped nagging her about it. And since both scenarios seemed highly unlikely at the moment, there was little point in opening up hostilities again. The best she could hope for was détente. Maybe now Devan was getting out more, his obsession would fade. He might even start investigating the options he'd mentioned, like sailing and the Open University. She could only hope.

Kraków took Connie's breath away. And temporarily set her free from both Jared and Devan. It was a busy thirteen-day tour, stopping at Berlin, Kraków, Auschwitz and Warsaw, places she'd never seen before.

'Will you look at that?' Audrey Mason, from Wisconsin, gasped as the group arrived in the Rynek, Kraków's huge expanse of market square, clutching Connie's arm and staring all around in wonder. It was an extraordinary sight, with its elegant medieval townhouses, St Mary's Basilica to the east, the famous fourteenth-century Cloth Hall.

Their guide today was Mirek, a tall Pole with a blond crew-cut and light blue eyes. Connie was going on all of the tours. Not only was she longing to explore this amazing city, but she also didn't want time alone. Thinking only made her anxieties screech round her brain, like cars on a racetrack.

By evening, the Rynek looked magical, lit up and

glowing, café tables dotting the square, humming with people chatting and strolling in the warm June evening. Tim and Julian, retired teachers from Norwich, both tall and rangy, tanned from regular rambling weekends, asked her to join them for supper. They'd found an outdoor table in a little café tucked into the corner of the square.

'*Na zdrowie!*' Julian raised his shot glass of vodka late in the evening. 'Here's to an inspiring tour.'

Tim and Connie followed suit, although Connie had dispensed with the vodka long ago in favour of white wine. But the delicious potato pancakes, the meaty *pierogi* and the vanilla cheesecake – all in portions that would have fed the three of them for a week – were fighting with the alcohol in her stomach and making her feel a bit queasy. She wanted to lie flat on her bed and undo her black jeans, but she couldn't be rude: they were both so charming.

'Are you coming tomorrow?' Tim asked, suddenly sober. He was the quieter of the pair, Julian the talker.

She nodded.

'So you think it's right we go? I'm curious, obviously, but is it OK to gawp at somewhere so ghastly? Isn't it voyeurism?'

There was silence.

'No, it's an important memorial,' Julian said. 'We need to see just how terrible it was, so we never let it happen again.'

'I get that,' Tim said, 'but fitting it in like a tourist attraction between beer and *pierogi* seems somehow disrespectful.'

'Connie?' The two men looked to her for an answer.

She thought for a moment. 'I think it is a crucial memorial, as Julian says. We'll be paying our respects. I've never been there, so I don't know, but Mirek was telling me it's an immensely powerful place, evocative and so heartrending . . . There aren't tour guides shouting and waving umbrellas, or people taking selfies. I feel it's right to go, personally.'

Connie let her gaze wander across the square. It was still full of people, although after eleven now. Something caught her eye: a figure, walking behind their table in the half-darkness. She twisted round, her heart hammering. But whoever it was had gone by the time she'd turned. There had been something familiar about the set of his shoulders, the way he walked . . . *Jared?* She shook herself. *Christ, Connie, get a grip.*

'Everything all right?' Julian was saying, concern in his sharp blue eyes.

'Yes . . . I thought I saw someone I know.'

Julian continued to eye her. 'You look shaken, Connie.'

'Do I?' She forced a smile. 'Too much vodka, I'm seeing things.'

Both men laughed. 'We ought to be heading back,' Tim said reluctantly. 'Tomorrow is going to be gruelling.'

She strolled between them on the short walk to their modern glass-fronted hotel, attempting not to think about Jared. Once in her room, the bright lights, patterned fabric and clean lines, the twenty-first-century version of G-plan furniture – all so anonymous and safe – calmed her. It was unthinkable that he would be wandering the Rynek at the exact time she was eating there. Although even the vaguest thought that he might be both disturbed and excited her – the recollection of their last encounter setting her body on fire so that she found it almost impossible to sleep.

What struck Connie as they arrived in Auschwitz was its stark enormity. Like everyone else of her generation, she'd seen countless films and photographs of the camps over the years, but they didn't take into account the sheer scale of the place. The images, by reducing the scale, also drastically reduced the impact. The reality – with that deadly railway track running straight through the middle, like an evil truth – was overwhelming.

The temperature had dropped and it had rained heavily overnight, the balmy summer wiped out in a stroke as if it had never been. Which seemed appropriate, in a way, their coach arriving at Auschwitz in the sullen grey light of mid-morning. Not all of the tour group were present. Audrey had cried off at the last minute, another five of her passengers had never had any intention of going, and Connie didn't blame them.

The buildings seemed solid, almost prosaic, at first. Not immediately ghastly. Not until she faced the infamous glass cases of shoes and matted hair, the suitcases and spectacles. Then Connie went cold. And the silence. Queues and queues of people, hundreds probably, at any one time, filing slowly past the exhibits in the purpose-built barracks, and barely a sound to be heard.

'You first.' Tim stood aside to allow her to enter the wooden hut. It was freezing inside, the floor just mud, the visitors stepping across duck boards. Most of the wooden huts had been burned, but this one had been preserved: a death hut for women too ill to work, not worth gassing, just left to die. 'And this is the summer,' Tim whispered, shivering like Connie, although she had on her Uniqlo padded jacket, he a professional-looking anorak. 'This happened in my lifetime, Connie . . . Can you imagine?'

On the coach back to Kraków no one spoke. Some of the tour had gone on to Birkenau and a chilling walk through a gas chamber; others had declined, staying in the café by the car park. But all of them were mute with shock.

The group was scheduled to eat in the hotel that night, and sitting in her seat, watching the Polish countryside slide past in a blur through the steamed-up coach windows, Connie wondered how any of them would find words to express what they had seen. Or if they would even try.

In the end, dinner had been drink-fuelled and noisy, her charges letting off steam in a boisterous manner that seemed to verge on hysteria. *We just want to celebrate life*, Connie thought, but was glad to reach the quiet of her room when the meal was finally over.

She took off her make-up and slipped into the light blue voluminous T-shirt she slept in on tour, took off her watch, plugged in her phone and sank beneath the soft hotel duvet with a sigh of relief. She felt properly warm for the first time that day. England, still on day-light saving, was currently two hours behind Poland, so this might have been the time to ring Devan, to share some of the horror that still clung to her, like a scab, with someone she knew would sympathize.

But, these days, she was so unsure of the reception she might receive that she couldn't face calling. The last thing she needed right now was to talk to a husband who was either drunk or remote – or both.

She lay back on her pillow and closed her eyes. The bedside light was still on, but she didn't want to be in the dark yet, the images from the day still rolling silently round her head. She must have dropped off, though, because she wasn't totally sure if she heard the knock on her door, or whether it was in a dream.

Groaning silently, she stumbled out of bed to check. *A passenger who can't undo his toothpaste*, she thought, irritable at being woken.

'Who is it?' she asked through the door.

'Me,' said a voice she instantly recognized.

11

Connie, still clutching the door handle, didn't move, didn't even breathe.

The voice again, more cautious this time: 'Connie?'

She hesitated for a second longer, swallowing hard, then slowly pressed down on the handle and pulled the door open a crack.

Jared stood in the corridor, looking uncertain. When he saw her, his face broke into a broad grin. 'Phew!' He spoke quietly. 'I thought maybe you'd swapped rooms with one of your people and I'd be frightening some poor eighty-year-old to death.'

'You nearly frightened *me* to death,' she retorted. Although the sight of him made her stomach lurch, she said, with as much firmness as she could muster, still through the crack in the door, 'Jared, go away. You can't come in. It's the middle of the night.'

Jared looked surprised. 'Don't be angry, Connie. Please.' And, when she didn't move, he went on, 'Can I come in . . . only for a minute? I just had to see you again.'

His voice trailed off as a young man in the grey uniform of the hotel walked swiftly along the corridor, staring at them both as he passed.

Connie panicked, terrified that some of the group might still be up and spot a strange man outside her room. She pulled the door wider and ushered Jared quickly inside before anyone could see him.

Finding herself face to face with him in the dimly lit hotel room, she didn't know what to do or say, very conscious that all she had on was a T-shirt that barely reached her knees. She crossed her arms, didn't ask him to sit down and he made no move to do so, just stood close to the door.

'So, it *was* you . . . last night, in the square?'

Jared looked puzzled. 'Me? I've only just arrived.'

'Really? I could have sworn I saw you, around eleven, walking across the Rynek.'

'Not me, Connie. My plane got in at eight this evening.'

She went and sat down on the bed, her whole body trembling with surprise, and finally indicated the only chair in the room, a wooden armchair with padded, patterned cushions. 'You really can't be here, Jared.'

He sat forward, forearms on his thighs, hands clasped, seemingly intent on making his case to her. 'I'm on my way to Warsaw to meet this new design group.' She must have looked puzzled, because he quickly explained, 'I've just sold my kitchen design business, and I'm looking for partners in a new venture.'

Connie waited. *So that's what he does*, she thought. It made him slightly less mysterious, but he had questions to answer. 'Are you telling me you just happened to arrive in Kraków at the exact same time as me? And that you just happened to stumble across the information that I was staying in this hotel?' Her voice was low but fierce. She wished she could stop trembling, but the combination of his presence in her bedroom and her naked lower half was not exactly helping.

Jared smiled sheepishly. 'I won't lie to you, Connie. I checked out your tour website and timed my meeting to coincide because I wanted to see you again.'

'*Jared!* You can't just follow me around Europe when the fancy takes you.'

His look was hard to read. 'I had to see you, Connie. That night at the lake . . .'

Now he stood and came over to her. She felt quite incapable of stopping him as he sat on the bed, put his arm round her shoulders and drew her close. His jacket was cool and smelt of the outside – it reminded her of the night at the lake too. She wanted to bury her face in it, to inhale the scent of him.

'You shouldn't be here,' she repeated weakly, closing her eyes as she tried to resist the surge of desire his touch engendered.

He didn't reply. His hand was lightly stroking the skin of her upper arm, his thigh lay tight to her own bare one.

Connie managed to pull away but did not stand up. She wasn't sure she could. 'You have no idea what a day I've had,' she said desperately, not looking at him, not daring to.

'I have. I went last year.'

She gave a shaky sigh. Without thinking, she allowed him to take her in his arms again, feeling the agonizing pleasure of his hair brushing her forehead, the pressure of his arm, holding her close.

'It was so unbelievably awful,' she whispered, trying to distract herself from the arousal she couldn't suppress. 'Incomprehensible. We all know about it. Know every grim detail. But seeing it close up . . . imagining those families . . .'

'That's the thing. People just like us,' Jared said. 'Hell.'

Then she felt his fingers under her chin, raising her face to his. For the longest second, they gazed at each other before he kissed her. It was slow and soft and exquisite – but not demanding. It turned her body to water, nonetheless.

'We can't,' she whispered, although every inch of her told her they must.

He didn't reply, just pulled her up from where they sat and lifted her in his arms, laying her gently on the bed, pulling the duvet over her. She watched as he peeled off his jacket and shoes, his jeans, until he was in his cotton shirt and boxers. Then he slipped into bed beside her.

Turning her gently on her side and bringing his body close, he wrapped his arm loosely across her body. 'Go to sleep,' he said quietly.

But Connie couldn't and, judging by Jared's quick breath on her neck and the tension fizzing off him, it was clear he couldn't either. She longed so much to make love to him right now, she could scarcely bear it. *Is it wrong?* she asked herself, as she lay, hardly daring to breathe, trying to control her desire. The cold, the anguish and hate that had stalked her day, the smell of terror that still haunted the place, seemed to reproach her. She felt ashamed that she was alive and free, able to enjoy the sensuous warmth of Jared's body against her back. But the life surging through her veins right now was irresistible, impossible to deny. She took a shaky breath, then turned to him.

Connie must have slept very deeply because when she woke Jared was gone.

A note, written on hotel stationery, was propped on the bedside table. All it said was 'Warsaw? x'.

She stared at it for a moment, remembering. The sex had been blissful. Quick, intense and cathartic, their bodies were so ready, so pumped with desire, that all thought of what she was doing – and whether she should be doing it – was temporarily banished. She had just let go. Now, through the haze of sleep, her pulse couldn't help but quicken at the prospect of seeing him again. Shame seeped around the edges of the thought, but she was too discombobulated, as she hauled herself out of bed and got ready for work, to give it proper attention.

Miles and Deborah Loader from Worcester – in their mid-seventies, a lively, inquisitive couple – accosted Connie as soon as she got out of the lift. They had obviously been waiting for her, but she was late down to breakfast, having dressed and packed on autopilot, her thoughts consumed with Jared.

'Connie, dear,' Deborah began, both of them flanking her as if they were worried she might make a run for it, 'we don't want to fuss, but we wondered if you could help us with something.'

Connie tried to focus. Something was wrong because Deborah, usually so engaging, looked pale and upset this morning. 'Of course,' she said, with her best smile.

Miles seemed a bit embarrassed as he took over. 'We're going home.'

'Oh . . .' Connie was surprised. No one had ever left early from one of her tours.

Before she had a chance to ask why, Deborah hurried on: 'We haven't told anyone, because we didn't want to make an issue of it, but some of my family died in Auschwitz.'

She bit her lip and Connie thought she might be about to cry. She took her arm and guided her to one of the chairs in the lobby, urged her to sit. 'I'm so sorry.'

'Yesterday was a journey I'd always vowed I'd make one day,' Deborah went on. 'But it's taken it out of me. I don't feel able to enjoy the rest of the trip now.'

Connie's head was banging with tiredness. She ran through the company protocol for a situation like this, dreading the hours she might have to put in to sort things out. 'I understand,' she said. 'I imagine you'll want to fly home?'

'We've booked a flight for later today,' Miles assured her. 'Our problem is, how best to say goodbye to everyone. Deborah doesn't want anyone to know the real reason – we only told you because we didn't want to lie to you. You've been so kind. But we thought you might have a suggestion.'

You've come to the right person, if you're after a plausible lie, she thought, guilt suddenly washing over her, like an icy wave, as she confronted Deborah's grief for her dead family in light of her betrayal of her living one. 'You could just say you haven't been well, that the tour is more tiring than you expected?'

Miles nodded, but hesitated, glancing down at his wife, who was sitting very still, head bowed, as if she were in another world. 'We wondered . . . would you mind saying it for us?' he finally asked. 'Then we could just slip away. Deborah really isn't up to all those questions, the hugging and stuff.'

Connie knew what he meant. 'Of course I will,' she said, swallowing hard because she suddenly felt nauseous. She dithered, not wanting to rush off and leave them in the lurch but worried she might actually be sick. She tried to breathe, but the waves of cramping nausea pulsed through her body, like the incoming tide. 'Will you excuse me for a moment? I'll be right back,' she muttered, fleeing to the Ladies behind the foyer before they had a chance to reply. When she reached the safety of the cubicle, she flopped down onto the seat and bent over, head between her knees, rocking backwards and forwards, finally confronting her betrayal.

People in the throes of an affair, Connie had often observed, often appeared buoyed up – the damage and distress coming later, of course – carried away, initially, by the blind thrill of it, as if it were the most glorious thing in the world to cheat on the person you love. Connie felt sick, not elated, as the reality of last night hit her. Yet she seemed completely unable to stop the juggernaut. *Warsaw*, she thought, as she sat there, head resting on her folded arms in the hotel toilets. *Tomorrow night.* And her body melted in direct defiance of her shame.

When she returned to the foyer, Miles and Deborah had gone.

How Connie got through the packed day – sorting out the Loaders' departure, the journey to Warsaw, the settling of the group in the new hotel and supper with five of them – she would never know. But get through it she did. Now it was nearly midnight and she lay on her bed, fully clothed, too enervated even to undress.

Jared had not been in touch. But, then, he never told her what he was planning. In a way, though, the random nature of his visits made their affair – because what else could she call it now? – seem less solid, less premeditated . . . but, she was ashamed to admit, also more exciting. *Will he come tonight?* She hoped not. Sleep was the only thing she needed right now.

Connie awoke a couple of hours later, still dressed and lying on top of the duvet, the bedroom lights blazing. She was cold and disoriented, her mouth sour from the wine at dinner. Dragging herself to sitting and swinging her legs over the edge of the bed, she shivered.

We're only in Warsaw for two nights, she thought, as she stumbled out of her clothes and into the bathroom, wondering how she would feel if Jared didn't appear.

'Hey, Mum, glad I caught you.' Caitlin's voice sounded cheery.

Connie was waiting in the lobby for everyone to assemble and be told the plans for the day when she took the call.

'I haven't heard a peep out of you,' her daughter was saying. 'I wondered if you'd been swallowed up by a salt mine or something. They have a famous one in Poland, don't they? I've read about it somewhere.'

Connie smiled. 'They do indeed. But for some reason they crossed the salt mines off the itinerary this year. Could a salt mine need renovating?' The sound of Caitlin's laughter was so welcome . . . and so uncomfortable.

'So where are you now?'

'Warsaw. Such a beautiful city. Did you know that they rebuilt a lot of the old structures after the war to precisely what they looked like before Hitler flattened the place?' She went into tour-guide mode, to fend off the truth of what she'd been doing in Poland. 'You'd never know the old town wasn't exactly that, to look at it.'

'Wow, hope I'll get there one day . . . when Bash is a bit less challenging on the travel front, perhaps. What's been going on, then, Mum? Any passengers getting up your nose?'

Connie cleared her throat. She had a persistent frog, as if her sins were choking her. 'Not so far . . . I'll tell you about Auschwitz when I see you. I want to hear about Bash.' She changed the subject and for the next ten minutes her daughter filled her in on the minutiae of her grandson's life. Caitlin's words soothed her, her pulse dropping for the first time in twenty-four hours. Listening, she was reminded of the normal round of her life, where she was a mum and a grandmother, a wife and a member of a solid, supportive community, all of whom she loved. Another universe to the one she inhabited with Jared. *I'll tell him,* she promised herself, as she ended the call to Caitlin. *If he turns up tonight, I'll tell him he can't come in.* But her promise rang false, even to her own ears.

Unlike before, in the G-plan hotel in Kraków, she made no attempt to resist, aware of nothing except his hand sliding softly up under her T-shirt and finding her naked breasts.

And also unlike before, this time Jared made love to her so slowly. He would not let her come. He teased her, tormented her, brought her close, then withdrew until she begged him. She thought she would literally die from pleasure. He was always in control and she found, to her surprise, that she liked it, enjoyed the agonizing way he was playing with her senses, caressing her body so that all her nerve endings were on fire. In the end she was gasping, half-conscious, the rippling surge through her body like nothing she had ever experienced before.

Afterwards he lay beside her in the darkness. The air in the room seemed to swirl and vibrate with their lovemaking. Her body tingled all over, her skin glowing from his touch. She closed her eyes, a wash of pleasure floating, like a fragrance, around her head. She felt his hand reach for hers and held it lazily, too dazed to move.

Jared had appeared out of nowhere, as always. Connie had spent the afternoon strolling past the colourful buildings and famous churches along the impressive Royal Way – sometimes referred to as 'the Champs-Élysées of Poland'. She was with some of the group, poking into small shops and stopping for coffee and delicious pastries. It was hot again, the June sun a welcome relief from the previous two days of rain.

She had come out of a trinket shop, Audrey from Wisconsin hanging on her arm and bending her ear about her grandson's extensive collection of snow-globes. Sitting at an outside table in the café next door, sipping iced tea from a tall glass, Ray-Bans and hair glinting in the sun, was Jared. He looked up as Connie and Audrey passed, raising his eyebrows just a touch in greeting. Connie jolted, held her breath, but was unable to stop a small smile in return. Audrey waffled on, oblivious. *Tonight*, she'd thought, her heart banging like a gong she thought the whole of the boulevard must hear.

For the rest of the day, Connie had fretted: she knew they would make love again – just the thought of it made her stomach flip, her heartbeat thump out of rhythm. But without the blind, almost furtive haste of that Kraków night and the cover of the duvet, she was suddenly conscious of her age, her breasts, her belly, the not-so-firm skin of a woman over sixty. Jared was still young – younger than her by ten years, anyway. Dressed, she passed muster, perhaps, but it was a whole different thing to strip off in front of a man she barely knew. In her mind's eye she ran through her underwear: bog-standard M&S, nothing frilly or even remotely enticing enough. How could he possibly still want her, her body revealed in all its nakedness?

But, in the end, nothing mattered. He had walked through the door – having texted first from the lobby this time – and that had been that. She forgot about her shortcomings. There was no self-consciousness between them, only desire.

Now she heard him turn and rolled to face him. His fingers brushed a strand of hair back, tucking it behind her ear. She took his hand and cupped it to her cheek. Then she said softly, 'You made me laugh today, sitting like a spy at that café table, with your shades and your newspaper.'

'It was in Polish,' he said, chuckling. 'I couldn't read a word.'

They fell silent.

'We're leaving tomorrow . . . Well, it's today now.' Her words sounded loud in the quiet room. They went unanswered: Jared was asleep.

*

Connie watched through half-open lids as Jared hauled his naked body from the bed. He was tanned and lean, the muscles of his back well defined. She had no recollection of falling asleep, but she must have done, because the summer light was poking through the blinds at the hotel window. The last thing she remembered was the feel of his breath, soft on her cheek.

He did not speak or look at her as he pulled on his jeans and buttoned his blue shirt, brushing his long hair back from his face with both hands as he padded to the bathroom. She heard him splashing in the sink but lay there, her body still tender and sensitive, in a blur of remembered pleasure.

12

Connie realized with a shock, as the Eurostar slid out of the tunnel on the English side, that she had barely thought about Devan in the days she'd been away. Now she felt the first stirrings of panic at the prospect of seeing her husband. He was the last person on the planet she felt able to face. He knew her like the back of his hand. Surely, surely, this time he must read something in her eyes.

Because she had changed. From being an unthinkingly faithful wife, she had morphed into a person who would willingly open her body to another man, lie naked with him, press her mouth to his in lust, and dream of him during her waking moments. Not just once, either. How could that not show in her eyes, in the way she spoke and breathed, even in the hue of her skin? She cringed at the thought.

Her next tour was in two weeks – five nights in the Scottish Highlands. Between now and then she needed somehow to remove herself firmly from Jared's orbit and slot back into real life. Although her mind still burned with the possibility of seeing him again. *Will he come to Scotland?* It didn't seem to matter to her brain that she despised herself for these perfidious thoughts. It ran on regardless, almost minute by minute, replaying those moments with Jared until she knew every one by heart.

The house was silent when Connie got home around three: no dog, no husband. Devan hadn't answered her call about picking her up from the station – she'd had to take a taxi – or any of her subsequent texts asking where he was. She wasn't even sure she'd told him when she was getting back, their communication having ground almost to a halt. Not that she minded his absence. It just put off the evil moment, gave her time to unpack and settle in, wash off the journey – and, hopefully, Jared – before she had to face him.

When she finally heard the front door open early in the evening, and the scuffing of Riley's paws on the wood floor, she was showered and as composed as was possible in the circumstances. She steeled herself for the blank indifference that seemed currently to be Devan's default position, her body tense as she put aside the local paper – merely a prop, her thoughts had been drifting elsewhere all afternoon – and took a sip from the mug of mint tea, long since gone cold.

Devan's face appeared round the kitchen door. Even with all that had happened, Connie felt a momentary pleasure at the familiarity of his handsome face. But his expression as he said a soft 'Hi,' was hard to read. She eyed him cautiously as he came into the room and took a seat opposite her.

'Sorry I missed the pick-up. Only just got your messages,' he said.

Connie bent to greet Riley, burying her face in his furry brown neck and fighting off his eager tongue with a laugh. It gave her a moment to catch her breath. 'Didn't matter, I got a taxi OK.'

When she straightened up, Devan was gazing at her. 'Can we talk?' he said.

It was a strange question for a husband to ask a wife, and Connie felt a frisson of alarm. *Is he going to say he doesn't love me any more?* Her heart was pounding. He seemed so serious, his hands on the table fiddling nervously as he rubbed hard at a spot on his index finger. She waited. He didn't speak for what seemed a long time. She could almost see the words bunching on his tongue.

'I know things have been shit between us for a while now,' Devan began eventually, 'and that's partly my fault.' He twitched his eyebrows in an apologetic half-smile.

Surprised by his opener and still nervous, Connie dithered in her response, wondering where this was leading. He was talking again.

'It's been weird . . . not sure how to explain . . . but I had a serious crisis after you left this time, Connie. I was so low, lower than I can remember being my whole life.' His head, previously bowed, lifted, his eyes finding hers. He hesitated before going on. 'I feel like we've been locked in separate rooms recently. Like I've lost you . . . and all sense of myself too.' He took a long breath. Connie did not interrupt: she was too moved by his words, and the obvious bewilderment in his eyes. 'It was bad. I barely got out of bed. I wasn't even drinking, just lying there, doing nothing . . . crying a lot.' He gave her a rueful grin. 'Pathetic, I know.'

'Devan . . .'

He held up his hand to stop her. 'Please, let me finish. It's been going round and round in my head, all this, and I want to get it out.'

This made her smile. Her husband wasn't comfortable with confessional mode. 'I've tried to analyse what happened to me when I stopped working.' He paused. 'It's hard to articulate . . . but it was like being trapped in myself. I couldn't see or feel or care about anyone or anything around me. On one level I knew I was pissing you off, I knew I was letting myself go, but it was all happening at a remove . . . It didn't really touch me.'

Connie nodded. She didn't totally understand, but it made sense.

'I know you were frustrated with me because you thought I was depressed and in denial about it. But I kept telling myself that none of what I'd been feeling fitted my professional view of depression.' He gave a wry laugh. 'Shows how crap we professionals are when it comes to self-diagnosis.'

Devan fell silent, even his hands now still, his head bowed again.

'So . . . something changed?' Connie asked cautiously.

He shrugged. 'I don't know exactly. It was like I'd reached the bottom. There was no feeling at all. I wasn't even scared, lying in that no man's land. Then I woke up one morning and realized I didn't feel like crying.

Which was progress in itself.' He gave a short laugh, raised his hands in the air. 'This probably all sounds loopy. Maybe not drinking for a week helped, who knows? I've been seriously knocking it back for a while, as you know.'

She nodded, waited for him to continue.

'I even felt like getting out of bed. I was suddenly desperate to. Which may sound small, but it was huge for me.'

'I wish you'd been able to let me in, Devan, not felt you had to go through it alone. It's been really hard, seeing you so unhappy.' Her words sounded uncomfortably false to herself, in light of how little thought she'd given her husband during the Polish tour. But she meant it. The months of watching him suffering like that had been agonizing. Now, remembering Jared, guilt hit her, like a smack in the face.

'Yeah, well, we haven't been exactly on the same page recently.'

Connie nodded in agreement. She was trying to take in what her husband was saying. After battling for so long, Devan's sudden moment of epiphany was bewildering. Like leaning on a heavy door until suddenly it gives way and you fall flat on your face.

'Anyway,' he went on, 'in the last few days I've slowly begun to appreciate things again . . . like sunshine . . . bacon.' He frowned, adding, 'You know you've got a lot of fans out there, Connie.'

She gave him a questioning look, puzzled by the non-sequitur.

'Jill, Gloria, Stacy, Neil . . . They've seen what's been going on between us.'

'You've been talking to them about our marriage?' Connie was taken aback. She'd left for Poland with a husband who was hardly speaking to her and returned to find a man who was smelling the bacon and baring his soul, not just to his best friend but to everyone they knew.

'Why not? They're our friends, Con.' He paused. 'They're rooting for us.'

Connie fidgeted uneasily. She didn't deserve her friends' support of her or the McCabe marriage. Not any more. When she looked at Devan again, his face was lit up with his old smile, not the jaded, tacked-on version of recent months, which faded almost before it had begun. It was tentative, as if he were unsure whether he was allowed to charm her like this. But it was there.

He got up and came round the table, hovering beside her. She rose. For a moment they stood in silence, as if they – who had been married for over thirty years – had forgotten how to hug each other. Then Devan opened his arms. Connie breathed out, feeling tears press behind her eyes as she leaned against him and felt overwhelming guilt, love and relief fight for pole position inside her head.

'I'm sorry,' Devan said, into her hair. 'I'm so sorry things got so out of hand between us, Connie.'

She looked up at him, her vision blurred by tears. 'I'm sorry too,' she said, then laid her head back on his chest with a long sigh. *Although he has no idea what else I'm sorry for,* she thought.

Devan let her go and she sat down, so weary suddenly, the air going out of her, like a deflating balloon. She was exhausted from everything that had happened on the Polish trip: the nightmare of Auschwitz, the sleepless nights with Jared, her overriding guilt and conflicted thoughts. Now she was also bemused.

Devan went to the side and picked up a bottle of Rioja, waving it at her with a question in his eyes. She smiled, nodded, and he brought two glasses from the cupboard, set them on the table and poured a little into each. He sat down opposite her and held his glass aloft. 'To us?' he asked hesitantly.

Connie chinked her glass against his. 'To us.'

Is this real? She didn't want to question his volte-face and jeopardize this precious moment between them, but after months and months of negativity, she felt she didn't recognize this version of her husband.

'You don't look too thrilled, Con,' Devan was saying. He sounded puzzled, bordering on hurt.

Connie dragged herself from her thoughts with effort. 'No, I am. I'm really pleased for you, of course I am. And for us . . . It's just all quite sudden . . .'

Devan did not immediately reply, and Connie tensed. But when he did speak, his voice was gentle. 'For me, too. I still feel a bit raw. But hopeful, at last.' He sat up straighter, seemed suddenly determined. 'Listen, about the dreaded R word. Let's just leave things as they are, see what happens.' He put his hand over hers. 'I know how much you love your job and there's no way I'm going to browbeat you, Con. The last thing I need is a resentful wife!' The final sentence was accompanied by a broad grin.

She laughed. She knew she should feel vindicated, relieved, grateful that the logjam of hostility had finally been freed. But it wasn't that simple. There was her gross betrayal . . . There was Jared.

'Where did you go this afternoon?' Connie asked Devan. It was dusk and a beautiful evening as they strolled through the village with Riley, the horizon beyond the houses shot with a luminous raspberry gold that made her gaze in awe. Devan took her hand as they walked, but she didn't feel entirely comfortable.

She'd been increasingly on edge since Devan's announcement. She knew more than ever that she must forget Jared now.

Carrying on an affair during a serious rift in her marriage was bad enough, but might be considered understandable by some. Now that he'd started to re-engage with her, though, it was unthinkable. *This is what I've longed for, isn't it?* she chided herself. *To see the love in Devan's eyes again.* And it was. But it was hard instantly to push Jared from her mind, or the confusion of the previous year, just because Devan was so unexpectedly onside again.

Now Devan said, 'Oh, out and about. I took Riley for a walk, then I dropped in on Bill for a cuppa and a chat. He's after a nineteen-seventies Alfa now.' She glanced at him as he spoke, detecting something oddly shifty in his tone. But he was staring at the sunset. He turned back and smiled, and she decided she'd imagined it. 'With all that's been going on in my head, I'd forgotten you were coming in today.'

They walked on, the air cooling as the sky faded to navy. Connie shivered and pulled her cardigan round her body.

'Tell me about Poland,' Devan said. 'I want to hear all about Auschwitz and Kraków.'

It's been an age since he's shown any interest in my tours, she thought. But although he was finally making an effort she found she couldn't enjoy it as much as she wished to.

When they got home, Connie wanted to delay going up to bed for as long as possible. She'd seen the eager light in Devan's eye since supper, the way he gazed at her across the table, and took it to mean he might want to make love to her later. The thought made her panic. Jared's erotic teasing had brought her to heights of pleasure she had never experienced with Devan. *Will he know?* She was hot with shame.

She also realized, as she slowly began to undress, that she felt bamboozled by her husband. *He's all sunshine and sorry, expecting me to respond as if nothing's happened. I'm obviously supposed to just roll over, forget.* Like painting over a crack in the wall. She knew he didn't mean it like that. He was just being enthusiastic about finally feeling free from his despair. About loving her. But, Jared notwithstanding, it didn't seem quite fair to expect too much from her, too soon.

Devan, already in bed, was watching as she self-consciously removed her bra, stepped out of her knickers. *Two nights ago* . . . She struggled to put it to the back of her mind as she lifted the duvet and slid in next to her waiting husband.

He was kissing her before she'd had time to catch her breath. His mouth was eager, his hands quickly finding her breasts, as if he were in a tearing hurry.

'Whoa, wait, *wait*, Devan.' She pulled away, staying his hand. 'Let's take it slowly, OK?'

His eyes didn't seem focused as he stared down at her. 'What's wrong? What have I done?'

She wanted to close her eyes for fear he would see the scene in the hotel bedroom playing there. 'Nothing's wrong.' She kissed him gently. 'It's just been a long time, that's all.'

He tensed and she saw his mouth working. Then he sighed and flopped back on his pillow. 'I know . . . and I'm sorry. I've just missed you so much, Con. I know I didn't show it, but seeing you looking so hurt every time I pushed you away these past months tore me up. Only I couldn't seem to stop. It's like I was punishing you for how I felt.' He turned to her. 'I just want to show you how much I love you, now . . . for things to go back to how they were before.'

She lay there, wanting to respond as he deserved, but feeling Jared lurking between them. Things would never be the same – it was naïve to think they might be.

'Come here,' she heard Devan say, and was painfully aware of the echo of Jared's words that night in

Warsaw. It was all she could do to repress a shiver of arousal. She felt Devan's arms pulling her against him. It was such a familiar gesture, but she couldn't relish the closeness, or relax into his embrace as she knew she should, and normally would.

But Devan seemed to understand. He didn't try anything more, although she could tell he was aroused as he spooned into her back when they turned on their sides. She wished he would move away. His breath on her neck was like the hot wind of shame. *What am I going to do?* She felt tearful, but dared not give in to tears, with Devan so close. *If only he'd said all this before Poland,* she thought ruefully. Although, in truth, she doubted it would have made much difference – hard though this was to admit. *If Jared comes to my room next week, will I be strong enough to resist?* The question kept her awake, despite her utter exhaustion, for most of the long night.

13

Connie was leaving again. Inverness and the Highlands. An easy tour, as long as it didn't rain the entire time, or the midges pester them to death. Devan had been almost painfully attentive in the days since she'd returned from Poland. Nothing was too much trouble as far as she was concerned. Which Connie appreciated after so long a dearth, but also found oppressive. He was trying so hard. And her heart went out to him in his efforts to show his love for her. But she wished he would just relax, let them settle into a new rhythm, rather than jumping up and down like Tigger, trying to make things instantly perfect. But Devan had never been one for letting the grass grow under his feet – until his retirement, that was – and now he clearly wanted to move on, forget last year ever existed.

Connie did, too, but she knew she couldn't throw herself wholeheartedly back into her relationship until she had finished with Jared, once and for all. She hoped he would pitch up in Inverness, then she could tell him – although she felt sick at the prospect. She was well aware that ending it wouldn't erase him from her mind – she wasn't stupid. Her betrayal would stay with her for ever. But at least she could begin to put their affair behind her, place it in one of the locked rooms Devan had mentioned and throw away the key.

She and Devan had finally made love for almost the first time in two years, although Connie had still found herself hesitating. But the night in question she'd known she had run out of excuses. So she'd drunk too much wine at supper, until her head was spinning, until thinking clearly – or at all – was impossible.

When they reached the bedroom, it had been she who took the initiative, almost rushing him – as previously he had her – in an attempt to prove that she could do this, that things were right between them. Devan was receptive. But the whole thing felt wrong to Connie. Both of them were over-zealous, as if they were showcasing their sexual skills rather than making love, neither fully confident in each other's bodies after the years of disconnect. As if they were strangers.

Afterwards, they did not speak, there were only brief smiles, no cosy cuddles. They just turned over and went to sleep, Connie using drunkenness as her escape. But it seemed like a necessary hurdle and she was relieved it had been jumped – although the sex itself had left her feeling restless and empty. Left her feeling cruel.

Connie had spent the day ironing and filling her case. It was trickier to decide what to take for UK tours, with scant chance of warmth and sunshine. As with the previous trips that year, she was desperate to get away. But not for the same reasons. Before, she had needed an escape from the tensions of her marriage. Now she felt she needed a break from Devan's unintentionally guilt-inducing love. His gaze was constantly upon her, willing her to be loving and happy – to share his enthusiasm that they were getting back on track. She felt she was playacting through her every waking hour and it was exhausting. *One more day*, she kept telling herself, as they ate macaroni cheese in front of the television that night. She refused to think of what lay in store for her in Scotland.

Later, as she came through from the bathroom to the bedroom, Devan, sitting hunched on the bed with his back to her, jumped and quickly clicked off his phone. She wanted to ask whom he was calling, but his body-language seemed so guilty, the words dried in her throat.

'Hey.' Devan carefully laid his phone face down on the bedside table and turned as he got up and began to undress. 'Looking forward to Scotland?' he said, with forced heartiness, his smile self-conscious as he pulled his T-shirt over his head.

What's going on? Connie gave him a quizzical smile. 'Sort of . . . Will you miss me?'

'Of course I will,' he said, not meeting her eye as he climbed into bed. 'So, tomorrow . . . I was thinking, instead of cooking on your last night, do you fancy a pub supper? We haven't been out in ages.' He was gazing at her oddly now, a small grin playing around his mouth. But she couldn't work out what it all meant and was too tired to ask.

'OK,' she agreed. 'That would be nice.'

Her husband's eyes were still fixed on her as he watched her taking off her gold Russian-ring bracelet and laying it beside her glass of water. 'What?' she asked, impatient suddenly.

'Nothing . . .'

In the morning, after an unsettled night, Connie woke to find Devan's side of the bed empty. It was just after seven and he usually slept much later. Rolling onto her side, she pulled the duvet around her ears and closed her eyes, not wanting to face the day.

But only a couple of minutes later, the bedroom door banged open and Riley bounced in, followed immediately by Devan, carrying a tray upon which were two croissants, a ramekin of strawberry jam, white paper napkins, white china mugs and a cafetière of coffee. An envelope was propped between the two mugs.

Dragging herself into a sitting position against the wooden headboard, Connie gave a puzzled frown as he set the tray alongside her on the bed.

Standing with arms crossed and a big grin on his face, Devan said, 'Happy anniversary!'

Oh, shit, Connie thought. She had never, in all the years of their marriage, neglected to mark their anniversary. She tried to bring a smile to her face, when all she felt was dismay. Devan's expression had fallen. He obviously hadn't even considered she might have forgotten. But that must have been what his strange look had implied, the previous night, when he suggested they go out for supper and she'd responded so casually.

She smiled up at him, contrite. 'This is gorgeous! Thank you, Devan.' He perched on the bed as she opened her card. The outside was a bunch of beautifully hand-painted poppies. Inside the message said simply, 'I love you so much, Connie, xxx'.

She felt tears spring to her eyes and a wash of fatigue at the unstoppable guilt that plagued her. 'I love you too,' she said. And this time it was heartfelt.

Devan leaned forward and kissed her lightly on the lips. 'You forgot, right?'

Connie gave him a sheepish grin. 'I'm so sorry . . . I never, ever have before. You should have said something.'

He poured some coffee into one of the mugs, handed it to her. 'Don't apologize. With the way things have been . . .'

'That's for you,' Devan said, pointing at a square package lying on the counter, when Connie arrived in the kitchen. It had been a lovely breakfast, both of them propped up in bed, sipping coffee and strewing croissant flakes over the sheets, laughing about it. She'd had the first moment of peace since that night in Lake Como and Jared's kiss.

Connie raised her eyebrows. 'A present as well?'

He shook his head as he washed out the coffee grains from the cafetière. 'Not from me, I'm afraid.'

She picked it up. It was light. Pulling open the cardboard box, she was confronted with bubble wrap, which finally revealed a small snow-globe. Peering at it, she recognized the Royal Palace and the Sigismund Column in Warsaw.

Connie's heart missed a beat. *Please, no*, she thought, trying not to run from the kitchen, the globe singeing the skin of her palm.

'What did you get?' Devan was at her shoulder, peering at Jared's gift.

Silently she showed him because she couldn't speak. If it wouldn't make her appear completely mad, she would have hurled it straight into the bin. Instead she watched her husband tip the globe upside down and then the right way up, gazing at the gently falling snow.

'Dear Audrey,' Connie said. 'One of my passengers. Her grandson is obsessed with them so she buys one wherever she goes. I told her about Bash and she said I should start a collection for him too.' She didn't look at her husband as she lied with unnerving assurance. 'How kind. She must have got the shop to send it.' The shop outside which Jared had been sitting, Polish newspaper in hand, the sun burnishing his hair gold.

'Good idea,' Devan said, handing the globe back to her. 'Give him a sense of the outside world. Although he's a bit young to appreciate that yet.'

Connie stuffed the globe back into the bubble wrap, then the box. She didn't want to see it *ever again*. Neither did she have any intention of giving it to her grandson, this emblem of her infidelity. The thought made her shudder.

'We can surprise him with it, next time we go up,' Devan, back at the sink, was saying.

*

That night, Connie took a long time getting ready. She wanted to look good for Devan, but her efforts felt hollow, a sham. Like disguising a second-hand gift in pretty paper and a bow. When she finally entered the sitting room, where her husband was sitting, smart in a pressed white shirt and navy chinos, she felt ragged with fatigue.

'You look lovely,' Devan said, smiling at her. Putting his phone away, he sprang up from the sofa and came towards her, pulling her into his arms and looking down at her, his gaze tender. 'I'm a lucky man,' he said, kissing her firmly on the lips.

I'm not at all lovely, she wanted to shout. She hugged him fiercely, pressing away her deception. It seemed oddly difficult, getting used to this new, romantically charged incarnation of her husband. But she told herself it would get easier. She had, after all, loved Devan for a lifetime.

It was a soft July evening, the sun low on the horizon, partially covered with light cloud. She shivered, although it wasn't cold, as they walked the short distance to the pub. Devan had his hand clamped securely round hers as they drew level with the Skittle House. But he pulled her past the door.

'What are you doing?' she asked.

He grinned at her but said nothing.

'Devan!' She snatched away her hand and stopped on the corner, turning to face him, arms defiantly crossed.

'Play along, Connie,' he said, putting his arm around her shoulders and encouraging her gently across the road.

She reluctantly allowed him to guide her, realizing there was only one place they could be going to: the Kitsons'. She'd been hoping for a quick steak and a glass of red at the pub – Stacy's wife, Nicole, did a mean sirloin and chips – and an early night so she could close her eyes and stop having to hide her real feelings from Devan. As her husband opened the latch on the low gate to their friends' front garden, Connie sucked in a breath and steeled herself.

Bill greeted Connie with open arms, his broad, affable features already tinged pink, his breath redolent of whisky. She saw him wink conspiratorially at Devan as he ushered them into the kitchen.

A rose-draped banner had been strung across the row of copper pans on the far wall: HAPPY ANNI-VERSARY CONNIE AND DEVAN, it said, the pink balloons tied to one end bumping each other gently in the breeze from the open French windows.

Neil and Brooks, their faces expectant along with Jill's, were standing in a group, champagne flutes in hand. They all raised their glasses and called, 'Congratu-lations!' Connie, so engulfed in her inner confusion, felt almost assaulted by the attention – although it was obvi-ously so well meant. She sensed herself being reeled in from a long way off, like a trout on a hook, and with the same sense of helplessness. *Smile*, she whispered silently, *for God's sake, smile*.

Jill and Bill had gone to a lot of trouble: rosé cham-pagne in copious quantities and a supper of marinated leg of lamb, melting *pommes dauphinoise* and buttered green beans was laid out in the back garden, pale pink roses in little glass vases glowing in the candlelight on the wooden table.

Connie was touched and, at any other time, would have been delighted. But tonight it felt like pressure . . . to be happy, to be thrilled that everything was all right with the world now that her troubled husband had seen the light. Her friends obviously *were* thrilled.

Halfway through the meal she got up, ostensibly to go to the loo. She didn't need to, just wanted a moment to herself. As she reached the hall, she felt a hand on her arm. Turning, she saw Neil's worried face.

'What's wrong, darling? You look like someone who's pretending to be Connie.'

She swallowed hard. 'Is it that obvious?'

Neil stroked her arm. 'No, you've been putting on a good show. But I know something's up. You've definitely been avoiding me recently.'

She sighed, biting her lip to stop herself crying. 'I've been away a lot.'

Neil put his head on one side, waiting.

She couldn't tell him about Jared. Not when she was about to end it. 'It's Devan stuff,' she muttered. 'Listen, I need to pee,' she added, opening the door to the cloakroom. Neil frowned, but she knew he wasn't going to push her. Not here, anyway.

'Coffee at Angie's soonest,' he said.

'I'm going away tomorrow,' she replied, as she shut the door.

*

The meal was over. A ripe, runny Époisses with charcoal crackers had followed the lamb, then strawberries and cream. Connie had tried to eat normally, but her stomach churned at the garlicky potatoes, the rich, herby meat, the pungent cheese. She'd noticed Neil watching closely in the candlelight as she pushed food around her plate, but there was nothing she could do about it, except smile and smile. Luckily, she didn't have to say much, just let the others carry the evening with their usual amusing banter. By anybody's standards, it was a lively, luxurious, loving party and Connie wished she could fully appreciate it.

They walked home, Devan once more clutching her hand, his tipsy laughter loud in the silent village street as he recounted his secret phone calls with Jill about the surprise dinner, and how Connie had nearly rumbled him the night before. But she wasn't really listening. She knew he would want to make love to her when they got home – it was their anniversary, after all. And she wanted to show him how much she loved him. He'd gone to a lot of trouble arranging the evening – driving Jill nuts, apparently, in his need for perfection. It had to be actual champagne – no Prosecco this time – and the very best salt-marsh lamb, cheese at the perfect ripeness, the most succulent strawberries sourced from a local organic farm. He'd insisted on paying for everything, too, although Bill had begged to contribute. She had been very moved by his determination to please her.

The evening was a salutary reminder. It told her,

loud and clear, that her marriage was her priority, not negotiable. She would definitely *not* be seeing Jared in Inverness. Or anywhere else, *ever again*. What she had with Devan – warts and everything else included – was way too precious to compromise.

14

It rained. The sober grey stone of Inverness, the cloud-darkened water of the Ness flowing past their spa hotel, and the fact that she had left her favourite Ilse Jacobsen raincoat on the sleeper, was not improving Connie's mood. She had not wanted to go away at all this time, even though she still felt a constant nerviness around Devan as they both continued to try to make everything seem like it was before. But mostly she dreaded the almost certain knowledge that she would see Jared. Not giving in when he was standing right in front of her – when she could see the desire in his eyes and know that her own mirrored his – seemed beyond the bounds of possibility, the bounds of her so far shabby willpower.

This was the evening of day four, however, and there had been no sign of Jared. Each night she'd gone to her hotel room and paced the patterned carpet in sickening anticipation. But he did not come.

It's good he's not coming. It saves me having to end it, Connie told herself firmly. She knew she should feel relieved. But instead she felt desperate, finally admitting to herself as she lay on the wide expanse of pristine hotel sheet, pillow clutched to her body for comfort, just how much she'd been looking forward to seeing him. *I would have told him it's over* – that wasn't in question. But her resolution didn't stop her guiltily wanting to be with him. One last time.

The day had been long and wearisome. They'd done the Strathspey Steam Railway in the morning, taking in what should have been spectacular views of the Cairngorms and the River Spey – if anyone could see through the steamed-up carriage windows and the driving rain, the mist obscuring anything more than three feet from the tracks.

Her party had been stalwart and philosophical at first, but the site of the battle of Culloden – where hundreds of rebelling Jacobites had been mown down in an hour by 'Butcher' Cumberland and his English forces in 1746 – reduced them to dull silence. It was a spooky, haunted place, even on a sunny day, but in the sodden murk of late afternoon it was almost as if you could smell the blood and cordite, still hear the dying screams of the slaughtered Scots. They had all returned to the hotel – and a nice hot bath, a stiff drink and a good slab of Scottish venison – with patent relief.

That night, Connie had fallen into a fitful doze when she was startled awake by her phone beeping and vibrating on the glass of the bedside cabinet, the screen illuminating the darkened room like a searchlight. She picked it up, thinking it would be Devan – he'd been messaging her a lot since she left, with pictures of his bacon sandwich, or Riley, or what was supposed to be a squirrel but was just a blur – making her laugh. *I'm outside* the text read.

Jared's name on the screen jerked her fully awake. For a moment she just stared at the display, her breath fluttering in her chest. She could almost feel his presence on the other side of the door. Hesitating, for a moment she pretended there was a decision to be made: ignore him or open the door. But her body had already decided, carrying her out of bed and quickly across the room to catch him before he walked away.

Jared was soaked, his hair plastered to his head, face glistening, jacket sopping wet. But he was grinning confidently as he stood on the threshold of her room. 'Christ,' he said, 'I'd forgotten how bloody wet Scotland can be.'

Connie stood her ground, although she trembled at his presence, so close. 'Listen, Jared, I'm sorry, but you can't come in,' she began, sounding unnaturally sensible and businesslike – reminiscent, in fact, of Mrs Barnes, her primary-school head. 'The tour finishes tomorrow. Maybe we could talk after I've seen them all off.'

Jared was clearly surprised. 'Oh . . . right . . . if that's what you want.' He continued to stand there, however, looking bedraggled but determined, not moving a muscle. She saw him shiver slightly. 'It's just . . . I'm really wet and I didn't book a room. My stuff's in the car.'

Connie still managed not to crack. There was a strange impasse as they stared at each other in silence.

'Could I just borrow a towel and dry myself a bit?'

She clung weakly to her resolve, but it was as if the last remnants were clattering fast down the hill, like shale loosened by a hiker's boot. After another moment of agonizing hesitation, she moved back, waved him into the room and shut the door.

Jared regarded her in silence. Then, with a slight raise of his eyebrow – as if asking permission – he stripped off his jacket and hung it carefully on the back of the hotel chair. Connie, heart now thumping nineteen to the dozen, went through to the small en-suite to get him a towel.

He took it and thanked her as he vigorously rubbed his face and hair. When his skin was pink from the friction, his hair wild and still damp but at least not dripping, he handed back the towel. Connie did not speak. She didn't dare.

He began to put his sopping jacket back on, not looking at her as he spoke. 'I drove from Glasgow because I love that road. But the bloody hire car got a flat the other side of the bridge. So, I walked, thinking the hotel was closer than it was.' His turquoise eyes settled on her now, taking in her T-shirt, her tousled hair, her bare legs. 'I'm sorry, did I wake you?'

She thought of the car, another long, wet walk away. But she knew, even if the car had been parked right outside the hotel's front door, even if he had a cosy room lined up along the corridor, it wouldn't have made any difference to her decision. All of her intentions deserted her the instant she allowed herself to meet his gaze. Like a magnet to metal, she found her body pressed tight against his, felt his lips meet hers, his hands caressing her skin through the thin cotton of her T-shirt.

*

Maybe because Jared sensed, from Connie's reluctance to let him in, that he was on borrowed time – and because she definitely knew they were – their lovemaking felt even more charged. Slow and exquisitely lingering, his fingers found places on Connie's body she didn't even know she had, enticing her to the peak of arousal – time and time again – until she was a tangled mass of feeling, no longer solid flesh.

It took her a long time to come down afterwards. The room felt hot and confining, her skin too sensitive to touch. She wanted air, but the hotel window wouldn't open more than an inch. She flopped back onto the bed in the semi-darkness, the only light falling in a weak glow from the bathroom. Jared was lying on his side watching her. He reached out his hand, placing it against her bare thigh.

'Mmm,' he said, smiling.

Connie closed her eyes. In that moment, she didn't care about anything. She couldn't think of herself as a bad person, or an unfaithful wife, a coward and a liar. She was just sensation.

'It's late,' she heard him say, 'or early . . . There's light outside,' he added.

She didn't want him to leave but, turning her head, she saw the glow of the digital clock saying 05:17. She groaned. 'Thank goodness they're going home today. I just have to hold it together until I've seen them off.'

His fingers were stroking her thigh in soft, circular movements. 'Then what?'

'I'm on the sleeper. Leaves at seven tonight.'

'Well . . .' Jared said, rolling over until he was lying on top of her, a strand of hair flopping on her cheek as he bent to kiss her '. . . that sounds suspiciously like an opportunity to me.'

The last of Connie's passengers were on their way by lunchtime and her case was with Reception. She felt dehydrated and lightheaded, almost wobbly on her feet after the previous night with virtually no sleep. She longed to lie flat somewhere and close her eyes. But the room was no longer hers, and Jared – who had kept himself out of the way during breakfast – was now sitting in an armchair beside the large picture window in the foyer, quietly waiting for her.

He stood as she approached, a mischievous smile on his face. But Connie's mind was in turmoil. *I have to tell him.* Her hand was clutched around her mobile, on which a lovely text from Devan had just arrived: *Can't wait to see you, Con. Have a good journey home. Love you xxx* it said, making her tired body twitch with self-reproach.

She sank down into the armchair opposite, pushing thoughts of her husband from her mind.

'Walk?' Jared asked. 'It's such a beautiful day.'

'Not sure I can put one foot in front of the other,' she said.

He grinned. 'OK, well, there's a nice bench about a hundred yards to the right, overlooking the river. Could you make it that far?'

'I might.' She found herself smiling back, almost

enjoying her feebleness. As usual, her time with Jared felt separate, unreal. It was just the two of them. The outside world – including Devan – did not exist. But she knew what she had to do, and the bench, away from the inquisitive eyes and ears of the hotel staff, would be a better place.

Getting up, Jared said, 'Coffee on its way.'

He strode off, coming back with lattes in takeaway cups and warm sausage rolls, the grease already staining their brown-paper bag in patches. She had no idea how long he'd been gone: she'd just sat on in the cosy, squishy, forgiving armchair in a dream-like stupor.

Bright sunshine flashed off the river, making Connie wince and squint. But the warmth of the sun on her back and a few sips of coffee were reviving her. The river looked more benign today, clean and clear and grey-green as it flowed swiftly past to the Moray Firth, the red sandstone of the stately nineteenth-century castle on the hill glowing pale gold in the afternoon sun. It was very peaceful as they sat on the wooden bench and ate their sausage rolls in silence.

'We're like Mr and Mrs Dracula,' Jared said, dusting off the flakes of pastry from his jacket and briskly rubbing his hands together to dislodge any remaining crumbs. 'We normally come out at night. This sunshine could finish us off.'

Connie smiled, but she knew this was the moment. Turning to him and taking a deep breath, she said, 'I can't see you any more, Jared.' The words plopped flat between them like stones in a pond, dull – and ultimately unconvincing.

He raised his eyebrows. 'You say that every time.'

'I know, but I mean it this time.'

'Why?'

'What do you mean, "why"?' She was almost snappish. Her head hurt and she didn't want to be questioned. The frailty of her purpose would not stand scrutiny.

'I mean, what's different?' He didn't appear ruffled, but she couldn't read the expression in his eyes. 'Nights like that don't come around very often in a person's life,' he added, with a slight smile. 'Not in mine, anyway.'

Connie gave an exasperated sigh. She hadn't shared with him the problems she'd been having at home: that wouldn't have been fair. But he must have guessed. Why else would she have been so vulnerable to his attentions? 'It doesn't matter why. I just absolutely can't.' She took a breath. 'Not ever again.'

After a long moment he said quietly, 'OK.' Then shrugged, turning back to the river.

She stared at his profile. *Did he understand what I just said?* She tried again. 'Devan and I were going through a bad patch . . .' She found herself explaining, anyway.

Jared raised his hand. 'I said it's OK, Connie.' When he turned his eyes on her, his expression was blank: there was no light in them now. She saw him swallow. 'Your call.'

The effect on Connie of his immediate acquiescence was searing. Maybe she'd thought he would put up more of a fight. Not that it would have made any difference, of course. She groaned, tears filling her tired eyes. 'I'm going to miss you.' She immediately cursed herself for her weakness, but it was the truth.

Jared nodded. 'So . . .'

She gazed at him. He had such a quiet face. Devan's was so expressive by comparison, his emotions flitting boldly across his features for all to see. She had no idea what Jared was feeling. Had no idea about his life at all, which perhaps was what made it so easy for her to compartmentalize him in this bubble. *Where will he go when he leaves me? Who will he be with? What will he do?* She wanted to ask, but instead she said, 'I can't keep on lying to him. Or, more to the point, I don't want to.' Because it was as simple as that.

Jared seemed to be considering what she'd said. 'We aren't hurting him.'

'Yes, we are. On some level.'

'He hurt you, I think.'

'It doesn't matter. I love him,' she said. What she said was true, but even she heard the equivocation in her voice. Which was not about her love for Devan, but about never seeing Jared again.

Jared, gazing off into the distance, picked up her hand and placed it between his two warm ones, resting it in his lap. She could feel his thumb stroking her palm. 'It's a different world you and I inhabit, Connie. It doesn't touch Devan. I've never stopped you loving him.'

'You don't exactly help.'

He laughed, and she did too.

'This isn't easy for me . . . Please try to understand,' she said, staring at his profile, her voice rising in her need to make herself clear. 'I can't make love to him when I'm remembering how it is between us . . . when I'm waiting to be beside you again. I can't meet his eye across the breakfast table. I can't say, *I love you*, when you're filling my thoughts. *I can't do it any more*, Jared. I just can't.' Her voice dropped for the last sentence, weariness washing over her. She slumped against the bench.

Jared rose, stood with his back to her, his hands in his jacket pockets. She held her breath. Getting up too, her eyes were fixed on his still frame. The sun was gone now, and a breeze blew sharp off the river. She shivered, battling the scratchy stupor from a sleepless night.

'I should get going,' he said. He did not turn to her and she felt a tiny pang of rejection she knew was unjustified.

Jared began to walk back to the hotel, Connie following in silence. *What will he do about his hire car? When does his plane leave?* It seemed easier to think about the practicalities, her tour-manager muscle automatically flexing, but she held her tongue.

He turned to her when they reached the hotel. 'I hear you, Connie. I do.'

She felt the finality of his words, like stones in her gut. An involuntary flash of last night's lovemaking made her catch her breath. *One more kiss*, she thought, but knew that was something she could not ask for . . . and would never have again.

'Goodbye, Jared,' she said.

Their eyes locked. She saw the turbulence in his and closed her own, feeling them both swirling upwards together, like leaves in the wind. When she opened her eyes, he had turned away and was walking slowly towards the bridge.

15

Normally the night train to Euston was a series of rattling, swaying, jolting patches of fitful dozing. Connie hadn't expected anything more. But last night she'd passed out, still fully clothed, as soon as the train started to move, only waking when the steward rapped sharply on the door of her compartment, informing her they were an hour from Euston.

In her bleary state, London seemed painfully loud and frenetic as she manoeuvred her wheelie-case through the crowds to the Underground and Paddington for the journey home. She kept picturing Devan at the station, imagining that smile of his, the enthusiasm he would show at her return. Because she wanted to prepare herself, plant herself firmly on the path back to her marriage.

But her night with Jared intruded. It was like trying to master the breathing exercises in her yoga class. 'Focus on the breath,' Nadia would say. 'Acknowledge your thoughts, then let them drift away, bring yourself back to the breath.' *How long will it be like this?* she wondered, in despair.

Devan, however, appeared subdued in the days after she got back. He was loving and attentive, but the burst of enthusiasm he'd shown around their anniversary seemed to evaporate on her return. He kept looking at her as if he were trying to gauge something about her. Connie found it hard to meet his eye. She couldn't allow him to see what lurked in the depths.

'We should talk,' Devan said, one evening. Supper was on the table, the doors to the garden closed against the teeming summer rain outside. It was hot in the kitchen, and Connie had drunk at least two glasses of white wine while she was cooking the chicken and vegetable stew.

Her husband was leaning on the back of one of the wooden chairs, although she had doled out his chicken into one of the Delft-patterned bowls she'd picked up in a charity shop, and pushed the dish of buttered peas towards him. With seeming reluctance, he pulled out the chair and sat down. But he didn't begin to eat.

Frowning, she said, 'What?'

He flicked his eyebrows up, his blue eyes clouding as they looked at her. 'I sense you're not onboard, Connie.'

It was fair comment. There was no point in denying it. She said nothing, glancing down at her food and helping herself automatically to some peas. The silence stretched, like claggy pizza dough, and she knew she had to answer him. But she also knew that whatever she said would be only a fraction of the truth. She hated herself for the deception.

Taking a deep breath, she began: 'OK, well, you're right. I'm not finding it easy.' Devan's face showed nothing, so she ploughed on. 'I know you've been struggling for a while . . . and that's nobody's fault. But it's been hard for me too, Devan. I tried to pass it off, knowing you were in a bad way, but still . . . I'm only human, and so many months of rejection felt pretty personal . . .'

He slowly shook his head. She didn't know whether it was in denial of her words, or discomfort at what he'd put her through. But he said nothing, so she went on, trying to stop her tone escalating with the hurt she couldn't help still feeling. 'Then one day I come home and everything's changed, literally overnight. You're all loved up. Your backache has mysteriously vanished and you want me again. You organize a surprise party behind my back – something you've never, ever done before. Which is lovely, but it's not fair to expect me to fall instantly into line as if the last two years never happened . . .' She trailed off.

'For God's sake, Connie,' Devan spoke quietly, but she could hear the weary frustration in his voice, 'I was trying to be nice . . . You're making me out to be some sort of monster.'

'I'm not. I'm just trying to tell you how *I've* been feeling.' Resentment almost made her add, 'This isn't all about you, Devan.' But she held her tongue, hating how peevish she was sounding.

Devan took a mouthful of wine and set his glass carefully on the table, as if he were trying very hard to control himself. 'OK. Well, obviously I'm really sorry it's been so difficult for you,' he said, the words sounding sincere, but the edge to his voice telling her something different. 'But I think we have to share the responsibility, don't you?'

Connie frowned at him. 'For what?'

Her husband sighed. 'Honestly, Connie, you're so bloody stubborn. I don't know what to say that I haven't said a million times before.' He stopped, looking quizzically at her, as if it were her turn to speak, to tell him she really did understand . . . and was ready to comply. When he saw she wasn't going to respond, he went on, in a voice full of patience, 'Surely you agree that we should have made a plan for our future. I couldn't settle to my life without knowing how things were going to pan out over the next few years. You talk about fairness, but what I was asking wasn't so unreasonable, was it?'

Although part of her still seethed, she accepted that what he was saying was probably true. But she knew, too, that she'd often tried to help him find something he could settle to, and had not been heard. The fault perhaps lay in lack of communication on both sides . . . and that he hadn't taken responsibility for his own life. Instead, he'd made her feel *her* retirement was the solution to everything. But she was on the back foot, now, weakened by guilt and without the energy for a coherent defence. 'Please,' she said, looking him directly in the eye, 'let's not do this any more, Devan. If you want me to retire, then I will.'

Her words fell like molten lead in the hot room, shocking her as much as Devan. Connie realized she was trembling. Something had snapped, like the painter on a boat in a storm, wrenching her away from the shore. She knew her guilt over Jared had partly provoked it. But she was also aware of an overwhelming desire to change the narrative, move on from this interminable dichotomy.

Clearly taken aback, Devan was eyeing her suspiciously.

'Are you serious?' he asked evenly.

Riley, sensing the tension, came up to her and laid his head in her lap. She stroked him absentmindedly, barely conscious of where this was taking them, but feeling out of control and angry. 'If that's what you want,' she said stiffly.

'It's not just about what *I* want, Connie.' Devan's voice was gentle. 'Don't say it if you don't mean it.'

Connie clenched her teeth. But her voice was level as she said, 'I can't have this conversation even one more time, Devan. It's destroying us both.'

The room was very quiet, the impasse rendering them both immobile. Riley had given up and was curled in his bed again. The chicken stew was cold in their bowls. The rain poured down.

Her husband's hand crept over hers and she allowed it to rest there. But she could not let go inside. In the ensuing silence, she listened to her breath: short, tight little gasps as she realized what she'd just agreed to.

'I love you, Con,' she heard Devan say.

That was the tipping point. She closed her eyes and reminded herself that this was home. This was her husband's hand over hers. This was safety, warmth, familiarity, history. Over thirty years of it. If she had to compromise, she would. She just hoped the resentment would go away.

'Connie?' Devan was staring at her. 'We can sort this out, can't we?'

She gave a small nod of acknowledgement. *Let it go*, she urged herself. *Accept the olive branch, such as it is.* If she didn't, she realized the chasm between them would widen so much that neither would be able to vault to the other side.

'You still love me, don't you?' His voice was tinged with anxiety now.

'Of course I love you,' she whispered, the words springing from somewhere deeper than conscious thought.

The meal she had put together so absentmindedly, her thoughts elsewhere, lay untouched on the table as they sat on in weary silence. Devan got up but seemed not to know what to do next. She saw him eyeing the wasted food. 'It'll do for tomorrow,' she said.

The silence continued as they packed away the stew, cleared the kitchen and made their way slowly up to bed. Connie wanted to cry, but not to have to explain why to Devan: it was for the sheer weight of her betrayal and of everything that had gone wrong between them.

But as Connie climbed into bed, catching her husband's tentative smile in the half-light, her heart softened. *I love him*, she reminded herself. As she reached to kiss him, she managed to stop any thoughts of Jared.

He was another time, another place. Tonight, she was here in the room with Devan. His embrace was tender and comforting. It was about a long-held familiarity, a potent reminder of all that he meant to her ... how precious that was. And Connie gave herself up to it without question.

As she lay sleepily in the darkness, she knew there was still a great deal between them that they needed to face. Lying quietly in each other's arms, feeling the soft kisses he laid on her forehead – not asking for more – had brought her back to Devan's side for the first time in months. She hoped they could build on that now.

A few days later, Connie watched as Neil grimaced, his bare feet meeting the cold rock. It was six in the morning and he'd swung by Connie's house just before five. Although it was early August, the air was cool and the clouds heavy with impending rain. Just how they liked it. There was no adventure to be had plunging into a river in the blazing sun with half the country for company. As usual, Neil had brought coffee in insulated cups and Connie had nursed hers, still half asleep, as Neil drove his 4x4 south along the M5. Neither spoke during the journey to the river, the silence peaceful between friends.

The river, full after a week of rain, was rusty-brown and frothing as it roiled over the rocks that spanned it. This place was called Salmon Leap – for obvious reasons – and was one of their favourite wild-swimming haunts.

'Looks a bit fierce,' Connie commented, as she

stripped off her clothes and laid them on the grass. They swam naked – one of life's great pleasures – so they always arrived early, hoping not to put any unsuspecting fisherman off his cheese-sandwich breakfast, but the riverbank was deserted.

Neil went first. 'Remember the pull at the bottom,' he warned, as he picked his way across the slippery rock to the natural stone slide – now beneath the water – that delivered them into the calm pool downstream. He wobbled and laughed as he poised at the head of the slide, water gushing round his ankles. Then he sat down and was immediately engulfed, swept the length of the slide as he disappeared from view.

'Oh my God, oh my God!' he shouted, head popping up the other side of the rocks. 'It's bloody knackering.'

Connie shivered as she followed Neil's path across the rocks and stood where he had. The morning breeze wafted cool over her skin, and she waited for a moment, savouring her nakedness. 'Here I come.' Tensing as the water seized her, she felt the smooth stone beneath her bottom, the fierce tug of the river. Then she let herself go, the cold making her gasp and shout until she was submerged, the rusty water closing over her head as she slid into the pool beyond.

They swam vigorously to and fro across the river, reeds tickling their bellies in the shallows near the bank. As their bodies adjusted to the temperature, they lay on their backs and looked up towards the trees and the sky, listening to the pounding of the water on the weir.

Later, damp and cold but exhilarated, they huddled in the car and drank the last of the coffee, gazing down at the river through the rain. A heron landed on the rocks where they'd just been standing, perching delicately on its spindly legs, its sharp yellow beak swishing slowly from side to side, as if it were surveying its kingdom. They watched in silence. This was what Connie loved about Neil. He knew how to just *be*.

Draining his mug and slotting it into the well between the seats, Neil turned to her. 'OK . . . I've been pretty patient,' he began, 'but you're hiding something, Constance McCabe, and I want to know what it is.' He accompanied his words with a severe flick of his eyebrows. The swim had left his short blond hair sticking up at all angles and softened his handsome, angular face.

Connie, cuddled in a thick wool cardigan, warm and relaxed after the swim, which was like a meditation for her, did not really want to engage with his demand. But she owed him an explanation. 'I've told Devan I'll retire,' she said.

Neil looked shocked. '*Seriously?* But you were so dead against it.'

'I wasn't really conscious of what I was saying at the time. I just wanted it all to stop. But since then I've come to realize it's the only way, if I'm not going to waste the rest of my life wrangling with him about it.' She sighed. 'Otherwise, it's stalemate. As I told him the other night, I just can't do it any more.'

Neil frowned. 'Me and Brooks thought you were back

on track, what with the anniversary dinner and Devan telling us how good things are between you now.'

'Yes, and he's been trying really hard, I'll admit. It's just he's rushing me, Neil. He thinks because he's back onboard with our marriage, I should be too. It's what I want, of course, but I'm not finding it easy.'

Neil didn't speak for a moment, just sat staring out of the window. Then he said, 'You can't let him railroad you, Con.'

'I know. But maybe he's right. Maybe I am being unfair to him.' She took another sip of lukewarm coffee. 'I really want us to be OK again. All this sniping and bickering is exhausting.'

Another silence.

'Yeah, but next spring comes around, and you have no tours, no work.' He turned his kind blue eyes on her. 'How are you going to feel?'

Connie shrugged. She'd done the same projection. 'I'll feel bereft,' she admitted. 'But I'd feel even more so if my marriage fell apart because I was being "stubborn", as Devan puts it.'

Neil laughed. 'Men, eh? Can't live with them, can't live without them.' He rubbed his hand over the stubble on his chin as if considering something. 'Could you perhaps cut down next year, see how it feels?'

'I've thought of that. Part-timers tend not to get the tours they want. Those go to the keen beans, for obvious reasons. But I've proved my worth over the years . . .' She paused. 'I could try.'

Neil picked up his phone, checked the time, pulled a

face. 'Sorry, I should get going. Have to be in Bristol by twelve and I need to clean up.'

As they drove home in silence, Connie wished with all her heart she could tell Neil about Jared. *What a liar I've become. Mum would be horrified*, she thought, glad for once that her mother was no longer around to witness her daughter's shame. Talking to Neil without mentioning the momentous thing that had happened to her these past weeks was like making a cake with one vital ingredient missing. But she knew it would be selfish and pointless to give life to something that was now over. It would expand in the telling, be given a new reality, and colour all her exchanges with her friend – change Neil's relationship with Devan for ever. Telling Lynne was bad enough. But her sister was discreet to the point of pathology – and not part of Connie's day-to-day life.

The affair is over. I love Devan. My marriage is the most important thing in my life. She ran these resolutions around her mind, like a playlist on a constant loop, as she stared out of the car window. But she was leaving for Tuscany on Friday and a familiar question had begun to nibble at the edges of her thoughts: *If Jared knocks on my bedroom door, will I be strong enough to send him away?* If she had her doubts, she was pretty certain Jared would too.

16

Connie thought at first it was the heat. Tuscany was roasting in August. It was day six when she started to notice she wasn't feeling well. The coach had taken the winding road up to San Gimignano in the morning. It was a spectacular hill town with medieval towers, built by various warring noblemen with the sole purpose of showing off and outdoing their rivals. After a potter round the sights, they'd driven down into the surrounding countryside, arriving at a rambling villa with faded ochre walls, green shutters and a terracotta roof, situated at the end of a long avenue of cypresses.

Two Italian chefs in toques and pristine whites had taken the next two hours showing them how to make ravioli filled with pork and red wine; *panzanella* – Tuscan bread salad; and custard-filled *bomboloni* – baby Italian doughnuts.

Connie's cooking triumphs were sporadic and unpredictable, but she loved cookery programmes and leafing through glossy recipe books, closely scrutinizing the mouth-watering photos for dishes she knew she would probably never make. So she'd been looking forward to the demonstration, which was held under shady trees in the corner of the villa's extensive vegetable garden.

But by the time the deliciously warm, sugary *bomboloni* were being handed round, served with a little demitasse of strong espresso, she had a headache and was feeling slightly shivery. *A bloody cold in the middle of August?* she thought resentfully. But she hadn't been sleeping.

The tour had gone well, so far. The magic of Tuscany – with its soft light and purple hills, its ancient culture amid such quiet beauty – always seemed to cast a spell over her charges. She felt she was seeing their best selves. One American complained about the lack of handrails on the steep streets of Siena, and she lost some of her group for half an hour during a climate-change protest in Pisa, but otherwise the only problem, with so many older travellers, was the searing heat.

There had been no sign of Jared. *He must have meant what he said,* Connie thought, as she lay awake night after night. She was ashamed to admit how dismayed she felt. But she knew that now she needed to shut down every thought relating to her time with him. Allow the images to fade, box up the bewildering pleasure she'd experienced in his company and lock it into the attic of her mind where, in years to come, she might bring it out and smile guiltily at the memory.

Life would gradually return to normal. *It's what I want*, she told herself repeatedly. Her husband was irritating her at the moment but, then, whose spouse didn't? She just had to be patient. These exhortations, however, did little good. Through the hot Tuscan nights her faithless body still ached to be lying in Jared's arms again. But he didn't come.

By the time Connie was lying sweating in her hotel bed in Turin – their stopover on the journey home – she knew this was more serious than a summer cold. Decongestants and copious quantities of paracetamol from the medicine chest she always carried on tour had staved off the worst during the remaining days in Florence, allowing her to function, just about. But she'd developed a nasty cough and her chest hurt, her head throbbing constantly. A couple of passengers commented that she didn't seem well, but she brushed off their concern with a smile. She'd purchased hardcore cough mixture from a sympathetic Italian pharmacist near their Florence hotel; he'd also suggested she see a doctor – which she stubbornly felt she didn't need – but the stuff made her drowsy and increasingly didn't seem to touch the problem.

Connie made it to St Pancras in a feverish haze, holding on by her fingernails until she'd said goodbye to all her passengers and seen them off on their various journeys home. By now she barely knew who they were, their faces swimming in and out of her vision in a baffling way over which she seemed to have no control. She prayed she wasn't saying weird or stupid things. But apart from one of her clients who said in farewell, 'You should get that chest seen to, Connie,' no one had seemed to notice that anything was wrong.

Scheduled to stay the night in London, because the Eurostar got in too late for the connection home, she only had to make it to the hotel in Great Russell Street and then she could sleep. Sometimes she overnighted with Caitlin when she returned from a trip and couldn't get back, but she had a meeting with her boss the following morning in the hotel – just a yearly catch-up – so it was easier this way. *I'll be fine tomorrow,* she thought. *I just need a good night's rest.*

The next thing Connie was aware of was waking up in the bath in her hotel room. She was shivering, her skin blue and mottled, the water long since gone cold. But when she tried to pull herself up, her limbs wouldn't obey and she thudded back hard on her bottom, chilly water sloshing up and over the side. *What's happening to me?* she wondered dizzily. Taking a deep breath, she tried again, but her arms were like string cheese and she failed to get any purchase. She began to panic, her heart thumping double speed in her chest. But the adrenalin gave her dazed brain a window of clarity. *Must get warm and dry . . .*

Galvanized, she heaved herself head first over the side of the tub, crawling forward until first her torso, then her legs slid onto the bathmat. For a moment she lay there, the effort rendering her wheezy and breathless. She just wanted to stay where she was and sleep. But she knew she couldn't. *Get up,* she urged herself. *Get up, Connie, you must get up.*

Using every ounce of strength left to her, she pushed herself onto her knees, managing to grab the lip of the basin. Muscles screaming, she heaved, flopped back. Tried again. On the third go, she found herself wobbling but upright.

Snatching the large white towel from the rail, she

huddled in the folds, feebly rubbing herself dry as best she could before staggering unsteadily through to the bedroom. With shaky hands, she put on all the clothes she must have stripped off earlier – although she had no recollection of doing so – including her jacket. Throwing herself onto the bed, she rolled the duvet round her until there was nothing free but the top half of her head. Then she lay there and shivered until she began to feel the warmth seeping back into her body.

But with the warmth came fever. One minute she thought she might die of cold, the next she was burning up. *Think*, she exhorted her pitching brain. *Think. Do something.* But what she should do was not clear. *Phone* . . . The word came and went. She knew it was important, really important, but the thought kept slipping away, like soap in the bath, before she had a chance to catch it. She gave up and closed her eyes again.

The next time she opened them and tried to focus, someone was sitting on her bed, a hand on her forehead. She shook it off, irritated by the intrusion.

'Connie . . . Connie, wake up . . .'

The voice was familiar and sounded urgent. She wished it would go away.

'*Connie* . . .' Now hands were shaking her gently, pulling off the duvet, opening the buttons of her jacket. The weight on the mattress was temporarily absent, then a blessed coolness was being pressed to her forehead. She forced her eyes open. Jared, his face pale with concern, was staring down at her, holding the hotel flannel to her brow.

'What . . . ?' Some part of her brain told her he shouldn't be there, but she was so pleased that he was. She untangled her hand from the duvet and took his free one, comforted by the feel of his fingers closing round hers.

'You rang me.'

She considered this information through the haze, then said, 'Are you sure? I wouldn't have done that.'

A small smile crossed his face. 'I've called a doctor.'

The word 'doctor' rang alarm bells. She struggled to pull herself into a sitting position, banging her head on the padded headboard as she did so, trying to make sense of what was happening.

Jared laid the flannel on the bedside table. 'You really gave me a scare,' he said. 'You were incoherent on the phone. Couldn't even tell me where you were.' He stroked her damp hair back from her forehead. 'I was getting to the stage where I thought I'd have to call the police, but suddenly you said the hotel name as clear as a bell.' He let out a long breath. 'Lucky I wasn't out of the country.'

She nodded, although her head throbbed so much she wished he would be quiet.

'Reception came up and opened the door for me when I explained that I thought you were ill.'

She was aware of a loud knock on the door. Jared rose from the bed to answer it and a man appeared, dark stubble on his chin, rumpled and middle-aged, carrying a doctor's bag.

'You're her husband?' the man asked Jared, in an

accent Connie could not place. She saw Jared nod, but was too dazed to correct him.

'What time is it?' she suddenly wanted to know. Something was odd about all this, her brain still not really comprehending how she'd got to be fully dressed in a hotel bed, with Jared and a strange doctor in attendance.

'Three in the morning,' the doctor replied patiently.

When Connie woke next, early-morning light was streaming through the uncurtained hotel window. *Where the hell am I?* she asked herself. She was no longer fully dressed but had on her night T-shirt. Jared was lying asleep beside her in his blue cotton shirt and boxers. The sleep must have done her some good, because her mind seemed clearer as she blinked in the bright sunlight, although her head was heavy when she tried to lift it from the pillow, and she began coughing as soon as she moved.

The cough subsided, leaving her breathless. She lay there, attempting to piece together the events of the previous night. The bath, her icy body, the panic, the doctor . . . Jared. *Did I call him?* She had no memory of it, but how else could he have been present in her room? Realizing she needed to pee, she gingerly pulled herself upright, swung her legs over the mattress and tried to stand. She felt dizzy and weak, though, and sat there, waiting for it to pass.

'Morning.' Jared's voice was sleepy.

Connie turned. Her feelings were mixed as she

looked down at his crumpled form. Gratitude for her rescue was overlaid by the knowledge that he really shouldn't be there. *Why didn't I ring Devan or Caty?* she asked herself, bewildered.

He sat up, rubbing the sleep from his face with both hands. 'How are you feeling?'

'Not as bad as last night.'

Jared yawned and got out of bed, coming round to her side and standing over her, placing his hands on either side of her head and gently raising her face until she was looking at him. 'You scared me to death, Connie.' He bent and dropped a kiss on her forehead.

'Don't, Jared. Please.' She twisted her head free of his hands. 'Listen, you were amazing last night. I don't know what would have happened if you hadn't turned up . . .' He was still standing there, and she eventually glanced up. His face was expressionless so she had no idea what he was thinking. 'I shouldn't have called you. It was wrong after what we agreed in Scotland. I'm so sorry.' She saw a muscle flicker in his cheek, and then he smiled, the sun illuminating his turquoise eyes like precious stones. She found herself staring into them, then collected herself and dropped her gaze.

'I'm just glad I could help,' he said, moving away to stand by the window, looking out across the London skyline.

Connie really needed to get to the bathroom. She tried again to stand. It was better this time, there was no dizziness, but her legs were soft as butter. She didn't want to ask for Jared's help, after what she'd just said.

But he was by her side in an instant. He held out his arm and she leaned on it gratefully as they made their way across the room.

She was shocked as she peered at her image in the dimly lit mirror. Her skin was grey, eyes bloodshot and bruised, hair lank. She was sure she smelt, too, after all that feverish sweating, but she didn't feel strong enough to brave the shower. *I look about ninety*, she thought, embarrassed that Jared should see her like that.

When she emerged from the bathroom, he was dressed and sitting on the side of the bed, lacing his trainers. 'You should ring your husband,' he said.

Connie nodded, pushing away the thought that she should have called him hours ago.

'I'll ask at Reception for an extension to the room. They'll be OK with it when I explain. And you should take another dose of antibiotics. It's every four hours . . . eight, twelve, four, eight.' His tone was businesslike as he rose to his feet and went to collect his jacket from the chair.

She felt a sudden tension. 'Jared?'

He turned, his hand groping in his pocket, perhaps for his keys and his mobile. The look he returned was empty. She stepped towards him, but he made no move to embrace her. 'Thank you,' she said, and was horrified to see his beautiful eyes swimming with tears. She wanted to pull him into her arms, but knew she couldn't. Jared was wiping his cheeks with the back of his hand.

'Oh, Connie,' he said softly. 'I honestly thought you were dead.'

Taken aback, she put a hand on his arm, just lightly, although she was aching to comfort him properly. But even in her feverish state, she held back. Their gaze met. 'I'm sorry,' she whispered.

For a moment neither spoke. Then he took a deep breath and seemed to shake himself. A second later he'd yanked open the door and was gone.

17

'I'm going to ring Dr Wright,' Caitlin said, as she tucked Connie into the spare-room bed in their Shoreditch flat, which was in a converted warehouse, with huge casement windows, high ceilings, exposed brick, and a roof terrace where she had installed terracotta pots of all sizes, filled with herbs and other plants.

'I've seen a doctor,' Connie protested. 'I've got the drugs.'

Caitlin looked worried. 'He was probably from some dodgy out-of-hours service the hotel uses. He'd have just thrown you the first pills that came to hand so he could get back to bed.'

'He seemed to know what he was doing,' Connie said, although her memories of his brief visit were sketchy. 'He said it might be a virus, but he didn't know. He gave me antibiotics just in case, because the cough was so bad.' When her daughter still did not look reassured, she went on, 'If it's a virus, we can only let it run its course.'

'Hmm . . .' Caitlin sat on the bed. 'I still think we should get her to check you out.'

Connie, who just wanted to sleep, replied, 'There's really no need. I feel much better, sweetheart. I think I was just exhausted from holding it together on the tour.'

Caitlin nodded slowly. 'You should have called me, Mum. I could have fetched you.'

'I knew Ash was in Paris this week.' Although the thought had not occurred to her last night.

'Yes, but I could have bundled Bash into the car. How on earth did you get a doctor, anyway?'

'I can't remember much. I was so out of it . . .' *Which is true*, she thought, before she added the lie. 'I must have phoned Reception and they sent one.'

Her daughter got up. 'Right, well, what can I get you? Tea, maybe . . . Are you hungry?' She checked her watch. 'Dad said he'd be here around three. But I think you should stay tonight at least – as long as you want, Mum.' She gave Connie a sympathetic smile. 'It must have been so scary, being ill and alone in an unfamiliar hotel room.'

'I think I was too far gone to mind,' Connie replied, although she remembered the relief she'd felt, seeing Jared's face.

'Tea?' Caitlin repeated.

'Maybe just water for now. I think I'll sleep.'

When Caitlin had set a jug of water and a glass on the bedside table and gone to fetch Bash from nursery, Connie rolled over on the clean, smooth pillow and closed her eyes. But she found she couldn't sleep. Jared's face kept coming back to her. He had been so frightened for her.

Never before had he shown Connie any signs of what she meant to him. He'd come and gone in such a casual way – his past, his emotional life, pretty much a closed book. Once, in Warsaw, she'd mentioned to him that her mother had died recently, and asked about his parents. He'd looked away. 'Nothing special,' he'd said. She could feel the sudden tension, but she persevered, 'Are they still alive?'

There had been a long pause. 'My mother was a single parent, I was an only child … She … she had problems.' Connie had waited for him to say more, but it was a long time before he added, 'Dinah is the closest thing to family I have now.' The challenging look in his eyes dared her to ask any more, and she dropped the subject, not wanting to upset him.

So, all they really had between them was breathtaking sex and a passionate love of all things Italian. With no future to consider, there seemed to be less requirement to delve into the past, to discover the ins and outs of a childhood, a career path, a family history. For Connie, such knowledge would only have meshed her and Jared more closely. And the truth was that she'd been drawing back from day one. Unsuccessfully, of course – because she was too weak to resist – but knowing too much, getting too close, would just have made things more painful to untangle.

What did he expect from me? she wondered now. He'd always known she was firmly married – although she had to admit her actions didn't exactly back that up. She remembered the allusion Dinah had made to a past relationship of Jared's – which had obviously gone wrong. But when Connie had tentatively asked him about Charlotte, the night they were in Warsaw, he'd been vague.

'We had a misunderstanding,' he'd said.

'What sort of misunderstanding?' Connie had asked, although she could see he was uncomfortable talking about anything personal, as usual.

He'd shrugged. 'We just didn't want the same thing. Dinah got all excited – she's so dying to see me "settle down",' he held up his fingers to put ironic quote marks round the words, 'but Charlotte had other ideas.' For a split second his eyes darkened. Then he deftly changed the subject. Connie was none the wiser about what had really gone on.

Lying there now, she worried that Jared's tears – his anxiety for her safety – implied he felt something more significant for her than just sexual attraction: an emotional tie that she'd not previously been aware of. The thought was disturbing.

When Devan arrived, Connie was sitting up, nursing a cup of tea and some Marmite toast she had little interest in eating. She'd slept for at least two hours, her cough bothering her at intervals, only properly waking because her grandson was standing by the bed, gently patting her face.

'Nana,' he said, in a stage whisper, 'Nana, wake up.'

Caitlin was immediately at the door. 'I told you not to disturb her, Bash.'

Bash shot his mother a triumphant look. 'It's OK, Nana's eyes are open.'

Devan barely said hello to Connie before going straight into professional mode. He'd even brought his bag of tricks, and pulled out his stethoscope. He listened to her chest, took her pulse and blood pressure, examined her throat, palpated the glands in her neck and finally pressed the sensor of the thermometer into her ear. Then he sat on the bed, his face a mask of worry, and began firing questions at her, leaving no time between each in which to respond.

'Christ, Connie, your chest sounds like a skip full of gravel. How long have you had this? When did the cough get so bad? Did you have any fever before last night?' He looked around the room. 'Where are the antibiotics the doctor gave you?'

Connie, dizzy with the onslaught, did her best to reassure him. 'It's just a bug, Devan. I'm on trains and with people all day long, it's not surprising I occasionally pick something up.' She was waiting for some barbed comment about the dangers and unsuitability of this sort of work for someone of her advanced age. But, mercifully, he held off.

He took her hand. 'I can't believe you didn't call me last night. You realize collapsing alone in a hotel room could have had quite serious consequences?'

'Yes, but, please, don't fuss.' She spoke weakly, just wanting him to leave her alone.

'I'm not fussing,' he objected.

'OK, but you can see I'm better now. In fact, I think I'll get up and have a shower. I must pong to high heaven.' She didn't really want a shower – even the thought of standing upright seemed like a challenge too far. But she wanted her husband to stop looking so worried.

'Caty says we can stay and I think we ought to, for tonight, at least.' Devan got up. 'I'm not sure I can face that drive again today. And you certainly shouldn't.'

That evening, after Devan had helped her wash and tidy herself, she was settled on the large sofa in the sitting room, wrapped in her daughter's fleecy dressing gown and hiking socks and covered with a soft wool throw. She was still shivery, despite the August temperature outside being in the mid-twenties.

Even Bash looked worried at this strange version of his grandmother – usually bright and laughing and energetic – and snuggled quietly into her side as they watched a kids' animation show about a squirrel club, while across the room Caitlin and Devan prepared supper. She was aware of them whispering to each other and occasionally casting glances in her direction but felt too tired to challenge them.

Neither, when she was eventually handed a bowl of minestrone, could she eat more than a couple of mouthfuls. The soup, although beautifully prepared, tasted rusty and made her want to retch. She needed desperately to go back to bed, but the fussing she knew this would provoke made her hang on till she was practically incapable of getting there.

They stayed with Caitlin for another three days, Connie giving in to her family's kind ministrations. Then Devan carefully drove her home. It was such a relief to be in her own bed. Devan had insisted on a visit from Caitlin's doctor, who had changed her antibiotics to stronger ones because she feared pneumonia. But the chest X-ray, which Dr Wright arranged, was clear of any nasties. 'I'm fine,' she kept repeating. But no one, including herself, really believed her.

Over the next few days Connie slept as much as the cough would allow, but was dismayed not to feel significantly better. When she was awake, she tried to block Jared from her thoughts. But she knew something had changed for him the night he'd rescued her, something significant. She just wasn't sure what. It was as if, by asking for his help, she'd opened up feelings in him that previously had not existed. Because, despite not remembering, she definitely *had* called him, according to her work phone records where she'd stored his number after his first text in Desenzano. How she wished, now, that she hadn't.

'Heavens, Con, you look like shit,' Neil announced cheerfully, when he dropped round a week after they'd got home. Connie was up for short periods of the day now but was still exhausted and frequently racked by coughing spasms. It felt like a sprightly demon was trapped in her chest, trampling about and ripping painfully at the lining of her lungs. She thought if she could only cough it up, she would be OK, but it point-blank refused to be expelled.

Now Neil hugged her. 'And you're skin and bone.' He drew away to look her up and down, a worried frown on his face. 'What the hell have you been doing to yourself?'

Connie placed the teapot on the kitchen table and turned to take the milk from the fridge. 'It's just a stupid bug, but I can't seem to shake it off. It's been nearly two weeks now, and I don't seem to be improving much at all.' She felt her chin wobble and tears form in her eyes. Swallowing hard, she tried to fight off the tears, but faced with her friend's anxious blue eyes, she felt suddenly helpless.

'Oh, darling.' Neil was by her side and embracing her again. He felt warm and strong and she leaned against him for a moment before collecting herself and pulling away to blow her nose and pick out some mugs from the rack by the stove.

'You know what they say about lungs, don't you?' Neil said, when they were seated with their tea. Not waiting for her to reply, he went on seriously, 'Louise Hay, she claims lung problems are associated with grief.' He looked sideways at her. 'What are you grieving for, Connie?'

Taken aback, she tried to smile. 'Don't know what you're on about. Why would I be grieving?'

Neil shrugged. 'I'm still not getting the whole story.' He wagged a finger. 'You should know by now, you can't keep secrets from Uncle Neil. Not for ever, anyway.'

Connie didn't know what to say. But before she had a chance to offer yet another denial, he threw up his hands in horror. 'You don't think you got this lurgy because of our swim, do you? It was bloody freezing that morning.'

She laughed, on safer ground now. 'Of course not. Cold swims are supposed to boost your immune system.' She took a sip of tea, which, like everything else these days, tasted rancid and bitter. 'It'll be something I picked up from the trains.'

'Hmm . . .' Neil was eyeing her. 'So you're not going to tell me?'

She heard the front door open. 'Nothing to tell,' she said softly, before rising to get her husband a cup for his tea.

Later, when she was alone, she thought about what Neil had said. *Am I grieving?* Sex with anyone, even Jared, was the last thing currently on her mind, but she was forced to acknowledge that it was a loss. She had gone to a place with him where she'd never been before. Knowing she would never go there again was a grief she was not allowed, but that did not make it any less real.

She had also lost her peace of mind. Devan was being so loving, so solicitous – she could not have asked for a better husband. But guilt made her jumpy and Jared still encroached, unwittingly, upon her thoughts. She wanted to be fully present with Devan, but memories snuck back through the cracks, unbidden, like mice into an empty house. It was hardly surprising, thinking about it, that she'd fallen victim to the nearest virus. She remembered Devan saying he just wanted things to go back to how they were. Even knowing the impossibility of this, Connie wanted it too, more than anything else in the world.

18

'I talked to Monica today,' Connie said to Devan, as they drove the twenty minutes to Glastonbury. It was a month since she'd collapsed in her hotel room and she was on the mend at last. But the cough persisted and drained her energy, making sleep – even drugged to the hilt with knock-out syrup – intermittent. She was sleeping in the spare room now, because trying to control her cough and not wake Devan just made the spasms worse. 'She groaned when I said I couldn't do Croatia either.' Connie had cancelled her Jungfrau Express tour, which should have started a week ago, as soon as she realized she wasn't shaking off the chest infection. But she'd assumed she would be well enough for the Croatian trip. It took in the beautiful Plitvice Lakes and the Postojna Cave, which she'd not yet seen and had been really looking forward to. It was a thirteen-night tour, though, which she knew would be exhausting.

A thought flashed across her mind. *Will Jared know I've cancelled?* She silently chided herself. But a small part of her still had not fully accepted that she would never see him again. 'So that's me done for the year,' she added quickly. Croatia was her last booking before the European tour season ended.

Devan shot her a sympathetic look as he drove. But she knew he must be secretly relieved. He'd been really worried about her. Too much medical knowledge was sometimes a burden, with mutterings of pneumonia, collapsed lung, broken ribs and heart problems as he watched her body torn apart with the paroxysms. 'Are you upset?' he asked.

'Bit disappointed. I'm never ill, as you know.' She thought back to when she'd last spent a whole day in bed and couldn't recall a single one.

There was silence. Then Devan glanced at her again. 'Listen . . . You don't have to retire next year if you don't want to, Connie.' He was concentrating on the road again. 'I know you said you would. But you love it so much . . . you can always change your mind.'

Connie's eyes filled with tears. Her husband had controlled himself valiantly since she'd been ill, not once digging at her about the job being too much for her. But as she began to show signs of recovery, she had thought he might bring it up again. Although, quite honestly, the thought of going anywhere at the moment, let alone on a long train ride across Europe managing forty passengers, made her feel quite faint.

'Thanks . . . Maybe see how things go,' she said, reaching over to lay a hand on his arm as they pulled into the car park next to the abbey. But Devan was scrabbling about in the well under the dashboard for coins, almost as if he were self-conscious about finally meeting her halfway on the issue.

If she wasn't touring, though, the thought of doing

222

only what they were doing today, maybe for the rest of their lives, filled Connie with mild dread. Devan's cunning plan for building up her strength was working so far. He kept arranging leisurely jaunts into the countryside, where they would walk short distances, rest, walk some more. They might visit a church, a beauty spot, or do what they were doing today – poke around the brightly coloured shops of Glastonbury – making Connie exercise without realizing it. She was always wiped out by the time she got home, but she was grateful to her husband. And she enjoyed the days out, after weeks cooped up, too wobbly to make it to the end of the road. But they also made her nervous. *This is what retirement could look like*, she thought, as they passed yet another purple-painted crystal shop on the crowded pavement.

They found a seat outside a vegan café on the town square and ordered mint tea for Connie and a black Americano for Devan, with two banana and peanut butter cupcakes – about which Devan was highly suspicious.

'I hate feeling like this,' Connie said. 'I've been so dependent on you, so whiny . . . and I feel really vulnerable when I'm out in crowds. I seem to have lost my nerve.'

'That's normal. You're convalescing,' Devan assured her, biting cautiously into the cupcake, then nodding slowly in appreciation.

'Yes, but I feel so old, Devan. Like really crocked and *old*. It's horrible. And I worry it's a slippery slope . . .'

She looked towards the spire in the centre of the square, around which a number of tanned young people in shorts and hiking boots were hanging out, laughing and smoking, tinnies in their hands, lumpy backpacks lying at their feet. She pointed to them. 'This is where we started,' she said, with a smile, remembering the medical tent at the festival as if were another life, she and Devan other people.

Her husband turned to look. 'I thought you were the craziest girl I'd ever met.'

'Crazy? Me?' Connie was astonished. He'd never said that before. 'Gaby was the crazy one.'

He laughed. 'She was stoned. You were crazy. You kept dancing barefoot around the tent to the music, your gorgeous hair all over the place, legs covered with mud, laughing like a lunatic and saying things like "You look so *weird* in those trousers", which were perfectly standard jeans. I was sure you were on something too.'

Connie stared at him. 'You're making this up. I don't believe you.'

Devan's face was alight with mischief. 'You don't remember, though, do you?'

'I do! I remember everything. You did look a bit peculiar in those tidy jeans. But I liked it.' She frowned. 'I remember the mud . . . Did I really dance around the tent?' Her memory was of being the sober, responsible friend, saving Gaby's life.

He nodded. Now they were really laughing.

'I probably *had* been drinking,' she admitted.

'You probably had,' Devan agreed. Suddenly serious,

he added, 'You've always been someone who grabs life by the balls, Connie. I love that about you.' He reached over and took her hand 'You're so not old. I think you're gorgeous.' His words made her want to cry, especially given the dilapidated state she was in. She felt like an animal who'd just crawled out of her cave after a long winter in hibernation. Her hair was faded and wild – badly in need of Janine's ministrations – her nails were flaking, her skin felt like the surface of a prawn cracker and was pretty much the same colour. She was still too thin. 'Gorgeous' did not really cut it.

September plodded by. It was now six weeks since Connie had become ill. Six weeks during which she'd cried with despair that she would ever be well again. Six weeks of being home, being cosseted . . . being loved. And six weeks since she'd seen or heard of Jared. She was a lucky woman, she knew, and tried not to think of how much she didn't deserve Devan's love. Not when the occasional dream of Jared still made her body vibrate and quiver, like a leaf in the breeze. But she thought about Jared less and less. Her brain was quietly beginning to wrap her memories in the convenient mists of time.

Today, Saturday, Jill picked Connie up after breakfast. 'Are we bonkers, driving all the way to the Forest of Dean?' her friend asked, as they headed west towards the M5.

Connie laughed. She loved food festivals: cookery theatre and sampling cubes of local produce, hot lunch in pots with little wooden spoons, mini plastic beakers of cider, beer and wine to test, and the general good humour and friendliness foodies inspire. But that morning she had almost cancelled.

She just couldn't seem to get her spirits up – or her enthusiasm for anything. Her life seemed just a grey trudge from hour to hour, day to day. Although physically she was no longer ill, the cough only plaguing her occasionally, it felt like a monumental effort to respond to Devan, let alone the few friends she'd been in touch with recently. A whole day with Jill – who liked to talk about things on which Connie might have to concentrate – rendered her a bit panicky.

'It'll be worth it,' she assured her friend.

'Should be. Although, according to the app, rain's forecast. Shame for all those stallholders.'

Connie sat in the warm womb of the car and couldn't think of a thing to say. She wanted to close her eyes, but knew she must not: it was barely ten o'clock.

'You know old Mr Solomon's cottage, down by the post office?' Jill said.

'The one with the wooden dolphin outside?'

'That's gone now. The son-who-never-visited has done the place up and is renting it out, according to Chloë, my mate at Tovey's. I bumped into her with that yappy terrier of hers that always growls at me as if I'm a burglar.' Jill fell silent for a moment as she negotiated a right turn, as instructed by the satnav's imperious Astrid, then added, 'Someone's taken a six-month lease, apparently.'

Connie wasn't really interested, but she made noises as if she were. 'It'll be weekenders, I expect.'

'It's only two bedrooms, and one's a cupboard, apparently. Probably a couple who live in London and have a yearning for fresh air and farm shops.' She sighed. 'Another one empty most of the year.'

The fair was packed and cheerful – music playing, lots of small children, delicious smells all vying with each other to make her mouth water. Connie blindly followed her friend around the stalls, responding to Jill's enthusiasms. The predicted rain didn't arrive till later, but it was chilly and Connie – who felt permanently cold these days – wished she'd worn more jumpers under her anorak. They ate beef, olive and sultana empanadas from a Chilean street-food stall, then shared a cone of hot, sugary *churros* with chocolate sauce, and sampled numerous beverages from plastic cups, some of them alcoholic, which Jill sipped, then passed to Connie to finish. So by the time they reached the car – a tiring trek across a bumpy, muddy field – Connie was pleasantly tipsy. It had been a good day and she was glad she'd made the effort.

She slid into the passenger seat of Jill's Mini Countryman and sighed with relief, her body limp with fatigue. Eyes half closed, she glimpsed in the side mirror a man in a Barbour, his bushman hat pulled low against the rain, walking past the rear of the car. He stopped to speak to Jill, as she went to open the boot in order to change out of her wellies. After a minute, he strode off along the row of parked cars. Although she couldn't hear what was said from where she sat, the raised tone of his 'goodbye' struck a chord in her sleepy, slightly intoxicated brain. After a second, she knew whose voice it reminded her of: Jared's. It jolted her out of her lethargy.

'Who was that?' Connie enquired, as Jill climbed in and banged the door, throwing her bag onto the back seat.

'Nice man. Lost his car keys, poor sod.'

'Heavens . . . What's he going to do?'

Jill started the engine and put on the wipers. 'Go back and have another look around the fair, see if someone's handed them in. Although he didn't hold out much hope. Then call a garage, I suppose. He didn't seem as upset as I'd have been.'

'What was he asking you?'

'Nothing. I think he just wanted to share his misery.' Jill gave her a sharp look. 'You OK?'

'Fine . . . Just thought I was going to sneeze.'

Connie laughed silently at herself. As if Jared would turn up in a muddy field at a food festival in the Forest of Dean! *I'm going senile as well as getting doddery.* But during the drive home she sat in silence, her thoughts unwillingly returning to the times they'd shared in the various locations around Europe. As she slumped in her old blue anorak and jeans, her face gaunt and pale, her limbs weak from ill health, she wondered if those nights had really happened. Now she was back in the slow, rhythmic flow of home life, it seemed almost impossible that she was that woman . . . that she had allowed herself to be.

Do I regret it? she'd asked herself over and over. And the answer was both yes and no. She was ashamed of – and deeply regretted – the breach of faith in their marriage, which she could never recover now. Some people thrived on the thrill of the lie. Not her. The guilt had made her physically ill.

But on the no side, however wrong she knew it to be, and however much she felt regret for those nights, she was aware that she would not have missed them. As she crept into her seventh decade, a man celebrating her body in the way Jared had – especially at a time when Devan had seemed not to find her the least bit attractive any more – had been nothing short of a miracle. *If he could see me now,* she thought tiredly, and almost smiled.

Devan had cooked supper. He'd been practising while she was ill, having no choice unless they were to exist entirely on supermarket ready meals. Tonight, it was grilled lamb chops, flageolet beans, baked tomatoes and a green salad. Connie helped herself to mint sauce, then handed the jar to him.

'Thank you. This looks lovely,' she said.

As they ate, Connie regaled him with her day at the fair: an English wine she'd tasted, the goat's cheese she'd almost bought, and a demonstration of knife skills. 'Jill forced me to try one of those slithery rollmops and I thought I was going to throw up.'

Devan smiled, but she could tell he wasn't really concentrating on what she was saying. 'OK,' he began, widening his eyes at her, 'so something happened today, which I'm rather excited about.'

She nodded but didn't interrupt him.

'You know Sylvie Masters, the doctor who did locum work for the surgery for a while?'

'Vaguely.'

'Well, she rang this morning. Apparently she's setting up this hospice in Weston . . . and she wanted to discuss me joining the team part-time.'

She sat up straighter. 'Wow, Devan. That would be great, wouldn't it?'

'Oh, Con. It's so up my street. I always found it so heartbreaking when a patient was dying and I had no time or facility to help.' He took a large gulp of wine. 'It won't be up and running for a couple of months or so. But if this works out, it might be two, three days a week . . .'

Connie laughed with delight at seeing her husband so invigorated, the light back in his eyes.

'And I really like Sylvie,' he went on. 'She's so straightforward and professional. I'm going to drive over next Monday, meet her, check the place out.'

They spent the rest of the meal discussing the potential job. *This,* Connie thought, *is what we've both been waiting for.* She wasn't thinking in terms of her tours, just that Devan would finally be busy and engaged again.

'Then me and Bill got chatting to this guy in the pub at lunchtime.' Devan interrupted her thoughts. 'Says he's just signed up for a six-month rental on Mr Solomon's place. Plans to move in in a couple of weeks, apparently.'

'Jill heard the same from her friend at Tovey's. Weekender?'

'Nope. Wants to try living in the country, he says. Seems to be on his own, didn't mention a wife or girlfriend. I liked him. Youngish, seemed intelligent and well-travelled. It's nice to have someone under sixty moving into the village, for a change.'

19

By mid-October, two months after Connie had fallen ill, she felt back to some semblance of her old self. She'd finally had her hair coloured and trimmed – the grey roots she'd been seeing in the mirror every morning only adding to her sense of decline – and treated her nails to a rare luxury manicure. She was almost back to her normal weight but, most crucially, she could feel the veil of torpor lifting.

These days, she woke with cautious optimism, mentally scanning her body as she lay in bed for signs of weakness, finding none. It seemed as if she'd been through some sort of test . . . and emerged undeservedly unscathed. Although part of her still listened for the buzz of the aircraft overhead, the moment when the bomb would finally drop and she would be punished.

This morning Connie turned to her husband. Watching his face as he slept, she realized that the lingering tensions between them were much reduced, as Devan had got stuck into working with Sylvie. She wondered what lay ahead for them, in these last decades of their lives.

She'd promised herself – and Devan, who seemed happy with this compromise, in light of his new commitments – that although she might not retire completely, she would cut down on her tours next year.

She couldn't afford a repeat of this summer on any level. Her vulnerability to Jared had scared her. The length of time it had taken her to recover from the virus had scared her too – one no doubt feeding into the other. And whereas there was fault on both sides for the breach in their marriage, Connie had been the one to cross the line. It still shocked her that even a marriage as seemingly strong and solid as theirs had shown it wasn't invincible.

She gently placed a hand to his head, feeling his soft hair, his warm cheek against her palm. *I love you*, she whispered silently. Devan stirred, opening his eyes. He blinked and smiled, taking her hand in his. He reached forward to kiss her and they snuggled into each other's arms under the warm duvet as the autumn dawn began to light the room.

'Just popping to the shop,' Connie shouted upstairs. She was glowing, satiated from the lovemaking that had followed the cuddle, rosy from a hot shower, her body revitalized in a way she had not felt for a long time. 'We're out of bread.'

Old Mrs Mounce – whose son owned the village store – was behind the till, as she was most mornings. Connie thought she must have been eighty if she was a day, her plump face covered with liver spots, her hands shaking as she took Connie's wholemeal loaf and the newspaper to scan.

'Nasty out,' Mrs Mounce commented, probably for the twentieth time that morning – she never talked about anything but the weather, which never failed her in its fickleness.

'Going to rain all day, they say,' Connie dutifully returned.

Mrs Mounce pushed the paper and loaf back across the wooden counter, handing Connie her receipt. Gathering her purchases, she turned to leave, bumping into someone standing too close behind her.

'Sorry,' she said.

'Sorry,' echoed the man.

She froze. That voice. *No*. She hardly dared look up. But when she did, it was straight into the turquoise eyes of Jared Temple. She thought she must be hallucinating. The newspaper slid from her shaking hands.

Jared bent to pick it up, neatened the pages and handed it calmly back to her. He had a quiet smile on his face, as if this were the most normal encounter in the world.

Connie, checking round and seeing the shop was empty except for Mrs Mounce – who was fiddling with the cigarette packets on the shelves behind the till – hissed at him, 'What the hell are you doing here?'

Jared seemed a bit taken aback at her tone. 'I . . . I just wanted to see you, Connie.'

She felt as if she'd been Tasered. Here she was, standing in her village shop, a mere three minutes' walk from her house and her husband, talking to the man with whom she'd enjoyed clandestine, abandoned sex. 'You can't be here,' she said, desperately. 'I can't be seen talking to you.'

He frowned, but did not speak, did not move.

'Please . . . please, Jared. Don't do this.'

When he didn't instantly disappear and stop the nightmare, she took a steadying breath. 'OK, listen. Meet me at the windmill . . .' she was trying to calm her delirious brain enough to remember what she and Devan had planned for today '. . . about eleven thirty? It's only five minutes away.' She didn't wait for him to agree, or explain which windmill or where. She just fled the shop, Stacy from the pub holding the door for her on his way in.

'Hey, how's it going?' he said, with a cheerful grin.

'Yeah, good. Sorry, in a bit of a rush, Stacy.' She shot past him and ran to her door, not daring to look back and see if Jared had followed her. It felt as if she'd been gone ten years, but the house was quiet, Devan still in the shower – she could hear the growl of the pump. Plonking the bread and the paper on the table, she sank into a chair, trying to control the trembling in her limbs.

A moment later, she realized the shower had stopped. She quickly got to her feet and opened the fridge for the eggs, milk and grapefruit juice. It was Saturday: they would have their usual scrambled eggs. She laid the table mechanically, unaware of her actions. Riley bounded into the kitchen and came snuffling around her, but she gently pushed him away. *Devan mustn't suspect anything's wrong*, she told herself, as she boiled the kettle and broke eggs into the Pyrex mixing bowl. Attempting to rearrange her agitated face, she stretched her mouth and squeezed her eyes shut, shaking her head from side to side as if to dislodge her panic.

She heard her husband's tread on the stairs and held her breath, not turning as he came in and walked straight across to where she stood, putting his arms around her and nuzzling her neck.

'That was superb,' he said, chuckling to himself as he let her go and stretched up his linked hands to the ceiling, loudly cracking his knuckles. 'Great start to the day.'

'Hmm . . .' She smiled but went on whisking the already thoroughly beaten eggs. When she swung round to the stove the butter was nearly burned, and she snatched it off the heat with a curse.

'Think I'll do the supermarket after breakfast,' Connie said, as she spread her toast and ground pepper over her eggs, although her appetite had deserted her.

'I'll come too,' Devan replied. 'I want to get a chamois for the car. That cloth we've got is useless – it just makes the windscreen worse.'

'I'll get it,' she said quickly. Devan didn't particularly enjoy supermarkets, and she thought her plan was safe.

He shrugged. 'OK. We need fruit and loo paper.'

She let out a careful breath. 'We could do something this afternoon . . . Pub lunch, maybe?'

Devan nodded, but was absorbed in an incoming text. Watching his bent head, she felt a sudden fear for him, for the hurt she might inflict on him, if he were ever faced with how she had betrayed him. *Jared's just doing what he always does*, she consoled herself. And, to be fair to him, she'd never complained before when he'd made a random appearance. In fact, she'd been waiting eagerly for him every time, to her shame. Not any longer. Definitely not any longer.

Connie was certain she just needed to impress upon Jared that she would not be succumbing to his charms this time . . . or ever again. *Not ever.* She'd had no indication that he was a vengeful, vindictive person – although she was aware she knew little about him. *Surely there'd be no mileage in compromising me*, she thought, months after their affair had ended. With these soothing thoughts, she readied herself for the rendezvous at the windmill.

Dashing round the supermarket as if she were a contestant on *Supermarket Sweep*, she bought the weekend's provisions in record time, settling for staples like shepherd's pie and pasta, the ingredients for which were stamped on her brain, like the words of a school hymn, and needed no concentration. Her mind was all over the place. *He'll be gone by lunchtime.* She prayed no one she knew would be up at the windmill today. It was more of a tourist stop, and she very much doubted that on a chilly late-October Saturday anyone would be there at all.

When Connie arrived, she was relieved to see no other cars in the lay-by near the gate to the tall whitewashed stone tower. She sat there for a moment, listening to the silence. *Will he come?* She tried to remember what she'd told him, but her brain wouldn't focus on the earlier conversation. All she could remember was blind, gut-churning panic.

She got out of the car. There was quite a wind up there, the air damp, more rain on the way. Pushing open the gate, she walked towards the mill, glancing nervously around. No one. She shivered. *Maybe he got the message*, she thought, clinging to a slim thread of hope.

Ten minutes later, she was still alone, gazing across towards the Cheddar Gorge. It began to rain, and she decided to wait in the car. As she turned away from the windmill she saw him on the other side of the gate, Barbour buttoned to his neck, hair dusted with drizzle. He must have walked, because there was no sign of a car. She hurried over to him.

'Let's sit inside,' she said, pressing the fob and pulling open her door. Jared, who had said nothing so far, gave a brief raise of his eyebrows in greeting, but made no attempt to reach for the door handle. There was none of the characteristic amusement in his face today as he stared at her over the roof of the car. 'Get in,' she urged. He gave her a half-smile, which didn't convince her, finally opening the passenger door and sliding into the seat.

Skewing herself sideways so she could face him, she spoke softly. 'What are you doing, Jared?' Seeing him there, on her home turf, the absolute manifestation of her worst nightmare, made her body feel leaden, cold as the stone of the windmill tower. The unrestrained lust that in the past had ignited at the sight of him was now like the ashes of a dead fire in the morning.

Jared bowed his head, hands clasped in his lap. When he raised his eyes to hers, he appeared defiant. 'I was worried about you, Connie. You were in such a terrible state when I left you. How was I to know that you hadn't died right there in that grim hotel room?'

She saw his point. But she had to make hers. 'We agreed this thing between us was over,' she said evenly. 'In Inverness, I said it had to stop, that I couldn't see you any more . . . and you agreed, Jared.'

'To be fair, I didn't agree,' he replied, his tone also reasonable. 'I said I understood what you were saying.'

Alarmed and frustrated by his semantics, she responded more sharply: 'Can't you see what you're doing to me by being here? You must go. Please, Jared, *please* . . . Just leave me alone.' Connie could hear the anguish in her voice, and clearly he could too, because his outstretched hand was prising hers from where it was clamped, white-knuckled, to the steering wheel. He folded her icy fingers gently into his warm palm. 'Don't,' she said weakly, wrenching free.

Another car pulled up beside them. Heart hammering, she peered through the rain-spattered window at the occupants, then let out a small moan of relief: it was no one she knew. 'Jared?' she prompted, as he still didn't acknowledge her entreaty.

'I would never do you any harm, Connie, you know that,' he said eventually. Then he fixed her with his turquoise eyes. 'I love you,' he said simply.

His words stunned her. '*Love?*' she croaked, her throat closed with fear.

He nodded, suddenly at ease with himself again, now he had played his trump card. 'That night when you needed me . . . in the hotel room . . . you looked so vulnerable, Connie. I realized then, as I watched you sleep, that it went far deeper.' He smiled. 'Although sex like that? Wouldn't you say it's a powerful touchstone? One that indicates the absolute strength of our connection?'

Connie tried to control her pounding heart. 'For God's sake, Jared, what part of "I'm married" don't you understand? You talk as if Devan doesn't exist.' *How can I make him see?* she asked herself desperately. *How can I make him go away?*

He shrugged. 'He obviously doesn't make you happy. If he did, you'd never have let me do all those things to your gorgeous body.' His voice had dropped to an intimate purr.

A sharp, unconscious frisson of desire stirred through her loins at the familiarity of his tone, the reminder of 'those things'. It shocked her that he still had that power over her. Now, when she feared him, almost hated him for being there. She looked away, tried with all her might to tamp it down.

'Would you?' he asked, a smile in his voice, as if he knew exactly the effect his words would have on her.

She shuddered. 'Stop it.'

There was silence in the stuffy, enclosed space. Through the steamed-up windows, she watched the people from the other car get out – a middle-aged couple in matching purple anoraks – open the gate and walk slowly across the turf to the windmill.

Connie took a deep breath. 'I told you . . . we were going through a bad patch. But things are better now.' She bit her lip, struggling for the right words to convince him. 'I should never have betrayed him.' Jared gazed at her but didn't speak. 'You dazzled me. I was overwhelmed,' she added, feeling the need to acknowledge what had happened between them. 'But *this*,' she waved her hands expansively, 'this village, with my house, my husband, my dog, my friends, is my life.' She wanted her next words to have the fullest impact. 'Please, you have to listen to me, Jared. I will *never* leave Devan. What happened between us is *absolutely over*.'

He nodded, as if he understood. Then he said, 'I've taken Foxwood for six months. I moved in two days ago.'

Foxwood? The name meant nothing to Connie. She tried to process what he was talking about, but her brain cells were in chaos, compromised by the mass of adrenalin pumping through her veins. Then the penny dropped.

She gaped at him, open-mouthed. 'You're the one renting Mr Solomon's cottage?'

He nodded. 'They've done a good job on the renovations. The kitchen's a bit small for my liking, but I'll be nice and cosy over the winter.' Grinning, he added, 'Pop round later and see for yourself.'

Connie was lost for words. She hunched in her seat, her arms crossed rigidly against her chest in an attempt to stop herself screaming.

'Bring Devan,' she heard him say, through a fog of

disbelief. 'I had a great chat with him and his friend in the pub the day I signed up for the cottage.'

The silence in the car was profound, as if she'd suddenly gone deaf.

'Are you completely out of your mind?' she whispered, all strength gone from her body.

With a puzzled frown, he leaned over and put both his hands firmly on her crossed forearms, staring intently into her eyes. 'You look terrified, Connie.' He drew back a bit. 'Oh, my God . . . you're not worried about your husband finding out about us, are you?' He sighed. 'You know I'd never betray you. I will never tell a living soul what happened between us, not in a million years.' He smiled his gentle smile. 'I just want to be near you.'

20

'You've been ages,' Devan commented, raising his eyes from the newspaper as Connie hefted the bulging shopping bag onto the kitchen counter.

She glanced at the wall clock. It was nearly one thirty. She'd been with Jared barely half an hour, but she was in such a state as she watched him walking back towards the village that she knew she couldn't go home straight away. Those last words of his, spoken with such chilling reasonableness, had felt like ice forming around her heart. She could hardly breathe. It didn't seem possible that they came from the same man whose casual, smiling flirtatiousness had got her so willingly between the sheets.

She'd driven around blindly, in a haze of distress, stopping by another gate somewhere west of the village and bursting into tears, her body shaking with dread. Jared had repeatedly assured her that their secret was safe. But revealing the truth or not was just the end of a long road stretching miserably ahead, littered with his presence in her life at every turn. How was she to survive that?

'I kept bumping into people. You know how it is.'

'Did you find the chamois?' Devan was up, pulling things out of the bag, opening the fridge and stacking the packets inside, tearing open the plastic mesh round a bag of satsumas and tipping them into the wooden fruit bowl, emptying an old carton of cream that was off when he sniffed it. Connie stood and watched. It was as if she were witnessing the last moments of her life as she knew it. *The chamois*, she thought. *I forgot the sodding chamois.*

'Sorry, they only had the huge ones . . . which were twelve bloody quid.' That was two lies in less than five minutes. And she knew it was only the beginning.

Jared is living in the village. She tested the words, unable to believe what she was hearing in her own head. Mentally, she began the journey to his house. Walk down to the corner, past the pub, turn right, then left through the small arcade of boutiquey shops, and the cottage was across the road, sandwiched between two identical ones. It was pretty, red brick with cooking-apple-green painted window surrounds and front door. A large bright yellow mahonia was flowering by the gate, the garden tidy and mature. Connie knew it: she walked past regularly, taking Riley for a walk. She'd watched the progress of the renovation, even chatted to Dougie, the young guy doing most of the work.

'Connie?' Devan was waving his hand in front of her face. 'You haven't heard a word I've said, have you?'

She came to as if from a dream. 'Sorry . . .'

'Are you OK? You look as if you've just seen a ghost.'

She tried to laugh, but it came out as a strangled cough. 'I'm fine,' she said, making a huge effort to compose her features.

Devan looked sceptical, but obviously his stomach took precedence over his curiosity. 'Shall we get going? I'm starving.'

Images of Jared seated on a bar stool, chatting cosily to Stacy, came to mind.

'Can we not do Skittles today?'

'Oh . . . I had my eye on one of Nicole's chicken pies.'

'It's just we always go there.'

'Fair enough. Where do you fancy, then?'

Connie's mind was blank. All she could think of was getting as far from Jared as possible. 'Umm, what about . . . There's the Pig?'

Devan's face lit up. 'Good plan. We haven't been there in ages.' Then he glanced at his phone. 'Will they still be serving lunch? It's a good twenty minutes' drive.'

I don't care if they are or not, she wanted to shout at him. Her stomach was so knotted, she doubted she'd be able to choke down even a mouthful of food, anyway. She felt on the verge of tears again, but knew she had to pull herself together. This was not going away. *He* was not going away.

Being with her husband was agony. Connie wanted to hug him close, whisk him away, rescue him from the mire into which she feared he was about to fall. Because even if Jared did as he promised and never told a living soul their secret, *Connie* knew. She would need to pretend, constantly pretend, always wondering what little thing he might be divulging – and to whom – that would blow her world apart. The toll was incalculable.

Devan would notice. He would suffer accordingly. *Unless I can persuade Jared to leave*, she thought, now, as Devan tucked into his beef brisket sandwich and she played with a fishcake on a bed of puréed spinach.

'I'm off,' Devan said, two days later, holdall in hand as he stood in the hall. 'Be back tomorrow lunchtime.'

He was attending a board meeting of the Royal College of General Practitioners – about GP education and support – in Bristol. Although it was less than an hour's drive, he was staying overnight. After the meeting, he and his doctor friends liked to settle in at the hotel bar and make a night of it, catch up with all the affronts they'd suffered at the hands of their patients, and the NHS.

She put her arms round him and gave him a tight embrace. 'Have fun,' she said, breathing in his warm scent and loving him so much.

Connie had not seen Jared again. But, then, she'd barely been out, except to scurry to the car or hurry up the road in the opposite direction to his cottage when she took Riley out. She'd almost managed to convince herself that he wasn't really there. But the tenderness she'd been showering on Devan was already making him wonder what was up.

'You're being very nice to me,' he'd commented the day before, when she'd helped him tidy the garden shed, then made cheese scones for tea.

She'd laughed nervously as she poured his tea. 'Am I usually such a harridan?'

'No,' he'd replied, then looked across the table, suddenly serious as he buttered his warm scone. 'You know I wasn't ever really questioning our marriage before. That would have been nuts.' He grinned. 'Especially as you make such delicious scones.'

Connie had grinned back. Now that the initial shock of bumping into Jared had worn off a little and she had some perspective, she was feeling more optimistic. *I can make him see sense,* she told herself. *He's not going to stick around once I've made my position clear.* Now, watching her husband drive off to his board meeting, she had only one mission: to see Jared and make absolutely sure he left the village.

She waited till dark. The last thing she needed was gossip. The Williamsons, in the cottage to the right of Jared's, were old and would be firmly ensconced in front of the television, curtains closed, as soon as they'd finished their tea. She'd been past often enough with Riley to know. The house on the other side was another of the many owned by weekenders: a young London couple who rarely came down outside the summer months. 'Please, please be in,' she muttered to herself, as she walked briskly through the village streets, Riley in tow as cover.

As she approached, she breathed a sigh of relief. The lights were on, and she could see Jared through the window, stirring something at the stove. Heart in her mouth, but still determined, she opened the catch on the low picket gate and walked up the path to the door. It was cold tonight, colder than it had been so far this autumn, but she didn't feel a thing.

'Connie!' he greeted her, wooden spoon still in his hand. 'Come in, come in. You're just in time to sample my pumpkin soup.' His smile and easy greeting implied this was the most natural event in the world, her popping round with the dog for a spot of soup.

With trepidation, she followed him into the warm kitchen. Everything looked new, a bit too clean and organized. A bottle of red wine was open on the table, and without asking, he fetched a glass from the cupboard and poured some for her.

'This is a nice surprise,' he said, lifting his own drink and holding it out to chink with hers. '*Salud!*'

Connie found herself complying as she touched her glass with his, but she did not echo his good wishes, taking only a tiny sip of wine, as if it might poison her. He was looking at her, waiting for her to speak. But now she was here, the words she'd rehearsed so often dried on her lips. It felt oddly normal in the kitchen, Jared relaxed, looking younger, she thought, in his jeans and a white T-shirt, his arms still tanned from his mysterious wanderings, brown hair streaked gold by the sun. She quickly looked away.

'Take a seat,' Jared said, lifting a couple of soup bowls from the open shelf at the end of the row of kitchen units, and placing them on the table. 'Spoons,' he muttered, finally plumping for the drawer to the right of the cooker. A row of foil and clingfilm rolls greeted him, and he shut the drawer and tried the one on the other side. 'Geronimo!' He brandished two spoons at

Connie, then put them both on the table beside the bowls. 'Still getting used to the place,' he added.

Connie experienced a strange snapshot, as if she were in an alternative version of her life, where Devan didn't exist, and she lived in this cottage with Jared and Riley. She watched Jared pour the thick orange soup. 'Sorry, no parsley. Have to make do with a little drizzle of olive oil and a grind of pepper,' he said, pushing her bowl across the table and turning to find the oil and pepper.

She did not touch the bowl. Smelling the soup, she realized she was very hungry – she'd barely eaten in the last few days. But she was not going to drink a single drop, aware that the onion-scented warmth of the dimly lit kitchen was having an irresistibly soporific effect on her fatigued state – the toll of so many sleepless nights. She sat up straighter on the stool, pinching the skin on the back of her hand until it hurt. She was here for one reason only. She must stay alert, force Jared to see things from her perspective, not give in to the seductive domesticity he was peddling.

'I didn't know you cooked,' she said into the silence.

'A kitchen designer who doesn't cook would be a tad peculiar.'

He was smiling at her, and she smiled back. Jared refilled his wine glass and began his soup. He glanced across at her untouched bowl, 'I thought you liked pumpkin,' he said.

'Sorry . . . not hungry,' she replied. He gave a calm shrug.

When he'd finished eating, neither of them speaking, he stood to clear both bowls, then bent to the under-counter fridge and drew out a packet of choc ices from the freezer compartment, laying a cellophane-wrapped bar in front of her – again without asking if she wanted it – and taking one for himself.

'Love these. Haven't had one in years. I saw them in Waitrose and couldn't resist.'

Connie also loved them, but she shook herself. 'Jared . . .'

He held up his hand to stop her. 'I know what you're going to say. I can't be here. I have to leave. I'm ruining your life . . .' When she didn't speak, he went on, 'But this isn't ruining anything. What's wrong with soup and a glass of wine between friends?' When she still didn't answer, he said, 'I'm not leaving, Connie.'

She winced at the resolve in his words. 'God, Jared. You're not being rational. There's no way on this earth we can be friends,' she said, her voice rising. 'After what happened between us? Surely you realize that could never work.'

He gave her a smile, which implied she was being simple. 'I really don't see what the problem is. I can be around you all day long and not give a single thing away. Can't you?'

Connie let out a frustrated sigh. 'You're missing the bloody point. What the hell do you hope to gain by being here?' She took a deep breath, preparing for another strike. 'OK, let me tell you again. I don't want to see you *ever again*.' She spoke loudly and slowly. 'Or have any contact with you of any sort . . . I just want you to leave the village, never come back.' It sounded harsh, even in the circumstances, and she winced at her own words.

He didn't seem upset, however. He nodded calmly. 'So you keep telling me, Connie. And I hear you.' He paused, his gaze suddenly fervent. 'But what you don't seem to get is that I can't just let you go. I can't simply discard the feelings I have for you, like so much rubbish, just because you're married. Your marriage has absolutely no relevance to how I feel about you.'

Struggling to make sense of what he was saying, Connie tried one more time to gather a coherent argument. Something that would finally convince him that he was whistling in the wind. 'Of course it has relevance, Jared.' She spoke forcefully, although she did not raise her voice – it was vital that he listen. 'It means we can't be together.'

Jared lifted his hands in the air triumphantly and grinned. 'You say that, but here we are, *together.* The sky hasn't fallen in. Riley still sleeps by my feet, the cottage still stands, Devan is none the wiser.'

Connie, up against the barricade of his skewed logic, felt only tired. 'You don't know what this is doing to me,' she said quietly. Her choc ice was still in its cellophane, untouched on the table – although Jared had munched through his, spraying shards of dark chocolate onto his T-shirt – and she knew that inside the shell it would now be mush.

Jared, hearing her despair, was instantly by her side.

Before she had a chance to stop him, he was leaning down to envelop her shoulders in his arms, but she stiffened, quickly pushing him off and rising from her stool to face him. 'Listen. I'm sorry if I misled you, Jared. Truly I am. But this has to end . . . right here, right now.'

He reached out and squeezed her upper arms between his palms. Shuddering inwardly, she shook herself free, moving back out of his reach.

'Never apologize, Connie,' he said, his words uncomfortably intense. 'If I hadn't met you, my life would be totally meaningless – like it's always been, till now.' She noticed the tears again, blurring the turquoise. But unlike last time, they did not move her. Instead they frightened her. *What the hell does he mean, 'till now'?*

'Riley!' she called sharply to the sleeping dog and turned to pick up his lead and her coat, both of which she'd slung on the hooks in the hallway. When she turned back, Jared was between her and the front door. For a split second she wondered if he would prevent her leaving – she couldn't read the expression in his eyes in the half-light.

She moved purposefully forward, heart pounding in her throat. At the same time, Jared stepped towards her, and swooped. His mouth was almost on hers, his arms reaching around her body, but she jerked away with a loud, 'NO!'

Riley, sensing something wasn't right, bounced up between them, paws on her jeans, driving his nose into her thigh, barking furiously. It was what he sometimes did when she and Devan kissed.

Forced to let her go, Jared actually laughed. 'Guardian of your virtue,' he said, rubbing the dog's head affectionately.

Coat under her arm as she clipped on Riley's lead, Connie straightened and roughly pushed him aside.

'Don't go,' she heard him call, as she yanked up the stiff iron latch and ran down the wet path to the gate, dragging the dog behind her. It was late and raining hard. No one was about at this hour. Without looking back, she crossed the road and reached the corner that led into the arcade, only letting out her breath when she knew she could no longer be seen from Jared's cottage.

Closing her own front door with relief, she let Riley loose and leaned against the wall in the dark hall, burying her face in her hands. She wasn't crying. She was too furious to cry. *Good job, Connie McCabe. Bloody great job. You've just made a bad thing a whole heap worse, you stupid woman.* She should never have gone.

21

Neil and Brooks adored fireworks, Connie loathed them, and Devan was ambivalent. But they always attended their friends' bonfire party, it being a three-line whip. Neil was simply unable to fathom why anyone would not enjoy such a life-enhancing spectacle. Every November, regular as clockwork, he would start on at her. 'You really need to get in touch with your inner child, Con.'

To which she annually retorted, 'I have. My inner child really hates fireworks, Neil.'

Now she and Devan were driving the dark lanes to Neil's house in the next village. Connie was dressed in so many layers that she felt as if she'd been mummified. But it was unseasonably cold, temperatures hovering around two degrees. On her feet she had an old pair of moon boots, found at the back of Caitlin's cupboard from a school ski trip – lilac, glittery, furry, with tiny images of Disney princesses, quite hideous. But at least numb toes were not going to be her problem tonight.

Devan glanced at her, chuckling as he drove. 'Were there any clothes left in the wardrobe?'

'You can tease all you like,' she replied, 'but when you've been standing on that windy terrace for three hours, no sensation from the knees down, your nose turning black and snapping off into your mulled wine, you'll regret your decision to choose style over substance – even if it is Barbour, even if you do always feel the need to compete with Brooks.' Which was a hiding to nothing, anyway. Neil's husband, a retired Barclays' executive, always dressed in immaculate Italian chic and had the honed, broad-shouldered physique of an athlete.

Devan was laughing as he turned into the open gates at the house. 'Smile, please. Don't want to curdle the mulled wine.'

Connie did smile, because despite putting on a jokily cantankerous show for Devan, she was secretly pleased to be there, to be out. It was the first time in two weeks – since that night in Jared's cottage – that she'd been social. She knew it was impossible for Jared to have become friendly with the entire village already, but she wasn't going to risk it.

'I still get really tired by the evening,' was the excuse she'd given Devan for not coming with him to a talk in the village hall. It was by a famous TV forager and naturalist, who was going to show them how to pick the right mushrooms – she'd bought tickets months ago. She was still coughing, and she did get tired, but still . . .

'I'm worried I'm coming down with something,' was the get-out for Fiona Raven's book launch in Bridgwater – to which she was supposed to be going with Neil. In other circumstances she would have loved to catch up with past colleagues and giggle with Neil at their old boss's predictable gush and swagger.

Devan had begun to notice. 'Are you sure you're all right?' he'd asked her a couple of nights ago, when she'd declared she was going to bed immediately after supper – really just wanting to get away from Devan so she could stop pretending. 'You seem so tense at the moment. Is something bothering you?'

'No.' She'd feigned surprise. 'I'm fine.'

He'd frowned and searched her face. 'You're not worrying about your job, are you? They're not going to sack you for being ill, Connie. It was only two tours you cancelled.'

She had barely considered her job, her mind so consumed with Jared that she seldom had any other thought in her head. 'I'm still feeling a bit below par, if I'm honest.' She gave him a reassuring smile. 'How would you feel about getting away? Fit in a week before Christmas, somewhere nice and warm. We could swim and lie about, read . . .'

Now it was Devan's turn to look surprised. 'It's a great idea. Where could we go?'

Connie didn't mind, as long as it was as far away from Jared as possible. *Maybe he'll have vanished by the time I get back*, she thought, like a child with a hand over her eyes – if she can't see you, you can't see her. In fact, she hadn't caught even a glimpse of him since that night.

Devan was on his laptop, searching winter breaks, almost before she'd left the room, although she knew it would change nothing.

Now Neil embraced her, then stepped back, a wide grin on his face. 'Very Scott-of-the-Antarctic, darling . . .

and I'm sure you had a gun to your head when you put *those* on.' His nose wrinkled as he noticed her boots.

In fact, her feet were stewing in them. The car had been hot and she felt her toes throbbing now. She longed to wrench the ridiculous things off.

Neil gave Devan a hug, too, and led them through the elegant 1930s art-deco house – flat roof, parquet floors, curved windows and a gorgeous timber staircase – to the wide terrace behind. About twenty-five people were there, many faces she recognized in the glow from the lanterns lining the low stucco wall and the huge bonfire that burned merrily at the bottom of the steps leading down to the garden.

Brooks, in a sleek, padded navy jacket and tartan scarf knotted European-style round his neck, was standing at a king-size barbecue, wielding tongs and holding forth to a group of friends clutching beers. On one end of the barbecue there was a capacious preserving pan and ladle, steaming with Neil's mulled wine. At the other, sausages and spicy lamb chops sizzled near skewers of prawn and vegetables, and crisping chicken wings. The pungent smell of roasting meat made Connie's mouth water.

Neil handed her a glass of his infamous concoction. The wine felt pleasantly warm between her palms. Despite the heat from the bonfire, the barbecue and the press of people, the air was cruel, icy on her cheeks.

Devan gave her a nudge. 'Not too bad so far!' And he was right. The wine was going straight to her head, she was beginning to relax . . .

It was a while later when Neil grabbed her arm. Piled plate in hand, she turned. 'Connie, I'm dying for you to meet Jed,' he said, indicating the man by his side. 'We bonded at the Raven's book launch.' She swallowed hard, coughed as if she might choke, her plate wobbling dangerously in her hand. The eyes that were staring directly into hers sparkled in the candlelight. 'He's a kitchen designer and he's just moved into your village.' His last words were almost lost in the heavy pulsing of blood in her ears.

Dizzily, she managed a weak 'Hello,' shrugging at Jared's outstretched hand, as she indicated her own, clamped firmly round her plate and fork.

'Hi, Connie,' 'Jed' replied, smiling that intimate smile of his.

Her stomach lurched. Devan was beside her, but with his back to them, talking to a man she didn't know.

'We had such a laugh,' Neil was saying. 'Jed had the exact same experience as me with our esteemed employer, didn't you, Jed?'

Jared nodded. 'Nightmare. She was all over me like a rash at first. Then I did something she didn't approve of – God knows what, I never found out – and she turned on me, made my life hell for about six months.'

Connie had a glassy smile nailed to her face. Neil was speaking again, but she had no idea what he was saying. Sounds of the party faded. The only thing in her field of vision, in her entire consciousness, was the man in front of her. As if they were all alone on the freezing terrace.

Then Devan, his other conversation over, wheeled

round. Connie almost gasped. But, astonishingly, her husband was grinning, holding out his hand to shake Jared's warmly.

'Hey, great to see you again.' He turned to her. 'This is the guy I told you about, Connie. Remember? Me and Bill met him in the pub.' He turned back to Jared again. 'So, have you moved in yet?'

'Been there a few weeks now.'

'How's it going? Not too quiet for you?'

'It's perfect,' Jared said, glancing at Connie. 'I've had things to sort out back at my other place but I've pretty much done that now. Just a few more boxes to go.'

'Listen, got to circulate,' Neil said, putting one arm round Jared, the other round Connie. 'But let's all get together and have a bitch-fest about La Raven, eh? We could do Angie's for a coffee . . . I'm around till the end of November now.' He grinned at Devan. 'You can come too, of course. But you might be shocked.'

'Shocked' was how Connie was feeling right now. Her head was spinning as she imagined the impossible scenario of her, Neil, Jared, and maybe Devan too, sitting cosily round one of the wobbly metal tables at Angie's, sipping Gajah Mountain blend and reminiscing about Fiona. *How come Jared worked for her?* It seemed an extraordinary coincidence.

The others were laughing as their host made off towards Brooks and had an earnest conversation in his husband's ear. Connie watched her friend. Anything but look at Jared, who was now asking Devan if he was interested in craft beer.

'I've got a brewer mate who's experimenting with a stout blend. I'm going over there tomorrow, if you fancy coming along for a tasting.'

Devan, who loathed stout, was nodding eagerly. 'That'd be great.'

Connie stared at her husband in horror.

'It's serious stuff. Tastes like singed soil, really gross,' Jared was saying. 'You can't drink much and stay upright.'

They chatted on, like the best of friends, the two of them side by side, glasses in hand, faces lit by the bonfire as they watched the extravagant display of fireworks. Connie edged away until she was standing on her own. She was both stunned and furious. *What the hell were you doing at the launch?* she asked Jared silently. *And how dare you pretend to pal up with my husband?*

In the car going home, Connie's head was pounding from too much mulled wine. 'You've always said stout was vile. Why on earth are you going for a tasting with that guy?'

He grinned. 'I know. But he's nice. I like him. And you always say we should be friendly to people settling in the village.'

She had no answer for that because she was assailed by a silent shriek of panic, of blind fury. *This cannot be happening to me* . . . The words smacked the sides of her brain like a hundred-mile-an-hour squash ball.

Late morning the following day, Connie phoned her sister. She'd been going crazy since the early hours, trying to work-out what to do, without success. She knew she needed someone else's advice. 'Have you got a moment?' she asked, after they'd exchanged greetings. It was a Friday morning and, remembering Lynne and Rhodri's rigid schedule, she knew they wouldn't be at the supermarket or at church or changing the sheets. Connie had waited till Devan went out to meet Jared. She had barely slept and now felt tearful. Swallowing hard, she tried to explain.

'Crikey,' Lynne said, which was as close as she usually got to swearing. 'He's living practically next door?'

'Three minutes away.'

'Why? Does he think you'll leave Devan?' There was a pause. 'Might you leave Devan?'

'No. *No no no!* Absolutely not. And I've told him that a hundred times.'

'Hmm. Weird. He's stalking you, Connie.'

Since his arrival in the village, she herself had reluctantly begun to use that word in relation to Jared. But it was scary: she didn't want it to fit. 'He doesn't call me, text me, send letters, leave stuff on the doorstep, boil bunnies, slash tyres . . . He doesn't *do* anything. He's just *there*.' She felt tears of frustration, which she'd kept under firm control for weeks now, finally breaking free.

'Please, don't cry.' Lynne hated tears. 'You say he's promised not to breathe a word. Maybe he won't.'

'How can I trust him, though?' Connie wailed. 'In fact, how do I know he's not telling Devan every single thing that happened between us even as we speak?'

Angrily she wiped the tears from her cheeks. 'But that's almost beside the point. Even if he never breathes a bloody word, I can't live like this, Lynne, with him breathing down my neck. I daren't even go out in my own village for fear of bumping into him.'

'He doesn't sound sane to me.'

'What he's doing is totally *in*sane. Although he appears completely normal to everyone else. They love him.'

There was a baffled silence at the other end of the phone.

'Well, perhaps he doesn't mean any harm, Con. Perhaps he means what he says – that he just wants to be near you.'

'And I'm supposed to roll over and let him be part of my life, am I? Ignore the Sword of Damocles hanging over my head, the threat that one day he'll get drunk and blurt out he had wild sex with me all summer?'

There was silence as Lynne digested this. 'So, he didn't mention he'd met you before, when you were introduced?'

'No. But he turned up at Fiona Raven's book launch. How the fuck does he know her? It's like he's found out every single detail about my life and is quietly infiltrating it all.'

'It's called stalking,' her sister repeated patiently.

Connie let out a frustrated sigh. 'Call it what you like. But I hardly think the police'll send out their armed response because I don't particularly like the look of some man who's moved into our village.'

'He'll get bored, won't he? If you ignore him,' Lynne said, after another short silence.

Connie hoped she was right, but Jared didn't seem to follow normal rules. 'God, Lynne. I know I did a really bad thing, cheating on Devan like that. And I know it serves me bloody well right. But this level of retribution doesn't seem quite fair.'

' "He who digs a pit will fall into it", Proverbs twenty-six, verse twenty-seven,' Lynne murmured to herself. 'There is a very simple solution, of course.'

'What?'

'Tell Devan.'

Connie felt her gut seize.

'Then Jared has no power.' Warming to her theme, Lynne went on, 'He really should know, Connie. It's such a big lie sitting at the centre of your marriage.'

It wasn't as if Connie hadn't considered telling Devan. Part of her was desperate to let the toxic secret slip from her grasp. Surely it would be a massive relief. But then she examined the fallout, the hurt and humiliation on her husband's face . . . the probable ruination of their marriage. And now Jared had compounded the potential mortification by becoming friends with Devan.

Connie began to cry. 'I can't, Lynne. I honestly can't tell him. Can you imagine? Devan would hate me for ever . . .' The thought froze her tears.

'How was the stout?' Connie had been on tenterhooks all day. Devan did not appear until gone seven and hadn't answered any of her texts asking where he was. Mad scenarios had built in her mind as the hours passed. When he finally arrived home, she searched his face for signs of stress. And found none.

'Foul. As you so rightly pointed out, I still loathe the stuff. But Torsten was a hoot. Looked like a cross between an overweight Viking and a computer nerd. I think he'd been sampling too much of his brew because he kept bursting out laughing at nothing at all. Jed said they were friends, but Torsten didn't seem to know him that well. Kept calling him Mr Temple . . .'

'And . . . Jed?' She only just stopped herself calling him Jared.

'Yeah, interesting man. He's been literally everywhere, Con. Seems to have spent his whole life travelling. Although he's also run a successful kitchen-design business, which he just sold for a great deal of money, apparently.' Devan bent to drop a kiss on her forehead as she sat at the kitchen table. 'He's good company. I said we'd have him over for supper one night next week. I'll cook, if you like. I'll make him my sausage pasta.'

22

Connie was sleeping so badly. She would fall asleep, then wake soon after as if to a loud noise, her heart beating like a drum. There was no actual noise: Devan was snoring peacefully beside her. What woke her was Jared's face, looming at her, wanting something, desperate. Wanting her? Then she would lie there, rigid with tension, unable to fall back to sleep.

What's he playing at? The question plagued her. *Is he waiting for me to see the light and leave Devan? Is he waiting for the right moment to destroy our marriage, so he can step in?* She knew it was pointless to ask. He never answered her questions straight. Maybe her sister was right: he'd tire of the game. But, meanwhile, it looked as if she would just have to accept him into her circle of friends . . . her life. It was like living with an explosive device strapped to her chest.

That morning she lay flat on her back on her yoga mat in the village hall. It was the first class she'd been to in ages, and she was stiff from illness and immobility, her joints aching as she attempted to keep up with poses in which she had previously been quite fluent. Nothing felt right, these days. She had even been worried Jared would take up yoga and be there on a mat beside her.

She walked the short distance home on wobbly legs, in a haze of tiredness – she'd almost fallen asleep during the meditation at the end of the session. A gentle hand on her arm as she reached the corner barely registered, until she turned to find Jared beside her. She pulled her arm away, looking right and left to check they were not being watched. But no one was around.

'Can we talk?' he asked, his expression anxious.

'No,' she snapped, turning to go.

'Please, Connie. I never see you alone. Will you meet me somewhere?' His voice was low and pleading.

Spotting a couple she knew quite well getting out of their Jaguar across the road, she was desperate to get rid of him. 'Shotgun Inn, eleven thirty,' she said reluctantly.

I don't need to go, she told herself. But, as she plastered a smile on her face and walked across to greet her friends, she decided she would meet him. It was worth giving it one more shot. If Lynne was right and he was a stalker, it wouldn't work. She had to try, nevertheless. The pub she'd chosen was down-at-heel, hidden in a small hamlet off the Cheddar road. No one would be there at this time of the morning – no one she knew, anyway.

What would I do without Tesco? she thought, as she collected the supermarket bags and waved to Devan – contentedly ensconced with his crossword and Classic FM in the sitting room, Riley snoozing at his feet. He was like a different man since his recruitment to the new hospice. Connie no longer detected the lost, dissatisfied look in his eyes. He met up with Sylvie once a week now, often talked with her over the phone. The plan for opening was coming together nicely, according to Devan.

It was still raining as she pulled up on the tarmacked pub forecourt of the low brick building. The only other car was Jared's black Golf. She took a deep breath.

He was sitting by the window, the gloomy interior stuffy, smelling of stale fat and furniture polish. He got up as she approached. 'Coffee?'

She nodded, sat down on a wheelback chair with a stained red cushion tied to the spokes.

'Nice place.' Jared raised a wry eyebrow as he set the two mugs of white coffee on the table. 'Don't run to lattes, I'm afraid.'

She stared at him. He didn't look quite his usual nonchalant self. Something about his eyes implied stress.

'I'm not here to be friends, Jared,' she said peremptorily.

He looked surprised at her tone. 'I just wanted to check on you, Connie. I mean, Devan is such a great guy. Our day with mad Torsten was hilarious. But now he's asked me for supper tomorrow, and I wanted to make sure you're OK with that.'

She shook her head in amazement, mouth agape. '*Seriously*, Jared? What part of the-man-I've-been-having-an-affair-with-coming-to-supper-with-my-husband would I be OK with?' She took a breath. 'You'll have to cry off.'

Jared shrugged. 'I get where you're coming from.' He took a sip of his coffee and pulled a face, set the cup down again. 'But if you're worried I'm going to blab at supper, you must know I'm not.'

She wanted to beat him over the head and scream in his face till he understood. 'You can't come to our house, Jared,' she said, her voice breaking with the effort not to attack him physically, but still sharp with anguish. 'You can't be mates with Devan . . . or any of my friends. And you can't be living five minutes from my door.' She took a breath, trying to control her leaping heartbeat. *I don't want to ever see you again.* She spoke in a low hiss, although the girl who had served Jared was nowhere to be seen. *Do you understand?*

Jared looked genuinely shocked. He frowned. 'Connie . . .'

Driving home her advantage, she leaned across the table, glaring into his eyes. 'I AM NOT GOING TO LEAVE DEVAN.'

He held up his hands, as if to fend off her words. 'OK, OK, no need to shout. I hear you.' But his expression was bewildered.

'You say that *every bloody time.* You keep saying it, but you *aren't listening.* You just carry on like you did before, turning up and doing exactly the same thing. Which means exactly what *you* want.'

'You used to want it too,' he said, almost flirtatiously.

Connie growled in frustration, throwing herself back in the wooden chair. 'I know I did,' she said softly.

Jared seemed to be waiting for her to go on.

'I don't want to live without you in my life, Connie,' he said, when she didn't say anything more.

A shiver of dread shot through her at his words. She felt she was pounding on a hamster wheel, going round and round and coming back to exactly the same horrifying place. But she could think of nothing to say that might halt the wheel. She had assured her sister that Jared appeared perfectly normal to Devan and Neil and his new friends in the village. But the look in his eyes right now, as he singularly failed to accept what she was telling him, seemed off-the-scale delusional. Exhaustion overwhelmed her. She felt too tired to argue any more.

Jared was smiling now, his face relaxed. 'Trust me, Connie. You have to trust me. I'd never do anything I thought might hurt you.'

As they got up, she remembered something. 'So did you really work with Fiona Raven?'

'Of course. We did some stuff on kitchens together, a while back.'

'"Stuff"?'

'She wanted to include kitchen design and how it works in one of her books.'

He spoke easily, seemed to be telling the truth.

'Bit of a coincidence,' she commented, as he held the pub door open for her.

'I prefer to think of it as synergy,' Jared said.

Connie walked out into the deserted pub car park. Turning to him one last time as she approached her car, she said, her tone cold and uncompromising, 'Just go away, Jared, get on with your life.' She looked him directly in the eye. 'Or it'll destroy us both.'

'Let's ask someone else with Jed,' Connie said to Devan, when she got back with the groceries. She was still hoping, vainly, Jared might do as she'd asked and cry off. But she knew that was unlikely. At least if there were other people as a buffer, his opportunities for mischief would be reduced. Her husband was sitting exactly where she'd left him, with the addition of a glass of red wine on the table beside him. He looked up and frowned.

'We could. But I thought it might be nice, just the three of us. You could get to know him better. He's a lot of fun.'

'We owe the Birtwhistles.'

Devan groaned. 'Please, no. They only ever talk about house prices and their super-clever Oxbridge grandchildren.'

She laughed. 'We've got to have them some time.'

'Yeah, but not tomorrow. Let's just have a cosy evening with Jed.'

Connie looked on in disbelief as she watched Devan and Jared, sitting at the kitchen table, begin to tuck into the pasta that her husband had cooked. *How did this even happen?* She was unable to raise a forkful to her own mouth. She knew she must, and praise Devan's cooking into the bargain. But she felt as dumb and inanimate as the fork in her hand.

'Connie travels,' Devan was saying. 'She's a tour

manager for a train company. Goes all over Europe, don't you?'

She stared blankly at her husband. 'Umm, yes.' She couldn't look at Jared.

But she heard him say politely, 'That's a difficult job, I imagine. All those people to herd on and off trains.'

'I love it,' she said dully.

'Tell Jed where you've been,' Devan urged, giving her a puzzled look. Connie was usually the best of the two at providing lively conversation at their suppers.

Forced to respond, she finally met Jared's eye with a half-smile. 'Oh, you know. The usual – Italy, Germany, France.'

For a second his gaze seemed fixed on her, his eyes so glazed and intimate she was sure Devan would notice. She frowned and he snapped out of it.

'Have you been to the Italian lakes?'

She held her smile steady. *This isn't a bloody game*, she wanted to shout. 'I do Como and Garda a lot. Beautiful.' Her answers, she knew, were monosyllabic and unconvincing. But to engage properly with Jared felt impossibly dangerous. She was certain she would give something away.

'Desenzano, on Lake Garda, is one of my favourites,' Jared was saying. 'Do your tours go there?'

Connie refused to rise to the bait. The night he was deliberately reminding her of, the one that had started it all, now made her feel sick with shame. Levelling her gaze, she replied, as calmly as she could, 'They do. I like the town but I prefer San Felice.' She deliberately named a town further round the lake, which had no associations.

Jared smiled. *He's enjoying himself, the bastard*, she thought.

'I feel I'm way behind you two in the travel stakes,' Devan said. 'I really need to catch up. I've been stuck behind the surgery desk too long.' He pushed the dish of sausage pasta towards their guest, who took another spoonful. Connie was struggling with her first helping. The food felt claggy and solid in her mouth, as if she were chewing tennis balls, but she choked it down and said again how delicious it was.

'I was in Warsaw earlier this year,' Jared, relentless, was saying. 'What an extraordinary place. The way they rebuilt the old city after the war is mind-boggling. Although I sometimes wonder if, by doing so, they've papered over the reality of what happened.'

Jared was gazing at her again, but luckily Devan engaged him about an article he'd read recently about the Warsaw ghetto and her heartbeat was allowed to subside, her cheeks to return to their normal colour.

'You were sent that lovely Warsaw snow-globe, Con.' Devan had turned to her. 'Where did it go? We were going to give it to Bash.'

'It's around somewhere,' she said abruptly, pushing back her chair and making for the door. She couldn't stand it a second longer. With the loo door firmly locked, she sank onto the seat and buried her burning face in her hands. She wanted to cry, but she knew she couldn't.

When she returned to the kitchen, Devan had cleared the pasta bowls and put a wedge of Manchego and a dish of mango chunks with pomegranate seeds on the table. The supper seemed interminable. But at least the men were still talking about the war.

'Bloody hell, Con, you made hard work of that,' Devan said, when they finally shut the door on Jared. 'You were almost rude to the poor guy.'

Connie, busy scrubbing the surface around the cooker, did not look up as she said, 'Sorry. Not feeling my best.'

But Devan was not to be brushed off so easily. He came over to her, carrying a handful of plates, which he placed on the side. 'I get the feeling you really don't like him.'

She didn't know what to say, but he was staring at her and she had to stop what she was doing and meet his gaze. *He must see it in my eyes*, she thought, miserably. She said, 'I don't really know him.'

Devan was frowning. 'It's so not like you, being sulky with a guest.' He was waiting for some sort of explanation, but she had none that was acceptable. 'And he's such a nice man. What have you got against him?'

She shrugged, throwing the cloth into the sink. All evening she'd held on, tried to contain her fury, the dread that Jared might be about to blow her life wide open – her anxiety overlaid by burning guilt. *What am I doing to Devan?* Sobs burst through her body and she began to shake. Devan's arms were instantly around her.

'Hey, hey, it's OK . . .'

She leaned against him, feeling his warmth, his love, and the tears only flowed more strongly. He pulled away slightly and was looking down at her. 'What on earth is it, Connie? What's going on?'

She raised her face to his. *Tell him*, a voice in her head whispered. *Tell him now. Get this over with.* But she simply wasn't brave enough.

'Don't know,' she mumbled, dropping her head to his chest again. 'I love you,' she added, squeezing him harder.

'I love you too,' Devan replied, although his tone was puzzled.

'Let's leave all this till the morning,' she said. 'I'm so tired.'

Her husband obviously realized that that was all the clarification he was going to get tonight, and nodded his agreement, turning her gently around and heading her towards the stairs and their bed.

23

'Hello, sweetheart.' Connie was so pleased to hear her daughter's voice. Caitlin and family had been away for three weeks in Los Angeles, where Ash was in negotiations for a miniseries with an LA-based streaming service. Connie had received lots of WhatsApp photos of Bash in the pool, on the beach with Mickey Mouse, eating ice cream in the sunshine, but she was glad they were back home now.

It was about ten days since Jared had been to supper. Since then, Connie had seen him once in the village shop, and rushed past him on a walk with Riley in the woods. Each time she'd barely acknowledged his presence. But she looked for him everywhere, twitched every time she left the house. And the vibrations of even these fleeting encounters haunted her for hours afterwards, reminding her of the speeding, out-of-control train that was about to derail her life. Their plans for getting away had fizzled out as Devan became more involved in the hospice project, so even that chance of a brief let-up in the pressure on her had been snatched away.

Devan met up with Jared in the pub at the weekend, but she declined to join them – her husband still bewildered by how she had taken against his new friend. She stubbornly refused to comment.

After a long catch-up, Connie said to her daughter, 'Now, Christmas.'

Caitlin chuckled. It was a fraught subject in their family. Connie loved Christmas and delighted in every aspect of the festivities. Caitlin was with her father in thinking it was a waste of time and money – although her attitude had softened since Bash was born. Ash's family, who were Hindu, always had a secular celebration in Manchester, but this year it was Connie and Devan's turn to host.

'Well,' her daughter said, 'I've talked to Ash, and we thought *we* could do the honours this year.'

'Really?' Connie was secretly thrilled. She certainly didn't have the headspace right now. Any excuse to leave the village and Jared's clutches would be welcome, too. It would be just like Devan to ask the bloody man for Christmas 'because he's all on his own'.

'We've never done it, Mum. It's definitely our turn,' Caitlin was saying. 'I'm quite excited. You and Dad can stay a couple of nights. We'll make a thing of it.'

'Ha! Do I detect an uncharacteristic enthusiasm?' Connie teased. 'We'll bring the turkey. They do delicious free-range ones at Sweeney's.'

'Great. I'm actually looking forward to staying put, for once. And you can help cook the bird – I haven't the first clue.'

Connie hung up in a better mood than she'd been in for a while. Her vision, since Jared had moved into the village, had become so restricted, she'd barely had another thought in her head. But Caitlin's call reminded her that she had so many good things in her life. She had a sudden burst of hope. Jared would surely give up and leave, now she wasn't giving their connection any oxygen. Or he wouldn't. And maybe she could gradually come to terms with that. Get used to him being around and ignore the threat that he might let the cat out of the bag. What had happened between them had been so unrelated to any sort of reality. *Maybe*, she thought, *it can stay in its own secret bubble for ever.*

She noticed she'd missed a WhatsApp from Neil. *Coffee at Angie's? 12? x*

See you there. DON'T ask Jed xxx she messaged back, remembering Neil's suggestion at the bonfire party that they all get together to bond over Fiona Raven.

??? Wasn't going to x Neil wrote.

They were ensconced at their favourite table by the glass doors leading to the wide green expanse of the recreation ground, Angie's delicious coffee hot and fragrant in their cups. There was a noisy table of hikers in the corner, but no one else. Connie always wondered how the place stayed open.

Neil looked preoccupied, Connie thought, as she sipped the unfamiliar Ethiopian/Brazilian blend.

'Why didn't you want Jed to join us?' he asked, after they'd caught up. He was looking at her closely and she began to squirm.

'Preferred just us,' she said.

He nodded but raised a questioning eyebrow. 'Right. It's just . . .' he hesitated, looking uneasy '. . . there's something you should know, Con. Jed and Brooks got tanked on margaritas the other night. I was in Cardiff on a shoot, and Jed asked himself over.'

Connie stifled a groan, keeping her face as neutral as she was able.

Neil took a deep breath. She noticed the small frown of concern. 'Thing is, darlin', when Jed was half-cut, Brooks said he got all confidential . . . sort of implied he'd known you in the past, sort of implied it was a little bit more than just "knowing".'

The blood drained from Connie's cheeks. The moment she had been dreading for what seemed like a lifetime had arrived. There was no way on this earth she could dissimulate. Not with Neil. 'What exactly did he say?'

Neil's eyes were wide with amazement. '*Seriously*, Connie?'

'Tell me.'

He shrugged. 'It's all a bit unclear, because Brooks was pretty wasted too. But Jed apparently said something about an Italian tour and a hotel room in Warsaw? And . . .' Neil seemed to wince '. . . he also implied he was really into you.'

Connie closed her eyes.

'So it's true,' she heard Neil say.

She nodded.

'Christ, Con. Why the fuck didn't you tell me?'

She opened her eyes, letting out a long sigh. 'Don't know. Lots of reasons. It didn't seem real . . .'

The hikers were scraping their chairs back, calling goodbye and thanks to Angie, drifting in clumps out of the main door, leaving a trail of cold air. Connie told Neil everything. As she did so, she saw incredulity burgeoning in his eyes.

'Wow,' he said softly, when she'd finished relating a potted version of the last few months. 'I told Brooks Jed must be crazy.'

Connie felt, in the telling of her secret to Neil, that she'd been shamefully exposed, as if someone had suddenly stripped her naked in public. Her friend was staring at her across the small café table, but all she could do was shake, tears not far from spilling down her cheeks. She must have looked pale because Neil, without a word, got up and went over to the counter.

'Can I have a glass of water, please, Angie?'

Angie glanced across to Connie. 'Everything all right?'

Neil said, 'Not really.'

'Connie's not ill, is she?'

'No.' He didn't elucidate, and his expression must have warned her off asking more questions because she went quickly to get the water, which he set down in front of Connie. She grabbed it and drank the lot in a few gulps.

'What are you going to do?' he asked, after a silence.

She shrugged. Although she was beginning to realize there was only one option. 'Tell Devan, I suppose.'

Neil sucked in his breath. 'God . . . poor man.'

'Don't.' She shook her head miserably. 'I loathe the sight of Jared now – or Jed, as he likes to call himself. But when we first met, it was this crazy attraction, a really insane lust I couldn't resist . . . or didn't try to. I still know virtually nothing about him. He'd arrive unannounced, we'd have astonishing sex – at my age, Neil – then he'd leave till the next time.' She paused. 'All of which now just seems creepy and horrible.' She gazed, bewildered, at her friend. 'Has anything like that ever happened to you?'

Neil nodded. 'Sort of. An older guy who came and went in my life for a while when I was in my teens. It wasn't great sex, though, he was just using me. I think I was flattered because he was famous.'

'Who was that?'

He waved dismissively in the air. 'Another time.' Reaching over to lay a comforting hand over hers, he said, 'You know, it could very well be curtains for your marriage if you tell him, Con. I can't see Devan taking too kindly to being cuckolded by the man he's currently having a budding bromance with.'

It was true: Devan was obviously loving his new friendship with Jared.

'Brooks won't tell a soul, I'll make sure of that. He wouldn't do that to you. So, it's only us three who know. And Jed, of course . . . so far, that is. The guy's obviously a loose cannon.'

'And Lynne.' It was already five people, she realized, with a shock. Four of whom could be trusted. But her secret seemed to have reached a tipping point. 'We can't be sure who else he might blab to.'

Neil nodded slowly. 'It would be so much worse if Devan found out from anyone but you.'

Connie gave a harsh laugh. 'I can't think how this awful situation could be even the slightest bit worse. But I take your point.'

'You never know, he might recall he was being a selfish pillock at the time.' But her friend was neither convinced nor convincing. And, anyway, it was a poor defence.

'Oh, Neil, how do I tell him?'

He winced but didn't reply.

'What will he do?' Now that she'd accepted she would have to confess, she was completely failing to imagine the scenario. Her mind was numb. All she could see was her husband's dear face in front of her . . .

'I'll talk to Jed, if you like,' Neil said.

Connie gave him a wan smile. 'Thanks, but it won't do any good. You'll just get the same old, same old – he's not hurting me, he's not causing trouble, he just wants to be near me . . .'

He frowned. 'Telling Devan . . . It's a fucking huge thing, Con.'

She nodded grimly. 'I don't think I have a choice. Jared, as you say, is a loose cannon. His whole life seems to be one big delusion. Take the Raven thing. Did he really work with her? He put up a credible story, but it seems like a stunning coincidence if he did.'

Neil thought for a moment. 'I saw him talking to Fiona . . . but I have no idea what he was saying.' He frowned. 'You think it was just part of the stalking?'

'Don't know . . . maybe. It would fit.'

*

Connie drove home, her stomach in knots. What she faced was so distressing – the disintegration of her whole life – that her mind skittered away from it. *Just one more normal day with Devan*, she begged silently. And maybe there'd be some miracle, Jared, suddenly out of their lives for ever. But she knew she was fooling herself.

By the time she parked the car by the house, she had determined to have the rest of the day with her husband. *I'll do a lovely supper*, she told herself, *sleep one more night with him.* Tomorrow, she would tell him. She felt like a condemned woman facing the gallows in the morning.

'There you are.' Devan was warming a can of chicken soup on the stove. 'Have you had lunch?'

Connie nodded, although she and Neil had eaten nothing. She knew she couldn't swallow even one mouthful of soup.

'You OK? You look as if you've been crying,' Devan put down the wooden spoon and came over to her, his face full of concern.

'Do I?' she said, with false brightness. 'It's just the wind. Bloody Arctic out there.'

Devan put his arms around her. 'You're freezing,' he said, rubbing his nose to her cheek. 'Sit. I'll make you a cup of tea.'

She sat down gratefully. Accepting the tea her husband made, she tried not to think that this might be the last cup he ever made her. The last time she would sit with him like this, while he crunched his toast and sipped his soup, the room warm and still in the early-afternoon light.

'I thought I'd do steak and Caesar salad tonight,' she said, knowing it was one of Devan's favourite meals.

But he pulled a face. 'That would have been great. But I'm meeting Jed. They're showing *Blade Runner, the Director's Cut*, at the film club and he got tickets. I know you hated it, so I told him not to get one for you.'

Connie was engulfed by a wave of despair. 'Don't go, Devan. Please . . . don't go out this evening.'

Her husband looked taken aback. 'I don't understand. Why ever not?'

She quickly blinked tears away.

'Is this about Jed again? I wish you'd tell me why you have such a thing about him.'

'I just felt like a cosy evening with you, that's all,' she said tiredly, aware of her promise to herself that she would tell Devan. *I should do it right now*, she told herself, her gut seizing with dread. *Get it over with*. But she was utterly unable to form the words.

Devan was peering at her. 'Am I missing something, Connie? You seem really upset. We can have steak and salad tomorrow, can't we?'

She found a smile from somewhere. 'Yeah, of course. Sorry. Don't know what's the matter with me at the moment.'

Still staring at her, Devan said, 'I can cancel Jed if you want me to.'

'No, no. I was just being silly. I know you love the film. It'll be good to see it on the big screen again.'

'If the projection works,' he said. 'Remember the last one we saw, when the whole thing was out of sync?'

She laughed. 'I think that was just the equipment objecting to having to run such an irritating film.'

Jared knocked on the door at six that evening. Devan was still in the shower, so Connie was forced to let him in.

'Hey,' he said softly, reaching to kiss her cheek.

But she stepped away, walked off into the kitchen. He followed.

She listened out for her husband and, hearing nothing, moved closer to Jared, lowering her voice. 'I saw Neil today. He says you told Brooks about us.'

He frowned. 'Of course I didn't. I'd never do that.'

She sighed wearily. 'Well, how did he know about the Italian tour and Warsaw, then?'

Jared looked bewildered and gave a defensive shrug. Connie watched his childishly handsome face, saw him sweeping back his over-long hair, recognized the navy cotton shirt he was wearing as the one he'd had on in Inverness . . . and felt no sexual attraction for him whatsoever. She wondered that she ever had. He seemed weak, lost, as he stood there gazing at her with the needy turquoise eyes she'd found so compelling in the past: the cuckoo in the nest. Seeing him now, she felt only revulsion.

'I'm telling Devan in the morning,' she said, very quietly.

He looked instantly alarmed. 'Don't, Connie. Please don't. There's really no need to do that. Things are

OK, aren't they? We're OK. I was so drunk the other night. It won't happen again, I promise. *Please . . .*'

Listening to him, Connie realized with a shock that for Jared this was about much more than her. He had bought into a community, friendships, a lifestyle – maybe for the first time. She was what had propelled him to this village. But now it was clear that he desperately didn't want the boat rocked. He wanted everything to stay exactly as it was.

She turned away. 'Devan will be down in a minute,' she said, as she walked out of the room. In the hall, she didn't know where to go. She needed to get away from them both, but Jared might follow her into the sitting room and Devan was in the bedroom . . . It was raining and bitter outside. She hesitated, then pulled on her heavy parka, grabbed her keys from the bowl on the side. She would drive.

24

Connie drove in the direction of the sea. It was about forty minutes, but she was unaware of the journey, only the destination. She wanted to stand on the edge of the land and look out into the blackness, the emptiness, feel the wind tear at her and the rain lash her cheeks, hear the thunder of surf on shingle and her own voice screaming to the blackened sky. She needed something violent and primeval to erase the image of Jared, who sat like an evil spirit, snug in her bright, cosy kitchen, in her home . . . with her husband . . . in the very heart of her marriage. It made her rigid with nausea.

It had stopped raining by the time she'd woven round the one-way system and parked on the seafront. No one was out in this weather. The pier to the west, its two iconic towers lit up, like a disco, with red, green and yellow neon, flashed out over the dark sea. She leaned against the guard rail and allowed the biting wind to whip off the hood of her parka, her hands numb on the cold wet metal, and closed her eyes.

She had brought Caitlin to this beach during numerous summers when she was small, brought little Bash once too. They'd both loved the donkey rides, splashing in the shallows, the ice cream melting down the cones and plopping onto the sand. That, she knew, would be another agonizing fallout from what she must say to Devan in the morning. Caitlin was kind, but she was also uncompromising. Connie cringed at the impact her announcement would unleash. Her daughter would never look at her in the same light again.

It had begun to rain. But her cheeks were wet with tears anyway. The unthinking recklessness of what she had done with Jared was like a knife twisting in her gut.

By the time Connie got back into the car, she was bone-frozen and soaked. She turned on the engine and waited for the heater to kick in and warm her numb fingers. Catching sight of herself in the rear-view mirror, she almost cried out in fright. Her damp skin was the colour of clay, her hair plastered to her skull, tendrils wrapping her face like seaweed, her normally light grey eyes so dark and crazed she looked almost inhuman.

For a mad moment she thought she might just keep driving, not go home at all. Escape Devan's pain – which felt like a real, palpable thing, throbbing in her hands, despite his not yet being aware of it. But there was no escape. She turned the car around and headed for home.

The house was silent and empty. Riley stirred when she walked into the kitchen, then dropped back to sleep. Connie was relieved Devan was not back – there was no way she could face him tonight, not in the state she was in. She plodded upstairs and ripped off her damp clothes, standing under a hot shower until she felt warm again, at least on the outside. Then she huddled under the duvet in her pyjamas, body scrunched up, mind whirring, agonizingly alert for her husband's key in the door.

The next thing she knew, Devan was climbing quietly into bed beside her. She'd been in a deep, numbed sleep and for a second she forgot the situation she was in, automatically turning to snuggle into his arms.

'Good film?' she muttered sleepily.

'Fantastic,' he replied, putting his arm round her and drawing her closer.

Then she woke properly and reality hit. She stiffened, sat up, accidentally knocking her husband's face with her elbow in her haste. She heard Devan's exclamation, then words began pouring, uncontrolled, from her mouth in the dark bedroom, as if disgorged from another person's throat. The sentences were sharp, staccato bursts, fired with unrelenting clarity. There could be no doubt about what she was saying.

When she had finished there was dead silence. Then the rustle of Devan sitting up, turning on the bedside light. The sudden illumination made her cower and hide her face.

'*What did you just say?*' Devan's voice was barely above a whisper.

Steeling herself, she turned to him. His dark eyes looked bewildered. She took a deep breath. 'I'm so sorry,' she said, almost laughing at the gross inadequacy of her words. Her husband was still staring blankly at her. She wondered if he had really grasped what she'd said. But she wasn't going to repeat it. She waited, hugging her bent knees, her body trembling. She wanted to get up, to move around and dispel the shaking in her limbs. But she felt anchored beside Devan, like a child to an angry parent.

'Christ,' Devan said, his voice low.

'I'm sorry,' she repeated vainly.

'Wait. Let me get this clear.' His tone had hardened. 'You've been having an affair with Jed . . . all summer.'

She didn't respond. There was nothing more she could add.

He wrenched her round to face him. Now, his eyes were blazing. 'You and Jed had sex? *You fucked him?*'

Devan seldom used that word. Connie winced to hear it on his lips.

'*Why*? Why would you do something like that?'

He was gripping her arms, his head inches from hers. She tried not to flinch, tried to be steady in face of his fury.

'Tell me, Connie. For God's sake, tell me.' He shook her, a short, sharp jerk like she'd give a wet sheet. She was limp in his grasp.

Taking a deep breath, she said, 'Nothing I can say excuses what happened.'

His grip slackened, but his voice was as cold as steel. 'I want to know why. *Tell me.*'

'I don't know, I really don't . . . Our marriage was in a mess . . . but I honestly never intended it to happen.' She knew she sounded weak and unconvincing.

He sneered, letting his hands fall. 'He was just *so* irresistible?'

'I can't explain, Devan.'

Her husband jumped out of bed and stood in his T-shirt and pyjama bottoms, glaring down at her with a stunned look on his face. She saw tears in his eyes. He put up a hand and wiped them away with his fingers. 'Maybe things weren't so great between us but God, Connie, I don't understand how you could go that far.'

She couldn't repeat 'sorry' again, so she gritted her teeth and stayed silent.

Devan began to pace, shaking his head in bewilderment. 'So fucking him in some Italian hotel room wasn't enough? You had to install him in our village, let me become friends with him? All these weeks . . . Jesus!' He swung away from her, shoulders slumped.

Connie jumped out of bed. '*No*, Devan. *No*, it's not like that.' She was desperate to make him understand. 'I finished it in Scotland. Told him I never wanted to see him again. I thought he'd accepted that.' She swallowed her own tears. 'But then he arrived in the village, completely and utterly off his own bat.' She realized, as she spoke, how improbable it sounded.

'Right.' He gave a harsh, cynical snort. 'Seriously, Connie? And I'm supposed to believe that? More like you thought you'd have your cake and eat it. Slip round the corner for a fuck whenever the fancy took you.'

'I promise you, we are *absolutely not* having sex any more,' she said wearily. 'The only time I've seen him alone was to beg him to leave. But I told you, he's deluded . . . a stalker.'

Devan's face sank into his hands and there was a painful silence in the bedroom. Connie tried to catch her breath.

'I can't believe this is happening,' she heard him mutter. Then his head shot up. 'Who else knows?'

She hesitated. *Why humiliate him further?* But there'd been enough deception. 'Jed told Brooks when he was drunk.'

'Neil and Brooks. Who else?' he demanded.

'Lynne.'

Devan threw back his head and let out a harsh snort. 'Ooh, I bet she just loved that. Me, getting my comeuppance at last.'

'Actually, she was shocked. And disapproving.'

Devan raised a disbelieving eyebrow. 'Who else?'

'No one.' Which Connie hoped was the truth.

He gave a shaky sigh, began to pace at the bottom of the bed, arms firmly crossed, head bent. She had no idea what would happen next. She felt oddly helpless, her life suspended. All she seemed to have done was swap one man's power over her for another's. She was finally free from Jared's threat of exposure, but now it was in Devan's hands as to whether or not their marriage survived. He could just walk away. Was she relieved she'd told him? She'd finally expunged her tormenting secret, certainly. But her husband's pain was excruciating. As she watched the dying embers of her marriage, she felt nothing but overwhelming regret. She wanted to tell Devan how much she loved him. But she knew he would laugh in her face.

Devan's expression was blank with devastation, his mouth set in a grim line. She waited for the next barrage, her body rigid. But he said nothing, just began to get dressed.

'Where are you going?' she asked, suddenly fearful that he might be intending to confront Jared. Her husband was not a violent man. As far as she knew, he had never raised a fist to anyone. But these were exceptional circumstances: he might do something he'd later regret.

Devan didn't reply, just bent to tie the laces on his trainers.

'Devan?'

'I don't know where I'm going,' he said, his voice hoarse and breaking. 'I don't know what the hell I'm doing any more.'

She raced to block his path to the door, putting her hands on his chest. 'Please, *don't go*. We have to talk, sort something out.'

'Worried I might be going to beat up your creepy toy-boy?' His eyes were contemptuous as he pushed her aside and was gone.

25

It was the longest night of Connie's life. Devan had taken the car, but she had no idea where he'd gone. She sat in the kitchen, nursing a mug of tea, wrapped in a thick cardigan and a scarf, but still numb with cold. She was desperate to talk to someone – Neil? Lynne? – and let out the misery that was choking her. But it was two in the morning. She cried softly to herself, on and on until there were no more tears, and then she finally dragged herself up to bed. But she knew she wouldn't sleep, and she did not.

Around six thirty, she heard the purr of the kettle, the clink of china, the slam of a cupboard door. She struggled from her bed, aching in every limb, and went downstairs, her heart pitching raggedly in her chest. Devan was sitting at the kitchen table, fingers looped through the handle of his coffee mug, staring vacantly into space. His face was gaunt and pale, dark smudges beneath his eyes. Riley rested his tan muzzle on his thigh, as if sensing his distress, Devan's free hand absentmindedly stroking his wiry coat. Both looked up as Connie came into the room. Riley wagged his tail but did not leave Devan's side. Her husband's stare barely changed.

'Where have you been?' she asked, not knowing what else to say to break the heavy silence.

'Nowhere.'

She went over to the cupboard and took out a mug for herself, poured coffee from the cafetière on the table. Then she sat down opposite him. She longed to reach out, to touch his hand, but she didn't dare. It was still dark outside, only the first faint glimmer of dawn in the sky. The kitchen felt close, the air stagnant. Connie wanted to open a window, but she didn't move.

His eyes were on her. 'Tell me about the sex,' he said, a brittle edge to his voice.

'Devan . . .'

He sat up straighter. 'Don't evade the question again, Connie. I need to know what was so bloody special that you'd go to these lengths – break up a lifelong marriage, humiliate me, destroy –' He gulped noisily and didn't finish the sentence.

She inwardly recoiled. 'I'm not going to,' she said flatly.

He raised a cynical eyebrow. 'I see. That good, eh?'

To her horror, she found herself blushing. Hot, shameful waves of guilt pulsing across her cheeks. But her eyes seemed glued to Devan's. Looking into them, he could surely see her naked body, Jared's, too, hear her cries, feel the sweat, the lust, the tangled sheets, like the playing out of a tawdry porn movie.

He jumped to his feet. 'Christ, Connie. You make me sick.' Picking up his coffee mug, he hurled it at the wall – on which was hanging a framed photograph of them both, kissing in front of the extraordinary façade of Gaudí's Sagrada Família in Barcelona. She remembered asking a couple of backpacking Japanese teenagers to take the picture. The mug shattered. Coffee sprayed on the white walls. The photograph wobbled but was unharmed.

Devan was breathing hard. He looked as shocked by what he had done as Connie did. Neither spoke as they regarded the mess.

He turned tearful eyes to meet hers.

'I rang Neil last night.'

She waited.

'He said not to be too harsh on you. It was just a stupid mistake – a low point in our marriage and you were vulnerable.' He gave a sardonic laugh, then levelled his gaze at her. 'Are you in love with him?' His tone grated on her strung-out nerves.

Connie shook her head firmly. *Love has never come into it*, she thought. *Obsession, yes. Intense, inexplicable lust, definitely. But never love* – not for either of them, she had been sure, until that night she'd collapsed and, blinded by fever, reached out to Jared . . . incomprehensibly altering the story for him.

Yet, in Devan's eyes, falling in love might be a more plausible excuse for her unfaithfulness. Casual carnal lust seemed almost obscene at her age. Although maybe her age had made her more susceptible. 'No,' she said firmly. 'I was never in love with Jared. Not for a single minute.'

Her husband's raised eyebrow told Connie he didn't believe her. But she stared him down.

'Doesn't change much,' he said sullenly, shaking his

head in disbelief. 'God. My wife and my new friend . . .' He held his linked hands to the back of his head and pulled his head down, letting out an anguished moan. 'Go away, Connie,' he said, with weary bitterness. 'Just go away. I can't stand the sight of you.'

Connie's phone, left on the table last night, suddenly pinged with a text. Devan snatched it up. 'Oh dear. Our beloved daughter.' He thrust it at her with a look of cruel self-satisfaction. 'Over to you.' Up at six thirty with Bash most days, and knowing her mother rose early, Caitlin often touched base in the mornings.

She took it but resisted checking the message. If it had been urgent, her daughter would have called. There was nothing she could say to her at this moment, anyway. Her daughter would hate her from now on. Let Devan be the one to break the good news. But both of them seemed rooted to the spot at the stark reminder of the family they loved.

'What do you want me to do?' she asked, blinking her dry, scratchy eyes, which had finally run out of tears. But she knew, as she asked the question, what she had to do. It was unimaginable, remaining under the same roof with Devan. Feeling guilty all over again every time she looked into his face, upon which his agonizing hurt and reproach would be writ large for the foreseeable future.

He was hunched over, arms crossed, standing there like a statue. He had not answered her question.

'I'd better go,' she said. 'It's not going to work, me being here.'

His head shot up and, with a spark of ludicrous hope, she thought he might be going to ask her to stay. But he nodded, his eyes blank. 'I think that'd be for the best.'

Devan didn't say any more, just pushed past her and left the room.

Connie packed a case. She was scarcely aware of what she was doing. Questions were screeching about her brain, like seagulls fighting over a dropped sandwich.

Where can I go? Neil and Brooks would always take her in. But Neil had his mother for a pre-Christmas week, as he and Brooks were flying to Costa Rica for the holidays. Anyway, it was too close to both Jared and home. Lynne might let her stay for a few nights. But Connie knew it would cause her sister too much stress, disrupting Roddy's routine with an uninvited guest. Jill and Bill? Bill was Devan's best friend. *Caitlin* . . . She couldn't think about her daughter.

Glancing absentmindedly at the pile of neatly folded clothes in the two sections of her wheelie-case, she pushed it aside and slumped onto the bed. Devan had taken Riley out, slamming the front door as if he were shutting it on their marriage. The silence was like a judge on his high bench, pointing a condemnatory finger at Connie, making crystal clear the price she must now pay. Which seemed painfully high.

Was she really packing a bag to leave behind her life and everyone who meant anything to her? She felt helpless. She refused to believe this would be the end of her marriage – surely that wasn't possible – but she knew now was not the time to fight for it. Devan needed space and she would give it to him. Although all she wanted to do was shove the suitcase onto the floor and climb into bed, go to sleep and pretend none of the events of the last twelve hours – the last seven months, indeed – had ever taken place. Wake to find everything the same as before that first treacherous kiss.

Flopping back on the duvet, she closed her eyes. *Where is Jared?* She'd told him she planned to tell Devan, but she might well have changed her mind, for all he knew. *What will he do when he finds out his cover is blown?* She shuddered at what a confrontation with her husband might look like. *He can't know where I've gone.* Then she gave a sad laugh. *She* didn't know where she was going either. Or for how long.

Exhausted, Connie slept, lying on her back and waking to a wrenching cramp in her stomach. Glancing at the bedside clock, she realized she'd been asleep for nearly an hour. Rain was pounding the windows and the bedroom was chilly. She dragged herself to her feet in a daze and reluctantly zipped her case shut.

I'll drive to a hotel for the night, somewhere I can rest, take stock. Then she remembered, with a jolt, that they had only the one car. Her trusty, rusting Fiat 500 had died a death two years before and they hadn't bothered to replace it, as her current job meant she didn't need to drive to an office every day. She could hardly add to Devan's indignities by leaving him stranded in the village, with only an hourly bus for transport. She reached for her mobile, hidden in the folds of the duvet, then put it down again, thought for another couple of minutes, finally lifting it and punching in a number.

'What's happening, darling?' Neil's voice was full of concern. 'Devan was off his head last night.'

'He still is,' she said grimly. 'Listen, could you drive me to Weston?' Connie was surprised at how matter-of-fact she sounded.

'Weston? Why? Where are you going?' Neil asked.

'London,' she said. 'I can't ask Devan.'

'Where are you going to in London?'

'Umm, a friend.'

There was silence. 'A friend? Which friend, Connie?' Pause. 'I don't like the sound of this. Where are you really going? You're not running off with *him*, are you?'

Connie gave a tired snort. 'Of course not,' she said. 'I just need to get away from here, Neil. I don't have a car, so I thought I'd be better somewhere I don't need one.'

'So, who's the friend?' he repeated stubbornly.

'Tessa. Not sure you know her. We were at school together. She lives in Hampstead.' The name sprang to Connie's lips almost involuntarily under the pressure of Neil's questioning. She'd barely spoken to her friend in the last ten years, beyond a sporadic exchange of emails. But Tessa's husband, Martin, had died in March and she'd gone to his funeral. Tessa had been in touch since, begged Connie to come and stay, saying how much she hated the empty house. For all Connie knew, of course, she was currently visiting her daughter in Hawaii, or had a houseful of other strays.

She heard Neil sigh. 'OK. But I'm worried about you.'

'I've just got to sort this out.'

'How will you do that from North London?'

'Neil, please, can we talk about this another time? I really need a lift. I'll get a taxi if you can't do it. I know your mum's staying.'

'There in fifteen,' he said.

She let out a sigh of relief. Terry, the village taxi driver, inhaled gossip as others did air, then blew it out again as soon as he had a captive audience. Word would get round soon enough, but she wasn't going to help it along.

Connie hauled her case downstairs. Glancing into the sitting room, she saw Devan on the sofa. He looked as if he'd just keeled over sideways where he sat, his head resting uncomfortably half on, half off a cushion, his feet still on the floor. In sleep, his face was sunken, his skin grey. He looked as if he'd aged years since she'd last seen him, his mouth twitching as if he were having bad dreams. She gave a quiet gasp, her heart leaping in her chest, so full of love did she feel for the man who had been at the centre of her life since she was in her early twenties.

She tiptoed over to the sofa and laid her hand on his head, stroking his dark hair, tears spilling from her eyes. She wanted to gather him in her arms, to rock him till his pain was gone. But she was the cause of that pain.

Devan's eyes sprang open. At first his glance was unfocused. Then he must have remembered. 'Don't,' he said, cuffing her hand away as he shot upright, his stare thick with confusion.

Connie moved back, shocked at his unqualified rejection, although she knew she had no right to be. *What did I expect?*

'Neil's taking me to the station,' she said.

Unlike Neil, Devan didn't ask where she was going. He merely nodded, his gaze flickering to her case. Leaning back against the cushions, he pressed his palms briefly against his eyes, then dropped them to rest on his knees. 'Jared's gone.'

Connie stared. 'How do you know?'

'I sat outside his house for hours last night. Banged on the door. There's no one there – you can tell. And his car's gone.' His smile was cynical, knowing. 'I suppose you tipped him off.'

She didn't bother to refute the accusation.

'Cowardly little shit,' Devan added.

Connie didn't know what to say, except 'Sorry' for the umpteenth time. But she knew Devan was too hurt to hear. The unwelcome thought sprang to mind that she need never have confessed to her husband. Just telling Jared she intended to might have been enough to see him off. But she knew it wasn't as simple as that.

Devan didn't get up at the sound of Neil's knock. 'Bye,' she said softly, reluctant to walk away from all that she held dear, but feeling she had no choice . . . for the time being, certainly. At least, she hoped it was for the time being. The thought that it might be permanent was unacceptable, too horrible even to contemplate.

26

When Connie woke the next morning in a strange hotel room and to the muted roar of traffic, she thought for a moment she was on one of her tours.

The room was the cheapest she could find, last minute – although not what she would have called cheap – in a Bayswater tourist hotel near Lancaster Gate. It looked as if it hadn't been redecorated since the eighties, the walls covered with varnished pine planks, twin bracket lights with singed pink shades, a patterned carpet in sickly browns and beige, the duvet cover and sheet a washed-out flesh colour. Even in Connie's distressed state, she'd shuddered as she got into bed the night before, smelling the flat, synthetic pillow with distaste and trying not to think of all the heads that had lain there before hers.

It was not yet daylight outside, the orange sodium glow piercing the thin cotton curtains coming not from the sun but from numerous city street lamps. She lay listening to the intermittent beep, beep, beep, beep of the pedestrian crossing immediately beneath her window, which had also lulled her to sleep. At least she had slept, so worn out by emotional turmoil that her brain had shut down and refused to function for another second.

Her phone said six fifteen. But clearly there were plenty of people already out and about, crossing the road outside with monotonous regularity. *Now what?* She was aware of the loo flushing in the next room, the banging of doors, the chatter of other hotel guests passing her door.

Connie was already regretting her decision to accept Tessa's kind offer to stay – which she'd secured late last night. Being alone, having some time to gather her strewn thoughts, seemed all she was capable of right now. But she couldn't stay here another night, and fancier places would have concomitant prices attached.

She was dreading her friend's unspoken censure. Tessa was no prude, and she'd never known her to be judgemental, but she'd recently buried a beloved husband of thirty-plus years. Connie had thrown hers away with a piece of spectacular indulgence.

There was no message from Devan – she'd expected none. No further message from Caitlin – the last one saying, *Just checking in, Mum. Nothing important. Speak soon.* Connie knew she would have to call her today and her heart contracted.

Nothing from Jared either, although he never contacted her . . . until he was outside her bedroom door. She blanched at the thought that there was even the remotest chance he might be out there now. *He's gone, running scared, like Devan said*, she told herself firmly, experiencing through her cautious relief a twinge of sadness, nonetheless, for a man who felt the need to behave in this peculiarly destructive way. She was confident there was no chance he could find her there, or at Tessa's, anyway. Although she didn't feel she could relax yet. Not until there was proof that the gremlin was finally off her shoulder.

The only message on her phone was from dear Neil: *Ring me, darling. Need to know you're OK*. She texted back: *I'm fine-ish. Thanks for asking♥*

Connie found a little café on the corner of one of the streets leading away from Hyde Park. Perched on a high stool at the window counter, the seats beside her empty at that hour, she savoured her first sip of hot coffee and watched people hurrying past on their way to work. She couldn't remember when she'd last eaten, but the seeded roll filled generously with thick slices of buttery bacon proved too much for her after the first bite.

Tessa was expecting her late morning. As she brought up the TfL map on her phone to plan her route to Hampstead, a call came in. *Caty*. Connie held her breath, glancing around the café, the mobile still buzzing in her palm. A small queue of people stood waiting to be served at the counter, but no one was paying her any attention, the café noisy with the coffee machine and breakfast radio, banter from the two women making up the orders.

'Hi, sweetheart,' she said dully.

'Mum? Where are you? What's going on?' Caitlin sounded panicky, which made Connie feel guilty all over again. 'I got this garbled call from Dad late last night, but I couldn't work out what the hell he was on about . . . except that you'd apparently gone off somewhere.' Her daughter gave a short laugh. 'He was hammered, so I'm sure it's all nonsense. But you know me, I hardly slept a wink.'

'I'm so sorry,' Connie said, wishing that Devan *had* made sense, that Caitlin already knew, that she didn't have to be the one to break the dreadful news.

'Mum?' Caitlin's voice was suddenly fearful.

Taking a deep breath, Connie filled her daughter in, her calm articulacy surprising her. She thought she must come across almost as cold.

The silence at the other end was profound. Connie could picture her daughter's face, shocked and disbelieving, unable to find any words with which to respond. But it was the wave preparing to break and she braced herself.

'You . . . *cheated on Dad?*' She sounded bemused. After a long pause she asked, 'Who with?'

'It's a long story . . .' Which Connie went on to tell in as sparse detail as possible.

'Oh, my God.' She heard Caitlin let out a sharp breath when she finished. There was a long pause, then simply, 'I don't know what to say.'

Connie didn't know what to say, either. She knew it would be a mistake to try to justify her behaviour in light of her problems with Devan at the time. And she could never explain the sexual obsession Jared had represented. Not to her daughter, not to Devan, not even to herself.

'So, this man's a nutter, a total fucking stalker,'

Caitlin was saying. 'Christ, poor Dad. That's so cruel.' A pause.

Connie waited. The wave had still not vented its true fury.

'Why didn't you stop him, Mum?' Caitlin demanded, her voice now steely. 'Why did you let this bastard move in and make friends with Dad? That's so fucking shitty.'

'I *tried*, sweetheart. I really did. I did everything in my power to get him to leave.'

But Caitlin wasn't listening. 'You should have made him, Mum. What the hell were you thinking?' She drew in an angry breath. 'You could at least have warned Dad. Not let this jerk cosy up to him. I mean, who does that?'

'I thought he'd go away.'

Connie heard Bash's voice in the background, Caitlin tempering her anger as she greeted her son, then Ash's concerned tones. *Ash, too*, she thought miserably.

'Listen, I've got to go,' Caitlin said. 'Talk later.'

Connie sat clutching her silent phone, realizing her hand was shaking. *Will we?*

She felt in that moment that she'd forfeited any agency over her life. She was at everyone's mercy, now. If Devan chose not to see her again, that was his prerogative. If Caitlin cut her out of her life, that was hers too. If Jared decided to find her and stalk her again, he could do that. And if Tessa didn't fancy having her in the house, then she could ask her to leave. She could – and would at some stage, when she'd had time to think – put up a fight to save her marriage. But Connie liked to be in control. It was as if Jared had loosened the strings on her life. In giving in to him, she had temporarily lost her grip on everything else, including the person she felt she used to be.

Tessa's house was in a quiet terrace a short walk down the hill from the tube station. Half brick, half white stucco, it had steps up to the front door and area steps down to a half basement. Connie, feeling like a refugee, hauled her case to the top of the flight and rang the bell. The street was almost empty mid-morning, eerily silent after the crowded busyness of the main road – just minutes away – with its numerous shops and cafés.

She hesitated before pressing the small brass bell, trying to settle herself to greet her friend. She felt as if her head was lying in a thousand pieces, but she didn't want to appear crazy before she'd had a chance to explain. When she'd asked if she could stay, she'd merely said she needed a few days away. Beyond that, she couldn't focus.

Nobody answered. She waited, then rang again. Nothing. Connie pulled out her phone. Tessa's mobile went to answer. She frowned. It was cold on the steps, the winter sun now fallen behind the houses. Although she'd managed to keep herself together thus far, she knew she was on the edge, just dying to be safe inside Tessa's house, maybe with a glass of wine, a hot bath, a bed on which she could rest for an hour or two. She felt tears stinging behind her eyes and blinked them away, imagining the neighbours tweaking the wooden slats of their blinds – the modern-day equivalent of nets – and wondering who this peculiar woman was, loitering outside Tessa's front door with a suitcase and in tears.

On the verge of bumping her case back down to the pavement, and going to find a warm café to sit in until her friend returned, Connie heard a shout and saw Tessa hurrying along the street, clutching a bulging mustard-yellow string bag in one hand and balancing a white cardboard cake box in the other. She was dressed in jumper and jeans, a red wool scarf round her neck – no coat – and sparkly silver sandals on her feet. Her right toe was swathed in a bulky bandage.

'Connie!' She arrived at the bottom of the steps pink-faced and breathless. 'Sorry, sorry! I just popped out for some lunch and the queue was horrendous.' She handed Connie the cake box and pulled out a huge bunch of keys, with a fluffy ball attached, from her back pocket. 'You must be frozen to death.'

As soon as the front door was shut, Connie let out a quiet sigh of relief. Tessa took the box from her. 'Come through, have a seat. Leave your case – I'll show you your room in a minute.'

The kitchen-sitting room was to the left of the front door, the sitting area on the street side, with a large, worn olive-green velvet sofa, a wall-mounted television and books floor to ceiling on either side of a gas-log fire. The kitchen was at the back, looking onto the garden. It was cosy and cluttered and the decor hadn't been updated for years. Connie instantly felt at home.

Plonking her purchases on the kitchen table, Tessa

came back to where Connie was standing and wrapped her in a welcoming hug. 'I'm so glad you're here, Con,' she said. 'You have no idea. I think sometimes I'm going crazy, all by myself.' She laughed and gave Connie a rueful smile. 'You know me. I never was one to relish my own company.'

Connie laughed. 'Me neither.' She searched Tessa's face, noticing the strain around her eyes, the look of vague distraction – as if she were not really present – that she'd seen in other recently bereaved friends.

Tessa was about her own height, with dark hair – now streaked becomingly with grey – in an untidy bob tucked behind her ears, the fringe brushing her large blue-grey eyes. Where Connie had small breasts, Tessa's were full, her figure straight-backed and athletic – she was a life-long jogger. But it was her open smile and extrovert charm that drew the eye. You always knew when Tessa was in the room.

By contrast, Martin, a financial journalist of some note, had been quiet, wary and thin. He had long since stopped bothering to be sociable, Tessa carrying the day for them both. She and Connie had been best friends at school, managing to keep up their close friendship for a while, until geography, husbands and children took their inevitable toll. But when they did get together, even after long periods with little contact, nothing seemed to have changed between them.

Overcome and feeling close to tears again, Connie said quickly, 'What have you done to your toe?'

'Oh, nothing. Just caught it on the edge of the bed,

stumbling around in the night.' She gave a half-smile. 'I've been at such sixes and sevens since Martin died. Bashed up the car – nothing major, but still – locked myself out at midnight, forgot one of my sessions at the bank ...' Tessa was a performance coach, employed by one of the big banks, having trained as an actress and worked in television for a while. 'I suppose it's inevitable.'

Connie felt so selfish. Here she was, feeling sorry for herself, when Tessa was dealing with a life-changing bereavement. She mentally shook herself and gave her friend another hug.

'Right, wine, I think.' Tessa grinned. 'And I got one of these delicious caramelized onion tarts for lunch. That deli will be the ruin of me.'

They poured the wine, cut slices of tart, spooned creamy celeriac remoulade onto plates, then settled down to talk, initially relating the bare bones of their last few months. In Tessa's case, Martin dropping dead one quiet Sunday afternoon in spring from a so-called 'widow-maker' heart attack – a huge blockage in the left coronary artery. Connie had heard versions of the story from people at the funeral, but she'd not been able to talk properly to Tessa that day and hear the real account.

'No warning, Con. We were sitting on the sofa in front of the fire, having our usual rant about the ludicrous bollocks we were reading in the Sundays, when he stood up and sort of gasped, fell back onto the sofa ...' Connie saw the shock still patent in Tessa's eyes. 'I tried CPR – I've done the bloody classes for my job – but it didn't work. He never came round.' She sighed. 'I always told him the Sunday papers were bad for his health.'

When it was Connie's turn to speak, she was brief, almost making light of her dilemma. It seemed so self-indulgent. But Tessa immediately saw through her restraint. 'What the hell are you going to do?'

Connie shrugged. The wine and Tessa's sympathetic ear had loosened her grip and she felt herself giving way to self-pity.

Before she could compose herself, Tessa said, 'Devan will get over it. He adores you. A single mistake in a marriage as long as yours shouldn't be a deal-breaker.'

'You think?' Connie was surprised at her friend's reaction. She'd expected more shock and disapproval.

'Christ, Con, we're only human. Cheating is never great, obviously, but it's hardly your fault the person you did it with turned out to be a bloody stalker.' She looked at her intently. 'He's totally out of the picture now, right?'

'Totally. Anyway, he'd never find me here.'

Tessa raised her eyebrows. 'You're sure about that?'

She nodded firmly, although she wasn't as sure as she was making out. On the way up to Hampstead earlier, she'd found herself scanning the tube carriage, the plat-forms, the pavement, just in case. Dinah, she knew, lived in Highgate, just the other side of the Heath.

There was silence as Tessa leaned back in her chair, wine glass clutched in both hands. 'Give Devan a bit of time to calm down ... to miss you. Then talk it through.'

It sounded so rational, so simple. But Tessa hadn't witnessed Devan's rage, his humiliation at Jared's hand.

'You can stay here as long as you like, Connie. I'm off up to Edinburgh on the fifteenth, having a few weeks with the family ... which I'm really looking forward to. But you can be here while I'm gone.' She frowned. 'Although Christmas holed up all on your lonesome doesn't sound like much of a plan.'

'I'll see how things go, if that's OK? It's so kind of you, taking me in like this, Tess.'

'Believe me, you're doing me a favour. And if you're staying, you can look after the cat.'

Connie had not seen any cat, but she smiled and agreed because nothing made sense in her life any more. One moment she'd been looking forward to a cosy family Christmas, checking out recipes for the turkey she and Caitlin would cook together, planning what to buy for her beloved grandson. The next, she was exiled in North London with only Tessa's cat – whose name, she later discovered, was Monty – for company.

27

Tessa had taken the night sleeper for Scotland five days ago. It was nearly two weeks since Connie had arrived at her friend's house, and the days had passed slowly. Tessa was working on and off, had presents to organize, other friends to catch up with. But they would have supper and a good glass of wine most evenings, talk like only lifelong friends can. Neither had solutions for each other's current sorrows, but it was comforting for Connie gradually to unwrap the chaos in her brain with someone who would listen, not judge.

Connie had waved off her friend with trepidation, clutching the house keys, her head spinning with instructions about closing the security grilles on her bedroom window in the half-basement, bin days, what and when to feed Monty, the fact that the gas hob no longer lit automatically, and how to regulate the central heating. Connie had written it all down as soon as she closed the front door, knowing she'd otherwise forget.

Now, waking to an empty house for yet another long and lonely day, she felt desolate. In the time since she'd left home, the only person she'd properly spoken to, apart from Tessa, was Neil. There had been complete radio silence from the rest of her family. Caitlin had not rung back – even to berate her mother. Connie had left countless messages, first apologetic, then asking to talk, then, when no response was forthcoming, just *Love you xxx*

Devan, on the many, many occasions that Connie had called – two or three times daily at first, heart in her mouth – had not picked up, and not returned a single call, although she'd left message after message asking him politely if he would please do so. Unlike with her daughter, she did not apologize to Devan again. She just wanted to talk to him directly, to try to explain. She wanted to apologize to a living person, not a machine.

'He's probably licking his wounds,' Neil said, the last time they'd spoken. 'Give him time, Con.'

'How much time, though?' she'd cried. 'I feel every day that goes by, he gets further and further away from me. Suppose he just point-blank refuses to speak to me ever again?' She stopped to catch her breath, overwhelmed by the thought. 'Help me out, Neil, *please*. Tell me what I should do.' Before he'd had a chance to respond, she rushed on: 'Have you seen him? How is he? Do you think he'll ever forgive me?'

'Whoa, Connie, slow down. *I* haven't seen him, but Brooks bumped into him in the pub. He was with Bill. Brooks said he seemed perfectly normal, smiling and friendly, as if nothing had happened.'

Typical Devan, Connie thought, *burying it all behind a public face*, but her heart constricted at the thought of him pretending so hard. Jill had rung Connie a few times, but she hadn't taken the calls, just texted back to say she would be in touch, although she'd decided it would be better if she wasn't. Bill was Devan's best friend. Jill would only be compromised if she got involved with Connie's side of the story.

'And Jared?' she asked, holding her breath in trepidation.

'No sign of him. I've done a couple of drive-bys, imagining what I'll say to the prick if I ever manage to corner him. I've even banged on the door, but it seems he's long gone.' Neil gave a harsh laugh. 'He wasn't going to hang about, though, knowing what's gone down with you and Devan.'

'You can never tell what Jared's going to do . . . But no, I suppose not.' She wondered where he was now. Would he have somewhere to run to, and if so, where? *Maybe to Dinah's*, she thought, and shivered at the proximity.

'Listen, Con,' Neil was saying, 'you didn't murder anyone. You've apologized. You made a daft mistake. Devan would be crazy not to come round in the end.'

'I've called him a million times and he won't ring back. He doesn't even seem to want to get in touch to yell at me. There's been nothing, not a peep, since the day I left.'

She heard her friend give a frustrated sigh. 'It's barely two weeks. You've got to give him time.'

Connie sighed. The conversation was going in circles. 'Would you talk to him, Neil? *Please*. Just sound him out?'

There was a groan.

'I know it's a lot to ask. But I genuinely don't know

where to go from here.' She waited. 'I'm *desperate*.' The word was no more than a whisper, she felt so utterly sapped by the situation. Even when she was talking to Tessa, watching television, trying to sleep, it played on and on around her brain in a persistent loop. Like a child repeating the same question until it is heard.

The other day, after another message left with no response, she'd almost jumped on a train back to Somerset, thinking if she could just see Devan face to face he would have to talk to her. But she wasn't sure she could cope with the door being slammed in her face . . . with another cold rejection.

'OK,' Neil was saying. 'But what do you want me to say?'

Connie had no answer. 'No, listen, it's probably a bad idea,' she said, after a moment's consideration. 'Forget I asked.'

He didn't reply at once. 'Thing is, we're off to Costa Rica on Monday. I could try to see him before I go . . .'

'Honestly, don't, Neil. Thanks for the offer, but this is my problem, not yours. And, as you say, it's not likely he'll be in the mood just yet.'

There was a short silence.

'God, darling. I really feel for you. Are you going to be all right while I'm away? We're not back till the sixth.'

'I'll be fine. I'm so sorry you've had to listen to me whining on. I hope you both have a brilliant time. People say it's an amazing place . . . all that walking above the clouds thing I read about. Love to Brooks.'

She was hanging on, forcing out her brightest self

for just ten seconds longer while they said goodbye. Then she took a juddering breath and burst into tears.

After lunch, Connie wrapped herself up warmly and took a walk to the high street. It wasn't that she needed anything in particular: she was heating tinned soup and eating a lot of toast instead of real cooking. She just needed human contact, even if it was only the barista serving her coffee or one of the friendly booksellers in Waterstones. It was raining, but the hill was crowded as usual, a sea of umbrellas jostling for position on the pavement.

She'd almost stopped looking around for Jared. Almost. That chapter of her life, she kept telling herself, was closed. The fallout was her main concern now. But as she crossed the wide road towards her favourite café, a man walking down the hill towards her – at least a hundred metres away – raised his black umbrella for a split second before turning right into the narrow side-street by the bakery. He was in jeans, muffled to the neck in a heavy parka, hood up, but even that tiny glimpse stopped Connie in her tracks, a cry discharging involuntarily from her throat.

Him? From the thrashing of her heart she was certain it was. But when she'd taken a few deep breaths, calmed down a little, although still staring fixedly at the entrance to the alley where he'd disappeared, she decided she must have been mistaken. *Just my crazy brain playing tricks*, she told herself, as she reached the café, with its steamed-up windows, coffee machine churning and cosy, all-pervading smell of damp wool. She found a seat at the back, her hands shaking as she unzipped her coat.

Over a large latte, she reviewed what she'd seen. The image was still clear in her mind, but it wasn't a clear image. There was the rain and the dim winter light, the other pedestrians, the umbrella and his hood. But she had seen enough, at least, to precipitate jumpy glances towards the door each time it swung open.

By the time Connie got home she was a bag of nerves. Every umbrella harboured Jared Temple, every brush against her arm on the crowded pavement was his hand, every shout was her name on his lips. She didn't feel safe. She went round the house checking all the locks, as if she expected him to have broken in, or maybe walked through walls, to be standing there, anyway, in the middle of Tessa's sitting room as if he had every right to be there.

The next day, Connie decided to stay at home. It was mayhem out there, she reasoned, Christmas frenzy building. But that wasn't why she stayed inside. She didn't trust herself not to invent a repeat of yesterday. Because, overnight, she'd come to the conclusion that the pressure she was under was making her mind play tricks, see things that didn't exist.

Connie, as Tessa had also claimed, wasn't used to being alone. She wasn't good at it. Even if she had known someone in London, though – which she didn't, other than her daughter, who wasn't an option – she was in no fit state to socialize. It was two weeks until her friend got back, during a time when almost every other person in the country would be indulging in some form of festive celebration with family or friends. All she could think about was her family: Caitlin and Ash and little Bash dressing the tree, Devan arriving, the warmth and laughter, the brightly wrapped presents, the fizz, the turkey they would share. It was sending her round the bend. *Aren't they wondering how I'm coping, all alone here?* she wondered plaintively, as she checked her phone yet again to find no messages from any of them. But they would assume Tessa was with her, of course.

For one more day she sat on the olive-green sofa, wrapped in the mohair throw, drinking tea and eating toast, Monty snuggled into her side. She ploughed through tiresome books about acting and economics – Tessa didn't seem to do light reading – or watched endless daytime television. She now knew all about the pitfalls of buying a property at auction, how to make perfect gluten-free mince pies, a certain sportswoman's mental-health issues, and how to tell a real Ming pot from a fake.

Enough, she told herself firmly, late in the morning two days before Christmas. *Stop being feeble. Take a walk, go to the cinema, buy some food that isn't bread. Get a grip.*

It helped that the rain had stopped, delivering a glitteringly bright winter's day. She couldn't help yearning for home as she wove through the shoppers on the hill, deafened by the noise of the traffic and a brass band bashing out Christmas favourites. Right now it would be heaven to be tramping in the frosty sunshine with Riley. Up through the woods they'd go, bursting out of the trees at the top to enjoy the stunning view across the Levels to the distant Mendips. She loved that view. Devan knew that when she died he was to scatter her ashes at exactly that spot so her spirit could enjoy it for ever. She pushed away the thought that he might not give a toss where her remains were scattered any more.

Thinking about home got her as far as the bookshop. She would browse for a while, find a nice fat detective novel with which to distract herself. Maybe buy a good bottle of wine, find a tasty dish she could stick in the oven from the ruinously expensive deli Tessa loved, and some mince pies to get into the festive spirit.

The bookshop was crowded and hot. Connie pulled off her gloves and woolly hat and opened the neck of her coat. She began to pick up books at random, taking her time and enjoying the hubbub, the company, the piped carols that filled the air.

She'd been there a while when she was aware of the opening bars of 'Away In A Manger'. Her eyes filled with tears. Bash's face swam in front of her: his nursery had sung it at their Nativity last year and all she could see were his dark eyes gazing dreamily from beneath the cotton-wool sheep's ears Caitlin had made. She found herself pushing past the other shoppers, almost running from the store.

Once on the pavement, she stopped and drew a shaky breath. The cold hit her and she realized she didn't have her hat or gloves. Cursing under her breath, she turned and went back inside. *Where did I leave them?* She revisited the various tables over which she'd lingered. But they were nowhere to be seen. In the end she found a girl with a bookshop badge and asked for her help.

'Come with me. We'll check if someone's handed them in,' the girl said, leading Connie through a door saying Staff Only to a large see-through plastic container sitting in the corridor. Unclipping the lid, she asked, 'What do they look like?'

'A green wool hat and brown leather gloves,' Connie told her. 'But I've only just left the shop. I'm not sure anyone would have had time to hand them in.'

The girl rummaged about, nonetheless, pulling out various hats – none of them green. She looked at Connie. 'Maybe come back tomorrow. We close at four.'

Outside once more, Connie found she was unreasonably upset by the loss of her hat and gloves. Devan had given her the hat for Christmas two years ago, when things between them were still good and a rift in her marriage was not even a speck on the horizon. She remembered trying it on and Devan taking a photo on his phone, them both laughing and agreeing it suited her perfectly, her husband teasing her that she looked like a mischievous leprechaun, such as his Irish grandmother had warned him about. Losing the hat felt like the last straw.

She stood still for a while, being knocked and bumped by the Christmas crowds, then began to plod slowly down the hill, head bowed, without any of her intended purchases. Once she turned the corner into

Tessa's road, leaving the roar of the high street behind her, she was aware of her phone ringing. Fumbling as she tried to extricate it from her coat pocket – where it was tangled in a tissue and the house keys – she pressed the green button frantically over and over. But the caller had clicked off. *Caty*. Tears of frustration clouding her vision, Connie immediately returned the call, but her daughter didn't answer and it went eventually to voicemail. *Noo*, she wailed silently, staring at the screen in disbelief. She didn't walk on immediately, as if the very fact of her stillness would enable Caitlin to get through. She tried the number a couple more times, but with the same depressing result. It was like being starving hungry, a delicious bite of something dangled before her, then snatched away before she could taste it.

The house was gloomy, silent, and she felt something go inside her: she had completely run out of steam. Struggling out of her coat, she lit the gas fire with a wobbly hand. Grabbing the throw, she flung herself down on the sofa and curled up into a ball, the cat in the crook of her knees, her head on a gold satin cushion, slippery and cold beneath her cheek. She was beyond tears as she lay listening to Monty's soft snores, the hiss of the gas-fire, the tick of the carriage clock on the mantelpiece. Cars braked for the sleeping policeman in the road outside the house, then accelerated away; footsteps tapped along the pavement, sometimes accompanied by snatches of chatter; the mohair from the throw tickled her nose. But inside her there was only numb silence.

Lulled by the warmth from the fire and the cat's comforting proximity, Connie dozed. When she woke the clock said it was just past five. She rolled onto her back, dislodging Monty, who scrabbled and jumped heavily over her legs onto the floor. *I ought to feed him*, she thought, reluctantly dragging herself upright, still groggy from the daytime nap.

Turning on the kitchen light, she washed Monty's bowl and took a new pouch from the row of cat food Tessa had left beside the kettle, Monty purring and threading himself in and out of her legs in anticipation. As she was lifting a fork from the drawer, her mobile blared. Since the earlier missed call, she had ramped up the ring to the loudest possible, dreading another disappointment.

She dropped the pouch and the fork, racing to pick up the phone pulsating on the coffee table. *Caty*, she thought.

'Ash?' She was taken aback. He seldom called and she instantly worried it boded no good.

'Hi, Connie.' Her son-in-law sounded cautious, but friendly. 'How are you?'

She gave a sad laugh. 'Been better, I suppose.'

'God, I'm so sorry about all this.'

'It's me who's the sorry one, Ash.'

'Listen, I know Caty tried you earlier . . .' He fell silent. 'I'm sure she'll try again later, it's just with Devan here . . .' He stopped. 'But she's worrying about you. And missing you, as we all are.'

Tears misted her eyes. 'I miss you all too. Terribly.'

'It's been pretty hectic –'

'How is Devan?' she interrupted, although she didn't really want to hear Ash's answer.

'Umm, not great, if I'm honest. He doesn't mention you much, just rants on about Jared. And his back's bad again.'

Connie winced. There was a direct correlation between Devan's back pain and his emotional state, his previous bout disappearing, like snow in summer, as soon as his mood improved. Now she could imagine her husband's dark-blue eyes, bruised and flashing with hurt. She let out an involuntary sigh. 'I can't tell you how much this call means to me, Ash,' she said. 'I'm truly sorry for everything . . . not least ruining your Christmas.' She wanted to hug him for being so kind, knowing what he must be dealing with at home. She wondered if Caitlin had asked him to call, or whether he'd done it off his own bat.

'No worries. You know I'm not a fan of the festive season.' He chuckled. 'We're off up to Manchester on the twenty-seventh, where Ma will no doubt feed me till I burst. Roll on January.'

Don't go, she thought, as she sensed Ash winding up the call. She wanted to ask about Bash, to hear about this year's Nativity and what he was getting for Christmas. But before she had a chance, Ash was speaking again, this time sounding furtive, in a hurry to be off the phone. 'Listen, let's arrange something as soon as we get back. Have you over . . . Bye, Connie, lots of love.'

28

Ash's call was a fillip for Connie. Her mood instantly improved. She knew nothing had really changed, but at least the agonizing wall of silence had been breached. It was a ray of hope. She knew she could manage her despair if there was the prospect of seeing her daughter and grandson – dear Ash – in the new year, even if Caitlin was still angry with her. About her future with Devan she dared not think. That was much, much more complicated.

On Christmas Eve, she spruced herself up – replacing the jeans she felt she'd been wearing since the last century with her black ones – and went out to do some shopping. She'd decided she really would get into the festive spirit now, buy lots of delicious things, then hole up, be patient and wait it out. *There's nothing I can do about anything until after Christmas*, she told herself.

The deli looked as if the good folk of Hampstead were preparing for a siege – and a very expensive one at that. The queue for the counter snaked onto the pavement, while the aisles were rammed with panic and sharp elbows, baskets bulging and weighed down with treats. The mood, far from brimming with good cheer, was focused, everyone hell-bent on the task in hand.

By the time Connie struggled out of the shop with

her meagre waxed-paper bundles of cheese and salami, a pot of olives, a chicken and leek pie and a slab of serious 85 per cent chocolate, she was stressed and sweating. Next on her list was alcohol. Devan always chose the wine, so the rows of bottles meant little to her, beyond knowing she wanted something dry and white. She left the shop with a Chablis that the man serving her insisted would 'set her taste buds dancing'.

It was nearly lunchtime, and Connie made her way towards her favourite café for coffee and a sandwich rather than going back to the empty house. Leaving Tessa's earlier that morning, she'd felt stalwart and resolute. The furtive glances she cast at the other shoppers were a natural reaction, she told herself, to what she'd recently been through. But even as she ate her delicious smoked-salmon and cream-cheese bagel, with the newspaper she'd just bought open at the quick crossword, she kept flicking her gaze upwards with every ting of the café door. All who entered, however, were blissfully strange to her.

Still unwilling to shut herself up for the rest of the day, Connie lingered on the hill, gazing into shop windows at things she had no desire to buy, wandering back into the bookshop to check whether her hat and gloves had been found – they had not – and buying a couple of books, checking the times of the services at the Unitarian chapel she'd noticed, close to where she was staying.

She and Devan were sporadic attendees at the village church – although Devan had been a devoted bell-ringer before his back had started playing up. But Connie's mother had been a lifelong Unitarian and this Christmas she felt drawn to the chapel for that reason. *If only I could ring Mum now*, she thought, as she viewed the noticeboard in the chapel porch. Sheila would've been upset with her daughter for what she'd done, Connie had no doubt. She'd been no soft touch when it came to moral issues. But she would have listened, talked it through in a sensible manner, not condemned her out of hand. Sheila had loved Devan, but was realistic about relationships, her own fraught at times as Connie's father had become anxious to the point of disorder as he grew older.

Now, she turned down the street towards Tessa's house. It was getting dark and the shops would be shutting soon, everyone making their way back to their families. She imagined Caitlin and Ash's brightly lit flat and the huge floor-to-ceiling tree in the corner of the room. Ash, despite his feelings about Christmas, was given to expansive gestures, claiming a small one in their warehouse space would look ridiculous. She pictured the coloured lights strung, like a twinkling necklace, across the wide expanse of window, smelt the canapés her daughter would be preparing to go with the champagne: chipolata sausages with mustard dip, warm, meaty samosas and maybe aloo tikki with spiced chutneys, some smoked salmon on squares of brown bread . . .

The family had a tradition of not eating a proper supper on Christmas Eve, just pigging out on plates of little eats. Sometimes, wherever the family was, there would be other people, friends dropping in for an hour or so. Bash would be round-eyed and crazy with tiredness, but Ash kept to the fond theory that the later he went to bed, the longer he would sleep – wishful thinking, of course. Connie sighed as she reached for the front-door key. *Stop*, she told herself firmly.

Unpacking her shopping from Tessa's string bag, she laid it out on the table. She wished now that she'd got something spicy – thoughts of the samosas had made her mouth water. She frowned as she picked up one of the packages. She didn't recognize it. Pulling open the flap of waxed brown paper, she found a cardboard tray stacked with ravioli, lightly dusted in cornmeal. Checking the sticky label, she read: 'Pumpkin and pecorino ravioli'. *Shit*, she thought, *I've got someone else's supper*. Thinking back to the scrum in the deli she was hardly surprised. She remembered putting her shopping bag down while she waited at the counter, so maybe someone had muddled hers with theirs. Or she'd swept it into her bag by mistake, along with all the other stuff. It was expensive, nearly nine pounds, but it was too late to return: the place would have shut by now. She felt guilty for a moment, hoping the person to whom it belonged was not counting on it for their festive meal. But she would eat it with pleasure – it was one of her favourites.

But as she held the tray, she felt a prickle shoot down her spine. It was triggered by a stab of memory that jumped out at her, like a hot coal from the grate. The pumpkin soup Jared had offered her, and him, one eyebrow raised, asking, 'Remember that pumpkin and pecorino ravioli by the lake at Como?'

She spun around. The dimly lit room was empty and silent, but Jared seemed suddenly to be everywhere. Was she going mad? But she could almost smell him. She dropped the tray onto the table, where the contents spilled onto the wooden surface. The hand she clasped to her mouth was cold and shaking. *No*, she thought, *no, no, no*.

Connie took a couple of deep breaths, steadying herself against the worktop. *Pumpkin's trendy, probably half of Hampstead's eating the same ravioli over Christmas*. Did she honestly think that Jared would be so devious as to follow her into the deli and lurk about until he got the opportunity to drop the packet into her shopping bag without her noticing? *I'm being stupid*. But her reasoning did nothing to soothe her nerves. She continued to tremble as she twisted open the wine – not even chilled yet – and poured herself a large glass, pulling the heavy curtains against the night, turning on the television to some shouty gameshow just to banish the creeping silence.

You've got to stop this, she pleaded with herself. She hated how vulnerable, how paranoid she'd become. It was like living with a chronic virus. Outwardly she functioned, just about. But inwardly she was now perpetually weak and afraid.

The absurd thing was, she couldn't easily define what was frightening her. It wasn't physical: Jared had never hurt her, and he'd never given the slightest sign of wanting to, of being in any way violent. He wasn't doing traditional scary stalker stuff – wasn't doing anything at all, in fact. She hadn't heard a peep out of him or set eyes on him in weeks. She downed the glass of Chablis too quickly, barely registering its deliciousness. The truth was all too clear. She didn't blame Jared for the breakdown of her marriage. That was on her. He had, nonetheless, become a bogeyman, haunting her every step, her every breath. He didn't even have to put in an appearance for this to be true.

Connie watched the show on television without seeing it. She was aware of her cheeks warm from the wine, her head slightly woozy, but she refilled her glass anyway, and contemplated preparing some of the food she'd bought. The ravioli, still scattering the table, mocked her. She should bin them, but that would be admitting she believed Jared had had a hand in their presence in her shopping bag, and she refused to do that. There was no chance, however, that she would ever be able to eat them and nothing else she'd bought for herself appealed.

Returning to the sofa, where Monty was once more installed, the sharp ring of the bell made her start. Immediately she was on guard, her heartbeat skyrocketing. Who would call so late on Christmas Eve? Holding her breath as she listened, she knew exactly what she was afraid of. *I'm imagining things*, she tried to tell herself. But she tiptoed as quietly as possible to the front door, gingerly sliding the cover of the peephole across and peering through.

Connie smiled and gave a huge sigh of relief. Turning the key for the double lock, she pulled open the door to the cold wetness of the night and greeted Tessa's American neighbour, Melanie, whom Connie had met a couple of times, coming and going in the street.

'Don't mean to disturb you, Connie,' she said, smiling, as she hovered on the slick steps, hands clutching her thick cardigan round her body, her dark hair glistening with drizzle. 'But Noah and I wondered if you'd care to join us for Christmas lunch? We've got a couple of friends coming by. Otherwise it's just us and the kids.'

Connie knew Tessa must have put her up to this. *How else would Melanie have known I was on my own?* She hesitated, acutely embarrassed by her situation and wondering what Tessa had told her.

'Wow, that's really kind. I'd love that . . . but I've not been feeling that great today. I'm worried I might be coming down with something.' Which was no word of a lie. And she was sure she looked a wreck.

Melanie frowned. 'Sorry to hear that. There's a ton of stuff doing the rounds. But if you feel better and change your mind, just come over around one. No need to call first.'

They wished each other a happy Christmas, and Connie closed the door gratefully. The Finemans seemed a lovely couple, but she couldn't face witnessing someone else's family engaged in what *she* would normally be enjoying.

She leaned her back against the door for a moment,

closing her eyes, then was jerked upright by another brief ding of the bell. *Melanie again*, she thought, and composed her features into a smile as she swung the heavy door open once more.

But the person she found herself face to face with was not Melanie this time. Jared, dressed in a heavy tweed coat, collar turned up, a striped scarf draped casually around his neck, stood, breathing hard, on the top step. His face was pink with cold. In his right hand he carried a small white-paper carrier bag. 'Happy Christmas, Connie,' he said, with a broad smile.

29

Connie thought her legs were about to go from under her. For so long she'd imagined – indeed feared – his presence all around her, seen him in every face in every crowd. But his actual presence, in the flesh, standing there on Tessa's doorstep as cool as a cucumber, was horrifying.

'May I come in?' he asked, his manners as impeccable as ever.

For a moment she was unable to respond, unable to move a muscle. She watched Jared start to step forward and her breath shot back into her lungs, her blood to her veins. She thrust out her hand, feeling the rough tweed of his overcoat as she pressed her palm hard to his chest. 'Stay right there, Jared.' She took a gulp of air.

He looked shocked and stepped back. Connie dropped her hand. It was freezing and she shivered in the wintry blast. 'Go away,' she added emphatically, as he showed no immediate sign of leaving.

He was staring at her. 'Are you OK? You look white as a sheet.' He reached out, but she backed away as she made to slam the door shut.

But he was quicker. He already had his fingers curled firmly around the door jamb. 'Two minutes, Connie. Please.'

'NO! *Go away!*' she hissed, threatening to slam the door on his fingers but not wanting him to turn nasty, to create an embarrassing scene on Tessa's doorstep.

'And stop bloody stalking me,' she managed, but her voice trembled.

Jared seemed genuinely taken aback, but he didn't shift, didn't remove his hand.

'I saw you,' she stated, more forcefully. 'The other day, on the hill. And you – you put those ravioli in my shopping bag.' She realized as she spoke that this was the only real accusation she could level at him, and it sounded insane.

He frowned, looking mystified. 'Ravioli? I'm sorry, Connie, you've lost me.'

Breathing fast with frustration, she wasn't going to be fobbed off this time. 'I know it was you.' She tried to remember which day she had seen him on the rainy hill, but her mind wouldn't focus. Their faces were too close as he leaned towards her, his eyes dark pools of purpose. She refused to give way, wouldn't leave any gap through which he could pounce as she waited for the moment when he would let his hand drop from the jamb and she could slam the door shut.

'Couldn't have been me. I've been in Berlin. Only flew in a couple of hours ago,' Jared said.

Connie stared at him. He seemed so calm. So frighteningly calm. She didn't believe him. But the fear that she had imagined it all, put a false spin on perfectly normal situations – his face under the umbrella, the parcel in her shopping – was almost more terrifying than Jared himself.

'Remove your hand.' She heard the venom in her voice. 'And if you ever, *ever* come near me again, I'll go straight to the police.'

He gaped at her. 'Police? God . . . don't say that.' But his tone was quietly rational as he continued. 'I thought, now Devan is off the scene . . .' When she didn't respond, he frowned as if baffled. But his next words were sharp, intense, his voice ratcheting up to something close to desperation. *'He doesn't love you, Connie.* Can't you see that? Where is he now, for instance? I mean, who leaves the person they love all alone at Christmas?'

'I said, remove your hand. NOW,' she repeated.

Jared was blinking fast, his cheeks flushed as if she'd smacked him. 'Connie, please . . .'

For a split second she almost felt sorry for him. He looked so pathetic, standing there in the glow of the street lamps, his face pink with cold, clinging to a ludicrous delusion as forcefully as he held onto the door jamb. And to think she'd once thought him Mr Cool: the handsome, seasoned traveller, the one in charge, who turned up and melted away again when it suited him, who'd been so confident in his way around her body that she'd lost her reason. It made her feel sick.

The night air seemed suspended between them as their eyes met. She held his gaze, hoping he would finally see her steely rejection writ large and glowing neon. He didn't flinch. Then, to her unutterable relief, she watched the fight slowly drain out of him. Stiffly, he released his grip and stood back.

'OK,' he said quietly. He held up the bag he'd been carrying in his other hand. 'This is for you.' Before she had time to stop him, he dropped it through the doorway, where it fell sideways on the mat.

Connie didn't wait a second longer, just slammed the door in his face, hastily twisting the key in the double lock and shooting the stiff bolts. She heard her short, rasping breaths as she leaned her palms against the door, eye to the peephole, terrified he would still be standing there, looming inches from her face. But the top step was empty.

Not believing he'd really gone, she moved quickly to the window, peering warily between the heavy curtains. He was nowhere to be seen, the street empty except for a couple holding hands as they ran across the road, their breath trailing smoke in the cold night air. But she still felt haunted and unsafe.

Realizing she was shivering, she pulled her heavy cardigan from the chair back and wrapped it around her, hurrying over to the fridge. She grabbed the bottle of wine, pouring herself a large measure with a trembling hand, wanting to scream out her fear, shout to the heavens until it left her in peace. And longing so much for her husband. His embrace would be the one thing guaranteed to calm her.

It was a while before she could think coherently, her brain still flooded with fight-or-flight hormones. But as she began to come down from the panic, her initial relief that Jared was gone started to wane. It was the final look he'd levelled at her that shook her the most: his eyes had appeared almost . . . fanatical. It was the only word that fitted.

Connie sat for a long time at the kitchen table, clutching her empty glass. Her head was fizzing, like a firework about to explode, her cheeks flushed from the wine and the heat in the room.

Did he get it this time? she asked herself, over and over. *Will he leave me alone?* She had never been scared before that he might hurt her. But she'd felt physically threatened tonight, terrified that he would push his way into the house. There was real craziness in his eyes . . . and she felt his obsession for her like a gun aimed at her head.

She got up, boiling hot and restless, ripping off her cardigan. She desperately craved escape from the claustrophobia of her thoughts, longed to take deep breaths of cold night air and clear her head. It would be heaving on the hill tonight: churchgoers off to Midnight Mass, revellers on their way home from Christmas Eve parties – this wasn't the country. For a mad second she thought she might join them, just to be among people, to feel the comforting presence of normal human beings. She even pulled on her coat and boots, found a Fair Isle beret of Tessa's hooked on the coat stand.

But when she got to the front door, her courage failed her. She knew she wouldn't be able to open it, to risk leaving the safety of the house. He was out there somewhere, even if she couldn't see him. Watching her.

Waiting for her. He might not approach her, but she would feel his eyes on her, maybe catch a fleeting glimpse of his face in the crowd – real or imagined. She leaned on the door, her painfully compressed heart suddenly making her breath ragged.

The searing pain took her by surprise and she staggered, gasped, clutching her chest. An iron band seemed to be crushing the air from her lungs. She couldn't breathe. She felt as if she were dying. *Please*, she thought, as she tried to catch her breath, *please don't let me die . . . not like this*. She weakly called out Devan's name. But all she got back was cold silence.

Connie had no idea how long she stood slumped against the door. It was the arrival of a taxi immediately outside, disgorging a party of shrieking, drunk girls, that startled her out of her stupor. The pain in her chest had lessened and her breathing was easier, although she was ice-cold and stiff, as if she'd been left out in the garden all night.

Shuffling back into the sitting room, she went to the fire, rubbing her hands together, letting the gas flames almost scorch her cold flesh. She knew she couldn't spend another minute on the sofa, or drink more wine, watch any more seasonal television. She should go to bed, but her bedroom in the half-basement seemed dark and creepy. She would never sleep down there.

Wandering about the sitting room, turning everything off, she made the decision to have a hot bath in Tessa's bathroom and sleep in her friend's bed – she was sure she wouldn't mind. She hoped Monty might choose to join her, as he often did Tessa, apparently, now Martin was no longer around to object. She felt in need of even the smallest comfort.

As she went to check the front door again – even though she knew for certain she had locked it tight earlier – her eye caught Jared's bag, scrunched against the hall wall where she must have trodden on it in her haste to slam the door. She stood eyeing it for a moment, then reached down and picked it up, holding it at arm's length as if it were a grenade about to detonate. But she was curious.

The parcel inside the bag was wrapped neatly in blue tissue paper and tied with a silver ribbon. The gift card had only two words written on it: 'Love, Jared', then three kisses. Connie's hand quivered as she gingerly pulled open the paper. What she found inside was a green woolly hat and a pair of brown leather gloves. Not hers. These were new, the labels still attached. But almost identical.

30

Connie awoke early on Christmas morning. In a strange bed and an unfamiliar room, having slept the sleep of the dead for a few short hours, her head spun as memories of the previous evening swarmed back into her consciousness. Jared's present had brought both relief and absolute fury.

Her sense of relief came from knowing she wasn't, after all, insane. She was now one hundred per cent certain it had been him on the hill that day. That he had also stolen her hat and gloves from the bookshop, slipped the ravioli into her basket. He had to have been watching the house, to know that she was alone. He must have been constantly watching her . . .

The fury came from the way he'd gaslighted her, lying so convincingly at every turn. Because now the deceptions all came back to her: claiming to have overheard Connie's name in the queue for the Doge's Palace, his friend with the crumbling palazzo, the supposed meeting in Milan. Then there was Kraków and the night she'd thought she saw him pass by the table where she was having supper with the two Norfolk teachers. He'd said then, too, that it couldn't have been him: he'd flown in just an hour ago. Not to mention the man who'd lost his car keys at the food fair, stopping to chat to Jill as she changed out of her boots . . . Fiona Raven's book launch . . .

As she'd stood stock still in the hall the previous night, staring at the green hat and gloves still lying on the tissue paper, the last of the scales now incontrovertibly torn from her eyes, Connie kept asking herself why she hadn't seen through him, questioned his behaviour, right from the beginning. Lynne and Neil had spelled it out. Just the way he'd turned up on her tours like that, always knew the number of her hotel room, was bizarre, by anyone's standards.

I wasn't looking, she thought. *I was enjoying it too much, carried away by the game* . . . until he'd arrived on her patch, where he'd fooled everyone else, too, of course. It confused her. The delusions he had about loving her were obviously acute – and crazy – but presented in such a reasonable way that she'd continued to think he might see sense, if she could only find the right words. But it was as if she were speaking Chinese to an Inuit. He simply didn't understand. Added to which, she couldn't imagine why anyone would have such an obsessive crush on her. Especially not at her age.

She'd eventually hauled herself out of Tessa's deep Victorian bath last night, dried herself and climbed into her pyjamas. The one person she ached to talk to was Devan. Without him, the hole in her life was bottomless. She'd always turned to him when there was a problem, enjoying his unquestioned support, the effortless back and forth of a marriage, without fully appreciating – till she lost it – how vital, how intrinsic it was to her life. In any other circumstances, she could imagine how they might now sit and dissect Jared's behaviour. Make sense of it . . . together.

She'd reached for her mobile on the bedside table. *I will call him*, she decided. But as her finger hovered over his contact details, she saw the time on the screen: it was the middle of the night. Devan would be fast asleep, full of delicious samosas and too much champagne, cosy in Caitlin's comfortable spare bed – where Connie had languished with that horrible chest infection in the summer. On Christmas morning, he'd be woken by little Bash and his cheeky grin, who'd climb in with his grandpa, all sleepy and warm and completely adorable.

Connie had put her phone down, too tired even to acknowledge the searing ache around her heart.

Now, she lay listening to the silence. No one was out and about at this time on Christmas Day. Even the persistent traffic hum from the hill had stilled. She wondered what on earth she could do with her day. There was a service at the Unitarian church at eleven. It was a bright morning: perhaps she could walk on the Heath. There was the Finemans' kind offer of lunch, or the chicken and leek pie if she stayed in. All of which were things she might enjoy. None of which she felt she could. So, she rolled over and gradually fell back into a fitful sleep.

She was woken by her mobile blasting from the bedside table. Snatching it up, her heart pumping from the shock of being pulled abruptly from sleep, she prayed it was

351

the family. But Neil's cheerful voice was wishing her a happy Christmas.

'This place is so bloody gorgeous, darling,' he went on. 'We've done rainforests and turtles on the beach and hanging bridges and howler monkeys ... you wouldn't believe.'

'Sounds amazing.' Connie couldn't help laughing at his childlike enthusiasm.

After a further excitable exposition of the wonders of Costa Rica, Neil's voice sobered. 'How's it going with you? Do I smell the toxic whiff of Brussels sprouts across the airwaves?'

'Afraid not. Tessa's up in Scotland with her daughter. It's just me.'

She heard a sharp intake of breath. 'You're all alone?'

'It's fine. Tessa's neighbours have asked me over for lunch. And it's a lovely day. I'll do a Heath walk, and there's a service ...' She thought she sounded admirably convincing as she lied her way through her reply. But Neil wasn't fooled.

'Hmm. So what are you really doing?'

She tried to maintain her composure, keeping her tone light. 'I'm lying in bed feeling sorry for myself, if you must know.'

'Bummer. I wish you were here. We'd cheer you up.' There was a pause. 'Any word from the old homestead?'

'Caty tried to call, but I missed her. Ash phoned, bless him. They're all OK, but clearly still avoiding me like the plague.'

'Cruel.'

'Listen, it's lovely to hear your voice, Neil, but don't worry about me. I'm surviving. You and Brooks have a great day. Let's talk soon.' She wanted him off the phone. Crying pathetically from three thousand miles away on Christmas morning was not a fair thing to do to a dear friend.

Neil said a reluctant goodbye and Connie hurled her phone down onto the duvet, the tears that had threatened while they were talking evaporating in a blast of irritation at her own maudlin self-pity. She forced herself out of bed and into a hot shower.

Washing her hair, rubbing her skin with the ginger and mandarin moisturizer she'd found in the bathroom and dressing in a clean jumper and jeans, she applied a quick smudge of foundation, a smear of lip balm over her dry lips and began to feel more human.

She went downstairs and made herself a treacly cup of coffee with some scary-looking full-strength Panamanian beans she found in the cupboard. With no real idea as to when she had last eaten, she knew she should make something. But she wasn't hungry, the thought, even of toast, knotting her stomach. She wondered what she should do now, as she sat at the kitchen table in the silence, hands circling her mug as the buzz of caffeine kicked in.

The clock, ticking so slowly it seemed like a fortnight between each tock, drew near to one o'clock. She was apprehensive about Melanie making another pitch to get her over for lunch. But the hour passed: no one knocked.

It was the sun shining in the bright blue winter sky – glimpsed through the window – that finally overrode her lethargy. It would be getting dark in a couple of hours, and then she'd be trapped inside for another long, lonely night with only Monty for company.

Wrapped in her coat and Tessa's beret – Jared's hat and gloves returned to the paper bag for delivery to the charity shop on the hill as soon as it opened again – she set off towards Hampstead Heath.

The air was sparkling with frost, the Heath crowded, families out taking advantage of the beautiful day. Connie walked quickly, keen to avoid the glances of people she passed on the wide paths round the ponds. She wanted them to think she was on her way to a gathering of some sort, not a lonely woman trying somehow to fill the day. Not that they were thinking about her at all, she was well aware. But she felt self-conscious, nonetheless. A woman surrounded all her life by friends and family, never giving much thought to what it would be like to be one of those who didn't have her privileges, suddenly cast adrift. *I will never take anything for granted again*, she promised herself, as she turned onto the path that would lead her home again.

She was also wary of catching a glimpse of Jared's face in the Christmas crowd. She could tell herself until she was blue in the face that he'd gone, that he was *out of her life*, but checking for his presence had become like a tic, a habit of which she was barely conscious. But at least she was out. No panic attacks on the doorstep today. Which was progress. *If you're watching me*, she thought defiantly, *then good luck to you. You'll never get what you want.*

What remained of Connie's day had been spent curled up on the sofa, gazing blankly at the gas flames, the book she'd bought open, but unread, a plate of olives and salami merely nibbled at. It was nearing ten now. Connie had wondered all day if she should try to phone the family. But, although her finger hovered frequently over Caitlin's number, she never made the call. She didn't want to be the cause of tension, possibly triggering more rants from Devan that would upset their day. Or face the disappointment of another voicemail and unreturned call. She'd hoped her daughter might ring again, but it was getting late now, and she knew she would be exhausted – Bash no doubt having woken them all at five, or earlier.

She'd received a text from Tessa, a short call from Lynne, a voicemail from Jill – because she hadn't picked up when she saw her friend's name on the screen. Every time, the sound of her phone had made her heart soar with hope – only for it to be instantly dashed. Now, when her mobile rang, she reached for it almost laconically.

'Mum?' Caitlin's voice was pitched low.

Connie, hardly able to believe it was her daughter after nearly three long weeks of praying, gasped her reply. 'Oh, darling . . . hello. *Hello.*'

'Listen, Dad's next door, so I can't talk too loudly . . .' she paused '. . . but I just wanted to say hi.' Another

355

pause. 'We're all missing you dreadfully. It's been horrible without you.'

'God, I'm missing you too, darling. I can't begin to tell you how much.' Tears pricked her eyes. 'How are you? How's Bash?'

'Yeah, he's fine, we're all surviving. It's been weird, though. Dad's in bits. Clingy and miserable . . . Angry, obviously.' Connie heard her sigh. 'He sort of assumes I'll take his side, which is exhausting. I'll be glad when it's all over, to be honest.'

'I'm so sorry, sweetheart. This is all my fault.'

'Let's not get into that now, Mum. I'm over it. Family's too important . . . I've had trouble getting my head around the whole thing, which is why I haven't rung before . . . I just didn't know what to say, didn't want to hear the details. Which was mean, I know, and I'm sorry.' Connie heard Caitlin take a deep breath. 'Anyway, enough's enough. We have to find a way to get Dad back onside in the new year. I'm not going through another Christmas like this one. Ever.'

Connie held her breath, overjoyed at her daughter's words. 'Do you think he might come round?'

'All I know is that he's totally lost without you. I mean, what's he going to do? Be stubborn and stay on his own for the rest of his life because he won't forgive you one lapse? After God knows how many years of marriage?'

'I really hurt him.'

Her daughter fell silent. 'I know,' she said. 'But you've apologized. We have to move on.' Her tone was tough, unequivocal, as only Caitlin could be.

'I love you so much . . .' Connie couldn't hold her tears a moment longer.

'Love you, too, Mum. Don't cry . . . please. You'll set me off.'

Connie felt Caitlin's love threading the silence that followed, like a warm hug. Her heart ached with the joy of it.

After they'd said their goodbyes – Caitlin promising to be in touch as soon as they were back from Manchester – Connie cradled the phone in her hand, in a daze. Hope, she realized, was the most agonizing thing. It was as if she'd been singeing her skin over a naked flame, hoping to speak to her beloved daughter. Now she felt weak with relief. And suddenly starving hungry.

The pie was delicious. Connie ate as if she hadn't for a month. She polished off the olives, the salami, gulped down the remains of the wine. Still not satisfied, she dug out crackers from one of Tessa's tins and layered them with some Kentish goat's cheese she found in the fridge. Finally, she sat back, replete.

It's going to be all right, she told herself, channelling her daughter's resolve. But having Caitlin and Ash onside was only half the battle. Facing Devan . . . She had no illusions on that score. Trust, which she'd always taken so much for granted in their marriage, had been blown out of the water. It might be a long, long time before Jared no longer cast his shadow.

31

Holding little Bash in her arms was heaven. Connie closed her eyes and breathed in his familiar smell. But the hug she valued above all others was Caitlin's. It was fierce and protective, and like a long, cool drink in a burning desert. The two women clung to each other for a full minute.

She had briefly embraced Ash, too, whose eyes were full of sympathy as he grabbed his leather satchel and left the two of them together. Now they were on the sofa, both clutching mugs of tea, Bash's small chubby hand resting on Connie's knee, showing her a wind-up robot he'd got for Christmas and telling her a long and garbled tale about Robot Man's adventures. She listened with half an ear, stroking his silky hair, her main focus on what her daughter was saying.

'Go on, text him again, Mum. Just say you really, really need to talk now. Me and Ash have been working on him over Christmas.'

'I can try. But you wouldn't believe the mountain of emails, texts and messages I've sent – all to no avail. I'm not sure he even reads them.' She shook her head. 'I'm always the one labelled "stubborn" in the family, but your dad takes prizes.'

Caitlin smiled. 'Tell me about it. But he's had time

to think.' Frowning, she added, 'You guys were the envy of my friends at school, you know. Sam's dad drank, Amelia's parents split up horribly, Maddie's mum worked in Brussels all week . . . I was almost embarrassed to have such solid parents who didn't fight and were always around.' She gave a small laugh. 'Just text him, Mum. Don't over-think things. It's Dad you're talking about. You love each other, remember?'

Connie could detect a slight note of impatience in Caitlin's voice. Her parents behaving like teenagers – especially after such an apparently exemplary past – was obviously taking its toll.

'You could do it now,' Caitlin was suggesting, holding her hand out for Connie's mug. 'I'll make a fresh brew.'

It was more of an instruction than a suggestion, and she did not argue.

Caitlin was right. Devan took only an hour to respond to the message she sent this time. *I'll ring this evening*, he wrote. Terse, but finally a communication. Connie was both relieved and heart-thumpingly nervous as she showed the text to her daughter.

'You see?' Caitlin was triumphant and, Connie thought, also very relieved.

But no amount of reassurance from her daughter made her feel confident about the impending exchange with her husband.

*

That evening Connie sat in the Hampstead house, waiting with a mixture of longing and dread. In the end, though, the call was a bit of a damp squib.

'Please, can we meet?' she asked, after a subdued greeting from her husband. 'We really need to talk.' She could hear the pleading in her voice, but she had put it there deliberately. He had to know how much she wanted to see him.

Devan made her wait for what seemed like a lifetime before he replied. 'I suppose we should.'

Connie made no attempt to hide her joy. 'Great, that's great. Thank you. Where would be good?'

Silence.

'I'm coming up to see the family at the weekend,' he said eventually, sounding as if the words were being pulled from him like teeth.

Connie bit her lip and took a slow breath. His use of the word 'family' was carefully chosen to exclude her, she was well aware. He didn't know that her daughter had purposely arranged for him to be in London . . . *Don't react*, she warned herself, and used a deliberately lighter tone as she replied.

'We could meet in a café? Or you could come to Tessa's? She's not back till Monday, now. It might be a better place to talk.' Tessa had rung to say she was staying in Scotland another few days. In fact, she sounded to Connie as if she were reluctant to come back at all.

'OK,' he said eventually. And Connie let out a breath she seemed to have been holding for a lifetime.

Whatever transpired between them, anything was better than stalemate.

Devan looked both strange and endlessly familiar as he stood on the doorstep at Tessa's house. He was thinner, Connie thought, and seemed older than she remembered, his eyes wary as he greeted her. They didn't kiss or touch each other in any way, just nodded their hellos. He brushed past her as she held open the door and waited silently in the hall.

'Give me your coat,' Connie said, her heart going out to him because he seemed so lost.

She had bought another pie from the deli for lunch, serving it with potatoes and buttered cabbage – Devan loved cabbage – and a good bottle of red wine. The pie was warming, the potatoes boiling, but it would be another fifteen minutes before the meal was ready. Her body was strung tight with nerves – she needed a drink to ease the awkwardness. She waved the Rioja at Devan, her eyebrows raised in question. He nodded his assent and she brought out two glasses, pouring for them both.

'Let's sit by the fire,' she said, taking the armchair and leaving Devan the sofa. 'That's Monty, by the way. Just push him over. I've been looking after him for Tessa and we've become firm friends.' She heard herself being bright and polite and swallowed any more niceties.

He sat down with a heavy sigh, cradling his glass in one hand, not looking at her as he stroked Monty absentmindedly, nudging him onto the other cushion.

Feeling on the back foot, the one who had sinned and therefore had no agency over the proceedings, Connie waited for her husband to speak. But he just sat there, staring into the fire. 'Devan?' she said, already overwrought by the encounter she'd been dreading and dying for in equal measure for three days now. She steadied her breath. 'I've really missed you,' she said quietly.

He looked up, his expression not as hostile as she'd feared. For a moment he didn't reply, just stared at her. Then he said, equally softly, 'I've missed you too.'

Connie wanted to cry. She hadn't expected that. She'd been bracing herself for something altogether more bitter and reproachful. A flood of apologies sat on the tip of her tongue but she held back, knowing the pointlessness of just repeating what she'd said so often before.

'I've been trying to work out if I deserved it.' Devan spoke into the silence. 'I know things weren't great between us these last two years. But was there something else, further back? Something I did that you never mentioned?'

'Of course not,' she said quickly, surprised he should ask.

'So . . . if not, why did you think it was OK to behave in that way . . . destroy all we had together, so carelessly?' His frown was bewildered. 'It was just a bad patch, Connie. Most marriages have them at some point.'

She couldn't look at him. His reasoning, although not the whole story, was painfully valid.

'Please tell me,' he went on, when she didn't immediately answer. 'I need to understand.'

Connie sighed. Then, selecting her words warily, she did her best. 'Why does anyone have an affair, Devan? I can't explain without sounding like I'm excusing my actions, which I'm not. But, as you said, we were in a mess at the time. I suppose I felt detached from you, upset at how you were treating me . . . and flattered that someone else found me attractive.' She gave a small shrug. 'Those tours are like a bubble, not real life.' She stopped. If she told him the real truth, told him how intensely she had desired Jared, she would hurt him beyond repair.

'You know . . .' Devan seemed to be thinking out loud '. . . I *almost* get how you could be lured into bed once. *Almost*. A drunken night, a foreign hotel room, some creep coming on strong, flattering you. And, if so, I need never have known.' He put his glass down and got up, walking towards the fireplace where he leaned on the mantelpiece with both hands, staring down into the flames. Then he turned to her again. 'But more than once, Connie?' His eyes were black with distress as he threw his hands into the air. 'I feel like the biggest fool on the planet. *Dr Mac*, the highly respected village doctor for three decades, just a pathetic cuckold.' He appeared to shiver at the thought.

'Nobody thinks you're a fool, Devan. Anyway, it's none of their business.' She sounded more sanguine than she felt about the village gossip mill. And his sceptical glance showed he wasn't taken in. She didn't know what to say. Didn't know what she *could* say that would change things for him. His next words, delivered in a dull monotone, made it perfectly clear.

'You still haven't told me about the sex.'

'Don't,' she said, lowering her face from his anguished gaze.

But, like a dog with a bone, he wasn't about to let it go. Standing uncertainly now, his palms rubbing up and down the sides of his jeans, he looked like a small boy. 'Please, Connie. I need to know . . . I can't move on . . . It's driving me mad.'

Her face was already flushed from the wine, so any blush would barely have shown. But she did not blush. Being reminded of those nights now was like watching a movie starring another woman. She was no longer remotely aroused by the memory. She sighed.

He waited dumbly, crossing his arms as if bracing himself for the blow.

'OK, if you insist.' She hesitated, cringing with reluctance. But however badly it turned out, she had to carry on or the question would keep being regurgitated, like kippers for breakfast. 'It was . . . exciting, I admit. It was secret. You and I hadn't made love for years. He made me feel sexy again.' Her sentences were bald. There was no hint in her voice of the trembling desire that had existed between her and her lover.

Devan's face remained shuttered and still. As if he were expecting more. As if what she'd said was not painful enough. Her answer was, indeed, unsatisfactory, merely stating the obvious. *He must already have worked this out for himself*, she thought. And any further revelations were out of the question. She wished she knew how to help him, wished she could soothe his painful obsession somehow. But she was as much of a novice as he when it came to mending such a dire betrayal of trust.

Before he had a chance to insist on more, she continued, 'Jared's still stalking me. I know you don't believe I had nothing to do with him appearing in the village, but he's followed me here too. Or found me, I don't know which. He stole my hat and gloves, sneaked ravioli into my shopping, dropped by on Christmas Eve . . .' Connie hadn't meant to tell him about Jared's visit, fearing that it would only inflame things further. The words just slipped out in her desperation to divert him from the issue of sex.

Devan was clearly confused. 'Ravioli? What are you talking about, Connie? Wait . . . you say he's been *here*? In this house?' His eyes widened. 'You let him in?'

'No, of course not.' Noting the instant suspicion in his eyes, she gave a brief account of what had happened.

'Christ, why did you indulge him, even on the doorstep?' he said, when she'd finished. 'It's like you feel sorry for the creep.' His voice was dull with anger. 'I can't believe you haven't called the police. The bastard should be fucking arrested.'

Connie was aware of a hissing coming from the kitchen and got up. The potatoes were boiling over, the starchy water pooling around the burners. She turned the heat down. Looking at Devan, she said, 'And say what? That someone I know is hanging about, buying me gloves and ravioli?'

'He doesn't have to do those things stalkers usually do – like constant messaging or damaging property or violence – with the new stalking laws. Believe me, Connie, I've checked it out. Even just following someone, watching them, if they do it persistently and you don't like it, is against the law and could end in a fine or a jail sentence, certainly a restraining order.' He frowned at her. 'Why won't you do anything to stop him?'

She hesitated, wondering if Devan was right. 'It's not that I'm dragging my feet. It's just . . . well, I'd feel idiotic trying to explain to the police. What he does is so nebulous, so hard to pin down. He moves in near us, but everyone likes him, welcomes him. *You* like him. Where's the proof that he's stalking? He might have just liked our village – plenty do. There are no texts or anything concrete. The ravioli could be interpreted in lots of ways. You know how plausible, how *polite* Jared is . . . and so far he hasn't harmed me . . . not physically, anyway. Although he seemed pretty crazy the other night.'

Devan was back on the sofa. He looked at her with sudden concern. 'Thank God you didn't let him in,' he said.

She nodded, grateful for the sign that he still cared about her safety. The atmosphere between them had changed. They were, temporarily at least, on the same side.

'Where is he now?'

'I've no idea. And I have no idea how he found me here. His godmother lives on the other side of the Heath, but unless he just happened to spot me . . . I don't know, Devan, he's like a phantom. Comes and goes at will. And every time I talk to him, I fool myself that this time I've found a way to convince him.'

Devan frowned. 'You think he might be out there right now, watching you?'

'No . . . Well, I don't know. Maybe . . .' As she spoke she felt the accumulative tension from Jared's relentless, sinister presence hit her, like a truck. Clutching the bottle from which she'd been about to fill Devan's glass, she began to cry. The sobs were savage, choking her. She gasped for breath, the wine sloshing dangerously.

Devan was on his feet in an instant, prising the bottle from her clenched fist and pulling her instinctively into a strong embrace. She had the chance to catch his familiar scent, feel his arms around her for a painfully lovely second. But the moment was over all too soon and she felt him pull back, as if he'd touched an electric fence. Despair returned. *It would have been better if he'd never hugged me at all*, she thought. The tantalizing moment of closeness made the rift between them seem all the more unbearable.

During a muted, often silent lunch, they talked about the family, about Christmas. Even the nightmare of recent politics seemed preferable to talking any more about the problem of Jared – to which there was no obvious solution – or opening up about how they were both really feeling. Connie was dying to ask, 'Where do we go from here? Can you ever forgive me?' But she didn't dare, in case his answers were not the ones she wanted to hear. *He's here*, she kept telling herself. *At least he's here.*

It was getting dark outside, the pie had been eaten, the wine and coffee drunk. She felt exhausted – it would be a relief when her husband left. The pressure of his wretchedness was wearing her down and she had no idea how to alleviate it. Although the day, on the whole, had been so much better than she'd feared.

Devan got up from the table. He looked drained, too. But his manner was edgy suddenly as he stood there, blinking hard, his hands so deep in the pockets of his cords it was as if he wanted to thrust his fists through the cotton.

'I'd better get going,' he muttered, then hesitated. His gaze, when he brought it to focus on her, was unreadable. 'I only came here today because Caty persuaded me to – for the sake of the family. For me, personally, I didn't know how I could face you.' He breathed in deeply. 'But as soon as I saw you, I realized how much I've missed you. And that makes me absolutely bloody, fucking *furious*.' She watched him snatch a breath, her own heart hammering at his attack. 'Because I don't know how to get past all this. I don't know if I'll ever be able to trust you again.' His voice was heavy with devastation. 'My beautiful Connie in someone else's arms . . . It breaks my heart.' He took a gasping sob.

Trembling, she got up. Devan was angrily brushing tears from his cheeks with his palms. 'Devan, please . . .' she said softly.

He glared at her, but the light of fury was fading now and she saw only a weary sadness in his eyes. Emboldened, she walked round the table before she'd had time to consider the possible consequences and circled him in her arms. Devan did not respond at first, just stood there, like the solid, unyielding trunk of a tree. He began to cry softly, his head gradually sinking to her shoulder, his arms slowly wrapping round her body. They stood there, two exhausted and traumatized people, clinging together for what seemed like a lifetime. She didn't feel safe or comforted, though, as she always had in Devan's embrace. It was as if they represented to each other the upturned hull of a shipwrecked boat – a slim chance of survival. *If I let him go*, she thought, *we might both drown.*

'I hate feeling like this . . . so much,' he said, when he finally lifted his head.

'I hate it too. These have been the worst weeks of my life.'

She waited for a sneering riposte. But Devan merely nodded as they gradually loosened their grip on each other.

Seeing him to the door, watching him slowly buttoning his coat, she held her breath in the hope that he would say something about seeing her again. At the last minute, he turned to her: 'We can talk on the phone?'

She nodded, gave him a smile. He frowned, then his

face cleared and he smiled back. It was a drained smile, but their eyes met. It was the connection she'd been longing for. A kiss or a hug was more than she could expect, but his smile was enough for now.

As soon as the door was closed and locked behind him, Connie flopped down on the sofa and took great gulping breaths, as if for the first time since Devan's arrival. She felt battered, but there had been some progress, she thought. Worn out, she fell into a numb, bone-weary sleep. It was two sharp beeps of an incoming text that woke her a couple of hours later. Not, as she hoped, from her husband. But Caitlin's message was almost as good: *Seems like things went well with Dad. He's looking so much better! Talk when he's gone home tomorrow xxx*

32

'I'm going to miss you,' Tessa said, as Connie dragged her wheelie-case up the stairs from her bedroom into the hall. 'You know you're welcome any time. For a weekend or if you need a bolthole again.'

Connie gave a wry smile. 'My life's so bloody bonkers, these days – anything's possible.' She hugged her friend tight. 'I can't thank you enough, Tess. You've been my absolute saviour. I genuinely don't know where I'd be now without your incredibly generous hospitality.'

Tessa brushed off Connie's thanks. 'You did *me* a huge favour too. I was so dreading the first Christmas without Martin, and your being here in the run-up was the perfect diversion.'

'Nothing like the McCabe soap opera . . .'

Tessa's face fell. 'Are you and Devan going to be all right?'

Connie shrugged. 'We've been talking a lot. Sometimes it seems almost like old times, and we begin to relax with each other. Then other times, one of us says something, or remembers something, and it's like the temperature drops by ten degrees. We fall apart.'

Tessa gave her another hug. 'Well, stick in there. It'll be worth it in the long run.'

Connie knew she was right. But the effort she and Devan had to make to get back on track seemed sometimes insurmountable. There was a long road ahead on which she knew she would have to tiptoe round her husband's hurt without a fuss. It was Connie who was on the back foot, and she accepted that. She had apologized so many times it was becoming almost comical. The apologies were heartfelt, but they appeared to be having no effect. Devan seemed to be waiting for her to say something in particular that would finally expunge his anguish. But she knew there was only one thing that might eventually do that: time.

Then one day in mid-January, two weeks after they'd begun talking, Devan had thrown something out, almost casually, at the end of his nightly phone call. 'You can't stay at Tessa's for ever, presumably?'

Connie had known immediately what he was really asking. It was a balancing act, though. She didn't want to push him. Or seem needy. Part of her was extremely anxious at the thought of going home, having to walk on eggshells, the imbalance his constant hurt would bring to their relationship. There would be village gossip to contend with, as well. But she longed with every bone in her body to be home again. 'No,' she replied. 'She says I can stay as long as I like, but she's just being kind.'

There was silence. Connie waited.

'I'm thinking of coming up at the weekend,' Devan said, with the same studied nonchalance. 'If you think it's a good idea, I could pick you up on the way back?'

After a moment's hesitation, Connie said, 'I'd like that.'

And there it was. No drama. Nothing really said. Nothing conceded. Just a tentative invitation to start again. She found, as she clicked off from Devan's call, that a huge weight had been lifted from her shoulders. Whatever the problems to come, Devan had shown her that he still loved her. That, despite all that had happened, he wanted her back.

Riley would not leave her side. His frenzied barking and leaping and tail wagging had been the best reception she could have wished for. It broke the ice between her and Devan too – the car journey home being a polite, mostly silent affair – and made them both laugh harder than the situation merited. A welcome release of tension. Connie felt an almost euphoric surge of hope as she rubbed her hand over Riley's coat. *Home*, she thought. *I'm home at last.*

They got fish and chips for supper. Devan lit a candle and placed it on the kitchen table. He produced a bottle of Prosecco from the fridge. There was a general air of quiet excitement between them as they ate. Connie wanted to know all the local gossip and Devan obliged, exaggerating his stories to make her laugh. His smile was the most charming, his blue eyes, as they rested on her, the most beguiling. All of it felt right . . . but also excruciating to Connie, in that she couldn't trust how long the current mood would last.

Where will I sleep? she wondered, as she took another

gulp of wine. *Will we have sex?* The notion, which in the past would have been so welcome, seemed like a huge hurdle to leap right now, knowing the images that currently plagued Devan's mind. Fuelled by the alcohol, however, she was in the mood to push through, ignore Jared's shade, and make love to her husband tonight, sleep in his arms. If they didn't do it now, maybe they never would.

As time wore on, tired as she was, she avoided being the one to suggest they go up. But the evening began to lose its sparkle and eventually they fell silent, both, she imagined, faced with the same dilemma.

Devan finally stood up, blew out the candle. He began sweeping the chip bags and remains of the battered fish and mushy peas into the paper carrier bag from the fish shop, screwing it up tightly and throwing it into the black bin. Connie, from habit, was about to protest that the paper should be recycled, but she held her tongue. Planet survival was not her main concern tonight.

She got up, too, and returned the ketchup and malt vinegar to the cupboard, cleared away the glasses. The stems were too long to fit into the dishwasher so she rinsed them in the sink, resting them upside down on a tea towel on the draining-board. All in silence. Her heart was beating raggedly. Unable to bear the tension a moment longer, she swung round. Devan was fiddling with his phone, plugging it into the charger on the ledge by the kitchen door. Resting her hands on the counter-top behind her, she said, 'What now?' It wasn't meant to sound aggressive, but she feared it had come out that way.

Her husband looked up, his expression hard to read. He gazed at her but didn't reply. Connie pushed herself away from the worktop and went over to him. She was shaky and unsure, her confidence waning in the face of his continued silence. 'Do you want me to sleep in the spare room?' she asked quietly.

He bit his lip. She felt his indecision stretching between them, like an unfolding yardstick, pushing them further and further apart. 'Probably best if I do,' she added quietly.

Devan nodded, but still seemed paralysed. She turned away, only to feel his grip tight on her arm, swinging her around. Before she had a chance to catch her breath, he was kissing her. His mouth was fierce, but she welcomed it. Welcomed, too, his hands pulling her across the hall to the sitting room, to the sofa, where they fell in a heap, tearing at each other's clothes. She was aware of his fast, rasping breath, his hands rough against her breasts, his knees pushing her legs apart. She cried out, wanting him so desperately it felt as if her life depended upon it.

They were quiet afterwards. The room had grown chilly, the heating gone off long since. Devan pulled the throw over them as they lay in each other's arms. Connie felt tearful. This was only the beginning – she had no foolish illusions. But the sex had proved something. Not love, not forgiveness, not even lust, but something bigger than all three at this juncture: a mutual desire to break down the barriers between them. For Connie, it was enough.

Connie found she was thinking less and less about Jared. In the early days at home, Devan was her entire focus. She ignored the question of why someone as obsessed – and mentally unhinged – as Jared would suddenly decide to throw in the towel and leave her alone. If he came back into her life now, she would go straight to the police. She and Devan would go together. The power he'd wielded so successfully in the past no longer scared her.

The village – in true English fashion – pretended on the surface that nothing had happened. But Connie was insecure as she began to show her face in the streets, the shops and cafés. A glance here, a nod there, a whispered exchange between two people, all were salacious titbits about her and Jared in her paranoid mind. And perhaps in reality, too. She had to brace herself every day, before going out.

Devan, previously so conscious of his perceived humiliation, seemed almost bullish by comparison. He had her by his side again, and that seemed protection enough against the gossip. 'Fuck 'em,' he said, when she expressed a reluctance to go to the pub. 'It's none of their bloody business.'

'I'm meeting Neil for a coffee,' she announced, ten days after she'd returned home. She was dying to see her friend, to spill the crazy patchwork of her emotional highs and lows to someone who would understand. Because her reunion with Devan, buoyed up by initial delight in the knowledge that they really did belong together, was not plain sailing. Not that she had expected it to be. The gilt was already wearing off the gingerbread: he seemed not to want her out of his sight.

'Where are you going?' Devan was instantly anxious.

'Angie's.'

'Will you be long?'

'Oh, you know me and Neil . . . gossip for Britain, us.' She was making light, smoothing the sudden tension.

'It's just if you're taking the car, I need to know when you'll be back. I've got stuff to do.' He sounded tense.

'OK. One o'clock, then?'

Devan glanced at the kitchen clock, frowned. 'Two hours for a coffee?'

'I haven't seen him since before Christmas . . .'

'Right.' He shot her a sardonic smile. 'Lot to catch up on, then.'

Connie chose to ignore his jibe. 'Come with me? Neil's your friend too.'

Devan pursed his lips. 'Think I'll pass. I might clog the airwaves.'

'I'll give him your love.'

'You could do,' he said.

She was unable to decide whether he was being sarcastic or not, but she didn't go there. If she was insecure, then her husband had every right to feel the same. But she knew if his constant questioning of where she was going and what she was doing continued, it would drive her mad.

Connie and Neil gave each other the longest hug. She felt it was the first time she could truly relax since the moment when Devan had picked her up from Tessa's house.

'No wonder you look frazzled,' Neil said, once they were settled with their coffee and she'd caught him up with her bizarre Christmas.

She grinned. 'Thanks.' A group of mums, babies in buggies and toddlers running about the tables, were chatting and laughing loudly, making quite a din, but she barely noticed.

'So how's it going, now you're back in the old homestead?'

'Up and down. It's difficult for Devan, I get that, but he does give me quite a hard time here and there.' She let out a long sigh. 'I don't really mind. I'm just so pleased to be home, Neil. And I know I deserve –'

'Stop!' Neil held up his palm like a traffic cop. 'Old news, darling. You've done your penance. Got to move on.'

She laughed wearily. 'Devan's not going to forget, though, is he?'

'It's more a case of absorbing than forgetting. Jed was part of your and Devan's life. Nothing's going to change that. But you can absorb him, now he's not an issue any more. Reduce him to just a thread in a long and steadfast marriage. You should both be proud of how you've survived.'

'When did you get to be so wise about infidelity?'

He raised his eyebrows slightly.

She frowned. 'You . . . *Brooks?* Surely not.'

Neil cleared his throat noncommittally.

'When? Why in God's name didn't you tell me, Neil?'

'Same reason you didn't tell me about Jared, I expect.' He waved a dismissive hand. 'It was one night. Years ago. We're long over it.'

Before she could take in what Neil was saying, or question him further, he was asking, 'So where's our beloved stalker now?'

'No idea. I'm telling myself he's gone for good. Which I'm trying to believe.' It was true that she hadn't sensed anything eerie or strange since being back, glimpsed no shape, no face, no image she thought might be his. The village seemed like a haven after the London streets, which she'd felt had actually vibrated with his presence.

Neil looked sceptical. 'He's finally given up? Do stalkers do that?' When she didn't immediately reply, he went on, as if she were challenging the label. 'He might fall short on the bunny-boiling cred, but he's definitely a stalker, Con.'

'Yeah, OK. It doesn't really matter what he is or isn't, does it? He's out of my life now.' Connie was irritated that Neil was making her focus on Jared, prodding the worry, like a child with a stick, that he might reappear. She wasn't sure her marriage would stand it. Devan had kicked off again yesterday.

381

They'd been walking in single file in the woods with Riley. It was a gorgeous late January day, almost hot in the sunshine. Connie was feeling good, until Devan, gazing straight ahead as they crested the hill, had re-opened the wound.

'Couldn't you see, right from the off, that there was something creepy about Jared?' he asked, sounding pained. 'Turning up like that at your hotels without you telling him where you were would have sounded loud alarm bells to me.'

Connie forbore to remind Devan that he hadn't found Jared the least bit 'creepy' when he'd met him. Neither could she let on that at the time it had felt exciting, flattering. 'The information's all on the website,' she replied. 'It was just a game for him, I suppose.'

'And you, Connie? Was it a game for you, too?' The bitterness was back, acrid as burned coffee. 'Way more fun than hanging out with your grumpy old man back home, I imagine.'

She stopped, taking a moment before she replied, anger churning in her gut, replacing, for once, the relentless guilt. 'Well,' she said, squaring up to him, arms akimbo in the winter sunlight, 'there is some truth in that, if I'm absolutely honest.' She saw him flinch. 'At some stage, Devan, you're going to have to stop bloody picking at this scab or we'll never move forward.'

She shocked herself with her uncompromising tone, and she had clearly shocked her husband. He looked at her aghast. 'You're making this *my* fault?'

'That isn't what I said. But listen to this: I withdraw pretty much all of the warmth, kindness, even sex from our marriage. I stop showering or dressing in clean clothes, drink too much and slump on my phone all day long, refusing any offers of help. I go on at you to give up something you love that you aren't ready to give up,' she took a breath, 'and outwardly question where our marriage is going.' Another breath. 'Would you be understanding and endlessly patient? Or might you be as childish as me, feel rejected, unconfident . . . and vulnerable to the first woman who seemed to admire you?' She was shaking, but she was shaking with relief. At last she'd said what she had not dared say, what had been festering in her mind for weeks now. 'Don't think I'm letting myself off the hook,' she added quietly, 'but there's only so much guilt a person can feel, so many times a person can apologize, without any sign they've been heard.'

Looking indignant, but also a bit punctured, Devan replied, 'I asked you to come home, didn't I?'

'Yes, and I'm so happy you did. But think about what I said.'

His face was set stubbornly. Then it fell, his body seeming to lose its strength as he slumped over, hugging his arms around his chest.

'I honestly thought you didn't love me any more,' she added, more gently.

Devan's face suffused with anguish. 'Oh, Connie. Of course I loved you. *I love you*. I've never stopped. Not even when I found out about Jared. I hated you, too, then. I never wanted to see you again. But I never stopped loving you.'

Connie, tears in her eyes, had just nodded.

Now, sitting opposite Neil, she brushed away the memory as she tried to concentrate on what he was saying.

'You should treat yourselves, Con. Get away somewhere warm for a few days. Change the record, change things up with your marriage. You've always been such a strong team – that still holds true, doesn't it?'

'Maybe,' she said diffidently, which caused Neil to frown.

'You do still love the man, don't you?'

Tears filled her eyes. 'Oh, God, yes. I love him so much.' She blinked. 'It's just . . .' Seeing Neil's face, she knew what he was going to say. 'I know, I know, give it bloody time. I haven't got any choice, have I? But it's so hard waiting for that moment when he looks at me again like he always used to – and it's just him and me . . . no Jared.' She was trying to control her wobbling mouth. 'I just don't know if that moment will ever come.'

33

The roof terrace was cool in the early-morning sun, which shone from a bright blue cloudless sky. Looking over the parapet, Connie had a breathtaking view across the city, the tower of the beautiful Moorish minaret sticking up above the flat red-brown Marrakech roofs dotted with satellite dishes, the Atlas Mountains on the distant horizon.

Connie and Devan, fresh from a swim in the chilly hotel pool, reclined in their white robes on rough-weave red and orange striped cushions. They sipped golden juice and strong coffee, ate hot fried eggs nestling in spicy tomato sauce, yoghurt and coriander, into which they were dipping chunks of crusty white bread.

'Heaven,' Connie pronounced, her mouth full.

She had taken Neil's advice and gone straight home to speak to Devan. 'We never got around to organizing that break we talked about last year. I think we need it now. Can you take a week off from the hospice?' It had opened in early January and Devan clearly loved working there.

He'd said he was sure he could, but had stipulated, 'Anything but a train tour,' with a sardonic grin.

And, so far, it had been a success. Neither of them had been to Morocco before. There were no memories, no associations. The hotel was beautiful, their room a vibrant pink and soft green, the bed huge, with capacious pink velvet armchairs to sit in and polished patterned tiles beneath their bare feet. Connie, despite all her travelling, had never stayed anywhere so elegant and luxurious.

In the five days they were there, they made lazy explorations of the medina, the souk, the famous Koutoubia Mosque. By night they ate harira soup, ordered tagines with fluffy couscous in local cafés, or ate on the hotel terrace at small wrought-iron tables. But the greater part of each day they just sat in the sunshine, utterly exhausted by the nightmare of previous months. Their chat was all about the city, the sights, the food, the hotel, the books they were reading, neither of them willing to ruin the time away with more rows and recriminations. It felt like a fragile peace, but peace, nonetheless.

Connie, however, hadn't managed to relax as much as she'd hoped since leaving the safety of the village. She couldn't entirely stop herself scrutinizing the passengers on the plane, the other guests, checking the faces in the busy medina, glancing about her in the narrow alleyways of the souk. A gift of dates, nuts and little oranges left in a dainty latticework dish on their bed set her heart racing. She kept her phone off at night, in case – ridiculously – there was a text saying he was outside the bedroom door. But there was no sign of him.

She put this unease partly down to something that

had happened on the day of their departure, although she did her best to push it to the back of her mind. As they left the house at four in the morning for their seven-thirty flight, she had noticed a little posy of snowdrops tied with string lying on the top of the low wall beside the house. The beam of her phone torch picked it out as she made her way to the car. *Anyone could have left it there*, she told herself firmly. Most likely a passing child had dropped it the day before, although it had been raining hard all night and the flowers looked fresh.

She'd found herself racking her brain as Devan drove in bleary-eyed silence to Bristol airport, trying to remember whether Jared had ever mentioned snowdrops, whether he might have thought they held any sort of significance for her. Nothing sprang to mind, but the old churning unease was set in motion once more. It made her want to weep with frustration. Would it ever end, this constant niggling, exhausting vigilance?

'I still don't get it,' Devan said, early on the morning of their last day. He was sitting propped up against the pillows, the light filtering through the half-open shutters dappling his face and naked chest. Connie was curled on her side, watching him sleepily, but his tone alerted her. She felt her body tense. 'I know I've got at you for not sussing Jared out earlier, but I was the same. I liked him. He really did seem . . . *normal*. He could have been a friend. How could we both have got it so wrong?'

This was the first time Jared's name had been mentioned on the holiday and it felt like something of a relief to Connie, despite her anxiety as to where the discussion might lead: as the days had gone on, the elephant still sitting in the room had been growing bigger and bigger in the silence. Devan was staring down at her with bewilderment. 'And he genuinely seemed to want my friendship, Connie – however twisted that might be. I think he was quite lonely.'

She pulled herself up to sit against the headboard, surprised at this sudden softening towards Jared. 'I reckon he did like you,' she said cautiously. 'You and the others were important to him – aside from how he felt about me. He didn't want me to tell you, to blow it all apart.'

Devan's mouth twisted and he let out a long sigh. 'Bonkers and utterly delusional to think that could work, but I suppose he just wanted to be part of the gang.' There was a pause. 'I'd still wring his neck, if I ever saw him again,' he added, a rancorous note entering his voice. But the bile obvious in previous similar comments was not quite so evident.

Connie reached for his hand and squeezed it. He returned the squeeze, then took his hand away and put it around her, pulling her close. They lay against the pillows in the dappled sunlight for a long time. There seemed no tension between them now. The silence was not loaded. His fingers stroking her bare arm were gentle and loving. A tiny orange-brown bird appeared at the open window, its head darting inquisitively to and fro. Connie watched it for a while, then closed her eyes, nestling into her husband's chest. She felt, even if just for this tiny, blissful moment, as if the barriers were down and it was just the two of them again. As if they had finally let Jared go.

It was raining and blowy as they drove home from the airport, the February night chilly. As Connie stared through the spattered windscreen at the blur of passing headlights, she felt a spurt of hope. Something had shifted between them since they had driven along the same road five days earlier. 'Change things up,' Neil had advised, and Connie sensed they might have done just that.

She looked forward to seeing Riley, who was staying with Bill and Jill until tomorrow. Looked forward to being able to think about ordinary things again, like making the annual batch of marmalade, catching up with her friends, clearing out the spare room, which had become a dumping ground over the past eighteen months. But what she most looked forward to was just waking up in the morning and not thinking of Jared.

Now that she was beginning to feel free of his hovering presence, she realized what a toll it had taken on her. She'd always been optimistic, equable, someone who enjoyed life to the full. Jared had reduced her to a neurotic mess. She cried easily now, her tears always close to the surface, and felt fragile, fearful in a way she never had before. As if she'd lost a layer of skin.

Morocco had been good, but now she wanted nothing more than to hole up at home with Devan and

Riley, stay in the safe confines of the village with a few close friends. Physically, she was always tired, these days, often the victim of headaches and sleepless nights. Jared had made her feel young at first. Now, because of him, she felt so much older than her years.

The house was lovely and warm when they arrived home. Jill had been in to turn the heating on. She'd left milk in the fridge with a shepherd's pie from a local home-made range and a bag of salad. The note on the kitchen table said, 'Welcome home. Brunch at ours in the morning? We're keeping Riley for ever, btw! xxx'

Connie laughed. 'Sounds like that dog's been on a charm offensive.'

Devan yawned. 'Let's get the pie in and have a glass of wine. I'm starving.' It was a long time since breakfast at the hotel, the sandwiches on offer on the plane spectacularly unappealing after the delicious food they'd been enjoying in Marrakech.

They ate mostly in a companionable silence, both tired from the journey. Connie kept glancing at her husband, checking his demeanour to see if, now they were home and in surroundings that might spark a bitter memory, he would continue to be relaxed. But she couldn't detect any sign of tension in his tanned face, so far. In fact, she thought he looked better than he had for a long, long time.

Coming out of the bathroom later, toothbrush in hand, Devan said, 'Did you hear that?'

Connie frowned. 'No – what?'

'I thought I heard a thump.' He pointed his tooth-brush to the ceiling, above which was the attic, used exclusively for storage and accessed by drop-down steps from the landing ceiling.

'It'll be the wind. The window up there's always been loose and it's blowing a bloody gale outside,' Connie said, as she got into bed.

He shrugged, went back into the bathroom. When he slid in beside her a few minutes later, he was looking preoccupied. 'Maybe we've got mice,' he said. 'I'll go up and check in the morning.'

They lay together, Devan tucking his length into Connie's curled body, his arm across her shoulders. He dropped a kiss on the side of her head. 'That was a great holiday, Con,' he said.

She turned her face to his. 'It really was.' She snuggled into her soft, familiar pillow, wrapping the duvet cosily round her neck, aware of the comforting warmth of Devan's body. She sank into sleep with a deep sense of contentment, gratitude for her husband, and her life.

Something nudged Connie from sleep. Blinking, she saw the clock display read 1:34. She rolled over onto her back and peered into the semi-darkness of the room, wondering what had woken her. Then she froze, her every fibre buzzing, instantly on high alert. She could just make out a figure, looming in the shadows at the end of the bed. She gave a loud gasp, lurching upright, the duvet clutched to herself in alarm.

Paralysed with fear, she managed to reach out a hand and violently shake her husband, her eyes still fixed on the dark intruder, who said nothing, just stood there, stock still.

Devan shifted, mumbled, 'What?'

She shook him again. '*Wake up, for Christ's sake.*'

This time he heard her. He turned over and jumped when he, too, caught sight of the shadowy form, cursing as he fumbled for the bedside lamp.

Jared blinked in the light. 'I'm sorry,' he said quietly.

Her husband leaped out of bed. '*What the fuck?*' His body rigid with tension, he hovered, fixing Jared with a wary stare, but clearly not sure what to do next. Glancing at Connie, he discreetly patted his hand down by his side as if to say, 'Tread carefully.' It occurred to her that he thought Jared might be armed.

'I needed to be here.' Jared spoke again. 'I hope you understand, Connie.' He was dressed in jeans and a navy polo-neck sweater, but his normally smoothed-back hair was flopping over his face and he clearly hadn't shaved in a while. He was kneading his fingers together in front of him.

Connie was trembling so much she could barely get the words out, but she spoke as calmly as possible. 'What are you doing, Jared?'

Devan began to edge round the bed, his eyes fixed firmly on the intruder. She watched, hardly breathing. The air in the room seemed to vibrate. 'Don't . . .' she whispered to her husband, terrified that Jared might pull out a knife.

As Devan got closer, Jared held up his hands to fend him off, backing against the door.

'Please, I'm not going to harm you,' he said, twisting his palms to and fro in the air, as if to prove he didn't have a weapon. 'I just . . .' He stopped and seemed disoriented for a moment. Looking pleadingly at Connie, he said, 'Can we talk?'

Devan, ignoring his request, pushed him aside and reached for the door. But it was firmly locked. 'Where's the key?' Devan demanded.

Jared shrugged, blinked. 'Do you know how important you are to me? Both of you. You've been so kind –'

Her husband cursed and swung round, shouting, 'Ring the police!' When she didn't immediately move, he added, '*Now*, Connie!'

Hardly daring to tear her eyes from the two men, she scrabbled blindly for her mobile on the nightstand, but it wasn't there. She lunged frantically across the bed for Devan's, forgetting in her panic that he always left his charging in the kitchen overnight. There was no landline in the bedroom any more. 'My phone's not here,' she said, her voice shrill in the silent room. It had been, she was sure, when she went to bed. She always kept it by her in case Caitlin ever needed them in the middle of the night.

'I took it,' Jared said simply. 'I don't want the police.'

His words were beginning to slur oddly and Devan eyed him closely. 'Have you been drinking?'

Jared shook his head, his gaze on Connie again, yearning and desperate. 'I thought we meant something to each other, Connie. You and I, we were a team, weren't we? I thought . . . I thought . . .' He shook his head as if to clear it and began to move towards the bed. But Devan put a hand firmly on his chest and pushed him roughly back against the door. 'Stay where you are,' he barked, as he ran his hands down Jared's body, searching his pockets for the door key or a mobile – and obviously finding nothing.

Jared passively allowed Devan to rummage, but his eyes never left Connie's face. 'I thought you felt the same . . . that connection.' He shot her the facsimile of a flirtatious smile, a pale imitation of the charming one with which he had wooed her back in the Italian lakes. 'It was special, no? You and me . . . Remember that night . . .'

Connie froze. *No*, she begged silently. *Please, no.*

Devan had taken him by the shoulders and was looking intently into his eyes. 'Christ, you stupid bastard . . . You've taken something, haven't you?'

Jared didn't reply, just stared blankly at him, eyelids flickering.

'What is it? What the fuck have you taken?' Devan shouted, face inches from Jared's, shaking him so his body thudded back and forth against the solid oak door.

Jared just closed his eyes. Devan gave him a final shake, then let him go with a frustrated curse. Jared hovered for a moment, then slid slowly down the wall until he was slumped, half sitting, head lolling to one side.

Devan began wildly rattling the door handle. Connie was up now, pulling on the jeans and sweater she'd worn on the plane. She went over to the two men, looking down at Jared as he lay collapsed on the floor. 'You think it's an overdose?'

'Fucking door. Can't get any purchase on it,' Devan said, banging it violently with the flat of his hands in frustration. Then he growled, 'Yes, he's taken something. Though God knows what.'

Connie bent and laid a hand on Jared's shoulder. At her touch, he seemed to come to, focusing his gaze on her again. 'I'm sorry. I'm really sorry to put you in this position,' he repeated grabbing her hand. 'I just can't live without you, Connie.'

She was shaking and speechless as she tried to wrench her hand away. But his grip was like a vice.

'I want to die . . . with you.' Tears filled his turquoise eyes – eyes she had found so beguiling in those moments that now seemed from another world. 'Will you let me? Will you stay with me, Connie?' He slid further to the side. 'Don't get help. Please . . . no help . . .'

Connie looked across at Devan, who had given up on the door and was staring at Jared, breathing heavily, an unreadable expression on his face

'OK,' her husband said, giving a cool shrug. 'If that's what you want. You've caused enough fucking trouble.' He turned away.

Connie was stunned. 'For Christ's sake, Devan. We have to *do something*. We can't just sit here and watch him die.'

Her husband flopped down onto the bed, the back he presented to the room rigid. 'What the hell else can we do? He's trapped us in here ... And it's what he wants. He just said so.'

Quickly stepping over the recumbent body, she hurried round the bed and stood looking down on Devan's dark head. 'Stop it. Don't talk like that. You're a doctor, for heaven's sake – there must be something you can do.'

Devan glared up at her. 'There's nothing, Con. And why the fuck should I care, anyway? This creep has ruined our lives.'

For a split second, she allowed herself the thought. Finally, to be free. No longer having to look over her shoulder or place sinister significance in the most trivial things. To be able to rest in the knowledge that Jared would no longer haunt her every waking thought. She took a faltering breath. Laying her hands on Devan's shoulder, she shook him till he lifted his bowed head. 'We have at least to try to help him,' she said, with quiet strength.

After a second, Devan seemed to come to, his anger morphing into a dazed frown. 'How can we? Like I said, the bastard's locked us in, removed all means of communication.' He glanced around the room, shaking his head. 'We could stand at the window and shout, I suppose. But on a night like this, who would hear? There's only Mrs Browne next door and she's stone deaf.'

It was true. The house on the other side was a holiday let and empty at this time of year. The Methodist hall and a small car park were across the street. Stacy, on the corner, was the closest and he was completely out of earshot.

Connie looked desperately at Jared. His eyes were closed and he seemed to be having trouble breathing, his chest heaving ominously.

'He has to stay awake,' she heard Devan muttering, almost to himself. He got up, taking Connie by the shoulders, his gaze intense. 'But he needs professional help. Nothing will make any difference in the long run, unless we get him to hospital . . . *right now.*'

They stared at each other helplessly, panic and shock mirrored in their eyes. 'OK,' Devan decided. 'You try to rouse him. I'm going to climb out of the window. It's our only chance.' He strode over to the window and ripped back the curtains. They were on the first floor, and the paned sash window of the old house was small, stiff in the frame – they rarely opened it more than a foot. Outside, it was a drop of around fifteen feet to the ground.

'No,' Connie cried out. 'You'll never fit through.' It was also true that she couldn't face being left alone with Jared, maybe watching as he gave up his hold on life. Devan was much better qualified, anyway. 'I'll go. You deal with him.' She went over and pushed her husband out of the way.

He hesitated for a second. 'Are you sure?'

She didn't reply. She was terrified, but also driven as she twisted the lock and yanked open the window. Cold wind rushed in, a welcome breath of air after the heavy, fraught atmosphere in the room. She knelt on the windowsill and put one leg gingerly out into the night, squeezing her body through the gap, hanging on for dear life to the sill.

'Take my hands,' she heard Devan say. 'I can lower you.'

Balancing half in, half out, and loath to let go of the sill, she managed, nonetheless, to grab one of her husband's outstretched hands, then, after a moment, the other. She took a deep breath as she slipped her other leg outside. Her bare feet scrabbled at the wet brick as she hung there, clinging to Devan's strong grip as he leaned out, lowering her slowly towards the ground. She looked down. There was a ledge above the sitting-room window, but it was just out of reach and too narrow to hold her weight anyway. Paralysed, she cowered as rain lashed cold on her back, the wind blowing her hair across her face so she couldn't see. *Jump*, she urged herself. *Jump – it's not far.* But she couldn't.

Devan's voice cut through the storm, steady and reassuring. 'It's OK, Connie, you can do it.' She felt her hands – soaked with rain – sliding in his, her grip weakening. There was no choice: the strain on her arm sockets was unbearable. Her fingers finally broke free and she fell.

The impact knocked the breath out of her. Pain shot through her right ankle as she tried to stand, but she was in one piece and inhaled a huge breath of relief. 'I'm OK,' she shouted up.

Devan waved. 'Hurry,' he yelled back, and his head disappeared.

In their haste, they hadn't discussed the next step. She tried to think. She didn't have her keys, but maybe she could break a pane in the kitchen door? But it was bolted top and bottom. Oblivious to the pain shooting up her leg, she hobbled as quickly as she could along the wet pavement to the pub. Even if Stacy and Nicole were asleep, their two Alsatians would bark for Britain – that was their job.

Connie shouted the publican's name over and over, pounding on the heavy, varnished oak. Almost immediately she heard the dogs barking, scrabbling frantically on the other side. She held her breath. '*Please,*' she begged out loud, '*please, Stacy, wake up.*'

After what seemed like an eternity, she detected the sound of someone thumping down the stairs. Then Stacy's voice bellowed from the other side of the door, 'Who is it? What do you want?'

'It's me, Connie!' she shouted back, her voice sounding feeble, blown away on the wind. But Stacy heard. Her body shook with relief at the sound of the bolts being drawn back. Then her friend, in what must have been Nicole's pink towelling dressing gown, was speaking her name, dragging her inside.

'Fucking hell, Connie,' he said, as she gave him a brief, garbled account of what had happened. He ran behind the bar and she watched, shivering and almost unable to stand, as he lifted the receiver and dialled 999.

34

The police arrived first, assuring her the ambulance was right behind. Connie quickly led them round to the kitchen door, where PC Ben Thurlow, swinging a heavy red-metal cylinder, forced the frame, the glass in some of the panes shattering as the wood buckled and gave way. Stamping heedlessly over the shards in their boots, they ran ahead. Stacy, without a word, swiftly picked up Connie – still barefoot: in her haste to rescue Jared she'd forgotten her shoes – and carried her over the broken glass, setting her down safely in the hall.

They found the bedroom key, her phone and what must have been Jared's on the landing carpet. They were only inches from the door, but out of reach to anyone inside. Connie noticed the metal steps leading from the loft were hanging down. *It wasn't mice.* She shivered at the thought he'd been up there all the time they'd been arriving home, having supper, unpacking, getting ready for bed.

She watched, breathless, as Yvonne Youngs – a sergeant and the one in charge – fiddled with the key in the lock. *Come on, come on,* Connie whispered silently as the seconds ticked by. Then at last the policewoman was asking them to stand back as she pushed the door ajar.

The room was still in half-darkness. Devan was by

the window, clutching Jared round the waist, one of his arms pulled tight around his neck. 'Stay with me, Jared, stay with me . . .' he was intoning to the semi-conscious, lolling head, as Jared's feet dragged uselessly across the carpet.

Connie rushed over to help Devan, but Ben was quicker.

'Let me, sir.' The policeman tried to take Jared from Devan's arms.

But Devan clung on, kept walking. 'I'm OK,' he insisted. 'Take his other arm.' He glanced round briefly at Sergeant Youngs. 'Where's the bloody ambulance?' he demanded, before turning his attention back to Jared. '*Come on!* Wake up, Jared! For God's sake, wake up.'

Yvonne made a call to chivvy the emergency services. Connie watched and waited, shivering, on the other side of the bed, while they continued to walk Jared's dead weight slowly back and forth across the room, her nerves strung to breaking point as she listened out for the sound of the ambulance. It was probably only a matter of minutes before the green-uniformed paramedics clumped up the stairs and blasted, businesslike, into the crowded room, relieving Devan and Ben of their burden – although it seemed like a lifetime to her.

Devan had his arm around her shoulders as they stood in the corner of the crowded room watching the scene playing out in front of them. 'He's going to be OK, isn't he?' she whispered to him.

But the look he gave her was bleak. He didn't answer.

'Can't find a pulse,' she heard one of the paramedics mutter a moment later, as they prepared to bundle Jared onto the stretcher.

The next minutes passed in a blur for Connie. Nobody panicked. Nobody shouted. There was just a controlled frenzy around the body on the floor. Yvonne tried to make them leave the room, but neither she nor Devan would budge.

This is all my fault. Responsibility lay on her shoulders like a ten-ton weight. She thought back to that first fatal kiss. *I should have stopped it right there*, she thought. *He was vulnerable . . . and I chose not to see it.* She felt tears of exhaustion behind her eyes. *If he dies, I will never forgive myself.*

It could have been minutes or hours, but suddenly she realized the room had gone very still. Devan was pulling her into his arms. 'I'm sorry, Connie,' he said softly.

She stared up at him, clocking his expression. Gasping, she dragged herself away. Looking over to where Jared lay, she jolted. His body was in shadow, his face, previously so full of pain and distress as he begged her to stay with him, now pale and motionless, his turquoise eyes closed. *NO . . .*

Connie watched as Devan carefully picked up the bigger pieces of glass from the kitchen floor and swept the rest into a dustpan, tipping the contents into a cardboard box. Then she waited in numb silence, her sore ankle raised on a chair, as he followed the trail of splinters trampled through the house by the police and paramedics with the vacuum cleaner. She was still wearing her coat because it was ice cold in the house, although she'd replaced her damp clothes with pyjamas. The noise of the vacuum, in her sensitive state, sounded brutal and deafening.

When he'd finished clearing up, Devan held out a dusty bottle he'd found at the back of the cupboard. 'I've had enough tea for one night.'

The police had stayed after the ambulance, with Jared's body, drove off into the rainy darkness. Stacy took charge and made tea – which was fortunate, because both Connie and Devan were incapable.

Sergeant Youngs listened as Devan attempted to fill her in. But his sentences were jumbled with tiredness, scarcely coherent. Connie said nothing. She was beyond speech, beyond any feeling at all.

When Devan had finished the garbled tale, the policewoman was mercifully pragmatic. 'Listen, sir,' she said. 'Why don't you both come down to the station in the morning and we can take a proper statement? You'll be in shock, after all you've just been through. You need to get those wet clothes off, have some rest.' She'd paused, eyeing them both closely. 'Do you want someone to stay with you tonight?' She glanced across at her colleague, who nodded. 'That kitchen door's not secure . . .'

'No, thank you. We'll be fine,' Devan had said firmly, and Connie had breathed a sigh of relief.

Now she nodded. 'Brandy would be good.'

'We can take it up to bed. It's nithering down here,' Devan added.

Connie thought of the bedroom and what had recently gone on there. She trembled, her spine prickling, the hairs rising on the back of her neck, as if Jared himself had walked over her grave. 'Caty's room?'

The spare bed was chilly, too, but they kept their coats on and pulled the covers round them as they sat propped against the rattan headboard, their hands clasping the tumblers containing the brandy, which burned a warming path into Connie's system.

A shattered silence filled the room. It was gone five in the morning. Dawn wouldn't be for a couple of hours yet, but she knew she wouldn't sleep.

'This is all my fault,' she said.

Devan squeezed her hand. 'No, Connie. Jared took his own life. It was his choice.'

'But I encouraged him. I let him think . . .'

Devan gave a weary sigh. 'He was ill. You couldn't have stopped him. If it wasn't tonight, it would have been some other time.'

Silence fell.

'Would you really have left him to die?' she asked quietly, staring straight ahead.

Devan didn't immediately reply. Then he said, 'He made our lives hell, Connie.'

'So, if I hadn't been there, you wouldn't have tried to save him?'

'Of course I would have. I did,' he said, without

hesitation this time. 'I couldn't have lived with myself if I hadn't.'

Connie let out a long breath.

'I did my very best. I hope you believe me. His breathing deteriorated so rapidly . . . There was nothing anyone could do. He must have taken a narcotic of some sort, maybe Tramadol . . . They'll find out.'

She turned to him. 'I do believe you.' She felt tears pressing behind her eyes. 'I'm so sorry, Devan, for everything I've put you through,' she said.

'I'm sorry too, Con,' he replied, pulling her gently into his arms.

'Poor Jared.' Her tears turned into sobs as she thought of his body, lying motionless on the bedroom carpet. She remembered Dinah Worthington, and the love she clearly felt for her godson. 'Dinah's my only family,' Jared had said. *If I'd called her, told her what Jared was up to, would it have made any difference?* The idea had crossed her mind after Jared's Christmas Eve visit. But Dinah was over eighty, and Connie hadn't wanted to upset an old lady over something she could doubtless do nothing about.

A while later, as she began to sink into a twitchy but exhausted doze, Connie was aware of Devan clearing his throat. His voice was quietly serious as he began to speak. 'I haven't said this before, Connie, because I've been so bloody angry with you recently,' he said, 'but it's always been there for me. It's like a solid layer underpinning the crap on both sides.' He took a breath and she looked up at him in the half-light from the bedside lamp. His mouth was twisting, eyes blurring with tears. 'You . . . our marriage . . . You and me . . . It's the absolute . . . *absolute* bedrock of my life. The family is important, work is important, but at the centre of everything is the love I feel for you.' He blinked, biting his lip, obviously trying to control his tears.

She couldn't speak.

He gave a wan smile as he went on, 'We've been so lucky. Most couples don't survive what we've just been through. But we will survive, won't we?' He looked at her beseechingly, his blue eyes still bruised by the anguish of the recent past. 'Because I really, truly love you, Connie.'

Connie took a breath. 'We're very lucky. And we will survive. Knowing I might have lost you was a living hell,' she told him, laying her head on his chest. Devan's love for her was tangible, not just in the powerful tenderness of his words but in the strength of his arms, the touch of his cheek to her hair. She felt it vibrate through her body as she breathed her love for him into the warm hollow of his neck. 'I love you too,' she whispered into the silent room.

Acknowledgements

As usual, Michael Joseph have provided me with the most excellent support in writing this book. Thank you, Maxine Hitchcock, Clare Bowron and Hazel Orme. Also, Laura Nicol, Rebecca Hilsdon, Emma Henderson, Helena Fouracre, Catherine Le Lievre and Zana Chaka.

Also, thank you Curtis Brown, my wonderful agent Jonathan Lloyd, and Lucy Morris.

For research into being a tour manager, I could not have written this book without the invaluable help of my dear friend Suzie Ladbrooke.

Thanks go to Eddie Mair, the ex-presenter of BBC Radio 4's *PM*, for his extended set of interviews with a victim of stalking. It was this which gave me the idea for *The Affair*.

And thank you to my family, of course.